INHERIT
THE SEA

JANET GREGORY

A SIGNET BOOK
NEW AMERICAN LIBRARY
TIMES MIRROR

SIGNET TRADEMARK REG. U.S. PAT. OFF. AND FOREIGN COUNTRIES
REGISTERED TRADEMARK—MARCA REGISTRADA
HECHO EN CHICAGO, U.S.A.

SIGNET, SIGNET CLASSICS, MENTOR, PLUME, MERIDIAN and NAL BOOKS
are published by The New American Library, Inc.,
1633 Broadway, New York, New York 10019

First Printing, March, 1980

1 2 3 4 5 6 7 8 9

PRINTED IN THE UNITED STATES OF AMERICA

CHAPTER 1

I was born in 1825, the only child of Charles Millbrook and Helen Allison Millbrook, and lived with my parents in a large, rambling Tudor house facing the River Mersey. The house was fashioned from gray Lancashire rock, with the sky above forever gray from the foundry or rain clouds, or both. There were gray velvet draperies in the drawing and music rooms, and gray brocade draperies in the dining room and library. For some reason my mother seemed always to wear gray dresses that lent no life to her brown hair and fine, patrician features. My Grandfather Millbrook had named our estate "Greystones"; perhaps he had a presentiment of life there.

My mother was a coldly beautiful woman who had been educated in London private schools which were, at best, adequate. Her father, my Grandfather Allison, had been an adventurous sort who had managed, through acquired money and a stroke of luck, the difficult feat of moving upward a notch in the social structure. Not, however, to the level to which my mother aspired. Nor was marriage to my father the goal she had hoped to achieve.

Many years later I came to understand that my parents' marriage had been one of arrangement and disillusion. But from the time I was five years old I lived with the uneasy conviction that it was *I* who was the cause of the ever-present hostility that crackled in the air of Greystones. My mother did not like me, that much was plain. As to why, I could not even guess, though I spent much time trying. Papa was my only source of affection and companionship. He was forced to spend a good deal of time in France doing business, but when he was home he played games with me and laughed with me and gave me gifts lovingly chosen while he was away—wondrously dressed dolls, scarves and ribbons of brilliant hue, exotic stones that glittered in the sun. He made me feel that I was the most important element in his life.

My mother resented the love Papa showered on me, and every effort to draw her into our happy relationship only

strengthened her chilly reserve. Yet I longed for her to love
me. I wanted her to smile down on me and smooth back my
hair. Or pull me close when I hovered around her as she sat
in the rose garden. Instead, it was always Dandy, her stout
cocker spaniel, that her hand sought and stroked.

No doubt I was tiresome. No matter how often I was re-
buffed, I clung to the hope that soon my mother would see
that I was not willful or contrary, as she claimed, but wanted
only to please her.

I recall one damp spring afternoon when I was six years
old, and Papa was away in France. I had found a patch of
early violets in our woods and picked them carefully, at the
very bottom of the stems, not snapping the heads off as I had
when I was younger. Delighted with my find, I rushed into
the house in search of my mother, heedless of my grubby
hands and a leaf or two in my hair. I found her sitting before
the drawing-room fire with fat Dandy on the loveseat beside
her.

Glowing with pride, I pushed close to her, edging Dandy
out of the way and holding out my fragrant purple offering.

"For you, Mama. Aren't they pretty? Shall I put them in
the pink vase for you?"

"Oh! You filthy child!" she exclaimed, pulling away. She
scrubbed with her handkerchief where I had leaned against
her skirt, though there was no mark.

"Go and clean yourself up at once, Margaret! What a disgusting little hoyden you've become."

She turned her attention to Dandy, who had waddled to
the floor. "Here, darling boy, don't mind that rude girl, come
here, pet." Lifting the fat dog to her lap, she turned her back
to me.

"Did the nasty girl push you away, darling?" she crooned,
cradling the animal to her breast. "*Poor* Dandy."

I stole from the room, ashamed of my unworthiness;
ashamed that my mother's voice sharpened and shrilled for
me, and murmured over Dandy; ashamed of my foolish heart
that refused to learn. I threw the violets away, and longed for
Papa's return from France.

My mother never shared my father's bracing wit, his
ardent love of books, his devotion to the cultivation of orchids, or his fondness for convivial company. She considered
Papa's wit vulgar, his reading reclusive, his orchid glasshouse
a monstrous expense, and the rural gentry beneath her. She
could not come to terms with the fact that she was isolated

from the London society she aspired to—the London of wealth and position, of frivolous, inbred people whose lives were defined by gossip and flirtation, and the hectic round of parties each night that lasted far into the next day.

My father, an idealistic, kindly Lancashireman, had inherited a brandy and wine trade with the French. He owned five ships—one steamer and four brigs. Their holds were always topped off with brandy inbound and hard coal outbound from the Lancashire pitheads.

Papa was the son of a country gentleman who had done little except clip-clop about Greystones on a finely bred horse. Grandfather Millbrook married in his fortieth year and his bride was a beautiful young French girl. Grandmother Cherbier did not understand English, or at least she pretended not; thus, French was always spoken at Greystones while she and Grandfather Millbrook lived.

Grandmother's family, the Cherbier aunts and uncles and cousins, operated several vineyards in the Bordeaux region. When someone in the family suggested that the cases from Bordeaux be shipped directly into the Mersey for distribution in Liverpool, Manchester, and Leeds, the Millbrook Line came into existence. The Millbrook trade was a balanced one; our cargoes were guaranteed on both voyage legs, for the family had made long-term arrangements with the Liverpool coal brokers to lift many tons of steaming coal a year to France. Three small brigs of 130 tons burden each came into service while my grandfather was alive. Papa built one more trading brig of 190 tons and finally purchased at auction a steamer, the *Hibernia*, formerly on the Holyhead-Dublin mail station. The Millbrooks' fortune increased as the small traders plowed in and out of the Mersey, always low in the water, a fine sign for anyone in the shipping business.

Father prepared at Eton and completed his studies at Cambridge, where they turned out romantic activists—men who dreamed among great books and led unruffled, polite lives while trying to do the right thing. It was not the school of the callous, conscienceless men who were smoking up England even as they inched their way into our rural gentry.

Papa was not a man who could hammer together a commercial transaction, but he ran the business with attention to detail and cared deeply about the men who served aboard his ships. He had not the slightest idea that his trade was a captive one. The Millbrook wine cargoes were automatically booked on his tonnage, and he could assure the coal shippers a freight rate of about one shilling under the going carriage to France. That was the order of things; all was right with the world.

When my father was away there would be entire days when my mother did not speak to me. I was left to Miss Barnes, my tutor, who helped with the baking and resided in a cell-like room on the third floor back. A dull, unimaginative woman, her main concern was to please my mother, and she provided no stimulation or companionship.

I learned to detest that dehumanized house, the scarred valleys of Lancashire, and the presence of the permanent poor we had on our hands and our doorstep as the Industrial Revolution tore up England. I think I grew up unanchored. My roots weren't in Greystones, dug into the land it occupied, the society in which it existed, for I was allowed no friends. While my mother had no very high opinion of me as offspring, there was no one near my age—and in fact no family in our area—worthy of our attention, in her view. Worthwhile people lived in London; all others were beneath us. I know it was a grief to my father, who would have relished seeing Greystones full of guests and gaiety. Certainly it was a grief to me, for I lived a solitary, drifting life.

Only once do I remember our having guests to stay at Greystones—a recently widowed friend of my mother's from London, with her two daughters. The Sinclairs were journeying to Scotland, where they would take up residence with titled relatives. They would break their journey at Greystones, staying with us overnight.

There was an air of excitement and bustle about the house as we readied for their visit. Once again, Papa was away in France. That was, no doubt, a relief to my mother; no man could have measured up to the exalted standards she claimed for her girlhood friend.

The two Sinclair daughters were tall, voluptuous girls with tumbling dark curls and high color. Though Eva was my age, twelve, and Elizabeth only two years older, both girls were far more worldly than I, and full of airs and graces. I had looked forward for days to their arrival. But Eva and Elizabeth Sinclair were the kind of girls who had "secrets." They smirked and giggled and tossed cryptic comments to each other in a way that excluded me from their conversation.

The afternoon they arrived I showed them about the place, but they appeared to find nothing at Greystones so fine as they were accustomed to. Within an hour I was reduced to feeling pale and commonplace. When I ventured to say anything, neither girl would allow me to finish a phrase, much less a sentence. They would simply talk the louder, until I fell silent. I was to be an admiring audience for their wit, and nothing more.

When I went to my chamber to dress for dinner I was in a temper. I decided that I would not be treated so at the dinner table. Nor throughout the balance of the Sinclairs' visit. I longed for a colorful taffeta dress that would bedazzle those bombastic sisters! Eva Sinclair, who was only my age, had bragged that she would be wearing a green velvet dress trimmed with real lace. But no matter how I rooted through my meager wardrobe, it was hopeless. I had only plain, serviceable dresses. My mother felt strongly that pretty clothes would foster vanity in me. Papa had long since given up arguing with her on that score.

Still, on his last trip, Papa had brought me a gossamer-fine scarf of striped silk. Perhaps if I twisted it and tied it in my hair somehow . . . I remembered a picture I had seen of a great court beauty. Her hair had been dressed high on her head and looped with pearls and curling feather plumes. If I could achieve that effect, I would look less plain and unadorned next to the Sinclairs.

I twisted scarf and hair together atop my head and arranged an artful cascade of curls to bounce downward from the crown. For added elegance I looped a string of golden beads in among the curls and was well satisfied with the result. Perhaps it didn't match up with a brown merino dress, but that was what I had.

I had fussed so long that the others were in the drawing room ahead of me. I remember that I felt quite regal as I entered, and didn't care a farthing for Eva Sinclair's velvet dress. There was a glorious moment when I saw admiration dawning on Eva's face. And then my mother's laughter, as brittle as shattering glass, pierced my rosy dream.

"Margaret! Really! What ridiculous thing have you done to yourself? Oh, dear—" She clapped dainty fingers to her mouth, as if to stifle laughter. But I was not deceived. Her eyes were cold as they raked me over, and I felt my insides beginning to shrivel.

"Only *look* at the child," she caroled. "Have you ever seen anything so preposterous?"

Four pairs of eyes studied me. With my mother leading the chorus, the Sinclairs were soon rocking with laughter.

"Oh, Margaret, you do look too amusing," Eva gasped, her eager eyes narrow with malice.

My mother turned to a simpering Mrs. Sinclair. "The child has *no* taste. I find it such a trial, my dear."

She turned her attention again to me, and all pretense of amusement had left her voice. "Please go to your room at once and arrange yourself more suitably for dinner with our guests."

I was rushing from the room, intending to take shelter in my bed, but the damaging voice caught me up.

"Be back within ten minutes, no longer."

"I don't want dinner." Even the words choked me.

"That is unfortunate. However, your presence at the table is required. Ten minutes, please."

The rest of that evening I have managed to put out of mind. My embarrassment was painful and under it deep anger smoldered, for they enjoyed my discomfort, my mother most of all. There was real gaiety in her that evening, as if her good humor fed on my misery. That night I knew that my mother hated me. It was a relief of sorts; I no longer needed to strive for her affection. My mother and I, for her reasons, not mine, were enemies.

From that day onward, life at Greystones was made bearable only by the long hours I spent in Papa's library, immersed in heroic stories in dusty books. Sword fights on the long lines of Trafalgar vessels; explorations of mysterious islands with gold buried beneath their sands; strange maps slipped out of the pockets of sinister men in the dark of night; daring exploits by handsome, dashing soldiers of fortune—these were the tales that rescued me from that dreadful house in a desolate corner of England. I wanted to *live* everything I read in those books.

As for my mother, I relieved my hostility by thwarting her whenever I could. The crisis arrived when I broke one of her rare porcelain vases—half by accident, but perhaps half by intent, for I was angry at the time. When she saw the pieces lying on the floor, she slammed her heavily ringed hand across my face with stunning force.

"You incorrigible creature!" she screamed, her blazing eyes terrifying in that chiseled white face.

As the blood flowed into my mouth and I started crying, Papa seized her arm, throwing her away from me.

"Helen, don't ever dare to do that again! The child needs

love and attention, not a lashing, for God's sake. Come, Margaret, come now, darling, no need to cry . . ."

"You're a fool, Charles!"

Later that night, still sobbing and unable to sleep, I got up from my bed and padded down the long upstairs gallery hall, half hoping that my father would be sitting up reading and offer me comfort. Instead, I heard my mother's raised voice from their bedchambers, a group of four rooms in the west wing.

". . . a simpering little miss when *you're* about, all sweet smiles and pretty ways. But let me tell you, when you go away on one of your interminable trips it's all quite different. Little Miss Innocence shows her true colors then. You have spoiled her beyond reclaiming, Charles, deluded by a beautiful face!"

"I have tried to give Margaret the love and devotion she needs, Helen. God knows, she gets none from you! There was no excuse for being so vicious this evening."

"Indeed! Someone must teach her that beauty will not always buy her impunity when she misbehaves. . . ."

I crept back to my room in despair. Why did my mother always insist that the way I *looked* was somehow at the root of my misconduct? Certainly I had been at fault in breaking the vase and I could understand being blamed for my temper, but what did that have to do with my face? She seemed always to be angry because I was pretty, though what difference that made to anything I failed to see. She could as easily have said I was ugly and I would have believed it, for there was no one else to tell me how I looked, and in the mirror all I saw was the face I was used to. Would she have loved me if I were ugly? Would Papa have loved me less? All I truly understood was that I was desperately unhappy and that somehow I must get away.

I resolved that I would ask to be sent to a French school. Two of my father's business associates in Bordeaux had daughters who attended an academy in Berri, and on the few occasions when we visited these girls they told me of their life at the school, of trips into Paris and the important people who came to talk to the students. All of this had built in my mind; the imagery of France, being with friends my own age instead of a beet-faced, spinsterish tutor. As I already spoke fluent French, it seemed a way in which I could hope to escape from Lancashire and Greystones.

The following day I contrived to speak to my father alone.

Unfortunately, just as we began to talk, my mother came into the room and I fell guiltily silent.

Her eyes went from my face to my father's and back again. "Up to one of your pretty tricks again, Margaret? What are you attempting to wheedle from your father now?"

"I . . . nothing. Just . . . nothing, Mother," I stammered, afraid to raise my eyes.

"Nothing you wish me to know about, at any rate! Well, I'm afraid . . ."

I heard no more for I fled from the room and the house, across the broad lawns and around the lily pond to the summer pavilion. It was my refuge, a private place where I often spent hours reading, when the library did not offer sufficient protection from my mother's ever-critical eye. Screened from easy view by the climbing roses, I was lost in grief when I felt my father's gentle hand on my shoulder. I looked up at him through a glaze of tears and knew that I loved him dearly. White-haired and regal as ever, his smile compassionate, he shook his head ruefully.

"Oh, my poor Margaret, whatever shall I do about you?"

"Papa, I'm truly sorry that I cause you so much trouble."

"The fault is not with you, my dear. Your mother and I have some difficulties. You must try to be patient with us."

"If only I could get away!" It burst from me with passionate intensity and I saw my father bow his head.

"Oh, Papa, I don't mean forever," I cried, immediately contrite. "Just for a time, perhaps to school at Berri. The Gilmont girls from Bordeaux have told me how greatly they enjoy it."

Papa looked at me closely. "I see you have given the matter some thought." He gazed off, over my head, sighing. Then the warm, familiar smile was turned on me again. "So you wish to attend the school at Berri, do you?"

"If only I could, Papa! I cannot bear the isolation here. I'm fourteen now, and there is scarcely anyone to talk with except the tenants and Miss Barnes."

"I've realized the problem, little Margaret. If that is what you want, then I'll see what I can do about it. I feel sure Monsieur Gilmont can arrange the proper introductions in Berri."

I threw my arms around him in a flood of joy and excitement. I had won a first battle in my efforts to put Greystones behind me! Smiling, my father kissed the top of my head, but his eyes were sad. I realized with a pang that I would be leaving not only Greystones and my mother, I would be leaving *him*.

In the weeks that followed, excitement and the expectation of my new life built a wall against my mother's barbs. She became more rigid and strained each day. She construed my request to go away as a personal affront, and she was right in that. Papa had departed on business, and word from him was not forthcoming for almost a month, the most anxious month of my life. Then on a late August day a letter postmarked Bordeaux finally arrived for me. My mother, who took all mail from the post carrier, brought it into the tutoring room.

"Well, Margaret, I suppose this is the news you've been waiting for. I know your father has succeeded: I can tell by the thinness of the envelope. Bad news, with all your father's rationalizations, would require five times the paper. So, Miss Barnes, this is your separation notice. Your pupil is going to school in France. Isn't that extraordinarily good fortune?"

I felt bitterness and antagonism flood the small classroom with its one-pupil seat, its one-teacher desk, and its three blackboards where Miss Barnes, a chalk person, forever scribbled. The correspondence from my father meant that I would soon put both of these women and the worst of England behind me.

My mother was right. The letter was short and bore good tidings:

> My darling Margaret,
>
> I have just returned to Charente from Berri, where I had a long and pleasant discussion with Madame Bouchard, the headmistress.
>
> As you can imagine, there are many applications from prominent French families for seats at the Berri Academy, and they, naturally, do not take kindly toward British applicants, but we prevailed and you have a seat at the academy.
>
> I expect the best from you in your studies and social friendships, as I have gone to great lengths to satisfy your request. I know you will not disappoint me.
>
> Madame Bouchard anticipates you on the last day of September for the term, and I shall personally escort you to the school.
>
> With my love and endearment,
> Father

The weeks which followed were painful. Mother felt she had been vanquished, and her resentment was a heavy, hostile presence in the house. Any words she spoke to me came from tight, angry lips.

"You are feeling quite triumphant, aren't you, Margaret? You've managed to twist your father around your finger once again."

"Please try to understand, Mother. It's very lonely for me here. I wish to be with other young people, to have friends of my own age."

"Don't waste your pretty wiles on me, Margaret. You don't deceive me for a moment, you never have. But of course, that's why you wish to go away to school, isn't it? Because I see right through your little pretenses. Behind that smooth, deceptive face you are a wicked, willful girl, quite beyond your years. Well, no matter; I'm sure you will have your fit reward one of these days. Just don't come crying to me!"

I counted the hours and then the minutes until I would depart from Liverpool. I saw France in my dreams and I sang French songs to myself. The day finally came when the signal station at Bootle Head brought the news that my father's brig, *Tough Tom*, had cleared the pilot grounds and was now in tow into the Mersey Basin. I gathered up my skirts and ran to the livery stable to ask Ned, our coachman, to take me down to the quay to meet my father.

As usual, my mother sought to diminish my joy. "Margaret, how dare you request such a thing of Ned!" she exclaimed, overhearing me. "He has duties in the livery house. You will wait until your father arrives home."

As soon as she reentered the house I hastened to the stables and saddled the Arabian mare my father had given me for my ninth birthday. In a matter of minutes I was galloping over the crushed stone driveway, around the curve of the broad slope of lawns, to a cliff overlooking Liverpool and the basin of the River Mersey. Far to the east I could see the brownish smudge of coal smoke hanging on the horizon, being pumped up into once-blue air by the squads of factory chimneys. To the other side was the river, with its forests of masts and the fronts of wattle and daub houses. I gazed at all of this and then back at Greystones, feeling the malevolence behind that thick facade like a living spirit. Let me get away, I breathed, just let me get away from this place where even the vegetables from our kitchn garden taste of that hateful soot!

"Oh, Papa, how dreadfully I have missed you!" I cried when I reached our quay and flung myself at him, hardly aware of the tears flowing down my cheeks.

"What's this? Don't cry, little Margaret, everything is arranged. Surely you received my letter?"

"Oh, yes, and I thank you, Papa, but Mother is terribly angry," I said fearfully. "I don't understand why she doesn't want me to go when, truly, she doesn't love me!"

"Hush, darling, don't say such things. You know your mother's ways—"

"I know she wishes to *own* me, yes," I burst out, "though I seem to give her no pleasure."

"Ah, well, we must all grow up and live for ourselves, darling. . . ."

He was right, of course. I resolved not to let my mother spoil my anticipation of my new life.

After a week of final packing while my father attended to his business, we cleared the Mersey with our holds topped off, hauling "Welsh best" coal for the emerging French railroads. My mother was calm that day as I kissed her good-bye. She handed me a gift, an unattractive piece of needlework I resolved to lose on my way to Berri. I could see nothing in her face except a cold lack of forgiveness and a mocking assurance that I would regret my going. Papa, who was never one to catch the subtlety of a glance, seemed to think she was taking it well, but I knew better than that.

As the brig dropped her towline and the pilot departed, we made sail, and soon all sails were drawing and our bows were slapping through the white caps of the Irish Sea. I forgot about my mother's smoldering look. In half an hour England was only a slice of green on the horizon and then it was gone—for a long, long time, I hoped.

The voyage to Charente took five days, and the wind was fair and the weather temperate for early autumn. We coached up to Paris and spent two weeks in final preparations for my arrival at Berri. It was my second visit to the French capital. My father had taken me there when I was seven, but I had been too young then to appreciate all that the City of Light had to offer.

Now I was fourteen, almost fifteen. I felt that I was truly grown up, and it seemed to me that my father shared this view when, on our third day in Paris, he permitted me to select a number of new gowns for myself. In the *atelier* he sat patiently in an elegant velvet bergère chair while the *ven-*

deuse presented a parade of colorful silks and velvets fashioned in the latest styles. Though my head was fairly swimming with excitement, I limited myself to six creations which I felt would surely help to disguise my unworldliness among the other girls at the Berri Academy. When I had made my choices my father surprised me by adding a seventh gown to my collection, a sea-green silk taffeta with a neckline cut lower than I had dared to choose, and ruffled sleeves that fell just to my elbows, edged in finest *point d'esprit* lace and brocaded ribbon.

"Clear sea-green to match your eyes my darling," he said, his own eyes alight with pride as the boxes were taken to our carriage.

When we arrived back at the hotel my father suggested tea, but I demurred hesitantly.

"I should like to go to my room and try on my beautiful gowns again if I may, Papa," I said, half fearful that my new interest in my appearance might be an indication of the vanity my mother was always accusing me of.

He smiled at my flushed, excited face. "Of course you do, my little one. I fear there have been too few such pleasures in your young life." He kissed me. "Off you go, then."

Back in my room overlooking the Rue de la Franklin, I carefully unpacked my new dresses from their tissue paper and laid them on the huge bed. Then, standing in front of the full-length mirror, I tried them on one by one.

I could not but be pleased by the effect. I had always had my mother's assurance that I was more than ordinarily pretty, but since it was invariably given in an unpleasant context, I had never paid it heed. Now, for the first time, I took pleasure in the reflection in the mirror. My pale golden hair was lustrous and silky; my skin fair and delicate; my cheekbones high and well-defined. My neck was long and slender—that was patrician, I decided. My breasts were beginning to take their final form, no longer merely gentle swellings but full and round; I looked particularly well in the low-cut sea-green gown.

But what did it all amount to? If my mother was right in thinking me beautiful, she must also be right in thinking me deceitful. I was momentarily depressed, but my spirit quickly reasserted itself. Deceitful or not, I had seven new gowns, I looked well in them, and I was going to school in Berri to begin a wonderful new life!

We left for Berri with eight trunks of books and clothes, and the traveling coach was so pushed down upon its springs that I thought the wheels would surely come off. I felt that my father had become not only my best friend in the world, but also my trusted confidant since we had left Liverpool. Perhaps he felt it too, for he talked to me as an equal.

"You know, Margaret, that ours has not been a happy household. I feel that you are young to be going so far away to school, but perhaps it will be better for you than living at Greystones."

"I'm very grateful, Papa. I know I shall love Berri, and though I shall miss you greatly, I shan't miss Greystones."

He reached out and took my hand. "You are the most important thing in my life, Margaret. All I truly care about in the world is your happiness. You are leaving me now, but whatever happens, good or bad, you must come to me whenever you wish. Remember, as well as father and daughter, we are friends."

"Dear friends, Papa," I replied, giving his apple-red cheek a light kiss. "Forever."

"Forever," he agreed with a smile, and eased his head back upon the velvet of the carriage with a contented sigh.

How the coachman knew where he was going I could not imagine, for we seemed to be circling, moving up one cypress-bordered lane, down another, in and out of small French market towns, and all the while, the excitement of my first real adventure in life was coming closer and closer. It was almost noon and I must have been dozing a bit as the warm country air drifted through the coach. Suddenly I seemed to see again the expression on my mother's face as she bade me good-bye.

I shuddered and opened my eyes. Perhaps Papa had been watching me, for he said, "What's the matter, darling? Were you dreaming?"

I shook my head. "I don't know . . . no, I don't think dreaming, exactly. But I seemed to see Mother looking at me. She was telling me that I would regret leaving Greystones. That I can never go home again."

Papa managed an uncomfortable-sounding laugh. "Oh, nonsense Margaret. Greystones is your home, your heritage. That and the shipping line." He took my hands in his, bluffly hearty. "Of course you will return there whenever you wish."

But I was unable to throw off the chill foreboding of that half dream and my mother's cold-eyed malevolence. Finally, in order not to distress my father further, I pretended to accept his assurances that my mother would soon forget her pique at my leaving Greystones. The future was to prove him wrong about that. It was as well that neither of us could foresee the pain and sorrow that would result.

CHAPTER 2

The Berri Academy was set amidst a vast expanse of interlocking gardens, and my first view of it conjured up the pictures I had seen of Versailles. The great parterres with their brilliant flowers and low, clipped hedges drew the eye from one enchanting vista to the next, each receding toward the majestic château that had originally been the home of the Forquet family. It was not a large château, my father explained, but it had stood for over two centuries, and its castellated walls and corner turrets, its spires that seemed to touch the very heavens, seized my imagination. It was a scene of fantasy and romance, a setting which could produce only angels, I felt sure, and hoped fervently that I would prove worthy of my place amidst such beauty.

Everywhere I looked wonders unfolded before my eyes: descending terraces as lushly green as velvet carpet; a long corridor of close-shorn hornbeam trees and marble statues, framing a square lake dotted with swans; arbored retreats watched over by golden nymphs and cherubs. Over all hung the sweet scent of jasmine arching above trellis walks. There was a fleshliness here, adventure; after gray England I found it intoxicating to my senses.

That first day I felt myself scarcely fit to breathe the perfumed air. Glimpses of laughing, well-dressed girls strolling about the grounds, all of whom seemed to me extremely sophisticated and self-assured, made me uncomfortably aware of my lack of experience with people of my own age and social level.

We dined with Madame Bouchard, a huge woman who seemed to take up too much living space. She was impressed with my French to the point of saying I would make a fine addition to the school, even though I was English.

Papa, who could not bear to hear my talents in any way qualified, replied in impeccable French, "My daughter, Madame Bouchard, is almost French."

"How can one be almost French?" the headmistress said, closing her wide mouth on the salmon soufflé.

"Margaret's grandmother was a Cherbier, of the Cherbier family of Bordeaux."

"Ah, yes, the wine growers." Madame Bouchard breathed her approval and surveyed me with a somewhat warmer eye. From then on we were on pleasant terms.

After our heavy lunch, my father took his departure. There were a few parting tears, not as many as I had expected, and then dear Papa was off to Paris again; from there, down to Charente and home.

Happy as I was to be away from the filth and grayness of Lancashire and the never-ending hostility of my mother, surrounded by the beauty and grace that seemed to me special to France, I was nevertheless not entirely comfortable in my new environment. As I had suspected my first day at the academy, the isolated life I had led at Greystones had not prepared me for the world of Berri. My fellow students were among the richest young women in Europe. They came to the school with private maids, seamstresses, and livery staffs to care for their horses, which were in residence at exorbitant rates. It cost three thousand pounds a year to attend the academy.

Before I had come to Berri I had drawn a mental picture of the school: plain and comfortable buildings, tasteless food, girls in uniforms, mistresses who made unruly students sit straight in their seats and perhaps even administered the birch. I had been willing to accept the hardships of a difficult French academy in order to leave England. Instead, I found myself in a dream world of wines, fresh vegetables, soufflés, leather-bound classics, exciting lecturers from Paris, and athletic activities if one desired. In fact, everything one desired, for the school had a philosophy: do nothing if you please, do all if you please.

"A school is an opportunity," the headmistress would repeat. "It is to be cherished and used, or dismissed. It is a preparation for life, where we must all eventually decide things for ourselves."

I was ashamed at having asked Papa to send me to so undisciplined a school and fearful of the expense and sacrifice it must have taken. I decided that I would achieve the very best grades to prove my appreciation. Having a love of books and learning imparted by him rather than by Miss Barnes's tutoring, I found that achieving outstanding reports was not unduly difficult, especially by comparison with most of the other students. The headmistress was correct: one could find an excellent education at Berri or select nothing but the gratification of every whim. I soon found myself being called "the scholarly one."

In spite of the fact that they were so much wealthier than I and that they teased me about my bookish ways, the girls at Berri were not unfriendly. An outgoing lot, they talked endlessly of the latest Paris fashions, of who had been seen at the ballet and opera, of parties and young men. Their heads together, they giggled and exchanged confidences about holiday escapades. They would have been happy enough to include me, but I had little to contribute to these topics. After a time, "innocent" as well as "scholarly" came to be an appellation used for me by my schoolmates.

That was scarcely surprising, I thought ruefully, for up to that point I had known only two boys even to speak to, apart from the tenants' sons. One youth was the son of the local rector who came to tea twice a year at Greystones, and the other was a tall, gangling boy, the eldest son of Captain Marshall, who handled our steam vessel. If the two boys had been at all smitten with me, they had managed to hide it completely.

Thus I got along well enough with my companions, but I had no special friend—although I longed for someone with whom I could share confidences.

Papa wrote, wanting to know if I wished to return to Lancashire for the Christmas holidays. I asked if he and I could spend the holidays in Paris. My mother's forbidding face was still in my mind and, after France, I could not bear to return to the somber Cheshire coast and the harshness of Greystones.

Papa journeyed to Paris and we attended a round of parties at the homes of my fellow students. That holiday was the happiest I had ever known. On Christmas night, when we were finally alone, Papa suggested that we dine at a small cafe on the Rue Bonaparte where he was known to the proprietor.

"How is Mother?" I finally asked, with some diffidence.

"She seems happy enough, and preoccupied, I must say."

"Preoccupied, Papa? In what way?"

"Ah, that's difficult to say, Margaret. Your mother is often away from Greystones. At first she would say merely that she had started a small business venture in Liverpool. Though I often asked her the nature of the business, for a long time she was secretive. Finally she told me. Your mother has opened a small apothecary in the Duke of York Street. She travels there to oversee things three times a week."

I was astonished. Mother, with her social pretensions, going into trade? It seemed incredible, and I said so.

"Ummm, it is, rather, isn't it? But she claims that it takes her mind off the boredom of country life. Understandable, I suppose. I'm away on business so many weeks of the year. In any case, she seems to be a changed woman."

"Does she ever speak of me?" I asked, fearing the answer.

Papa paused and gazed at the table, fiddling with his side whiskers. "She hasn't mentioned you, Margaret," he admitted finally. "Of course, I keep her informed of how well you are doing. I'm sure, in her own way, she is proud of you."

I stretched out a hand to him. Dear Papa, so afraid of hurting me.

"It doesn't matter. I'm truly sorry to have caused her so much unhappiness, though I should think she would be better pleased by my absence than my company, wouldn't you? In any case, I couldn't stand Lancashire and that sad house any longer. You understand that, don't you, Papa?"

The old, keen smile broke across his strong face. "I understand perfectly, darling. Margaret, I would have lived in London for your sake and your mother's, if I could have. I have no more appetite for Lancashire and Liverpool than you do, but how could I operate a brandy and wine trade off the Mersey if I lived in London?"

"Perhaps we should have lived in Bordeaux."

"No, my dear. I am a buyer of the family's wines. In shipping, one must be based where the cargoes are sold, not bought. Buying the consignments is routine; selling them at a profit is the art of trading."

We finished the meal quietly. I wished to ask Papa a most delicate question, but we had never discussed financial matters. After much thought, I slipped in my inquiry as a declarative statement.

"Papa, the Berri Academy is so expensive."

"I know, but I want you to have the best."

"I appreciate that, but you see, the girls at Berri are from the richest families in Europe and—"

"And we are not?" he interrupted.

"Well . . ."

"Darling, there is no need to concern yourself on that account. The matter is taken care of."

He said it with bluff confidence, but I was not deceived. When Papa attempted to tell less than the truth his eyes darted away and he adopted too hearty a voice. But to pursue the matter further would hurt his pride and serve no purpose.

We parted in Paris, and I coached back to the school in a mood of renewed determination to keep my grades at a high level; I had to make Papa feel that he was educating a daughter for the sacrifices I felt sure he was making. But I was more and more aware of my underlying loneliness.

Then, at last, I made a friend. Her name was Adriana Rantana, and she was a striking-looking girl from a noble Tuscany family. Everyone admired Adriana. She was easily the most notable girl in the school; very tall, with a long, graceful neck and a willowy body. Her acquiline features reflected her Latin background, and her eyes were feline, aristocratic.

Every girl at Berri longed to be noticed by Adriana, so I was surprised and flattered when she began to cultivate my acquaintance. Before long we were spending all our free time together. For the first time in my life I had someone with whom to share laughter and sorrows, dreams and aspirations.

I almost worshiped Adriana. She was intelligent as well as beautiful and sophisticated. She knew about opera, ballet, theater, the latest books. Although she was only two years older than I, she was infinitely wiser in her knowledge of the ways of the world. I listened breathlessly as she told me stories—generally scandalous—about life among the fashionable, dropping names I had heard of but never thought anyone I knew would have met. At first I was shy, almost tongue-tied, about myself, especially since Adriana spoke very little about her personal life, but eventually I told her about the bleakness of my life in Lancashire. She listened sympathetically and pressed my hand.

Adriana never seemed to be concerned about her studies, and soon my own studying and classes drifted into a rather bothersome routine relegated to what time I could spare for them. When the weather changed that spring, we began riding over wooded paths every afternoon and sometimes even in the mornings. Often we took picnic baskets and rowed along the lagoons, eating cheese and fresh berries.

The term drew to an end and I received a correspondence from Papa, inquiring how I wished to spend the summer holiday—in Lancashire or with the Cherbiers in Bordeaux. I did not look forward to either, so I was elated when Adriana asked me if I wanted to spend the summer at her family's villa on Lake Como. I pictured long, sunny days with Adriana and with the other guests who would be there, all of whom I was sure would be brilliant and stimulating. And I thought too, of starlit evenings with handsome young men who might be there, for I was beginning to dream of smiles half hidden behind fans and stolen kisses in the moonlight and whispered good-nights—all of the things chattered about so incessantly at Berri.

I wrote to Papa, telling him that I would spend the summer in Tuscany and asking him if he could send me money, for I would need some as gifts for the servants and in the event of excursions here and there. I did not want to impose overly much on Adriana and the Rantana family. The money still had not arrived when it was time to depart from school, but Adriana made naught of my concern. And so we left for Lake Como.

CHAPTER 3

I will never forget my first view of the Villa Rantana. Our coach arrived at the landing and we were rowed by servants toward what appeared to be a dream castle, rising from the center of the Italian lake. Outlined against the blue Tuscan sky, its spires and turrets resembled an idyllic painting more than reality, with the northern mountains forming a hazy backdrop in the distance.

No doubt my face reflected my wonder, for Adriana laughed. "The villa is built on the foundations of a medieval fortress." She gazed at the vista before us and her eyes narrowed in thought. "Perhaps it is my favorite of our estates. There is an autonomy about it, an atmosphere of secrecy and power that appeals to my soul."

That statement was as startling as the view of the Villa Rantana itself, for Adriana had never before revealed any

hint óf her inner being. It was a portent of things to come.
The secrecy and power that appealed to Adriana Rantana's
soul were destined to wreak havoc with my life for many
years to come.

Our boat approached the Villa Rantana from an angle, for
the magnificent edifice was situated on a high plateau that
jutted out to one side of the island. Leading up to the house
were three broad flights of steps balustraded in stone, all of it
a soft gray-pink, as far from the harsh gray stone of my own
home as imagination could conceive. Magnificent baroque
gardens cascaded like a peacock tail from the villa down to a
sandy beach.

Wherever my eyes alighted was a vast panorama of flowering terraces and yew-bordered walks. Sparkling fountains
caught the sunlight and jetted forth showers of diamonds.
Statues of satyrs and nymphs stood or reclined in niches half
obscured with tumbling blossoms of brilliant red, against deep
green foliage. Over all swept the soft summer breezes of the
lake.

Within, the villa was spacious and opulent, combining the
fresh coolness of deep blue and white tiles with lavish silken
hangings. Luxurious furniture invited a mood of ease and
abandon. Each room led to another more delightful than the
previous; and in shady loggias, great hanging baskets of flowering vines perfumed the air.

My bedroom, a bower fit for a fairy-tale princess, was
hung in the palest of sea-green silk. The canopied bed was
flounced and festooned, its gauzy silk layers caught up with
bunches of beribboned violets. I owned no gown so beautiful!
The other furniture—chairs, small tables, the wardrobe, and
a graceful satin-covered chaise longue—were of ivory wood
carved with small flowers picked out in pastel colors. On the
tile floor was a deep-piled carpet like some vast velvet flower
garden of violets and sweet pea.

I gazed around, marveling. Adriana favored the Villa Rantana because of its "autonomy"? Its "atmosphere of secrecy
and power"? In my own view it was a fairyland of loveliness
and luxury beyond belief.

The Rantana family was large and everyone had invited
guests for the summer months. The island was a miniature
Europe, with guests from Russia, the various city-states of
Italy, Germany, and even Sweden. There were twenty-six of
us in all, and most appeared to be weak, indolent people who

thought of little apart from eating and drinking to excess, when not indulging in amorous byplay.

I was bitterly disappointed and shocked, but I did not confide my reactions to Adriana. I thought it would be rude of me to criticize the guests of my hostess's family, particularly since Adriana did not seem to find anything amiss in their behavior. Admiring her as I did, I began to wonder if I were being too prudish, too much governed by middle-class English morality. Besides, even more than at Berri I was beguiled by the charm of my surroundings. I loathed the west of England and wanted nothing so much as to root out every trace of it from my person and my mind. The bleakness of my life there had made me vulnerable to anything that presented itself in the guise of beauty and ease. How could any place so exquisite be evil? Although I isolated myself from the others as much as possible, spending all the time I could with Adriana, I found myself gradually becoming less disturbed by my fellow guests.

The indolent, laissez-faire mood of the Villa Rantana was not conducive to ethical examination of the soul. Berri had softened me, and the Villa Rantana offered merely a heightened version of the same sensual appeals. One ate exotic foods and drank tempting concoctions. One laughed and danced that newest rage, the polka. One professed to adore the vodka our Russian guests esteemed so highly—and soon the company seemed nicer and more scintillating. Little by little, I accepted the manner of living that surrounded me.

One night, realizing that I had drunk far too much—unaccustomed as I was to spirits, it took very little to affect me—I excused myself and went to my room. I had donned my nightgown and gotten into bed when there was a knock at the door and I looked up to see Adriana standing in the doorway. She, too, was dressed for bed. Through her sheer nightgown I could see clearly the soft curves of her firm body.

"May I come in and talk with you?" she asked, smiling.

"Of course." Although I was slightly dizzy from the vodka and wanted only to go to sleep, Adriana and I, both at Berri and here, often talked until late into the night in her room or mine, and I did not feel I could turn her away.

She sat down on my bed.

"You have beautiful hair, Margaret, like beaten gold. It was one of the first things I noticed about you at Berri." She slid her hand along the back of my head in an easy, natural gesture.

"Like heavy silk, as lovely to touch as to look at."

I remained still, smiling uncertainly, for although Adriana and I often complimented each other, there was something about the way she spoke that was new to me.

She took my hand in hers, gently, and began to talk of beauty in a general way, studying my face closely all the while.

Suddenly she stopped talking and leaned closer. One blinding moment later her warm lips were upon mine. I remained perfectly still, mesmerized by shock. I did not think of her kiss as passionate, for how could that be? She was not a male. But neither did I mistake it for just a further expression of our friendship. We had exchanged kisses and hugs many times, as schoolgirls do, but this kiss was far more than that. Precisely *what*, I was at a loss to know.

"Your lips are so soft, Margaret," Adriana whispered. She drew my head to her shoulder, murmuring that I was beautiful, that I was her love, her darling. At that moment I should have eased away, but I scarcely knew how to do it without appearing gauche. In the midst of my mental chaos I realized that her hand was on my thigh, exploring, and then it was too late. I knew I was making a great mistake, something I would be ashamed of later, but I was caught. I let it happen completely, and then she showed me how to please her.

I did not sleep that night. When Adriana finally left me, I lay awake staring into the darkness, unable to believe it had happened, shocked anew each time I realized it really had. The first time I had made love, it had been with a woman, not a man! Why had I done it? Answers came easily—the vodka I had drunk; my social and sexual inexperience; the fact that Adriana had taken me completely by surprise, showing an expertness that belied her eighteen years; the licentious atmosphere of the villa Rantana—but none of them provided any ease to my tortured spirit.

I resolved that I must leave the villa as soon as morning came. Money from my father still had not arrived, so that I would be forced to ask Adriana to advance me funds, but that could not be helped. Leave I must.

As soon as the first rays of light came through the windows I rose and dressed. I packed all my belongings and went to knock on Adriana's door. It was still very early and she was asleep, but she woke cheerfully enough and greeted me warmly.

When I told her that I was leaving, she was silent for a

moment, and then her whole attitude changed. She treated
what had happened as of no consequence.

"Oh, Margaret, you English are so bourgeois! Still, it's of
no importance to me. You need not leave on my account.
Most of the time I love men, old ones and young ones. Don't
flatter yourself that I'm interested in you as a lover. A friend,
yes. But lovers—poof, I have too many as it is. However,
leave if you wish. I will be happy to provide you with traveling money, but it will take me a few days to arrange for it."

More than a few days passed, but the money was still not
forthcoming. And I'd had time to realize that I did not know
where to seek refuge. I had decided that I could not go to my
relatives, the Cherbiers, in Bordeaux. In my present state of
guilt and shame, I was ready to believe that everyone on the
Continent—except for me, poor fool—knew of the infamous
Villa Rantana and what went on there. I did not want my
relatives to learn I had been at the villa.

As for going home to Lancashire, I was haunted by my
mother's words: ". . . you are a wicked, willful girl. . . .
I'm sure you will have your fit reward one of these
days. . . . Just don't come crying to me!" I was certain that
as soon as she looked at me my mother would know what
had happened—and that she had been right. I could not bear
to face her.

I had some mad notion that once I had relations with a
person of the opposite sex, I would be redeemed. There was
no shortage of willing partners at the villa, but of course my
endeavor was doomed before it was begun, for I went about
it with no feeling of love or desire. The event proved to be
embarrassing and mechanical. Without passion. Without even
affection on either side. I felt more sullied than I had before.
I stayed in my room and wept. It was then that Adriana, who
had been keeping out of my way, came to me. Her words
and gestures of comfort soon became something more. Lost
and confused, I succumbed again.

After that I felt that I was ruined, damned forever, that it
no longer mattered what I did. I might as well try to enjoy
the role I had been thrust into—that of a sophisticated
woman in a sophisticated world.

As the days drifted by, the pretenses of polite civilization
among the people gathered at the Villa Rantana dropped
away altogether. The laughter became more abandoned and
the debauchery more flagrant. There was a constant going
from one room to another, from bed to bed, indiscriminately.

The objective seemed to be for each member of that sum-
mer-long house party to try each other at least once. I joined
in, hesitantly at first, then with desperate abandon. I was
drinking heavily, and I tried not to let myself be aware of how
little joy there was in my frantic gaiety.

Although money from my father had finally come, with an
apologetic letter explaining that business problems had prevented its being sent sooner, I remained where I was.

When the first breezes of autumn blew down from the
mountains and the fires were started, I prepared to leave for
Berri. Adriana was not coming back to school. She was
eighteen, and it was time for the Rantanas to display their
marriageable daughter in the glittering capitals of Europe.
Before we parted she told me that she adored me, that she
would never truly love anyone but me, and vowed that someday we would be together again always. I paid little heed to
her words, sick at heart about the dissolute summer and
wanting only to put all of it behind me. I did not realize
then that Adriana was not someone to be cast off so easily.

CHAPTER 4

Back at school, my common sense reasserted itself. I ceased
to believe that I was damned forever or that I had destroyed
myself so irrevocably that it no longer mattered how I lived.
I determined to become "the scholarly one" again. There
would be no more adventures in love. What passed for love
had brought me no happiness or fulfillment anyway.

It was not, however, easy to exorcise the summer. Everyone at Berri seemed to have heard of the decadent pastimes
at the Villa Rantana—and of my part in them. Adriana had
fashioned a name for me at school the previous year—"the
white and gold angel"—and now I frequently overheard myself referred to as "the tarnished angel." All during the fall
and even into the winter I was still encountering sly smiles
and insinuating remarks, and I worried about how far the
stories had spread.

Several letters came from Adriana, describing her life in
Rome and elsewhere, and telling me how much she missed

me. Eventually the letters thinned and then ceased altogether. I assumed that she had found new diversions, and I was relieved.

What did concern me was the absence of letters from my father. I wrote to him faithfully once a month, but I received no replies. I told myself that he was busy and I would hear from him when he had time to write. I scarcely admitted to myself that not hearing from him was easier for me, for his letters would surely have renewed the feelings of guilt I still felt.

Then, in May of 1842, the letter arrived.

It was in my mother's hand, the first time she had written to me since I started in Berri.

> Dear Margaret,
>
> Had you found the decency to return to Greystones for the summer holidays, you would have noticed a great change in your father. He has not seen you this year in Paris because he did not wish you to view him in his present condition, always believing that he would return to health.
>
> This has not happened. He is dying. I suggest that you take leave of your school and prepare for a journey home, as distasteful as you might find that.
>
> Mother

I cried for almost a day. My beloved father was dying and I had failed him. At last I understood the reason I had received no letters from him. He had been too ill to write and my mother would not, except to impart news that she knew would hurt me. I dreaded going home, for fear my reputation had traveled before me, but I was going anyway. I was determined to reach Liverpool before my father died. I had to see him one more time.

The next morning I left for Charente. It took two painful days to reach the brandy-loading port. I walked down the dock under a drift of fine rain. Above, the clouds were boiling and tumbling upon each other in fast-moving patterns of gray curls. Wind-driven water lapped briskly at the quay, and further out the harbor was shredded with breaking waves. Overhead the gulls cried, and their keening echoed in my heart.

Within the hour I would be leaving France aboard a small
side-wheeler, the *Cognac*, bound for Liverpool.

I had been gazing at the frothy bay for some time, holding
an umbrella above my head and lost in thought, when I became aware that I was being watched. Near the cargo
"lumpers" who were swinging the brandy cases aboard stood
a tall, broad-shouldered man with a head of fiery red hair.
Even from a distance I could see the vivid network of
freckles that colored his face, the level gray eyes studying me
more intently than good manners would dictate. I allowed my
eyes to linger on his before forcing myself to lower them dec-
orously and turn away. That he was admiring me I had no
doubt. And despite my present unhappiness and self-con-
tempt, I knew on the instant that this was a man whom I
wished to know. From the moment I laid eyes on the flam-
boyant hair, the stalwart maleness outlined against a gray
French sky, I knew him to be different from the weak-faced
European youths I had encountered, in bed and otherwise.

From his breadth of shoulder and his look of bodily
strength, I could have believed him a laborer, a man who
worked with his muscles, lifting or digging things, except that
he was too well dressed to belong to the lower classes. There
was something about his stance, his lithe body relaxed and
yet alert, and in the devil-may-care tilt of his red head, that
put me in mind of the sword-wielding, treasure-seeking adventurers I had encountered in my childhood reading. I
judged him to be in his early twenties, and when he approached and spoke to me, his voice left no doubt that he
was educated.

"Am I correct in believing you to be Mademoiselle Millbrook?" he asked with a smile in which respect struggled to
overlay admiration.

"Yes, I am."

"I'm Oliver Jardine. I'm traveling with you back to the
Mersey."

We shook hands as the crew hauled my bags up the gang-
way. Once aboard, I found myself confused, for something
about the *Cognac* seemed vaguely unfamiliar. It was not until
an hour later, when I had unpacked and settled into my quarters just aft of the midship saloon, that I recognized the
source of my unease. It was not my memory playing a trick
on me; the *Cognac* had changed.

I knew the ship well, having traveled back and forth on

her from Liverpool to Charente many times, preferring the steamer to my father's brigs. As a little girl I had explored every inch of the vessel, and I always felt that I could find my way blindfolded around the side-wheeler. When the towline had been stretched to the steam tug and our hawsers slipped, I came up on the deck to watch the familiar sights of the Charente River slide by. Below I had noticed certain changes: the buffet table at the far end of the small saloon had been moved; the four cabin doors which had been varnished in years past were painted oyster-white. But on the busy deck, the alterations became more apparent. For one thing, I did not recognize the master and the mates, and I had thought I knew all our seagoing personnel.

These were new men.

Then there was the smokestack. Grandfather had used the insignia of two bands circling the blue stack, one white and one red. They were intended to signify our trading relationship with France. Someone had changed this; now there was a dark stack with a large blue band upon which was painted a blue star.

It had been several years since I had been aboard the *Cognac*. Naturally, I rationalized, a few things were bound to change in that period. The light rain began to increase. I retired below and was putting away a last few items when there was a gentle knock at the door. I opened it and the mate, a tall, sinister-looking man in a wet and dirty uniform, stepped into the cabin.

"It's about the passage fare, Miss Millbrook."

"Passage fare? What do you mean?"

"I'm here collectin' it."

"I made the arrangements with the agent in Charente."

"You booked passage through the agent, but you didn't settle the account, which is eleven pounds six."

"I've *never* paid for a passage on my father's ships!"

There was a long pause, and a slight smile came to his face.

"Your father hasn't owned these ships for almost a year. They were taken over by the Jardines."

The words stunned me! My father's shipping line taken over by the Jardines? That was why the stack symbol had been changed! My heart started to pound, I felt as if the secure base of my whole world had shifted off center.

"How did it occur?" I asked, when I was able to speak.

"I don't know, ma'am. I'm only the mate. I was told to collect the fare."

"I wish to speak with Mr. Oliver Jardine."

"Very well, ma'am."

The moment the mate was out the door, I burst into tears. My father close to death, the Millbrook Line gone! What terrible tragedy had brought my father to this state, and why had he not been able to tell me about it? Despite my inner turmoil, I managed to gain some control of myself before Oliver Jardine arrived.

"Margaret . . . may I address you as Margaret . . .?"

"Please do."

"The first officer tells me that you did not know about the transfer of the Millbrook Line."

"I had no suspicion such a thing had happened. Or possibly *could* happen. Why did my father sell it?"

"I don't know the circumstances because I was up at Glasgow University. All I can tell you is that I received a letter from my father saying that he had bought out the Millbrook interests. I've just been in Austria attending an engineering conference, and Father thought this would be a good opportunity for me to observe his new steamer. That's why I'm aboard."

"Did he say that my father was too ill to attend to his business?"

"He did not. I know nothing else, Margaret, but if you do not have the passage fare, I can make arrangements."

"Of course I have the passage fare. It is just that I thought I was traveling aboard my family's steamer and . . . well, now I find that it belongs to your family. Who *are* you?"

"My father, Matthew Jardine, commanded a royal naval vessel until he retired seven years ago. He had always wanted to get into shipping for himself. We live at Holylake, over on the Cheshire strand." The gray eyes fixed on my face were concerned. "I regret this incident, Margaret, and your distress. I thought you knew."

I was so steeped in sorrow and disbelief that I could not take the evening meal. I remained in my cabin and lay awake late into the night, trying to imagine the course of events back in Lancashire.

I was dimly aware that the vessel seemed to be plowing through very heavy seas, and when I woke from a short, fitful sleep, there was a shriek to the wind and a rattle of the yards and halyards, for the vessel had auxiliary sails set upon three masts. As I tried to fetch my bearings, I heard a throaty explosion and then the hiss of escaping steam; the vessel was lurching about, almost out of control, and above me was the continual crash of the swift sea and the sound of men screaming. I made my way through the saloon and carefully climbed the midships companionway. When I unlatched the double half doors, a tongue of wind and water darted in, almost knocking me back down the companionway ladder. In the brief second that I looked through the open door I saw that the smokestack had collapsed. Perhaps the boiler had blown up! Whatever the damage, the steamer was out of control and helpless, tossed like a cork by the mountainous waves of raging water crashing about her.

I was descending the ladder, shaking with fear, when there came another crash from behind me. The oil lamp went out. I stood in the darkness, too terrified to move. It had sounded like a waterfall! Though I could see nothing, I felt the swirl of icy water lashing and curling about my feet, and terror surged through me. That crash must have been the skylight over the large walnut dining table. Its colored glass had been shattered by a wave, and the ship was taking the seas through the gaping hole in the deck.

Certain that the vessel was sinking, I clutched the base of the companionway ladder, trying to hold back panic. Should I race for the deck or stay below? No place was safe.

Suddenly, cold as the water swirling about my feet, came the certainty that this catastrophe was no haphazard accident but a punishment being meted out to me. First, my father was dying; then the shipping firm no longer ours; now this unseasonable storm had leaped upon the vessel and next, I had no doubt, would come death. I had been judged and condemned. I could not remember a moment in my life when I had felt so guilty—and so irrevocably doomed.

Above the roar of the crashing storm, I tried to make my peace, calling out to God. "Yes, yes, I accept it. I am sorry, but do what You must!"

"Do what?" a voice came back to me. "Margaret? Are you down there? Come topside and get aft. Hurry!"

It was Oliver Jardine's voice, and as I hurried to climb the companionway ladder his hand reached down to help me. I grasped it and breathed a little prayer of thanks, for respite if not safety.

The ship was dying and I knew it; long sweeps of angry water washed over the deck, and I could not tell where the

sea stopped and the ship began. Several yardarms came out
of the blackness and crashed upon the deck, rolling to the
weakened gunwales, where they pounded the timbers apart.
Cascades of water were boiling through the midship skylight
as the sailors ran about like a pack of crazed animals, stumbling and seemingly directionless in their panic. The engine-
room gang had left their posts and crawled to the deck to
witness the horror, and the sound of escaping steam came up
from the belly of the *Cognac*.

The master had panicked. I could hear him shrieking one
order after another and countermanding them as swiftly, but
it scarcely mattered, as his voice was carried away in the
pitch of the gale. Oliver Jardine continued to haul me aft, to
the raised poop, where there was some safety. There he
lashed a manila line about me and secured the other end to
the mizzenmast.

"That will at least keep you aboard!" he bellowed.

"But we're going to sink!"

"No, Margaret Millbrook, we are not going to sink," he
shouted close to my ear. "We are going to survive!"

Oh, how I wanted to believe him; but the *Cognac* was
plunging deeper and deeper in the mounting seas, and I
thought him gallant, but a fool. He wasted little time remon-
strating with the captain, for even I could see that the man
was in a blind panic. While I watched, Oliver Jardine drove
his fist into that wild-eyed, whiskered face, bundled the man
toward the aft-deck hatch, and stuffed him below. Having asserted his authority in so forceful a fashion, he rallied the
crew and set them to useful work. While one group stretched
a tarp over the broken skylight, another set a small, steadying
sail, and Oliver Jardine took the helm, spun it, and headed
the vessel off downwind, where her response to the seas came
under control. Roped to my mast, I watched in amazement.
Here was a man of courage and skill, unlike any other I had
ever met. If I had found him attractive before, I thought him
doubly so now. When dawn finally flushed the darkness the
seas were still enormous, but they were not jumping aboard.
Simply being alive to see another morning seemed a miracle,
and Oliver Jardine a part of it.

Five days later, under our auxiliary, England appeared just
after dawn, much as I remembered leaving it—a thin slice of
green off the starboard quarter and over it the brownish
mantle of factory smoke. Lancashire.

Two hours later the pilot was aboard and the tug pulled us

into the Mersey; the forest of masts was thicker, the smoke darker, and the waterside more crowded and ugly than when I had left. When the lines were ashore, I looked up at our old quay and saw that where the sign had previously said, "THE MILLBROOK LINE," there was another emblem: "JARDINE AND SON, LTD."

"Would you like me to accompany you back to Greystones, Margaret?" Oliver asked as my bags were passed ashore.

"That won't be necessary. I'll take a hansom cab."

"I wish to see you again, Margaret, if you will allow it. But I don't know my schedule up in Glasgow. If I have to leave immediately, I'll send you a message, if I may."

"That will be most kind, Oliver. And"—I placed my hand on his arm—"please accept my thanks for what you did. I owe my life to you. We all do."

For a moment Oliver Jardine's hand covered mine, his strange silver-gray eyes smiled down at me, and I knew, for a certainty, that we two should meet again.

"No doubt you would have made a fetching addition to Heaven, Margaret—a sweet little blonde angel—but I doubt they would have allowed a redheaded rakehell in. So I'm glad you'll be gracing Lancashire instead."

"*Au 'voir*," I called softly, enchanted with the man and with his vision of me, and guiltily thankful that my face didn't betray my experiences in Italy.

The gloominess and depression of Lancashire smote me as the hansom cab crossed on the winch ferry and we started down for the opposite side of the fetid, nut-brown river. It had begun to rain, as usual, and I thought that was unfair; at least the sun might have shone on my return to Liverpool. Instead it became darker and darker, and my nostrils were tickled by the coal smoke which hung in the air. Then, nestling under the fast-racing scud clouds that are peculiar to Lancashire, the vaulted roofs and high chimneys of Greystones came into view. The outlines grew larger and larger, and once again the eerie sensation I had experienced when I first boarded the *Cognac* returned. I had found the *Cognac* strange, unfamiliar. Now Greystones, as we drew closer, seemed subtly different. The silhouettes of the roofs against the furnace sky . . . those black spikes pointing into the air at wild angles . . . As I peered from the window of the hansom cab the explanation struck me like a blow. There had been a fire!

I pushed aside the talk panel and asked the driver, "What happened at Greystones?"

"Burned about a week past. The master died in the flames. Hadn't been too well, they say."

My head plunged back against the velvet seat; tears rushed into my eyes and my hands began to shake.

I was too late. Papa was gone.

CHAPTER 5

The coach rolled up the crushed-stone driveway. Through my tears I saw the large black hole of what had been the bow windows with their tinted leaded glass. The great oak door, which Papa said had come from an old castle, was blackened and hung at an angle from the half-melted iron hinges. The cab drew to a halt and the driver opened the door, but I did not move.

"This is it, mum. This *was* it, I should say."

I stared at the ghostly wreckage of what had been my life. God knows, I was shaken at seeing the old house destroyed, but it was the feeling that I had deserted my father in the very end which filled me with overwhelming grief.

I had to see one room, just one room, and I asked the hansom driver to wait.

"I'll be walkin' you inside, mum, if ye wish."

"No, thank you."

I moved over the mounds of fallen slates which had tumbled from the roof, stepping this way and that, making my way through charred beams, and then I entered the dark ruins of Greystones. The beautiful chandelier which had hung in the reception room had fallen; it rested in a thousand sprinkled chips upon the heaps of burnt boards. The grand staircase, with its elegant banisters and Persian carpet runner, was ugly and still dripping. A high-pitched whistle of wind sounded throughout the opened house, and somewhere above me I heard the flapping of birds' wings—or bats. My heart pounded as I moved through the sodden debris of what had been the music room; and then I opened the ashened door to the library, the room in which I had spent so many hours with

Papa, where my imagination and love of adventure were nurtured by the kindest man in the world.

Surprisingly, the room had hardly been touched by the fire. The bookshelves had been emptied, but his large writing desk was still there with the drawers pulled open, and a few papers were scattered about the smoke-blackened carpet. A thousand memories and the face of my father flooded my mind. Trembling, I left the library and made my way past the kitchens, littered with rusted pots and pans, and out a back door.

I was glad to escape from that morbid house, from the sound of scurrying rats and the acrid smell that hung in the air. But once on the rear grounds, I became aware of how high the grass had grown; it must have gone untended for months. Clearly, Greystones had fallen on bad times long before the fire occurred. At the southeast corner of the house I could see Papa's prized conservatory, but I had no heart to visit it. Blackened wood and shards of broken glass were all that remained of that proud domed structure that had housed his precious orchids.

Papa had cultivated specimen roses when I was very small, but finally gave up in despair as Lancashire's smoke-burdened air, thick with noxious fumes, stunted their growth despite his efforts. Raising orchids under glass became his new enthusiasm. I could vaguely remember when he had had the orchid glasshouse constructed by Mr. Joseph Paxton, over my mother's strenuous objections. Only the fact that Mr. Paxton subsequently built the famed conservatory at Chatsworth, for the Duke of Devonshire, took away some of the sting for her, since she considered it a mark of importance that the duke's man had accepted a private commission from my father, costly though it was. I wondered whether Papa's more-than-fifty specimens of orchids had perished in the blaze—or been reluctantly parted with when money became scarce.

Poor Papa. His prized elderberries were a tangled clump reaching in all directions. The walks among the boxwood were covered now, and the plantings had closed in so that the shape and architecture of the back gardens had disappeared. Years of care and effort had suddenly been erased.

"Papa, Papa, what went wrong?" I whispered to the eerie desertion that surrounded me.

To the far rear, the stable doors were open and the horses were gone. I continued to move toward the rose garden, now a thorny tangle, but in the distance there was a mound of fresh earth and beside it a bouquet of flowers. My father's grave. The headstone had not been set yet, if indeed any had been planned, and I stood there in prayer for some minutes, seeking solace.

"I place fresh flowers on the grave every day," came a voice from behind me.

I spun around and saw Ned, our liveryman, standing there, his face tragic. I flew to him, throwing my arms around him as I often had in years past, when in trouble with my mother.

"I'm sorry, Miss Margaret. We're all sorry. We loved yer father."

When I regained my composure and was finally able to speak coherently, I asked the question that had been haunting me.

"Oh, Ned, what happened here? To Papa . . . and to Greystones?"

"Come back to the cottage and me wife will be fixin' a tea."

The old livery master, who had been with the family before I was born, helped me unload the hansom, and we carted my bags to his small cottage on the far side of the grazing pasture. Once inside, I regained control of myself. Ned took a lager and sat by the small table while his wife, Emily, brewed the tea, her large dark eyes darting compassionately toward me as we talked.

" 'Twas a terrible shock for ye, Miss Margaret, to come upon the house like that . . . and then the grave. . . ." Ned said.

"Oh, yes!" I struggled to control my voice. "The letters from Papa began falling off; I heard nothing for a long time. And then Mother wrote to me about his illness and I returned immediately. Did he—did Papa die in the fire?"

"He did, Miss Margaret, but he was sick long before that. Last year, little by little, yer father came into financial difficulty. Some of his ships were wrecked, I take it, and then yer mother spent more and more time away from Greystones. She had a business, ye know."

"An apothecary in Liverpool?"

"Yes, mum. She spent most weekends there. And yer father was left alone much of the time. Aye, we tried to care for him, but he was white as a snow duck and his old laughter dried up. We knew he was goin'."

"Did the doctor attend him?"

"Dr. Grimes from Birkenhead. Then of a sudden he seemed to improve a mite. We were all happy. He told us he had suffered great financial reversals, but asked if we would stay on at Greystones. Yer father promised that he would sell off some of the acreage for our wages. He was a decent man, he was."

"What of my mother?"

"She was hardly about, mum."

"And the fire?"

"Well now, the fire, that happened Sunday week. Yer mother returned home, but we saw little of her. She and yer father kept to themselves. They told the house staff they could have the weekend off. We thought that was a bit strange, because yer mother never went to the kitchens. Me wife's youngest sister, Laurie, who was visiting from Manchester, didn't know the staff had been relieved. She went into the house that night looking for Ellen—she's our daughter that did the scullery wash. Laurie thought everyone was gone, so she went upstairs to the master's chambers to have a little peek for herself. Laurie told us later that she heard conversation, and it was soon after that the smoke started to pour out of yer father's room, and Laurie ran and stumbled down the backstairs. She came to us half out of her mind, blatherin' that the big house was burnin'. Me wife and me ran out and saw a flame in every window. We tried to get in to save yer father and mother. We couldn't. The whole tenantry tried, mum. It was too late. We heard yer father screamin' and we saw him come to the window, and he was about to jump when the flames suddenly reached his nightgown and he was like a torch. The master disappeared from the window. We heard his last wail and knew he was gone."

I began to sob once more as Ned leaned over and took my hand.

"Mebbe it was too much to tell ye."

"I had to know, but Ned, did my mother die in the blaze, too?"

There was a long pause as he glanced down at the flaxen tablecloth.

"The mistress has disappeared."

"What do you mean?"

"There's two ideas, mum. Some say they saw a carriage leave Greystones just after the fire started. But yer mum has never been heard from. She didn't attend the services."

"What about her apothecary?"

"She hasn't been there, and the constable's searched Greystone's ruins. Nothin' has turned up."

"So she's probably alive?"

"We think so."

"About this conversation your sister-in-law heard, Ned. What was it?"

"Again, mum, we don't know. Laurie had a spasm over the fire. She was dazed like, and her father came down from the Midlands to fetch her back to Manchester."

"What is to happen to the estate?"

"Well, the judge at probate came for inventory a week Tuesday. He told us we'd be hearin' from him, and he awarded me a small wage to care for what was left."

"All the others are gone?"

"Yes, mum. See, the staff was reduced, week by week, there before the end. We're the last."

I spent the night in a small bed at the livery-stable cottage, and three times I woke from a frightful dream and went to the window to gaze at the remains of Greystones as the moon drifted in and out of the clouds. Around five in the morning, not being able to sleep, I felt a need to visit my father's grave again. There I wept, for my father and myself, and for fear of the changes all around me. Then I made two positive decisions: I would see our solicitors in Liverpool, Hampton and Robinson, and then I had to reach a friend, as I desperately needed someone. Oliver came to my mind.

After walking around the exterior of Greystones staring up toward the second story, I decided to enter the house once again. It was dawn; the long, awesome shadows came through the gaping windows, forced in by the low sun. I walked to the library again and opened every drawer of Papa's desk, but someone had been there before me. Then, gaining courage, I mounted the grand stairs, step after step creaking under my weight. I reached the top and started west, through the long, blackened gallery. Our many paintings were burned to tatters and only the outlines of the frames rested in their places upon the wall, blank pictures, all of them.

Long streaks of light fell through the open roof, and again I heard the flap of wings. At the end of the gallery I turned left, for I wished to see what had been my own room. I opened the door, and it was an entrance to nothing. The floor had collapsed, and what remained was a rubble far below me. In a way I was glad that the room where I lived as a young girl was gone. I moved toward my father's room. The door was burned through, so was the roof; but in his death chamber the evidence remained: there was a lump of heavy, charred curtains, and I assumed that it was in this inferno and upon that spot that he had finally died, unable to escape the flames. The bed was a skeleton, and so were the large Chippendale table and dresser. I left the appalling ruin with relief.

By the time I returned to Ned's cottage the sun was bright, and after a porridge-and-egg breakfast, the faithful old fellow saddled up the two remaining horses and drove the carriage into Liverpool to the offices of my family's solicitors. Ned offered to wait, but I said there would be no need, a statement I was shortly to regret. Twenty minutes later Mr. Robinson, a stern-faced, gaunt solicitor, stared at me coolly and imparted his stunning news.

"The inheritance, Miss Millbrook? There *is* no inheritance."

"What are you saying? Surely my father made a last testament?"

"Oh, yes, indeed. In fact, we're the advocates of probate, Miss Millbrook, but I'm sorry to tell you there's nothing but debts."

"What has gone on here?" I demanded, endeavoring to keep my composure. "My father had an estate—a shipping line. Suddenly he is burned to death in a mysterious fire and now you say there is no estate. Why? Why?"

"I'm surprised that your mother didn't inform you."

"We haven't been on the best of terms, Mr. Robinson."

"I see. Well, when your father died, he was in debt. It began about a year ago. Three of his ships were lost, and finally his line and his contracts were sold to the Jardine interests."

"So I learned, in the crossing from France. But surely there must be something left?"

"Absolutely nothing. Greystones will be auctioned off to settle the creditors."

"Then, I am suddenly—"

"Are you without funds, Miss Millbrook?"

"Yes," I whispered.

"I am truly sorry."

"But my mother has a business, I understand?"

"Oh, yes. We approached her about the debts and she told us to sell off the land."

"Do you know where she can be located?"

"I'm afraid not. I understand she disappeared after the fire."

"They said she didn't attend my father's funeral. Only the church warden and a few others were present."

My world was shattered. I was alone and poor. There were no close relatives whose help I could seek. I left the solicitor's office after obtaining the address of the apothecary, carrying my bags through the twisting and littered streets of Liverpool. I found my mother's business establishment, which appeared to be large and well run, and announced my name. It neither surprised nor impressed the whey-faced proprietor.

"Ah, yes. Miss Millbrook. We are instructed not to give out information. In any case, my employer has resumed her maiden name. She is known as Mrs. Allison now."

"But I'm her daughter. I have come all the way from France!"

"Mrs. Allison's instruction were very clear. No one is to be informed of her whereabouts."

"I am scarcely *no one!* I demand to know!"

The pale, indifferent face regarded me without interest apart from a malicious flicker of disdain. It told me that my mother's instructions had been clear in one regard, at least. *I* was not to be told of her whereabouts.

The door closed in my face and I sank to the doorstep in despair.

CHAPTER 6

There was nowhere to go and no one to turn to. If only I had accepted Oliver Jardine's offer to accompany me to Greystones! I thought of his assurance that he would call on me before he returned to Glasgow. But call on me where, now that Greystones was no more? Yet Oliver was surely the only person of substance closer than France who had the slightest interest in me. So Oliver it must be, I had no choice. Happy to welcome even so fragile a hope, I got to my feet and managed to get a hansom cab.

We crossed the Mersey and turned right, along the strand which rims the Cheshire coast. Called the Wirral Peninsula, this head of land runs for about thirty miles up to the mouth of the River Dee, which flows inland toward the Port of

Chester. At the end of the peninsula stood Holylake, seat of the Jardines.

In its own way it shared the morbidity of Greystones; perhaps it was even grimmer, for it was built of Cheshire shale and sat on a promontory of what was once a twelfth-century fortified monastery. The carriage turned by the gate lodge and we rode along a cobbled road which girded a scalloped harbor, and then the horses strained forward, pulling the carriage up the twisting road leading to the mount. Once through the gate, we halted in a courtyard. Holylake resembled more a military establishment than a home, and I wondered what sort of people, besides Oliver, lived in this pile of rough-hewn rock.

Well aware of my unconventional behavior, I held my head high, approached the door, and knocked, while the driver waited.

A very old retainer wearing fine and new-looking livery opened the door.

"I'd like to see Oliver Jardine. Miss Millbrook is calling."

"Master Oliver left for Glasgow early this morning."

"Did he leave any word for me, a message, perhaps?"

"Step in, miss, and I'll see."

I entered the chilly house and was shown into what seemed to be a minstrel gallery; the elderly man promptly disappeared through one of the doors which led off the large, dampish room. The house was still; the only sound I heard was the continual muffled crash of the waves on the rocks somewhere far below.

A door opened and a woman entered the room. The light streaming in from one of the high, mullioned windows washed out her face for a moment, but as soon as she spoke, I knew.

"Hello, Margaret."

"Mother?"

I moved forward, not understanding why my mother would be in this house, and so confounded that for a full moment I could only stare. But I was not mistaken. This was my mother, though in some way she appeared younger. Her brown hair was gathered into glossy side curls and topped with a lace cap. Her dress was of scarlet merino with a fringed paisley shawl. But her crisp voice and chill blue eyes had not changed.

"What are you doing here?" she asked, her voice as sharp as I remembered it.

"I'm—I'm looking for Oliver. And you?"

"After the fire Commander Jardine kindly offered me a place to stay. We heard that you had met Oliver."

"On the trip home. There was a dreadful storm and Oliver saved the *Cognac*."

At my use of the word "home" my mother's lips curved downward in a sardonic smile.

"Oliver left this morning for his university classes in Glasgow. I'm afraid you are too late." Again the scornful smile flickered.

"Surely he left a message for me?"

"No."

"But he said—"

I frowned, aware that she was enjoying my disappointment. "Are you certain?"

"Entirely certain."

A long pause ensued as I stood, ill at ease, under her chilly stare.

"Mother, please? *Please* tell me what happened? The fire—and why the line was sold?"

"The line was sold because it began to assume debts. I felt obliged to go to work. Fortunately, I met Commander Jardine, Oliver's father, and we went into business together."

"What business?"

"The apothecary, of course."

"And the fire?"

"A candle fell over. I tried to save your father, but it was too late. The flames consumed him and I barely escaped with my life."

"But . . . they say that you left in a carriage . . . !"

She inclined her head in barely perceptible assent.

"Your father was dead. There was nothing I could do."

"But you didn't attend Papa's funeral!"

"My condition was too delicate. Your father and I were only technically married, in any event."

"What am I to do?" I pleaded.

"I don't know. I suppose you have your life worked out."

"No—there's nowhere . . ."

"Well, I'm sure you'll find some solution."

"Is there no inheritance? Nothing?"

"You've already called around to the solicitors? I thought that would be your first stop."

"I have no funds, Mother. And nowhere to turn . . ."

"Awkward for you."

"But what am I to do?" I asked again, desperate for any crumb of hope or help.

"Margaret, the day you left Greystones you walked out of my life forever. You neither corresponded nor came home until I wrote that your father was dying."

"But I did! I wrote every month, even though I got no replies."

She merely shrugged and raised one disbelieving eyebrow.

"At least tell me what was wrong with Papa!"

"He had a disease of the lungs."

Tears flowed into my eyes, but my mother's hostility was adamant. She watched me without so much as blinking, though she knew I was begging.

"How am I to live?"

"That is your problem, Margaret. You exhausted your father's inheritance with your willful insistence on that school. I believe you have been living quite well."

"Could you advance me just ten pounds to reach Glasgow?"

"Certainly not. Furthermore, I forbid you to bother Oliver Jardine further! The Jardines are people of quality, related to the Howards of Norfolk. To the *Duke* of Norfolk!" For a moment her eyes lit with inner joy, as she savored that thought. But no part of the joy reflected on me. "A family of so lofty a caliber can have no commerce with your type!"

"What type?" I whispered.

"A deceitful, ungrateful young woman. The only reason you've come to me now is to plead for an inheritance. Well, you're wasting your time, miss! I've no doubt you are going to hell eventually. So far as I am concerned, you may leave immediately!"

"You've always hated me, haven't you?"

"You dare to pretend that I am the one who harbors an unnatural emotion? On the contrary, I was the only normal member of the family, as I am sure you are well aware. You—with your pretty, winning ways—you had a quite unfortunate attraction for your father. A weak man—though in the end he saw his error."

"I—what are you saying? I loved Papa and he loved me"!

She shrugged. "He's dead, and he left you nothing." She laughed, and her humor was as chilly as her eyes. "I match his bequest." She turned away abruptly. "I have nothing further to say to you."

"But I have no way to live! You are responsible for me until I am eighteen. I am not yet even seventeen, Mother, not for another six months. Could you not help me for a little while?"

The smile my mother turned on me then was triumphant. "*I* am responsible for you? Is that what you think? Dear Margaret, you *deserted* us, your father and me."

"Deserted! But that's ridiculous. I was sent away for an education."

She shook her head. "Your father and I disowned you for running away."

"Papa *couldn't* have done that. He loved me. And who paid the school bills at Berri if Papa disowned me?"

"When you demanded to go to Berri, Madame Bouchard requested tuition for two years. You destroyed your father financially and emotionally. He had to cut back on the crews and equipment aboard the ships. Three of them were lost and you are to blame, you little ingrate!"

"Oh, no! *No.* Papa would never have disowned me, no matter what happened."

"Ah, but he did. It was a very simple procedure. He signed a paper which our solicitors witnessed, and it was processed by the Queen's Bench."

"And I suppose you are going to say that it burned up in the fire?" I challenged.

"Oh, no, my dear, that was the one thing I saved. I knew you would arrive looking for the inheritance. I went to your father's desk and found it, even as the flames were closing in around me!"

She left the room and returned abruptly, thrusting the court order of disownment in my face. There was what appeared to be my father's signature, witnessed by Mr. Robinson, as she had claimed.

"You recognize your father's hand, don't you?"

I was not certain. "If it is his writing, he must have been persuaded to sign under some false pretense. Papa and I loved each other—trusted one another."

"You are very foolish, Margaret. When he became ill, he wrote to you constantly. I took the letters to the post three times a week, and every day he looked for some response. But there was never anything, so I can't bear to hear your hypocrisy now. You didn't love him! As he was dying he finally realized that, and so he signed the paper. And his anguish was so great that he set himself on fire."

"You said a candle started it."

"*His* candle. I was going to spare you that, but since you're being so obstinate—" She shrugged.

I looked at her supercilious smile and suddenly I was no longer devastated by her words, for I found I didn't believe them. Neither what she said about the disownment nor about the fire. Moreover, I found her behavior exceedingly strange; to go into trade was perhaps, as my father had said, logical in that she had been often alone and wanted something to occupy her mind. But to go into trade with this man Jardine, a career naval officer, not a chemist? What *was* Oliver's father to her? Apparently she had lived in his house ever since the fire. . . .

My mother picked that moment to walk toward a window, and I saw her in profile. She was pregnant! Though I was inexpert at judging such things, I surmised that she might be four months along.

"Did you try to save Papa?" I asked abruptly, not sure where my thoughts were taking me.

"Of course."

"I don't believe you."

"Get out of this house!"

"Yes, I will, for it's a strange house with a strange aura. Though perhaps that is your contribution. However, I intend to bring this matter to the Queen's Bench, for I know there is much more than you have told me and I'll wager that none of it reflects favorably on you. For example, whose baby are you carrying?"

She didn't answer, and the red flushed into her face as if a giant blood vessel had exploded, but her eyes remained steady, unflinching.

"I told you to go. Shall I summon the staff?"

I smiled. "No need, I'm leaving. I believe I will find truer answers to my questions without your help. Pray that none of them will hang you, Mama!"

With that I turned and stalked out of the room.

Actually, there was no place to go. I was down to five pounds, not enough for the trip to Glasgow, and certainly not enough for Berri, and I was not going to Adriana, because in exchange for her help, she would ask something I was not willing to give.

"Where shall I take ye, miss?" the driver asked as I returned to the hansom.

"Greystones."

"The house that burned?"

"Yes."

The carriage rolled away from Holylake and I looked at the spires and I smiled the way my mother had smiled at me. I had no doubt at all that someday, in some manner that would distress her most, I would make her rue today!

CHAPTER 7

"It's the devil's own handiwork, Miss Margaret," Ned stated, shock and disbelief etched on his weathered face as I finished telling him what had transpired at the solicitors' office and at Holylake.

"The devil's work, perhaps—and my mother's certainly," I assured him, determined to bring my suspicions into the open. I watched poor Ned struggling to be fair; he had never cared for my mother's chill haughtiness, unchanging despite his long years in her service.

At length he nodded. "I don't doubt the devil found many a willing hand to help him, mum. But as fer the master disowning ye, no, mum. I know better than that, ye see, fer I would walk with yer father every day he was well enough to walk a bit in the garden."

Ned's face set in stubborn Lancashire lines, and he shook his head in the slow countryman fashion that permitted no room for doubt. "He spoke of ye with pride, at yer fine school in France. It was his sorrow that ye never wrote to him—"

"But I did, Ned. I wrote every month, even though I received no replies. Not long letters, perhaps, but no matter how caught up I was in my life at Berri, I never forgot my father. I loved him very much. . . ."

Tears rose to choke me and I dropped my head to the table where we sat in Ned and Emily Carter's kitchen. I felt an awkward hand rest on my shoulder for a moment, and then Ned Carter said the words that made me sit bolt upright.

"And he loved ye, Miss Margaret, fer he told me so not two days afore he died. That's why I know as sure as I'm sitting here that yer father never disowned ye, no matter what piece of paper yer mother showed ye."

I held my breath, watching Ned strive to find the right words, both of us knowing that this was important.

"If ye say ye wrote to him every month, then I can only tell ye that yer father never received yer letters, mum. It was a great sorrow to him, like I said, but . . ." Ned's honest face sought to puzzle out his impressions of that last meeting with my father. "He was feeling a bit better, like. Not stronger, I wouldn't say, he was still thin as a pike and the gray look was on him. But happier in his mind, so to speak. 'Ned,' he said to me, 'I win! I win after all, Ned. My daughter will be safe!' "

Ned looked at me sharply. "Were ye in some danger then, Miss Margaret?"

I shook my head. "He was speaking of my financial situation, Ned. He must have been. If he were very ill and knew he could leave me no inheritance, that would weigh most heavily on his mind. Somehow he must have made arrangements for me to be 'safe,' to have a means of livelihood. But how? Why does the solicitor, Mr. Robinson, not know about it?"

We stared at each other in silence, trying to make sense of it.

"Was there nothing more?" I asked finally.

"Naught to speak of, mum. He said he would write to ye and asked that I post the letter when it was ready—"

"Not my mother?"

"No mum." Ned's shrewd eyes glinted for a moment. "Mayhap he figured out, mum, why he got no letters from ye, and thought the postal service worked equally poor in both directions."

I nodded, knowing at last why the letters my mother had "posted" had never arrived in Berri. "But did my father not give you the letter?"

"I never saw him again to speak to, Miss Margaret. That was two days afore the fire, ye see. Mayhap he hadn't found time to write to ye."

I didn't believe that. If my father had been excited and happy because he had made arrangements for me to be "safe," he would have wasted no time in trying to let me know. Especially if, as Ned thought, he had come to believe that his previous letters had not reached me and that I might have written letters that had not reached him. He would have been eager to reassure me. The letter had been written, I felt reasonably certain. But had it disappeared in the flames? Or had my mother come upon it before he could give it to Ned?

I looked at the two honest Lancashire faces across the kitchen table from me and thanked God that Ned and his wife Emily had been in my father's service before I was born and had loved and respected him as much as I had. They were my only link now with Greystones and my only friends in this leaden-skied world where I was obliged to remain while I endeavored to sort out the ruins of my life.

The drive back from Holylake had been exhausting. Although I had been suffering from shock and a sleepless night, my mind had seethed with feverish plans for vengeance against my stone-hearted mother, alternating with formless dreams in which I was once again my father's beloved daughter, safe and secure. I had had no experience of financial insecurity in the past, and to find its dark shadow enfolding me had filled me with panicky terror. I had worried in a desultory fashion during my stay at Berri that my schooling there must be costing my father more than he could easily afford, but I had never doubted that it would be no more than a minor burden to him. The ships and forward contracts of the Millbrook Line had always been the bulwark of my comfortable life. They were to be my legacy. They would endure. But they had not endured, and with no inheritance, not even funds to provide a roof over my head and food to sustain me, I had passed the trip from Holylake to Greystones awash in a sea of fear for myself and grief for my poor father.

When the hansom cab had finally deposited me before the livery stable at Greystones, it was dusk. I had returned to Greystones because I had nowhere else in the world to go. After paying the driver from my meager funds, I had followed the narrow footpath around the grazing pasture to the cottage, half prepared to find that Ned and Emily Carter too, would stare at me stonily and say they were "sorry" as they closed the door in my face. But they had heard my arrival and they came to meet me, eager to hear good news but far from expecting it, as their worried eyes betrayed.

When disasters come thick and fast, word has a way of sifting through all levels of society, and Emily Carter had an aunt in service at the home of Mr. Robinson, the solicitor who handled my father's affairs, so perhaps she suspected that my situation would be grim. Yet not even Emily and Ned were prepared for the news that I was literally penniless and that my mother, although apparently a woman of substance now, had rejected me out of hand.

They had taken me in and made me sit down while Emily Carter fixed me a light supper and Ned hung on every word of my account of my mother's reception of me. It was then, shocked by the wickedness of her tale of disinheritance, that Ned had remembered my father's happiness, just two days before his death, that I would be "safe," and his intention of writing me a letter to explain.

We sat in silence in the well-scrubbed kitchen with its homely furniture and heavy "china" dishes gleaming in the lamplight, each of us locked in wonderment at the strange ways of Providence. It was Emily, finally, who broke the silence.

"Tell Miss Margaret about the tub, Ned."

He frowned at her, but she set her round jaw and stared him down. "Ye know what I think, and more than likely ye think the same, though ye won't admit to it. The master was always good to us, Ned. It grieves me, it does, him dying like that when—" Her dark eyes flickered in my direction and her round chin quivered with determination. "Miss Margaret has the right to know. Let her make what she can of it."

Even then, Ned thought it over for some time before he spoke. "Me wife believes yer mother could have saved the master, mum. If she was of a mind to. There was a tub of wash water in the room, ye see. It was still there when the constables come, after the fire."

I stared from Ned to Emily as the import of that fact took hold in my mind.

"What *I* say, Miss Margaret, is why didn't she throw it over him? If it was me there in that room and Ned on fire, no power in this world would make me turn tail and run to save me own skin, leavin' him to roast."

Emily Carter's eyes were brimming with tears, and though I cringed at the picture her words conjured up, I knew I owed her a debt of gratitude.

They were very kind, Ned and Emily Carter. Good people. Not like me, God help me. They had a sense of justice, yes, and they suspected that my mother had been responsible for my father's death. But shocking as that was to them, it was outside their lives; touching on their lives, but apart. Not so for me. The thought that my mother, that cold, supercilious, arrogant woman who had always held herself above her marriage, could have saved my father's life and didn't—or more likely, I realized with a rush of instinctive knowledge, planned and executed his death—froze my very soul.

Perhaps there was some of her in me. Almost certainly there had to be. At that moment I felt her coldness rush through my veins. She had brought me into the world. I would help escort her out of it.

I cannot say how much of my emotion showed on my face, but I was conscious of the silence in the room, the ticking of the large-faced Lancashire clock upon the wall, the nervous movement of Emily Carter's fingers fussing at the lamp, turning it up, then turning it down, so that there was a tiny sputter of sound and shadows leaped on the walls.

I broke the silence. It was my problem and the solution would be mine. How I would achieve it I had no idea, but Providence would show me a way. Yet I shuddered at the thought that my mother's blood ran in me, that her deviousness and her arrogance held a foothold somewhere within me, and I hated her with an abiding hatred. As a kind of assurance that I would not become like her, I determined to face myself with honesty, to compel myself to say outright what I felt and intended.

"She murdered him. She is clever enough to have achieved it and to have got away safely. Or so she believes. I am her daughter, and I am clever enough to see that she will pay for it."

I waited then. It was for them to make whatever comment they chose.

Ned nodded first, his shrewd eyes hooded but approving in the bland Lancashire face. Emily, without looking to her husband for direction, stood up abruptly and squared her plump shoulders. Without a word being said, I knew we were partners, all three.

"Ye will live here, Miss Margaret, as long as need be. This is yer home until ye find a suitable one," Ned said. "If I can do aught else to help ye, ye have but to say the word. But this much I can do, give ye a place to call yer own so ye need not worry yer head about a roof and a meal." He turned to his wife. "Emily?"

Emily, her eyes again awash with tears of sympathy, nodded. "Evil flourishes everywhere, Miss Margaret. Ye're very young, dear, but mayhap ye already know that, being so traveled and all. We're simple people, Ned and me, but we valued the master, ye know. And," she added with a smile that triumphed over her emotional turmoil, "ye're more than welcome here, mum."

No words could convey the load that lifted from my shoulders then. I had a place to stay until I could think how best to solve my dilemma. I thanked them most sincerely and resolved to put no more burden on them than I could help. But despite my good intentions and my lack of sleep, I couldn't rest until I had explained my necessity to talk with Oliver Jardine in Glasgow at the earliest possible moment.

When Ned fully understood that Oliver was the son of Commander Matthew Jardine, the man who had bought out my father's shipping interests, who was my mother's partner in the apothecary shop, and the owner of Holylake where she now lived, he growled his agreement that I should indeed go to Glasgow.

"Aye, and the sooner the better. If this young Oliver Jardine was kind to ye on the voyage, mayhap he'll be kind enough to shed a bit of light on the present situation. I have money put by, enough to get us there and back safely, and the master's coach is in good order."

I was reluctant to make use of the Carters' hard-earned savings, but they overrode my objections, and I thanked them again with tears in my eyes.

I fully expected to lie awake another restless night. I was going to Glasgow. I was going to see Oliver Jardine again. I had to have faith that he would give me whatever help he could, for I had no other hope of learning what had happened to my family's fortunes during those fateful two years while I had lived in France. At the very least, he should be able to provide some insight into the strange coalition that appeared to exist between his father and my mother.

But as I fell asleep, it was not such practical matters that filled my mind. Instead, I saw Oliver Jardine as I had first glimpsed him on the quay at Charente, his vivid coloring and breadth of shoulder outlined against the slate-gray sky. He had stood there, studying me with an almost-bemused expression, like some alert and glorious animal faced with an intriguing, possibly dangerous, new experience. If I had thought then that I needed him to brighten the prospect of life in England, I needed him now for quite a different reason. Events had presented me with the necessity of seeking him out. With a rush of warmth I remembered his aura of confidence and raw vitality, and I realized how eager I was to see him once more. Yet somewhere deep within me I felt a flicker of warning. I would be playing with fire. Oliver Jardine, with his crop of fiery curls and red-gold freckles, was a far different man from the ones I had known in Europe. That thought was at once a challenge and an unexpected source of unease. He was going to influence my life. If I was determined to play with fire, and I was, then I would have to be very careful to keep control, or I would be consumed.

CHAPTER 8

When I had left Greystones two years earlier Papa had owned four fine Yorkshire coach horses, handsome bays with black and brown points. He had been proud of those high-stepping beauties with their elegant sloping shoulders and strong loins, and it saddened me to think he had been forced to sell two of them, as well as my Arabian mare, when financial disaster overtook him. Still, the two remaining horses were sufficient to pull the light coach, and I was pleased to see that Ned had kept the mahogany gleaming and the brass fittings bright.

Ned estimated that it would take four days for the long journey up to Glasgow, if there were no mishaps. We set out in relatively good spirits, but I soon found myself depressed by the landscape, viewed through a constant slanting rain that seemed to envelop all of the world. I had made the trip only once, years before, with my parents, and had anticipated enjoying again the view along the main road, which ran north to the Scottish border. But where I had retained an impression of fertile valleys running like long green fingers between undulating hills, and tilled, well-tended earth, I now saw only ruination.

Liverpool and the River Mersey were grim enough scenery, befouled as they were with the filth belched out by the mills and foundries that were spreading like a plague wherever the eye looked. But now I saw that the "furnace sky," that curse of English industrial progress, extended throughout all of Lancashire and beyond. From foundry hearths, spits of yellow ocher like batteries of distress rockets curved up and up, blasting the heavens with man-made ash and smoke. And

fused into this hellish light was the white steam from the
working engines that fed the blast furnaces and stirred their
spawn of pig iron. I could only pity the people who lived
within the sound of that fierce energy, for the cacophony, like
the forges, went on day and night.

Nor was that the worst of it, I realized as we traveled
north. What had been parks and woodlands was now waste-
land, its wealth of oak and birch harvested to fuel the fires
for mills and foundries. I could only imagine the plight of the
poor folk whose forebears had lived close to the land for generations and who now tramped off to the mills—men,
women, and children alike. They had learned, I supposed, to
keep time with belt-driven loomers and giggers that were to
restore England to prosperity; or they existed in the cold,
squirrel-gray workhouses that were springing up to conceal
the new "permanent poor" of the Industrial Revolution from
our eyes.

After that first day, the sun shone again and the countryside became less malevolent as we left behind the worst of
commercialized England. The coaching houses where we
stopped overnight were adequate, but by the time we neared
Glasgow I was in a fret of anxiety to see Oliver Jardine
again. I had advised Ned that I would stop at the Duke of
Cranford Hotel, because I recalled it vaguely from my previous visit so many years earlier.

We reached Glasgow at midday. If I had thought that
Liverpool rested at the entrance to hell, Glasgow, I decided,
must surely be beyond the gates. It was gritty, gray, and
pocked by gull drippings. Its people looked to be grim-faced
descendants of the Covenanters, watching narrow-eyed for
signs of the Church of England encroaching on their sacred
Presbyterianism.

Consumed as I was by eagerness to discover if I could
count on Oliver Jardine for aid, I wasted little time at the hotel. I secured accommodations that were satisfactory while
reasonable in price, and after a hurried meal which I had ordered to be sent up immediately, I prepared with great care
to present myself at the university. The dress I had brought
for the occasion was the most decorous that I owned in that
it was black, and therefore suitable to my present circumstances. Happily, it was also most becoming, for black con-
trasted to great effect with the fairness of my hair and my
complexion. And if Adriana was to be believed, added depth
to the green of my eyes.

I had Ned drive me to the university, a collection of dull stone buildings that spoke volumes about the serious purposes of the studies conducted within. The registrar was the traditional dour Scotsman, but not, I fancied, immune to femininity, for he was most courteous and arranged for me to see Oliver in a small private room off his study.

There was in Oliver Jardine some strange magnetism that had captured my imagination the first time I saw him. I was not, until a much later date, to understand it fully, but it was never more evident than when he strode into the small room where I waited. I felt again the same deep stirring within me that I had felt on the quay at Charente, an awareness of masculine vitality that exerted a powerful emotional attraction for me.

"Margaret Millbrook!" he exclaimed, seizing both of my hands in his. "How delightful to see you here. You received my message? I regretted having to leave Holylake so abruptly. . . ."

"I had no message, Oliver," I protested. "I called at Holylake but was told that you had left no word for me."

The slate-gray eyes under coppery brows darkened. "When I learned that Greystones had burned I wrote you a letter offering whatever help I could give. Mrs. Allison assured me it would be sent to you wherever you were staying."

"Mrs. Allison, as you call her, is my mother. Allison was her maiden name; apparently she has resumed it since my father's death."

Oliver stared at me blankly. "Really? I know her only as Mrs. Allison. She made no mention of you, though she knew that we traveled together from Charente. What sort of mother would behave in such a fashion?"

"A most unloving and bitter one," I assured him. "Perhaps I wasn't a lovable child. Though God knows I wanted to be—oh, that doesn't matter, she didn't love my father either, and he was surely one of the most lovable men ever born. We are . . . estranged. Until I saw her at Holylake I had no idea where she was, alive or dead, after Greystones burned."

Drawing me to a couch before the windows, Oliver Jardine bade me tell him exactly what my circumstances were and how I had happened to journey to Glasgow to find him.

I did, sparing nothing. When I had finished, Oliver shook his head as if to escape from a miasma of nightmares.

"My poor Margaret! How could any mother treat a child so—especially one as lovely and sweet as you—"

"I am sixteen, Oliver," I interrupted swiftly, stung by his words, for I had no intention of allowing so attractive a man to consider me a mere babe.

He looked momentarily startled and then threw back his head and laughed. "Yes, of course, one cannot mistake you for a child for long, Margaret." His eyes moved approvingly over me and a hint of self-mockery crossed his face. "Only you have an air of delightful innocence that is quite . . . disconcerting, I'm afraid."

Oliver Jardine frowned into the distance, thinking, and a slanting ray of sunlight from the window behind us shone directly on his hair with coruscating brilliance. I felt an almost ungovernable urge to stretch out a hand and run it through that tangle of loose curls glinting like new pennies. But this was not France. Victoria was on the throne of England, and since I was to live under her aegis, apparently, I would need to be circumspect if I wished to appear a lady. Or as circumspect as my strong attraction to Oliver Jardine would permit.

"Margaret"— Oliver spoke with sudden decision, again taking my hands in his and fixing me with those unreadable eyes—"our parents appear to be allied in some strange, secretive way. There is something clandestine in the very air of Holylake now. I have reason to believe that your mother has a great deal of money, yet she refuses to help you. My father, too, appears to enjoy the wealth of Croesus this past year, but—"

He broke off abruptly and drew me to my feet. "Let's talk of this later. Somewhere more private, for I feel we are destined to join forces. In the meantime, put your mind at rest. Since you cannot get funds from your mother, I'll contrive to get them from my father. Enough to keep you from penury, at least."

A smile, dancing with deviltry, broke over his face. "Perhaps it all comes from the same pocket."

We arranged that Oliver would come to my suite in the Duke of Cranford Hotel as soon as he was free, and we would continue our discussion over dinner. Ned drove me back to the hotel, my mind seething with new excitement, all of it centered on this compelling Jardine man. He had said we had a great deal of planning to do if we were to "solve our problems and realize our future ambitions." I told myself that that was merely a turn of phrase; hardly a reason to conjure up rosy, romantic dreams. My mind agreed, but not my heart. A delicious warmth stole through me at the very thought of my future securely linked to Oliver Jardine's. Though I had just left him, I could scarcely wait for the time to pass until I should see him again.

Oliver arrived at my hotel, elegant in black evening attire that justified my admiration for his broad shoulders. I took his cloak and beaver hat, and soon we were sitting in the small but comfortable sitting room of my suite, sharing confidences like a pair of conspirators over the champagne he insisted we must have to inaugurate our partnership. Sipping it, caught up in his story but unable to keep a part of my mind from falling prey to the sheer appeal of the man, I found my own excitement rising to match what I read in his eyes.

"First I must tell you that my father was not a wealthy man until roughly two years ago," Oliver began. "His pension from the Royal Navy and a small annual income that comes to him through our Howard forebears was the sum of our wealth. Enough to live on in mediocre style, but my father, who had long been a naval commander of the brig *McIntosh* on the Singapore station, was accustomed to high living. He fretted a good deal at his reduced circumstances, but not only because of that. He has a great hunger to be wealthy and regain what he considers his rightful place in society.

"Quite suddenly everything changed. From being morose and resentful he became feverishly intent on some new scheme, and spent long hours in his library at Holylake and on trips to Liverpool and London."

Oliver flung a quizzical glance in my direction. "It was by no means the first scheme he had involved himself in, but it appears to be the first time one of them had succeeded so lavishly."

He quitted his pacing long enough to replenish our champagne glasses, then seated himself across from me, at the small table before the bow windows looking down on the street.

"Margaret, I know nothing of your mother except what little you've told me. But I know something of my father and his hunger for wealth and recognition. He enjoyed power, you see, in his years of command, and more than a modicum of fame. But it all came to nothing when he was retired. He's been driven by devils ever since. And he has Howard blood in his veins. The Howards have controlled wealth and power in England since before Elizabeth's time, and my father feels very keenly the vast gap between his own position and that of the titled members of his grandmother's family. A legitimate link with royal blood, yet it avails him nothing! I believe since his retirement his imagination has fed on nothing but the determination to raise his own station: peerage through the power of wealth."

I laughed. "In my mother, he has surely found a match for his ambition. But Oliver, I fail to see how an apothecary shop can be the answer."

"No more do I. All the same, for the past two years, he appears to have had access to large sums of money. When your father's shipping firm fell into financial difficulties he was able to purchase it. In addition, he has spent a great deal on the repair and refurbishing of Holylake."

With a ferocious scowl, Oliver sprang to his feet and resumed his restless pacing. "And with all of this, he still refuses to consider the venture that means everything to me, unless he can impose conditions that would doom it to failure from the outset."

Oliver's air of anger straining at its leash was so forceful that I felt a tremor of foreboding. I would take pains not to incur it, I promised myself, for I felt he would stop at nothing if the temper that must accompany that head of copper hair once slipped his control. But what ambition was his father thwarting, that his resentment was so passionate?

When I asked, he shrugged and fobbed me off with the response that we would come to that in good time. "There is nothing that can be done about it until we learn what's going on behind the scenes." He gave me an uncertain look. "I suppose you are aware that your mother is pregnant?"

"And I suppose, since she is now living at Holylake, that your father is responsible?"

"I find lechery at their age distasteful," Oliver responded coldly. "No doubt with your father conveniently removed from the picture, and their shared affluence, they will marry in time to give the child a name."

The intelligent, strong-boned face above the white cravat and ruffled shirt became suddenly older. "Has it occurred to you how tidily events appear to work to their advantage?"

"You mean"—I could scarcely force the words out—"my father's death?"

"Fortuitous, in view of your mother's delicate condition. Also, your father's illness afforded her the freedom to pursue her new career."

"For every reversal my father suffered, those two reaped a gain," I agreed bitterly.

"Three of your father's ships were damaged at sea within months of each other, enabling my father to get control of the line. *Three* of them. Accidents apparently. Such good fortune defies credulity."

My heart seemed to stop, as all of my unfocused suspicions came together in a rush. I had accused my mother of being responsible for my father's death and, God knows, the core of hatred that seemed to be at the center of her being made almost anything she might do believable. Ned had suspected her, certainly. But this was Oliver Jardine, whose quickness of mind I was beginning to appreciate. And he was as good as implying that there was little he wouldn't believe his own father capable of. But why was he allying himself with me in this matter?

I found out in short order.

"Tell me again, Margaret, what makes you so sure your father left you provided for, in spite of the fact that the solicitor says the estate left only debts."

I repeated to him, as exactly as I could, Ned's tale of my father being in good spirits only a few days before his death, and his statement that he had "won, after all." That I would be "safe." To me, that was open to only one possible interpretation—my father had somehow found himself once again able to ensure my future. I told Oliver that I had thought perhaps some investment had suddenly produced an unexpected windfall of profit, something my mother knew nothing about, and that my father had secretly put it in my name, to protect it from his creditors.

As I talked, I became aware that there was a considerable amount of speculation in the look Oliver Jardine turned on me. For the first time I realized that the help he had so generously proffered might depend on the assumption that I would indeed have an inheritance. As swiftly as the thought was born, I let it slip away. I was under the spell of this cool-eyed man, and any vision of my future must have him in it. Only let me discover the meaning of my father's cryptic words to Ned . . . let me find and claim my inheritance . . . and I asked nothing better than to have Oliver by my side to share it.

And so I set about making sure that Oliver Jardine would find me of such interest that he might well forget why he wanted wealth in the first place. I arranged for dinner to be served in the cozy privacy of my suite. I flirted with Oliver throughout the meal, as if we were newly met at a grand dinner party with a score of other guests around us. But when we had finished, I pleaded weariness.

"Dear Oliver, we have much to talk of still. I know that you have suspicions you haven't yet confided to me. And I need your guidance in making my own plans for the future. But this has been a long and wearing day. Would you take it amiss if I were to put on a comfortable wrapper and take down my hair? Truly, these pins feel as if they're piercing my very brains."

He was on his feet instantly. "My poor Margaret, I've been inconsiderate to stay so long. I should have known you were tired. I'll leave immediately, we can talk tomorrow—"

"Oh, please, Oliver, no! My head is so full of confusion that I know I shouldn't be able to sleep. I should toss and turn half the night, trying to resolve all of our mysteries. Of course I mustn't take down my hair. That was merely a foolish impulse. . . ."

But the glint was already in his eyes. Nothing would do but that I unpin my hair immediately, and by all means put on a comfortable wrapper. . . .

I judged Oliver Jardine to be possibly five years or so older than I, and of considerable experience with women, for there was a sense of self-assurance about him that, combined with his build and obvious virility, had great appeal.

Oliver, I felt sure, thought that he was seducing an innocent. I did nothing to disabuse him of the notion. Having made the intial "error" of allowing an atmosphere of intimacy to establish itself in the sitting room of my suite, I had merely to gaze at him from a safe distance while earnestly seeking his advice—and let nature determine the outcome.

"Oliver, I feel I must start back to Greystones tomorrow. Ned has duties there and I dare not keep him from them too long. If only I could leave here feeling that we had worked out some course to follow—"

"You cannot continue to stay at the livery cottage, Margaret," Oliver declared, his gray eyes trying desperately to devour every inch of my body in the sea-green wrapper. "You must visit an estate agent and see what is suitable in the way of a cottage where you can live temporarily. I will make whatever arrangements are necessary."

"Yes, Oliver," I replied in a little-girl voice that seemed to see no further than his words.

"Near Greystones would be best, I think, and . . . nothing too grand, at the moment, I'm afraid." Whether from unease at what he was about to say or from some more basic need, Oliver was on his feet again, pacing. "It's your mother who holds a tight purse string where I'm concerned. She feels a proprietary interest in my father's funds. Protecting the patrimony of her unborn child, no doubt."

"I expect she dreams of a son," I commented, unable to keep the bitterness from my voice, "having been so disappointed in a daughter."

"While my father dreams of a daughter, you think? Some spiritless creature who will agree with his every vagary?" Oliver's strong thighs were dark against the lamplight as he moved closer to the chair where I sat. "Ah, well, they're riding the crest now, but we will have our own plans, beautiful Margaret, I promise you."

He sank to the floor at my feet. "Be ready to leave for Liverpool in one week, Margaret. Our first undertaking must be a trip to France."

Those words were pure joy to my ears, for while I had determined to avoid France in the future, to go there with Oliver was another matter. I sensed the excitement on his face reflected in my own, as he reached out and clasped my hand.

"I no longer believe in miracles, Margaret. The transfer of the Millbrook Line, with its forward contracts still intact, to Jardine and Son took human effort. I propose to find out how the matter was arranged. Those contracts interest me. The cargo from Charente to Liverpool, from the time your grandfather inaugurated the Millbrook Line, has always been wine and brandy from the Cherbier vineyards—"

"The Cherbiers are our relatives," I interrupted eagerly. "My father's mother was a Cherbier. You know how insular the French are about family, Oliver. If there is anything to be learned they will want to help me, I know."

Oliver Jardine nodded, his eyes on my face. "Yes, I think anyone . . ." He hesitated. "You have a quality, Margaret . . . a most appealing naïveté. . . ."

He reached out for me and I slid from the chair onto the floor beside him and into his arms, as naturally as an unsuspecting child. Tilting my head up, he kissed me softly on the point of my chin, and then drew back. One hand smoothed my hair back from my brow, as the opaque silver-gray eyes searched mine for—what? I slid my arms around his neck and with a groan, he began to kiss my face.

All of my resolutions to be clever where Oliver was concerned ebbed away. I seemed to have no strength in my limbs. I wanted only to cling to him, to have his hands, his lips, his mind, devoted to loving me. As for my future, all that remained of my clever plans was a prayer: let Oliver share it.

"Oh, Margaret. Little Margaret. What am I doing?"

In wordless response, I wrapped my arms more tightly around his neck and sought his lips with mine. For a moment he went utterly still, and then whatever pangs of conscience had assailed him were washed away in the flood of desire that had taken us both by storm. I clung to him as he carried me into the bedchamber, remembering with wonder the transient lovers I had known, as unreal now as passing shadows. Oliver Jardine undressed me, and, his trembling hands at my bodice, his lips at my breasts, burned away every memory of my past.

"Margaret. Lovely Margaret. Are you real . . . or a delicate Dresden doll brought to life just for me?"

There are many ways of making love, as I had reason to know. Oliver wiped out all previous experience. His love, whatever form it took—and that night it took many, for nothing seemed to be enough—was the only love that would ever matter to me. I knew it with frightening clarity and I didn't want to know it. I didn't want to pay the price of loving this man, for the price would come high. I knew it, yet I clung to him, cradled him, reveling in the feel of his coarse red hair against my cheek, in the warmth and strength and musky scent of him, sharing his driving need of me, and the exultation of knowing myself possessed, body and soul.

Later, I watched as he dressed by the soft light of the turned-down lamp, marveling at the long, hard-muscled lines of his legs and buttocks, remembering the feel of him against my flesh.

He leaned over me, running a finger along my brows, over the planes of my face.

"My beautiful little doll. Don't look at me with those big eyes, for they shame me."

I smiled up at him and he dropped to his knees beside the bed, his strong-boned face contrite.

"Oh, God, Margaret. I feel like some rake who has stolen—misused—innocence. My sweet little love, why did you *let* me?"

For a moment I wanted to wipe the troubled look from his face; to tell him the truth. I was no innocent. Tonight, held close in his arms, loving him, I had indeed felt as if this were

my first experience. But instinct told me that we must bear
our own burdens, and mine was the guilty knowledge of that
dissolute summer. I believed now that Oliver Jardine loved
me. I couldn't bear to see the tenderness on his face vanish
forever. No, the burden was mine. I must keep my past to
myself, and pray that Oliver would never learn of it.

CHAPTER 9

Despite my intention never to reenter the ruined hulk of my
old home, I found myself repeatedly drawn there during the
week that followed my return from Glasgow. I knew that
Ned and Emily watched worriedly whenever I left their small
cottage. I think they feared both my melancholy and the
physical perils of sagging staircases and falling roof tiles.

Greystones had been an unhappy home for me and I did
not make the mistake of enshrining it in memory because it
was gone. Yet it was my only link with my father. Walking
in its overgrown gardens, I thought I could sense his presence
and was alternately engulfed by grief and loneliness or fired
with strength, sure that he had loved me dearly despite my
mother's tale of disownment.

The last time I entered that unhappy house alone, Ned and
Emily, if they had seen me, would have felt their fears for
my reason well-founded. It was very late on a gray and dismal afternoon. I think that as the sun neared the western
horizon it tried to pierce the overcast, for the sky had a
strange, unearthly glow. The very air seemed dull yellow,
deepening into an ocher sky that had nothing of sunlight
about it but made me think fearfully of some strange nether-
world where nothing was as it seemed. It was then that I felt
my father's presence most strongly, as if he were just ahead
of me, behind the next clump of overgrown rhododendron,
around the next misshapen boxwood hedge, leading me
toward the blackened ruins of Greystones. Across the threshold, across the threshold, now come this way . . . this
way. . . .

Perhaps it was imagination, born of my fierce need to believe in my father's affection. Perhaps it was merely the cul-

mination of my mourning, demanding one last moment with
him before I could turn to the future. All I know is that I
followed, fearful of the shadowy depths of the house, for
even there the yellow cast seemed to penetrate. If he had led
me up the perilous grand stairs, would I have gone? Very
likely, for I was no longer aware of the charred, rain-soaked
stench that hung like a pall over the house. As I moved
through the entry hall I could sense, very faintly, the scent of
bay rum that I had associated with my father since my childhood. A drift of memory—or something more? I neither
knew nor cared, for I moved as one in a dream, with no
choice but to follow this strange compulsion. Through the
scarcely recognizable remnants of the music room, through
the open door of the library, swaying gently from the drafts
that circulated in every direction throughout the open-roofed
house, but giving the effect of having just been opened for
me.

Here.

I stood inside the doorway, peering into the dusky recesses
of the room, surprised again at how slightly the fire seemed
to have damaged it. There was little enough to see. Virtually
everything had been removed save my father's desk. I wondered who had taken away all of his books, so often shared
with me. My mother? Almost certainly my mother, for who
else would have emptied his desk, leaving only a few unimportant newspaper clippings scattered on the floor, clippings
related to the wreckage of his vessels. I had gathered them up
on a previous visit and placed them in one of the open desk
drawers. Who but my mother would have left nothing in that
room except for an oil miniature of me that my father had
had painted when I was twelve and that she had never liked?
Perhaps she would have taken that, too, I thought bitterly, if
the gilt frame had had some value.

I took what there was, the newspaper clippings and the
portrait, resolving to keep them always. Sad mementos, perhaps, but the only ones I had.

As suddenly as it had come, the compulsion to be in this
house left me. I made my way at a panicky run out of the
gloomy place—the acrid stench of burnt wood and carpeting
was back, strong in my nostrils, and I found myself holding
my breath until I was again in the open air. I ran all the way
to Ned's cottage as if the Devil himself were on my heels. I
arrived breathless, feeling that I had eluded evil by a hairs-

breadth but, for the first time since I had returned to England and Greystones, with a sense of inner peace.

From that day forward I left the past behind and nurtured my dream of the future. "Margaret will be safe," my father had told Ned. Very well, I would discover the source of that safety, whatever it might be. And with Oliver Jardine's help, I would try to discover how and why my father had died.

Oliver arrived, as he had promised, one week to the day from the time we parted in Glasgow. We left the Mersey Basin next morning aboard the Jardine and Son brig, *Tough Tom*, bound for Charente. As the last glimpse of the English coast slipped below the horizon, I couldn't help but contrast this leave-taking with that other, scarcely two years ago. Instead of my father by my side at the rail, Oliver Jardine stood with his feet planted apart and his adventurer's face turned toward the salt spray.

Something in the challenge of his stance, in his narrowed eyes as they checked the sails drawing overhead, the white-capped sea parting before us, suddenly piqued my imagination. The man looked a born pirate, lacking only cutlass and kerchief! In an earlier age he would have sailed with Cook, or he would have gone adventuring against the Armada and no doubt attracted the interested eye of a Queen with hair as red as his own.

Then he turned and found me gazing at him, and the illusion vanished.

"Take a good look at them, Margaret." He indicated the full-blown sails straining at their masts. "Soon they'll have only historical interest. Give me two years," he continued with pride in his voice, "and the Jardine Line will have ships with propeller-driven steam engines powerful enough to carry them across the Atlantic."

"And then I suppose we shall enjoy the delights of traveling under that same horrid miasma of ash and smoke that hangs over half of Lancashire," I replied, making no effort to hide my disdain.

Oliver rounded on me like a leopard. I swear his ears seemed to flatten against his head and his eyes lightened from gray to the opaque glitter of quicksilver.

"Don't play the fool, Margaret. Steam is where our fortunes lie, ours and England's."

I was to hear more on that subject before we reached Charente, but for the moment I was intent on the more personal aspects of Oliver Jardine's words. "Our fortunes," he had

said, linking us together even when he was angry with me. I
felt a smile start deep inside me. "Oliver and Margaret. Oliver and Margaret. Jardine." It ran through my mind, half
frightening me with the intensity of my emotions. If only my
dreams would become reality!

The crossing to France was admirably swift and free from
storms, as if the treacherous Irish Sea were seeking to redress
the balance after our dreadful voyage short weeks earlier. But
if the voyage itself was tranquil, my relationship with Oliver
Jardine proved to be alternately idyllic and stormy. I was excited at the prospect of five uninterrupted days—and
nights—in his company. The fact that we were conspirators,
determined to bring down whatever house of cards my
mother was carefully building, added spice. But unseen shoals
and reefs threatened to wreck our fragile alliance almost at
its start.

Our cabins adjoined and it was with a delicious sense of
expectancy that I watched Oliver close the door of mine behind us that first night aboard, when dinner was over. I had
had some notion of playing the coquette, in line with my determination to be, or more correctly to appear to be, a proper
lady. But Oliver Jardine gave me no opportunity for such
subterfuge. He fastened the door behind us and turned to pull
me close.

"Beautiful Margaret. Have you seen me looking at you all
day? Have you appreciated how circumspect I've been? Miss
Millbrook, would you care to stroll on the upper deck? Miss
Millbrook, may I fetch you a wrap? Miss Millbrook, may I
have the honor of escorting you to your cabin?"

With a laugh that betrayed his excitement, Oliver unfas-
tened my cloak and tossed it onto a chair. His arms closed
about me, his mouth over mine was hard and demanding. My
lips parted willingly and once more I marveled at how different Oliver Jardine was from the effete, would-be worldlings
who had played at love with me. They had left me cold and
untouched inside. When Oliver touched me, when I felt the
warmth and strength of his hands, I wanted them on my
flesh. If he hadn't stripped away my clothing with an expertness at dealing with fastenings that should have made me
wary, I would have done it as switfly myself. I wanted only
to feel his body fitting itself to mine, his hard-muscled arms
and thighs demanding my compliance. His head bent above
me, and my arms slid around his neck. My hands fastened

themselves in the thickness of that mop of fiery curls and I clung to him, completely wanton.

Oliver Jardine carried me to the bunk, and, as if wantonness was what he had been seeking all of his life, braced himself above me, laughing down into my eyes.

"Blonde vixen! You like it, don't you? Rather better than a well-brought-up miss should. No matter, we are alone here, with no one to question what we do to each other—and together."

I had been lost in a haze of desire, but some hint of patronage in Oliver Jardine's tone affected my sensibilities like a dash of ice water. I struggled to sit up, but his hands on my shoulders pressed me back against the pillows.

"Come now, vixen, there's no need for pretense between us, surely? Ah, but perhaps you prefer to be taken forcibly"—amused arrogance danced behind the silver eyes looking down into mine—"by the rough, red-haired brute. . . ."

I cursed him in the gutter French that was much in vogue with my patrician French friends, but he set about trying to take me as if my fury were some playful response to urge him on.

I struggled wildly to shove him away, to slide from under him, but he merely lowered more of his weight until I was gasping for deeper breaths, for my lungs had no room to expand. Worst of all, he evidently thought I was amenable to soft endearments, for he was murmuring my name, calling me beautiful little Margaret, his love, and I had no breath to scream at him, though God knows the words filled my mind. And all the while those strong legs of his sought to separate mine, as if we were playing some love game. I crossed my ankles and wrapped my feet together, determined that he would break my bones before I would yield.

Suddenly he was off me and on his feet at the end of the bunk. Before I could move he grasped me by my crossed ankles and flipped me over onto my stomach as neatly as he might beach a fish. With my face in the pillow I lay there, spent and sobbing, clinging to my weak rage in an effort to wipe out the knowledge of complete humiliation.

And then I felt him lift the damp hair from the back of my neck and his lips soft at my nape. The kiss was as gentle as if he were comforting a child. His lips and his hands traveled caressingly along my back, over my buttocks, down to the backs of my knees. And there I felt the flick of his tongue. Felt, too, an answering flicker deep inside me. When he slipped an arm under me and gently rolled me over onto my back once more, when his lips began their searching at my throat, my breasts, I kept my eyes fast shut and let it happen—first the tenderness, then the stirring of passion as his lips and tongue explored me, attuned to every tiny shiver of response.

In my head I cursed myself for a fool, but my arms reached out to hold him close. My body responded of its own volition and made him welcome when he took me, wrapped him around through a wild paroxysm of passion and tenderness that left us both exhausted.

Later, with his face buried in my neck, Oliver begged for my forgiveness.

"You rouse some devil in me, Margaret. I find myself caught halfway between wild, heart-choking love for the innocent you—and lust for the wanton. And afterward I must endure this terrible guilt, for no matter what excuse I make for myself, you are still a child, a trusting, wide-eyed child ... and the wanton is only my own evil imagining. . . ."

I prayed again then that Oliver Jardine would never discover what manner of life I had lived during that summer in Italy, for if he did he would surely kill me.

Those five days on the voyage to Charente were to stand out in my mind as one of the strangest interludes of my life. We were in a cocoon world of our own, isolated from what had gone before and what was to come afterward. I learned nothing about Oliver Jardine's sensual life before we met, despite discreet foraging expeditions into his mind when we were in one of the tranquil periods that followed our lovemaking. He sealed that part of his life away from me completely and in the end I was grateful, for I would not, on pain of death, have confessed to my own garish experiences.

But if Oliver declined to confide his sexual adventures to me, he talked freely enough about other aspects of his life. His background had been, in many ways, as emotionally sterile as my own. Remembering the austere gloom of Holylake on the one occasion when I had seen it, I could not be surprised. Nor could I believe that my mother's presence there now would warm its gray dampness. But to my amazement, Oliver saw Holylake as the one redeeming element of his childhood. And perhaps its proximity to the sea explained a great deal about him.

"Even on those brief occasions when my father was home from the sea, he wanted the feel of it around him. The

Jardines have been seafarers since the early sixteen hundreds.
We have lived at Holylake since seventeen-forty. My father
was born at Holylake, and so was I," Oliver told me with the
pride I might have displayed if I were able to claim Balmoral
Castle as my ancestral home.

To my eye, Holylake had looked like a huge, ghostly gal-
leon, perched high up on its gray granite mount, surrounded
by sea on three sides. It faced outward, and the road leading
up to it followed a long spit of rocks curving out from the
strand, then climbed steeply to encircle the gray walls and
towers of Holylake. The whole apparition, with nothing but
gray sky as backdrop, seemed to be one with the wet granite
boulders that surrounded it. Only a seafarer could feel at
home on so harsh a headland, where the Irish Sea would beat
incessantly and the shroudlike sea fog provide the only illusion of softness in that untamed, watery view.

The land area of the Jardine estate had appeared less grim,
marked by holly groves and with a lake that gave the estate
its name. The farmlands and the cottages of the tenants had
looked well-tended, but there was none of the lushness of the
inner plains, and I had felt instinctively that the soil would be
riddled with small chipped shells, relics of the never-distant
sea.

"Originally Holylake was a fortified priory." Oliver's eyes
dwelt in the past as he spoke of Holylake. "It was built in the
twelfth century and endured continual attacks from pirates
and ambitious enemies of the king. It was Queen Elizabeth
who gave the property, with its garrison and priory, to one of
our forebears—'Bold Will,' Lord William Howard, third son
of Thomas Howard, Fourth Duke of Norfolk."

My interest was immediately piqued. Oliver Jardine's
Howard blood, that link to royalty, stirred my imagination.
Too, I could picture him as a young boy, living his dreams in
that grim fortress, his solitary games the battling of pirates
and marauding barons who had colored his family's history.

"Holylake suits the Jardines," he concluded with a dignity
that warned off criticism.

I believed him. Despite his Howard blood and the warmth
of copper freckles and hair, Oliver Jardine had within him
the chill, unyielding granite strength that distinguished his
home.

That rocklike inflexibility of will was directed now against
his father, as I learned the night before we arrived at
Charente. We were in my cabin, as was usual, and I had ex-

pected Oliver to take me to bed without delay, for that too was usual. Instead, he opened a bottle of brandy, and after pouring us each a glass, prowled the confined space, brooding.

"What is it, Oliver?" I asked when it appeared that he might continue that way all the night.

He flung himself into a chair, long legs sprawled out before him, and studied me through narrowed eyes. "You dislike everything to do with the steam engine, Margaret? Or so I surmise from some of your statements."

I shrugged, unwilling to become engaged in a pointless argument. "I don't like living in their shadow, though I suppose they are the source of the new prosperity we hear so much about."

"One needn't like steam engines aesthetically to see that they are where the future lies."

I was determined to be reasonable. "Surely not at sea, Oliver. Those great heavy engines and all the coal that must be carried to feed them—"

"Especially at sea," he interrupted, his eyes dangerously bright. "Even a woman, if she cared to take thought, should be aware of the advantages of being in control of your source of power. Not having to go hundreds of miles off course in order to move at all!"

"The wind is free," I reminded him coldly. "One doesn't waste valuable cargo space lugging along mountains of coal that must be *purchased*. Where is the point in arriving at your destination more swiftly, if your holds are half empty of merchandise? How can you hope to turn a profit when you have less to sell, and the added expense of the coal into the bargain?"

"Quite simply, Margaret, by making the voyage in half the time or less."

"But to what purpose? All of this rushing about, to transport *what*? And to whom? What good would it have done my father to bring his cargoes of brandy to Liverpool in half the time? He was transporting all that the Cherbiers had to sell. And selling all that the English market could absorb."

"Ah, yes," Oliver said approvingly, as if I had given the response he had hoped for. "But the brandy trade with France is not strong enough to evoke a steady growth rate. Economic pressures at both ends limit the production and the market. But that is the brandy trade. There are other trades, Mar-

garet. The new wealth in this country won't be in the land, as
it has always been in the past. England's new rich are the
middle class, led by the mill owners."

"Even so! The largest part of their market is here, in England."

But Oliver Jardine was shaking his head in frustration.
Words tumbled out of him, telling me of the classes in trade
theory he had completed at Christ College, at Cambridge; of
what he called "the magnificent opportunity within England's
grasp, if only we have the wit to seize it!"

"Let me tell you, Margaret, we can turn out all the
worsteds in the world, all the pottery, all the cast and pig
iron, and if we don't secure new markets, it'll be a roar for
nothing. England cannot absorb her coal production nor her
new industrial output. The answer is in new markets. Markets
that steam vessels will open up."

"And when the new markets are secured, what then? Will
we produce more and more goods to ship to them, until all of
England is covered with smokestacks and we choke to death
in our own effluvia? I liked England as it was."

"Nothing remains as it was. It goes forward. Or it falls behind. And the world needs what England produces." Oliver
was on his feet marching agitatedly about the cabin. "You
are like my father, looking backward, always backward, as if
past glories can sustain us."

He swung around to glare at me, the coppery freckles
standing out starkly against a face white with emotion. "Both
of you with your eyes tightly shut against the future. Because
he commanded a ship that supported our trade in the East,
he cannot believe there are other markets than India and
China. For him, the traditional markets, the traditional cargoes, are all that matter. As for steam vessels . . ."

Oliver's voice changed to a deep bellow, like a foghorn
heard from a distance. "Hah, yes, steam vessels, Oliver? Perhaps, perhaps, but for the East, my boy. If you can contrive
a way to refuel. Hah, that's the problem, isn't it? But at least
set your sights on the right target, so a canny man may see
where the profit lies. The East, boy, the East—"

"While at your grim gray school in Glasgow, teachers and
pupils alike no doubt prate on about coal and commerce, and
work to inundate the rest of us in ashes! Have you no soul,
Oliver? At Berri we valued beauty and laughter and fine food
and we despised the grubby little minds that labored to make
all of life joyless and—and mechanical!"

Within moments we were engaged in a battle that left no room for a meeting on middle ground. I accused Oliver of being a philistine and he assured me that I was a hedonist at best, and possibly something worse. There being nothing that insults the pride so effectively as a shaft of unkind truth— even though the sender does not know it really is the truth— my temper rose like boiling milk and I flew at him with my nails bared. He seized my arms and flung me backward onto the bunk with my skirts flying upward and my heels in the air.

Before I could right myself, Oliver Jardine was leaning over me, his face pale and furious under the mask of brandy-colored freckles.

"Now, baggage, let us establish once and for all that I will tolerate no more of your evil tempers."

"My evil tempers!" I raged, struggling to sit up, only to be tipped over again onto my back, as helpless as a turtle. In a fury of affronted dignity, I realized that Oliver's eyes were enjoying the view of my flailing legs and heaving bosom. "Compared to you, sir, I am a model of gentility and decorum!"

"Gentility, indeed! You were going for my eyes, vixen. As for decorum, I've seen precious little evidence of it thus far. I am afraid you're one of those women, Margaret, who cannot be reasoned with, who understands only one kind of authority. . . ."

With a shock, I realized that Oliver's anger had changed suddenly into a quite different form of passion, and even as I thought it, he was upon me, hoisting my skirts and tugging at my underclothing like some village Lothario tumbling a scullery maid. This time there was no question of crossing my legs and giving battle, for his hard-muscled legs were between mine and forcing them open. And the more fiercely I heaved about, berating him with what breath I could spare, the swifter inevitability overtook me. My squirming became only a pretense, as my body disregarded my mind and arranged itself to accomodate him.

Damnation! Hell and damnation, why did my own flesh have to betray me? Why could Oliver Jardine, within minutes, change me from a raging virago into a willing—no, worse, an enthusiastic—partner in rape? Oh, I had been right in my foreboding, from the very beginning of our relationship. Playing with fire, is that what I had thought? Hah, I had

consigned myself to the flames and was reveling in the holo-
caust!

When it was over, I lay for a long time sleepless and confused, nursing my wounded pride and intellect—and the angry suspicion that my loving or hating of Oliver Jardine was
immaterial. Apparently, he had only to touch me and I was
his creature. Well, I was aware now. I swore to myself that
he would find me different game in future!

CHAPTER 10

Throughout the docking of the *Tough Tom* at Charente, and
the trip by hired coach to the Cherbier estate, Oliver and I
were coldly polite to each other. But by the time our carriage
crossed the long, many-arched bridge into Bordeaux, our antagonism had given way to excitement. I sat forward eagerly
when I recognized the old stone wall that bordered the road
on either side, marking the vast Cherbier holdings. We drove
past mile after mile of tiered grapevines until at last we arrived at the tall, arched gateway that led into a compound set
out like a village square. Here were the fieldstone winery
buildings, the presses and treading tanks, and the storage
sheds with their dark oak casks. The musky scent of grapes
and sunshine brought back memories of my childhood visits
with my father's French cousins.

Our carriage rolled past a thick screen of willow trees
marking the separation of the winery from the formal garden
of Château Cherbier, and then we were traveling a long, geo-
metrically straight drive bordered by tall poplars that led
back to the manor house. It presented a most impressive
vista. The house itself was large and half-timbered in the style
one associated with the French provinces, set with rows of
deep windows glittering in the brilliant sunshine. In the distance more vineyards, rising in terraced rows against a
cloudless sky, formed a backdrop for the house.

With a pang of conscience in so bucolic a scene, I hoped
that this household was far enough removed from Berri so
that they had never heard of my exploits, and still remembered me with kindness. Although Gustave and Jules Cher-

bier were my father's cousins and thus second cousins of mine, because they were my father's contemporaries I had called them Uncle Gustave and Uncle Jules, and their wives Aunt Mathilde and Aunt Fleur-Ange.

It was Aunt Mathilde who welcomed me. She came scarcely to my shoulder and was now even more round and rosy than I remembered her, but her black shoe-button eyes were as merry as ever, and she clutched me to her as if I were one of her own returning.

"But my dear Margaret, how tall and lovely you have grown! And how delighted we are that you have come to us. My darling child, what dreadful news that your poor father . . . ah, but it is the will of God and we must not question his ways. . . ."

It was as if I were again nine years old and mystified by Tante Mathilde's Catholic piety, coming as I did from an English household where God was considered a being far removed from everyday events who was certainly never introduced familiarly into conversation by my mother and father.

"Tante Mathilde, may I present Oliver Jardine, the son of Commander Jardine of Holylake."

"Ah, but of course, I have met your father, m'sieu. A most interesting man. I see you have the same *cheveux roux*." Tante Mathilde laughed.

Before we could ask how it happened that she knew Commander Jardine, the rest of the family trooped into the salon where Tante Mathilde had conducted us, and there was the usual effusive Frenchness of reunited relatives after the passage of years. Uncles Gustave and Jules hugged me, beaming through the luxuriant mustaches they both affected; and pale, shy Fleur-Ange lingered in the background until she could clasp my hand and whisper a welcome. All of them made much of Oliver, though it was plain they scarcely knew what to think of his accompanying me on this journey, since I had introduced him only as a friend and not as the fiancé they obviously thought he should be.

None of my younger cousins was present, for Jean-Luc and Phillipe, the sons of Jules and Fleur-Ange, were both away at the university in Paris, and their sister Solange was married and living in Lyons. As for the children of Gustave and Mathilde, François and his new wife, Marie-Reine, who lived on the estate, would be home later that evening. Pierrette, the cousin to whom I had felt closest because she was nearest my own age, had joined the Order of Ste. Agathe, Tante Mathilde informed me with a sadness I thought surprising, in view of her own often-expressed piety.

My uncles and my Aunt Fleur-Ange offered me their condolences on the death of my father. There was talk of his long illness and inquiries as to how my poor mother was bearing up, which I managed to parry. But it was only after a huge and very rich dinner which Oliver, for all his avowed distaste for French gourmandizing, enjoyed with gusto, that the opportunity arrived to discuss the purpose of our visit.

Uncle Gustave, leaning back at ease in a comfortable chair and with a glass of his own finest cognac at his elbow, smiled at Oliver expansively. "And so you are the son of Jardine and Son, with whom we now have so amicable an association?"

"The son, yes, but not presently allied with my father in his shipping firm. I am at the university in Glasgow studying steam engineering and its application to trading and passenger vessels."

Before the conversation could hare off into a discussion of steam, I plunged in. "Uncle Gustave, it is about your association with Jardine and Son that we wish to talk with you. When I went away to school two years ago, the Millbrook Line appeared to be operating successfully. Yet now my father's solicitors tell me that it fell into debt and was sold to Commander Jardine, and that my father's estate consists entirely of debts. Even Greystones must be sold to satisfy the creditors, and I am left literally penniless."

There was much clucking and worried sympathy then, with everyone assuring me that if such were the case I must come and live with them. I was, after all, family, albeit a foreign member, and I had fortunately been schooled in France—it would be admirably logical, and so on. It took considerable effort to retrieve the conversation while thanking them for their kindness. I did it, finally, by plunging into the account of my mother's strange alliance with Commander Jardine. They listened in astonished silence as I told of her partnership in the apothecary shop with a man who had lived on and for the sea most of his life; and the equally unlikely fact that my mother was going to have a child at her stage of life and was living under Commander Jardine's roof at Holylake.

Their dark eyes seemed to dart from my face to Oliver's throughout my story. But when I spoke of my mother's fierce enmity toward me and confided that Oliver and I thought she might well have been at least partially responsible for my fa-

ther's death, the room erupted with cries of *"Diabolique!"*
Only *"une femme sans pitié"* would ever have disowned me.
My relatives were intrigued with the idea that my father had
contrived somehow to leave me a secret legacy. They listened
to every detail when I recounted Ned's story of my father's
happiness shortly before his death. And they nodded portentously, vividly imagining themselves in my father's position
and wanting to believe that he had somehow wrung a minor
triumph from adversity.

When I had concluded, Uncle Gustave, as the senior member of the family, cleared his throat and dabbed a quite-genu-
ine tear from his eye. "My poor Margaret, to have suffered so
much pain at your tender age. And our poor Charles." He
flicked a glance at his brother. "Jules, I fear we contributed
to his misfortune and unhappiness."

"Through trickery, Gustave, not through bad faith. The
woman lied and we believed her."

Uncle Gustave nodded, pursing his lips. "But of course. A
female Judas, a Jezebel, but"—he spread his palms in a Gal-
lic flourish—"the Devil conspires with such to confound honest men."

He turned to me, his dark eyes warm and earnest. "I shall
tell you how it was, Margaret, and then we shall see what is
to be done. We received news that one of your father's ships
had been wrecked. Then, in swift succession, that a second
and a third had suffered disaster.

"As you know, we have for many years shipped all of our
produce aboard the Millbrook Line with complete satisfaction. But when three of Charles's vessels were no longer seaworthy, we became worried, quite naturally. Then, within
weeks, your mother visited us, along with Commander
Jardine. She was very pleasant. To be truthful, far more
pleasant than I had ever found her to be on previous occasions when we had met. And the commander appeared to be
a man of knowledge where things nautical were concerned.

"Your mother professed to be greatly worried about
Cousin Charles. He was seriously ill and unable to attend to
his business, or even to leave his bed, if she were to be believed. The illness, and the virtual wrecking of the Millbrook
Line, had worked great financial hardship on the family, but
Commander Jardine had come forward with a happy solution
to the problem. He was prepared to buy the Millbrook Line
at a most generous price—"

A low growl from Uncle Jules interrupted him, and

Gustave nodded. "Yes, yes, but with Helen Millbrook herself testifying to all of this, we had no reason to disbelieve it at the time, Jules."

He turned back to me. "The outcome was that Commander Jardine would purchase the shipping line and repair and refit the wrecked vessels in time to meet our needs. But everything hinged on our willingness to transfer to him our long-standing contracts with Cousin Charles."

Gustave shrugged. "So of course we agreed. We were convinced that Charles would otherwise lose everything. This way, there would be money forthcoming from the sale of the vessels, and your family would be provided for, at least in some measure. It seemed the only honorable course. Moreover, we were impressed with Commander Jardine's knowledge of our problems and willingness to meet our needs."

It was Uncle Jules who turned to Oliver. "This commander is your father? What is your interest in Margaret's difficulties?" His keen eyes narrowed in suspicion. "Surely your father's machinations work to your benefit."

Oliver's face paled a trifle. His mask of freckles appeared darker and his silver-gray eyes held a dangerous glint, but his voice was even.

"I hold no brief with thievery or possible murder, no matter who stands to benefit," he replied, frowning at Jules and Gustave in turn. "My father is what he is, an old brigand in many ways, but I don't deny that I'm fond of him. Margaret's mother, however, is quite another matter. I don't doubt she has put herself out to be pleasant to me. If appearance were the only criterion she would make a handsome match for my father, for she's a beautiful woman. But my father is a man who needs a restraining hand, not one that will nudge him to indulge in his own excesses. The Widow Millbrook is overly ambitious, and her coldness of purpose within shows through too plainly for my taste."

Oliver smiled a thin smile with a hint of tiger in it. "With a woman like that behind him, my father will end on the gallows."

My uncles nodded solemnly in sympathy with his sentiments and Tante Mathilde reached over to pat my hand. "Poor child, poor child."

There was much discussion all of that evening and before we took our leave of the Cherbier family next day. We learned no more useful information, but my uncles were unanimous in their conviction that I should try to find out what had actually occurred at Greystones at the time of my father's death.

"This woman who was in the house at the time of the fire, the one your servitor spoke of, why have you not talked with her?" Jules demanded.

"She lives in Manchester. She was so upset by her experience that her father was obliged to take her back home with him before I arrived at Greystones."

"Ahhh? Indeed . . . so upset, was she?" Uncle Jules asked, mustaches waggling with emotion. "Only fear, perhaps, at her own close escape? Or something more, something she witnessed? My dear Margaret, you must see her as quickly as possible. You have few stone to turn, *ma petite*, you can afford to neglect none of them."

Both uncles were at hand when we took our leave, patting Oliver's broad back in approbation and squeezing my hand as they assured me that they would arrange immediately with Hampton and Robinson to have funds deposited in my name. I was not to feel that I was alone and friendless, that I needed to depend on strangers for a home and sustenance. I was to call on them in future for whatever help they could provide. In the meantime we would let matters stand as they were with Commander Jardine and my mother.

"One must be circumspect, my little Margaret," Uncle Gustave warned. "Perhaps there is nothing"—his face expressed disbelief—"but it is always wiser not to alarm your quarry, *hein?*"

Oliver and I had much to talk of. We made good use of the long trip back to Liverpool, going over and over the new information we had gathered and making plans to go to Manchester to speak with Laurie within the week.

"I have a presentiment, Margaret, that time is the most important element now, time and secrecy. So far, everything has worked to their advantage—my father's, your mother's. They have no reason to feel uneasy, since apparently they overcome all obstacles without difficulty. But they have been the hunters, tracking their game, moving in for the kill."

The tiger smile I was beginning to know came and went swiftly. "That has changed. Though they don't yet know it. Now we are the hunters; very circumspect hunters, as your Uncle Gustave suggested."

The smile returned and lingered longer this time. "We will see how they fare as the game."

I was grateful that Oliver Jardine was on my side, though I had some misgivings about his motives. Did he really have so much animus for my mother, did he really fear for his father's future in her company? My uncles had appeared to find that convincing; I was less sure. I had reached the uncomfortable conclusion that Oliver was a far more complex and less trustworthy person than I had at first supposed. Oliver had reasons for everything, and reasons behind his reasons, none of which he revealed except as circumstances dictated. Perhaps that complexity of character added to his fascination for me. But it also added to my growing unease.

CHAPTER 11

Before Oliver was to return to Glasgow it was decided that we would take my Uncle Jules' advice and call on Emily's sister in Manchester without delay. By now she would have had time to recover her wits enough to remember what she had seen at Greystones that had frightened her so greatly.

Ned, as caught up in our venture as we were, had listened solemnly to my account of the Cherbiers' dealings with Commander Jardine and my mother.

"Aye, Laurie was there when yer father died," he agreed, "and mayhap she knows more than she was able to tell. 'Voices,' she said, and the place 'boilin' with smoke,' but we could get no sense out o' her after, what with the spasm and all, her being half daft from the fright. She stared at Emily and me like we was strangers, and Emily her own sister!"

With Ned driving the coach, the journey eastward, along the Mersey, took but a few hours. Again we were traveling through the worst of the new-ruined countryside, but when Oliver peered from the windows at every evidence of steam engines at their foul work, I restrained my tongue.

Laurie lived with her father, Thomas Oatway, in a small cottage on the near side of Manchester. She offered us a cautious welcome, while the old man scolded that he wouldn't have his Laurie worried, now that she had "come to herself again."

If Laurie had indeed "come to herself again," I trembled to

think what depth of terror she had known at the time of the fire. She appeared as wholesome and uncomplicated as Emily, and listened gravely while Ned explained that Emily urged her to help us in any way that she could. But she was clearly still badly shaken by her experience. It was only after I had pleaded with her to imagine our positions reversed, how she would feel if her own father had died in the blaze, that her kindly heart conquered her fear.

"Yes, mum, I do see how it must be fer ye. I'll do me best. I hope ye'll understand, mum, I'm not a sneak, it's just that I was lookin' fer young Ellen, she's my niece, Ned and Emily's girl as did the washing up at the big house. But there wasn't no one around that night, quiet as the grave it was."

Laurie flushed at her own choice of words; I reached across the deal table where we sat and patted her hand.

"I'd never been in a fine house before and I—I thought I'd just take a little peek upstairs. I didn't touch nothing, you understand, mum, I was only looking at the pictures in the long gallery, all those ladies and gentlemen in their fine clothes. I'd walked along a good distance from the grand stairs, see, and there I was, right by the master's chambers as Ellen had told me about, though she hadn't ever seen them herself, just heard from the others. Well—I opened the door and walked in, bold as brass, and I'm sorry enough I ever did it, but there I was all the same. That's when I heard the voices. I was that scared I didn't know which way to turn. You know how the master's chambers was, mum, this little hall like? And then the big room with the bed and all, and another room beyond, where the voices was. 'Oh, they're comin' out here,' I thought, and I went all funny, kind of shaky you might say. But there was this little room off to the side, with the door open, so I just ducked in there, mum, and hid behind the door."

Poor Laurie began to tremble. Before her father could object to her continuing, Ned Carter took command. On our arrival Oliver had presented Thomas Oatway with a bottle of fine cognac. I had thought at the time that a few bottles of lager would have been more appreciated, but it appeared that Ned and Oliver had their own scheme.

"Thomas, why don't ye give the poor girl a wee glass of that fine cognac Mr. Jardine so kindly provided? Nothing better than a sup of cognac to steady the nerves, in my opinion."

Thomas Oatway hesitated, but Ned turned to his sister-in-law. "Strengthens ye a wonder, it does, when ye take it in hot tea, lass. Shouldn't wonder but what we'd all be the better fer some, and Emily'd say the same if she was here."

Laurie, without further encouragement, poured out the ever-ready tea for all of us, and Oliver, at Thomas Oatway's nod, laced it generously with cognac. Upon tasting it, Oatway put another pot of tea to brew, and very shortly Laurie, her cheeks flushed, announced herself ready to continue.

"At first I scarcely listened, I was that petrified," she confided. "But then they began shouting at each other. I knew it had to be the master and mistress of Greystones, but their voices were all hard and hating. And then—oh, it was fair horrifying, it was—the master laughed, and it was enough to make the chills run down yer back.

" 'You're possessed of the Devil, Helen,' he said, 'and you'll be called to account for it, in this world or the next. In the meantime, you can consider the very substantial gift you left for me as part payment against a lifetime's debt.' The mistress wailed then, 'My fortune, my fortune.' " Laurie's voice sank to a whisper. "Like one possessed—as the master said."

Ned hurriedly replenished her cup and she half emptied it in a gulp. Then something quite strange occurred. Laurie no longer recounted a story, but spoke the roles of my mother and father in her own approximation of their voices, as if their words and even their inflections were graven on her mind.

"That box is mine, Charles, and I will have it! I put myself at great risk to earn all that it holds!"

"And sold your soul in the process to a red-haired pirate! My business lies in ruins, I am hounded by creditors, and the two of you smile, counting your profits."

"You beggared yourself for an ungrateful daughter, you fool, or you could have weathered those storms."

"How, madam, when you suborned my crews? But no matter. It's a fair exchange, my vessels for your treasure trove, so we'll say no more about it."

"Thief! Robber! Where have you put it? *I will have it*, I tell you, or—"

"Now, now, Helen. A prudent man with a greedy wife must be allowed his little secrets. This one will go to my grave with me, I assure you. Though perhaps not so soon as you think, for I no longer take those mysterious potions you prepare for me. . . ."

Dead silence fell in the small Oatway cottage as Laurie stopped speaking. With a sigh, Thomas Oatway got to his feet and stirred the fire on the hearth. The crackle of the leaping flames was the only sound in the room.

I leaned forward anxiously. "Laurie, what happened then?"

Laurie Oatway looked at me as if just roused from a deep sleep, her eyes dazed and her cheeks flushed. "I don't know, mum. I think the mistress struck him with something, fer I heard the sound of a blow and then it seemed as if the master fell heavily. I couldn't rightfully understand it, mum, fer there was such a dreadful ruckus, like they was struggling. The mistress was cursing him and shouting she would have what was hers or she would send him to hell. And the master yelling all the while that the curse was on *her*."

Poor Laurie looked at me with haunted eyes. "He kept on, mum, about some awful curse that would get her, and I thought the Devil himself must be there in the room with them, for I could smell the burning."

"Why didn't ye run, girl?" Thomas Oatway growled at his daughter. "It was none of yer affair."

"I started to, Dad. But then I saw her. She carried a candle and her face was like—like the master said, like a demon! He was screaming in the room beyond, 'I have written an account, Helen. You'll never find it—nor find your box without it. . . .' But the mistress took time to set her candle to the drapes and then to the bedding. The room was alight in seconds, mum, and then she was gone, past the room where I was and out into the long gallery. I ran then. I didn't care if she was Lucifer himself, fer the smoke and the flames was everywhere, and the poor master—I don't remember how I got out of that house, mum, I was that crazy with fear. . . ."

The tears were streaming down Laurie's face, and her father, overwrought as we all were after that dreadful story, began to shout that we had turned his daughter's mind again. But Laurie shook her head and put a hand on his arm.

"No, Dad. It's better that I told. Mayhap now I won't hear it anymore. Nor have the dreadful dreams."

If Laurie Oatway's mind was more at peace after her revelations, mine was in turmoil. Though we started back to Greystones immediately, I was unable to shake the black mood her words had conjured up. My mother was a murderess. I was her daughter and some of her character would be rooted in me. What did it matter that I had little admiration and less affection for her? It would be better if I were more like her in temperament, more admiring of her cold ambition. At least I wouldn't feel the revulsion that shook me at the thought of that malevolence, directed first at my father and now at me.

But Oliver Jardine had no patience with such imaginings. "You have lived too long in France, Margaret. You dwell on the metaphysical instead of practicalities. Set your mind along other lines and try to think where your father would have hidden this 'treasure trove' that matters so greatly to your future."

"Even that was hers," I reminded him bitterly, "however she got it. Blood money."

"Your father called it a 'fair exchange' for his vessels—and paid for it with his life. Are you willing to see that sacrifice go in vain?"

"It's already too late! She must have found it by this time. If it wasn't destroyed in the fire."

Oliver shook his head, and a solitary ray of late afternoon sun slanted through the carriage window to turn his hair to fiery gold. "No, because she has had no real opportunity to search. Neither Ned nor Emily has seen her about Greystones since the fire. She must have dared one stealthy trip by night, to take away his books and papers in hope of finding the 'account' he said he had written. But to search Greystones in the dark, to risk treacherous footing and falling timbers? She would have virtually no hope of finding anything in the debris. No, Margaret. Your mother is more wily than to conduct her search like a thief in the night."

"Perhaps it's destroyed anyway," I replied despondently.

"If her wealth was in paper money, would she have dared fire the house?" Oliver countered. "Surely you know her cool head better than that. No, it's gold and silver, something fire couldn't destroy, depend on it."

"If we are to credit every word that Laurie said, then she could never find it without the account my father wrote."

"That would make it easier for her, yes. But letter, note, who knows what form his writing took? With your father gone, she can search at her leisure, or so she believes. She is waiting because she believes she can well afford to wait. She has no notion that Laurie Oatway was in the house the night your father died. He was ill and unable to leave Greystones, so she feels confident the money is still there—somewhere. For the time being she has only to be patient—and take over the house after probate."

"Oliver, no!" I was finally shaken out of my lethargy.

"Moreover," he continued inexorably, his face grim, "my father will be well aware of the situation, and I know his nature. He will sift the sands of that house, if need be. Unless we can block him. Unless we can delay probate and find the treasure first."

I bowed my head in my hands and wept. Whatever we learned or deduced led only to further problems. There were no solutions and every road ended at a blank wall. My despair was a mixture of grief and discouragement; I felt I could face no more of this dreadful emotional upheaval that had swept, like a tidal wave, into every corner of my mind and my life.

Oliver took me in his arms and held me close while the carriage jounced its way over the rough road toward Greystones.

"Poor little Margaret, poor little love. Don't you know that I'll help you? We are partners, if you wish. If our parents are strong, we will be stronger."

Oliver's face, so close in the gathering darkness of the carriage, rested against my hair, and I pressed close to him, welcoming the comfort of his words and his warmth. In spite of the gravity of my present circumstances, I found myself strongly reminded of that day when I had first journeyed to Berri with my father. We had agreed then always to speak frankly with one another. My feeling for Oliver Jardine had no father-daughter sentiment in it. I loved him in quite another fashion. But his tenderness and concern for me melted the icy block that had been my heart ever since my father's death, and I spoke impulsively.

"Dearest Oliver, we will always be friends, will we not? Honest and open with each other, not afraid to speak frankly?"

"Oh, my little love, of course! And I am afraid I must speak frankly now of matters far beyond your age and experience of life, for halfway measures won't do if we are to fulfill your father's hopes for you. This undertaking must be as carefully contrived as an Elizabethan drama, for we are dealing with avarice and ambition unbounded by any trace of conscience. We must be prepared to pay whatever price is exacted of us. I know you are young, Margaret, and I believe you are also very brave. But—are you brave *enough*, little love? Can you trust, and be strong? I hope so, for both of our sakes."

It was impossible to see Oliver's face in the darkness of the coach, but I sensed the confident excitement in his voice and felt myself ready to do whatever would be necessary.

"Margaret, I know how little taste you have for my enthusiasm for steam engines, on land or sea. But listen to me, love, for I swear to you, I've seen the future. England's future—our future, the success and wealth we can so easily win, if only you are able to share my vision."

If I felt a faint stirring of unease, I swiftly buried it. Oliver Jardine, with his adventurer's face and his Howard blood, had captured my imagination as well as my passion. I could think of no more desirable fate than to share whatever visions he beheld, to link our lives securely together. So I listened, spellbound, as the words tumbled forth that were to seal my future.

Our first consideration, Oliver insisted, was to block the probate of my father's estate. Our parents must not be allowed to gain control of Greystones and conduct their search at leisure.

"Otherwise your father's sacrifice becomes no more than a momentary obstacle in your mother's climb to power and prestige. But to balk her will require both money and the cooperation of your cousins, the Cherbiers. You must write and enlist their support."

"But Oliver, they have already provided funds for my livelihood. I can scarcely ask them for more immediately," I protested.

"Not for money, Margaret, but for time. You must ask them to delay the probate by sending letters and statements demanding payment of debts, real or fancied. The more involved and debatable their demands, the longer the court findings will be delayed. Delay is all we ask. The rest is up to me. In the meantime, Greystones must be guarded day and night, for if the probate drags on too long, count on it, our parents will lose patience. Neither of them have it in abundance. We must be quick and quiet, so that we don't alarm them."

"All right, Oliver. I'll write to Uncle Gustave tomorrow."

"Good. But there is more. If Greystones is to be guarded, we will need money. I propose to get it from my father. . . ."

Oliver had spoken before of his dream of putting steam-driven vessels on an ocean route to America. He swore it was possible and practical, that his studies of steam and marine engineering at the university had convinced him beyond doubt. But he had no money for such a venture.

"My father will provide the money for the building of such a vessel, but only on the understanding that it will be designed for service to the East. All his dreams focus there. He sees it as the font of all wealth, for he still has powerful friends there from his days on the Singapore station. He longs to be a nabob and fancies the idea of the newest of ships being added to the Jardine and Son shipping line, but only the East counts, in his view."

Oliver fell into a moody silence, withdrawing the arm that had been sheltering me, locked in his own thoughts. I waited sympathetically, but unable to see how his dilemma concerned me.

"Margaret. I will make a bargain with you, and seal it here and now. I will get the money to protect Greystones, on the pretext that I am to design and have built a steam-driven vessel for the India service. My father is a canny old bird and it will take some doing to deceive him. But Greystones and your inheritance must be protected. In return, I want your assurance that when your money is found you will turn it over to me to form a company in which we will be equal partners."

Oliver turned toward me, seizing my hands in his. "Together we can do it! Without me, you have little hope of reclaiming your inheritance. Without you, I have no immediate hope—or very little—of finding the capital I need to build my ships and put them in service to North America. What do you think, my darling?"

What did I think? I gazed inward at the jumble of misconceptions that I had been harboring and saw, too late, where vanity had led me. I had thought Oliver Jardine in love with me? He was in love with his vision of the future. While I dreamed of marriage, he dreamed of a business partnership. Perhaps his single-minded passion allowed no room in his life for any other attachment. In one bitter moment my girlish hopes sank without a trace, and I viewed my situation coldly. If he wanted a business partnership, he should have one, for I needed his help. But I would join his venture with open eyes and closed heart. And I would make him struggle for his victory.

I swallowed the anger and sorrow that had flooded all of my being and pretended a blissful ignorance I no longer enjoyed. But I demanded with pretty hesitancy that Oliver must

convince me before I could agree. While I seethed inside, I
learned much about England's seafaring history, for Oliver
seemed determined that I should lack nothing in background
knowledge.

We were, apparently, no better sailors than anyone else—
less so, in fact. While the Vikings sailed, the Anglo-Saxons
rowed. While St. Brendan and his Irish monks ventured to
North America, our small cog vessels traded with France,
bringing back an assortment of spirits for merchants and
their kind. Early English ships, constructed by royal carpen-
ters who knew nothing of transverse stability, floatation,
buoyancy or hydrodynamics—fully understood by the Portuguese, Genoese, and Spanish—often went bottom up when
launched. Or if by some miracle they floated, they went on
the rocks with monotonous frequency, since our early voy-
agers had not yet learned celestial navigation at Prince
Henry's school in Portugal.

"In the meantime, the Portuguese and Dutch picked up the
spice trades out East and the Spanish scraped the gold from
the New World. Britain finally found a place in the merchant
trades, but even that was by royal charter, under the East India Company, which forced out and punished interlopers and
free traders. And now their day is over. The East Indiamen
are glossy and well-manned, but they are also fat and slow,
and no longer protected by the old trade monopoly. The door
is open, Margaret, for sleeker, faster ships that can keep to a
schedule and a direct course, and never mind the slant of the
wind."

"Or the price of coal, Oliver?"

"Coal! What's coal to England? We have more than we
can use. Look, girl, your father's own account books prove
my point. The *Cognac,* a side-wheel steamer, completed nine
more round trips to France than the other four brigs of the
Millbrook Line on her first year in service because her course
was *direct.* Those extra voyages paid for the employment of
three assistant engineers, five coal heavers, and two trimmers.
And the added annualized end-profit was seven hundred
pounds nine in cargo receipts!"

In the end, I allowed myself to be convinced, for I had no
other choice if I wanted Oliver's help. We would become
partners in the building of his steam vessels, I agreed, as soon
as my inheritance was safely in our hands. He responded
with immediate joyous affection. Behind my smiling response
I could feel my heart cooling and hardening as truly as any

product of his beloved blast furnaces. I knew then that if I was determined not to be like my mother, I was equally determined to root out of my nature every trace of my father's trusting compliance. I would be my own woman. I would go along with Oliver—for the moment—but henceforth I would put trust in intellect. At the moment Oliver Jardine thought he had acquired a partner in name only. He would learn to live with the hard reality as time went by.

CHAPTER 12

With the aid of Mr. Harburt of Liverpool, an estate agent who was full of commiseration that I should have to seek new living accommodations because Greystones was no more, I found a cottage that would be adequate for my needs. It had been built in the sixteen-hundreds, the home of a prosperous local family. Though small, it was sturdily built, with stone walls and a slate roof and handsome mullioned windows. The garden had been let go—it was surrounded by a wild tangle of roses, hollyhock, pinks, sweet william and lavender—but Ned promised to find me a local gardener to put it in order. Most important, it was conveniently near Greystones, so that Emily had agreed to come in half days to look after me. The price was modest enough to suit my restricted funds, and with Ned's help I set about making it habitable.

I was fortunate in the matter of furnishings. My eye, trained to recognize and appreciate simplicity of line and quality of workmanship during my stay in France, found little to like in the pretentious modern stuff that was becoming the new vogue in England. I chose pieces suited in scale to my limited space, discarded from grander homes when the gimcrack lure of red plush and mother-of-pearl inlay usurped their place in popular taste. If my small home would lack modernity, it would have at least the soft glow of French damasks and the gleam of well-polished wood free from curlicues and dark varnish.

In the midst of this domesticity, I posted a letter to Gustave and Jules Cherbier advising them that information we had obtained from Laurie Oatway had convinced us that the probate of my father's estate must be delayed. I pleaded for their help, asking that they do everything short of compromising their good name in demanding payment of debts against the estate.

In the meantime Oliver had not been idle. The men he found to stand guard over Greystones and its grounds day and night were rough enough looking rogues to discourage would-be trespassers. His arrangements may or may not have been legal, but they were effective, as I was soon to witness.

I had been spending every moment I could at the house, going over it room by room, with Ned's help when he had the time, alone when he was busy elsewhere. It was dirty, exhausting work. After the first cursory search, I had decided I must leave no pile of rubble unturned, no wall untapped for secret recesses where my father might have hidden his cache. Despite gloves to protect my hands and one of Emily Carter's capacious aprons, I would arrive back at my small house late each afternoon smudged, grimy, and bone-weary. My only comfort was that I no longer feared Greystones; familiarity with every inch of it had banished the earlier fancies I had felt within its ruins.

After two weeks, my belief and enthusiasm had waned. I was now convinced that my mother had managed to reclaim her treasure and I was searching for something no longer there. Lack of alternative kept me at it.

It was just past midday when the row occurred at the gate of Greystones. I was halfway along the curved drive that led from the house to the gates, on my way to eat, when I heard shouting and the whinnying of horses, then my mother's haughty voice raised in anger. I had no wish to confront her fury when she found herself balked at entering, so I made my way closer to the gates in the shelter of the overgrown rhododendron bushes bordering the drive.

Peering from that shelter, I saw my mother, elegantly garbed in lavender silk, descend from a glossy new carriage drawn by handsome black horses. Rigid with anger, she faced one of the guards of Greystones, and for once her cold composure had slipped. Her face was flushed with fury.

"I tell you I am Mrs. Charles Millbrook. I am the mistress of Greystones. You cannot prevent me from entering my own property."

The guard, a lout with shaggy black hair and a sacklike coat, stared back at her sullenly, shaking his head. "No, mum. She died in the fire, along of her husband. Whoever ye be, ye have no rights here, mum."

My mother's imperious voice was sharp enough to draw blood.

"Call Ned Carter, the liveryman, at once. He will certainly assure you of my identity."

"He don't have no say, mum. 'Tis the courts put me here to keep out thieves and the like. Beggin' yer pardon, mum."

The sound that came out of my mother then was one of pure rage. "She did this, didn't she? That little bitch!"

She climbed back into her carriage and peered out the window at the guard. "You may tell her for me that I'll see she regrets the day she was born. As *I* do!"

With that, she ordered the coachman to drive off, pretending not to see the guard's smirk at such carryings-on from the gentry. As soon as the carriage was out of sight I ran all the way to my cottage. Though shaken, at least I knew now that my mother had not yet found her treasure.

I intended to return to Greystones later in the day, but after I washed off the worst of the grime from my morning's work and ate the lunch Emily had left for me, I fell asleep, exhausted. When I awoke it had grown dark outside and Emily was busy in my small kitchen, preparing a roasted chicken and vegetables. She greeted me with a large smile and barely contained excitement.

"Ah, Miss Margaret, ye missed great goings-on this afternoon. Ye saw the mistress here at midday, so Painter told Ned? Well, mum, back she come this afternoon in her fine carriage with Mr. Robinson by her side. Oh, there now, mum, don't ye look so stricken, fer it did her no good. Painter wouldn't let the one nor the other of 'em onto the property, though Mr. Robinson strutted about, waving some fancy bit o' paper and threatening to have the law on the lot of us."

In spite of Emily's delight, I was uneasy. "Surely, if Mr. Robinson had written authority to enter Greystones—"

"'Twan't no authority at all, Miss Margaret," Emily scoffed. "My Ned can read a bit, ye know, and Painter sent for him immediate to come see. Just some piece of folderol, Ned says it was, with a scrap o' ribbon and a seal on it, to scare poor Painter, if he was fool enough to be took in by it all. *Which* he wasn't and nor was Ned!"

My mother's patience was coming to an end. Oliver Jardine's arrangements to protect Greystones had worked

well enough this time. But what device would my mother try
next? With Mr. Robinson aiding her, she could circumvent us
in short order. When I said as much to Emily, she flung me a
dark look.

"Him! If conniving can do it, mayhap she'll get her way,
for he's a trickster right enough, behind that pious face o' his.
You know that my aunt is in service at the Robinsons' big
house in Liverpool, and she's told us more than one story o'
Mr. Robinson's sharp way o' doin' business. But he couldn't
do nothing when he saw Ned's paper, mum, for it says
straight out that no one is allowed on Greystones property
and it's signed by the probate judge, see. Young Mr. Jardine
is a smart one, my Ned says. For all it might have cost him a
bit, he's got it tied up nice and legal."

"But if *no* one is allowed—surely that includes me?"

"Who's to know, mum? Them as pays the fiddler gets to
call the tune." Emily's round face broke into a grin. "And I'll
tell ye, Miss Margaret, yer mother and Mr. Robinson were
fair dancin' about this afternoon, they were that
fashed. . . ."

It was a damp, chilly evening and perhaps that accounted
for my melancholy mood. When Emily had gone and dinner
was over, I sat in front of the fireplace for a long time,
watching the flames, my mind in turmoil. Despite Emily's optimism and Oliver's efforts, I felt instinctively that we had no
time to lose. Time was our enemy, and I was no nearer
success after two weeks of careful searching than I had been
at the very beginning.

I sighed and wondered at the state of my father's mind
when he had been concocting whatever plan I was seeking
now to unravel. He had been in better spirits when last Ned
saw him, but hardly strong enough to go to great lengths to
achieve his ends. The treasure, whatever it might prove to be,
would scarcely be cemented behind the walls of the cellars,
for instance; the physical effort would have been beyond poor
Papa's capability. Nor could he have dug a pit of any depth
to hide it on the grounds, judging by Ned's account of his
pallor and frailty. All the same, he had done whatever he'd
done well enough to defeat all of my efforts.

A sensation of complete hopelessness overwhelmed me. I
was exhausting myself on a fool's errand. Tears of self-pity
welled in my eyes, and I was about to give in to them when
my natural contrariness rebelled.

I sprang to my feet and strode about my small room. My

father, ill and dying, had tried to make me safe. Yet here I stood, young and strong, bemoaning my ill fortune. Ready to let fate carry me, willy-nilly, where it would. I snatched my portrait from the mantelpiece where I had placed it when I first brought it back from Greystones, and studied the face it depicted. *My* face when I had been twelve years old. Surely there was strength of character in those wide-spaced green eyes set above strong cheekbones. Surely the soft lines of that girlish mouth showed, even then, the beginnings of courage and determination. I was about five years older now—almost seventeen. I would not bow my head in surrender to some whim of fate. I would accept nothing less than my due!

In the grip of deep emotion, I lifted my eyes to the low beamed ceiling above me and vowed that I would prove my father right in loving me. He had fought for my future up to the moment of his death. Whatever my past had been, whatever my present circumstances, I too would fight for my future, and somehow he would know!

Once again, like a benediction, I felt my father's presence. In a more rational mood I might have told myself it was the result of strong emotion, born of need. But I was not of a mind to be rational. I clutched the portrait he had cherished against my heart, feeling that Papa must often have held it so, like a talisman when his loneliness was most acute. The one link between us, and infinitely precious to me now. A corner of the green baize backing was loose and curling, and I felt a twinge of guilt.

I had placed the portrait on the mantelpiece; had heat from the fireplace caused the glue to dry out? Well, I would repair it and keep the portrait at a safe distance from the heat in future. In the back of my mind I knew, I think, that that was ridiculous; the heat from the flames that had destroyed Greystones must surely have been far more intense, even if little damage had been done to my father's library. But I wished to be busy at a trifle; I wished to preserve the closeness I felt with my father at that moment, so I carried the portrait to my small kitchen and sat down to examine how I would go about the repair.

Or perhaps, even then, I had a premonition. For surely I had never before seen an oil painting backed with green baize—or with anything else, for that matter. There was the sturdy canvas on which the artist placed his paint, stretched taut within its frame, varnished on the surface for protection but needing no protection on the back. All of this was famil-

iar to me from my art classes at Berri. This sort of backing
had been used only for the framing of watercolors, or for pen
or charcoal sketches executed on perishable paper or silk.

I turned up the oil lamp on the kitchen table and slipped
the tip of a knife under the curling edge of baize, testing the
glue that held it in place. Within a moment the green backing
lay on the kitchen table and I stared at the folded sheets of
thin paper that were hidden within. The square gilt frame extended perhaps a quarter inch behind the undersurface of the
canvas. There, my father had found his secret place, safe
from my mother's eyes, for the last thing she would lay hand
to would be a portrait of me.

With shaking fingers I took the folded pages from their
nest and opened them, half afraid to look for fear they
weren't what instinct told me they had to be. Eight pages of
thinnest paper, covered in my father's familiar neat hand, beginning "My beloved daughter."

Tears flooded my eyes and I wept as I hadn't since childhood. Here was the letter Papa had said he would write. But
why had he not given it to Ned, as he'd intended? Had he become too ill to leave the house? I could imagine him forcing
himself to descend the long flight of stairs from his bedroom
to the library, taxing what little strength he had in the careful
secreting of these pages in the one place he might hope I
would find them.

When my paroxysm of weeping finally ceased, I began to
read the letter. It took me a long while to finish it, for several
times I had to stop, blinded by tears and a torrent of conflict-
ing emotions. But there was comfort, too, for truly my father
loved me and had provided for me. That, above all else, was
clear.

My beloved daughter:

For months I have been heartsick at receiving no
replies to the many letters I have written you. I confess
that while making every allowance for your active life at
Berri, I was deeply hurt at the thought that you had
completely forgotten the father who loves you so dearly.
Loves you perhaps too dearly. In recent years I have realized that my love for you has been at the root of my
difficulties with your mother. She has a jealous soul, and
the deep affection that you and I share has always been
an affront to her. Jealousy does not respond to reason
and no doubt I sometimes erred in favoring you, for I

tried to compensate for the lack of love I know you have always felt in her.

Margaret, her rejection was not based on some flaw in your own nature. To reassure you of that (and also on another score which will soon become evident), I must tell you that the woman you know as your mother is, in fact, your stepmother. Your own mother, Anne Wilding Millbrook, a very beautiful young woman whom you much resemble, died in bearing you; and her parents in an accident a few months later. You were less than eight months old when I married Helen Allison, believing naïvely that she would be a loving mother to you and a loving wife to me.

I made myself blind for many years as to your stepmother's true character, something I can no longer do. She has made even that refuge impossible to maintain. Much as I should like to spare you the knowledge, I dare not, for your future will soon depend on what warning I can give you now.

I think, Margaret, that I have been as happy with my lot in life as most men. If my second marriage has lacked affection, I have had the compensation of a beautiful, intelligent, and sensitive daughter who has brought me infinite pleasure, and I truly believe most men are not so fortunate as that. My life has been fairly comfortable, fairly tranquil, fairly successful—so perhaps it is also "fair," if hard to bear, that my last years should be the troubled ones.

Having reassured you as best I can of my lasting love for you, and my acceptance of the adversity which has befallen me, I will try to explain as straightforwardly as possible the position in which I now find myself. I do this for your protection, Margaret, as you will shortly understand.

Perhaps two months after I left you at Berri, my difficulties began, though I didn't recognize that fact at the time. Your stepmother deeply resented your going away to school, but once it was accomplished, she appeared to wash her hands of both you and her life here at Greystones with me. I discovered that she had undertaken a business venture, partnership in an apothecary shop, with a Commander Matthew Howard Jardine of Holylake, an estate not far distant from here, on the tip of

the Wirral Peninsula. She is now, I believe, carrying his
child.

Jardine is a man of strange character and stranger
reputation. I have made it my business to learn what I
can of him, for your sake. It is always wise to know
your enemies. The Jardines are directly related to the
Norfolk Howards and hence to the royal family, albeit
distantly. Apparently there was some blemish several
generations back (which I find easy to believe) that prevented the family from achieving the peerage that would
ordinarily be theirs by birthright. Your mother, as you
know, would consider an association with a Howard,
peer or no, to be a means, at last, to achieve her own
dreams of position. The man was retired from the Royal
Navy some seven years ago, and a certain amount of
speculation has followed his career since that time.

I am now in a position to apprise you, not of speculation but of fact, but I must caution you that the
knowledge I am going to impart is dangerous, only
slightly less dangerous than if I were to leave you in ignorance. I cannot warn you too strongly, Margaret, that
you must keep your own counsel on this. Use the
knowledge only to protect yourself, for you are far too
young and inexperienced to undertake the meting out of
justice, either on my behalf or on behalf of society in
general.

In the guise of running an apothecary shop, your
stepmother and Commander Jardine are engaged in the
business of smuggling opium into England and selling it,
through their shop, to the poor wretches whose insup-
portable lives are spent in Lancashire's dreadful mills
and foundries. I hope, my beloved child, that you never
come face-to-face with the toll that industrial poverty
now takes of human life and spirit throughout much of
England, and nowhere more horribly than here in Lancashire. Men, women, and children alike work eighteen-
hour days in appalling conditions for scarcely enough
money to keep body and soul together. Illness is ram-
pant, but no reason for not being at your loom or furnace six days of the week. Opium, if it must be bought
at the expense of going without bread, makes it possible
to endure—for the short span of so tragic a life.

Do I sound as if I fault the poor creatures for finding

what surcease they can, at whatever cost? Not so, Margaret. But to traffic in their misery seems to me to be as heinous a sin as men can conceive of!

This is the business to which your stepmother now devotes her life. You may say that it is no more dreadful than the virtual enslavement of England's poor, chained to their machines by deprivation as surely as if they wore iron bonds. Perhaps that is true, but it compounds the ill and tightens the fetters. Behind such sins against humanity are greed and avarice—on the part of those who own and operate the mills and foundries, and those, like your stepmother and Commander Jardine, who add the curse of drug addiction to the already overburdened.

It may be, Margaret, that I have some time left on this earth. After my discoveries of recent days, I am permitting myself to hope. However, if that is not to be, for all of my faults I will go with a clear conscience in one respect. I have tried to look after my own. Of all the men who worked for me on my vessels, none was ever hurt on the job but that I took care of his family with a reasonable pension if he could no longer work. I paid fair wages and expected a fair return in labor. I was seldom disappointed in a man, and to the best of my knowledge treated each one humanely.

It was only after I became ill and could no longer look after my interests that good men were replaced with dishonest ones and dishonest ones bribed to sabotage three of my vessels during storms that could easily have been weathered. Well—that is of no importance now, for I was forced to sell the line for a pittance to Commander Jardine when I became so ill, and before I discovered what manner of business he was in. And what manner of illness was afflicting me. At the time, I was glad enough to have a purchaser at any price, for I was unable to leave my bed and was grateful that my wife had found someone who was willing to take the burden from my shoulders.

Margaret, I have learned, I hope not too late, that your stepmother has been systematically poisoning me for many months. The realization dawned slowly; at first a vague suspicion quickly put out of mind, now a conviction that I can no longer disbelieve. I have proof that my illness was not the will of God, but the ill will of my wife, visited upon me in the guise of remedies prescribed

by the doctor, but in fact provided by her apothecary
shop. The worm of suspicion, once entrenched in the
mind, is surprisingly agile at seeking out corroboration
to feed upon. While your stepmother was often away for
days at a time tending to her business in Liverpool, she
was most unnaturally attentive to me when she was here,
particularly in the matter of administering my medica-
tions. Since they appeared to do me no benefit, several
days ago I began to consign them to the slops when she
wasn't looking. While my illness has in no way
abated—I feel that the damage done may be irrevers-
ible—I have at least been spared the dreadful symptoms
that have always followed her previous ministrations.
Yesterday, when she again left for Liverpool, I determined to search for whatever foul poison she might be
using.

I will spare you the details of my enfeebled efforts as
I hobbled about Greystones, searching drawers and cup-
boards to no avail, for in the end I found what I sought.
You will remember the green iron chest which has sat
for many years in the corner of your stepmother's bedchamber? An Armada chest, a relic of the sixteenth century which her father brought to her from Spain shortly
before we married. The chest is a novelty in that the lid
contains seventeen locking mechanisms which can be
opened only by a complex system of moves that rotates
each lock in turn. Knowing my wife's nature, I never
told her that her father, full of brandy and pride, had
also confided the secret of the locking mechanisms to
me, for it would have spoiled her pleasure in his gift. I
should have saved my strength and looked in the chest
first, for it was there that I found a small washleather
bag of what I feel certain is white arsenic, along with a
king's ransom in five-sovereign gold pieces.

You may be sure, my beloved daughter, that I stared
at that hoarded fortune with mixed emotions for a long
time. I swear, it smelled of evil, breathed it forth in chill
emanations that made my very soul shudder. How many
deaths did it represent? My own—not quite yet, but
desired and hastened at the very least—and countless
others, those poor wretches whose lifeblood had been
traded for opium.

Margaret, in the course of my life in the shipping
trade I have heard many a curious tale of a curse, the

Curse of the Flowers, some call it, that afflicts anyone who seeks to profit from the traffic in opium. Fortunes built on that nefarious trade, they say, are swiftly lost, along with health, family, sanity, and every vestige of happiness. But even that seems not to satisfy grim fate, for the Curse is said to visit the sins of the fathers on their children, their entire households, down through succeeding generations. If the stories are true, then it is a sorry legacy I leave you. But more than I fear tales of the Curse of the Flowers and of men whose seeds of destruction were surely within themselves, I fear for your future as a penniless girl, alone in the world. I prefer to believe in a gentler God, Margaret, and so I have hidden this ill-gotten fortune and trust that your own innocence will cancel out its inherent evil.

I hope, my dearest child, that I have decided rightly, and that my efforts have not been in vain. When one is contriving the demise of a "loved one" to look like a work of God, one must be diligent as well as cautious, so there is every chance that your stepmother may return to Greystones today or tomorrow. I dared not wait, but removed her treasure trove immediately—or rather in slow and laborious stages—to my own quarters.

We have little help in the house nowadays and they were happy enough when I declared an unexpected holiday so that I might do my work in privacy. I lowered the gold in pillow covers, by means of ropes, from my bedchamber windows to the ground two floors below and, after much effort, the chest itself. I had thought to dig a pit to hide it in the earth floor of the livery stable, but my strength would not stretch so far. Beneath the windows of my bedchamber the rhododendron bed had been freshly turned over and I managed, at length, to make a hole deep enough to hide the chest and its contents.

I have left the lid unlocked, Margaret, for to explain in a letter how the locks open defeats me. I feel sure that the burial spot looks no different from the rest of the bed; at least this morning I could see no trace of my handiwork. When I am stronger, as I pray I may soon be, I will contrive a safer spot and write to you again. But for the moment the rhododendron bed must suffice. Today, after yesterday's labors, I was very poorly and have only sufficient strength to sit in a chair and write to you. Tomorrow, I will find Ned and give him this letter to post. In the meantime I have devised a safe hiding place for it, too, for I fear my wife's temper if she should return to find her treasure missing before I am ready to cope with her wrath.

My dear daughter, if all goes well I shall weather that storm and see you again. But do not, under any condition, Margaret, leave Berri and return to Greystones before I can assure you that you will be safe. And should worst come to worst and I am not here to protect you, you must retrieve this fortune I bequeath to you without delay and with utmost secrecy. I cannot stress too strongly the danger to you if your stepmother were to suspect that you might have it. I trust you to use that fine intelligence which has so often in the past made me proud of you. Protect yourself, for I love you dearly and *will not rest* unless I know your future safe.

This is a sorry burden to place on your young shoulders and I wish it could be otherwise. I pray that I have chosen the lesser of two evils in the decision I have made. At least you may comfort yourself with the knowledge that no taint of inherited evil comes to you through the bloodline of Helen Allison Millbrook. Whatever befalls, keep that thought firmly in your mind. God bless you, Margaret.

Your loving father

My palms damp, shivering uncontrollably, I put the letter down upon the table and stared into the future. I had been horrified that my mother was a murderess, that my father had died a victim of her ungovernable temper and vaulting ambition, but this was infinitely worse. My father's words afforded me a glimpse of cold malevolence that would stop at nothing, and I thanked God I was not her daughter by birth. Hers was a calculating evil. It had destroyed my father without a qualm. It would now be directed against me.

A wave of truly primitive terror overtook me. With shaking hands I located a bottle of cognac and gulped some down, then ran to hide in my bed, dropping my clothes where I stepped out of them and pulling the covers over my head, as if that childish retreat would afford me safety. The blessed warmth of the cognac stole through my body and the shivering stopped, but not the vision of hell that unrolled like a tapestry before my eyes. I finally slept, pursued in my dreams by a fiery-eyed demon, demanding my soul in exchange for her gold.

CHAPTER 13

The guards posted at Greystones were there to keep trespassers off the property. They paid scant attention to the activities of Ned, who had the official title of caretaker while the estate probate was delayed. The entire surroundings of the house were littered with fallen roof tiles and brickwork, charred timbers, and every sort of fire-blackened debris. Because the fire had started in my father's quarters, the southwesterly corner of the house was the worst damaged, though there was little to choose between one area and another.

Ned, with a large barrow, scrabbled around the foundation, ostensibly gathering fallen pieces of wood for his fireplace, should any of the guards show interest.

"None o' them did, mind ye," he scoffed later, in the shelter of his own cottage as he unloaded his gleanings to reveal the green iron chest he had gone to fetch. "Too afraid I might ask them to lend a hand, I don't doubt. A vacant-minded lot, they are, fit fer bluster and loud threats, right enough, but not the ones to turn a hand to labor. I had no trouble findn' it, mum, for yer poor father was unfit for such labor and barely managed to sink it out o' sight."

I nodded, eyeing the familiar Armada chest with misgivings. It looked, from Ned's efforts, to be very heavy.

"Still and all, mum, we'd best transport it to yer house in the carriage and not trust to the barrow. They might take it into their heads to examine anything I trundled off the grounds."

With Emily and me shoving and Ned tugging on ropes attached to one handle, we managed to slide the heavy chest up inclined boards and into the carriage. Getting it out by the same method at my cottage proved somewhat easier, though we were all red of face and winded by the time it was safely ensconced in the darkest corner of my bedchamber.

I had decided to tell Oliver of the contents of my father's

letter, but no one else, not even Ned and Emily, beyond what they had to know. I would continue to refer to my stepmother as my mother, and guard the secret of her nefarious trade in opium, for I shared my father's fear of her and wanted to stir up no gossip that might eventually reach her ears.

When Ned and Emily had made their departure, I opened the chest to examine my legacy. True to his word, Papa had left the lid unlocked, the hasp fastened in place with a twist of cord that was easily cut. It was a murky afternoon and I had turned the lamp up to light my work, so perhaps I should have expected the sight that widened my eyes when I lifted that lid.

I had thought of the value of the contents, what it had cost in human misery, but little more than that. So the sight of lamplight gleaming on heaps of gold, more gold sovereigns than I would have thought existed in all of England, stopped my breath in my throat. The glittering hoard seemed alive, dancing with reflected light, when I plunged a hand into its depths and let the coins fall back in a heavy stream of clinking, coruscating wealth.

My father had felt emanations of evil from it? Not I. Excitement mounted through my body in one great rush of glorious emotion—exultation, a sense of power. I was no longer poor and terrified of the future. All of this was *mine*. I knew then that I would never, even under threat of death, release it to my mother.

It would buy me a place in the world!

I did not think of my new wealth as a means to fine clothing and an impressive mansion, servants, comfort, luxury. I had had those things, not on the grand scale of Adriana Rantana, perhaps, but without having had to give them more than a passing thought. They were pleasant, certainly, but what I hungered for was independence. My terror at finding myself alone and penniless in a world where I counted for nothing had gone deep. Mr. Robinson, safely behind his solicitor's desk, blandly impervious to my misery; the whey-faced clerk in the apothecary shop who had fobbed me off with thinly veiled contempt; never again, *never*, would Margaret Millbrook stand humiliated before such men.

This—and I forced my arms into the depths of gold so that sovereigns overflowed the bounds of the chest and spilled, clanking, to the floor—this was power, and I would use it so.

I set to work to protect my patrimony.

Oliver arrived six days later, in response to the letter I had

had Ned post, telling him only that the matter of our finances had been resolved and the proposed partnership could be arranged for whenever he was ready.

I was surprised to feel myself quite calm and in control of my emotions when Oliver walked into my small house, dwarfing the salon and all of its contents. He appeared as stalwartly handsome as ever, vibrant with an air of suppressed excitement.

Smiling, I led him to my bedchamber and opened the large brassbound trunk which had gone with me to Berri and which had finally arrived back in England, with the balance of my personal possessions I had left behind in France. I had had Ned purchase four large strongboxes for me in Liverpool and transferred my wealth to them, and thence to the trunk, covered over in layers of clothes. Ned had reburied the chest where my father had hidden it. Let my mother make of that what she might, in the event she found it.

Oliver, at first struck dumb at the sight of such a profusion of wealth, fell on his knees as I had done, plunging his arms into the hoard of gold pieces. Then, jumping to his feet, he threw back his head with a great roar of exultant laughter and grabbed me around the waist.

"We've foxed them, by God, we've foxed them!" he shouted, whirling me around the room in a wild gavotte. "Now let them settle the estate as they will, for you've skimmed off the cream. Puss, right from under their noses!"

Around and around we went until I was dizzy and weak from laughter and exertion and had to beg for mercy. When he released me, I fell into a chair, panting. But when Oliver began to speculate on the source of the gold sovereigns, I knew I could no longer postpone showing him my father's letter. I watched silently as he read it, his face reflecting deepening horror as he learned of his own father's complicity in the opium trade and, by association, in my father's ruin and death.

When he finally looked up to meet my eyes, Oliver Jardine's face was stark-white beneath its coppery freckles, with a strange vulnerability its strong bone structure had always disguised from me before.

"Devils, both of them! Battening on human misery and spitting in God's face! Although I still cannot believe my father a murderer. Nevertheless, he's bad enough even without that." His eyes, searching inward, were as bleak as the gray granite rocks of Holylake. "At least you have the consolation of knowing no taint of their evil runs in your blood, Margaret. I wish I were as fortunate."

It was a sentiment I shared, for many misgivings about Oliver Jardine lurked in the back of my mind. But to banish the gloom that had overtaken us, I fetched a bottle of French cognac and poured us each a glass.

With a great show of gaiety, I proposed a toast.

"To good fortune, and to us, Oliver, partners and comrades!"

"Partners, comrades—and lovers," he added softly, his eyes holding on mine over the rim of his glass as he drank the toast.

Half against my will and entirely against my judgment, he had me in his arms and, seconds later, on the bed. How can I say what I felt then, for I myself scarcely knew. As always with this lusty, imperative man, I found myself responding entirely as he wished, letting my clothing be stripped from me, even helping.

I seemed to be two separate beings. One his eager partner, seeking his hands and his lips, completely wanton in my hungry need for him; the other, within my head, holding back, even as my body kept time with his. I feared that Oliver used passion, used me, as coolly as he would use whatever tool came to hand that would further his driving ambition. That suspicion was a cold black cinder lodged in my heart when the fire between us was banked.

Oliver stayed with me that night. I wondered if he was incapable of leaving the aphrodisiac presence of the gold. Long after he slept, I lay awake staring through the dark at the draperies of the bed, conscious of Oliver's warmth at my side and husbanding the new coldness in my heart. I would need it to protect myself, for I was bound to a bargain I had little stomach for.

Despite my misgivings about Oliver, and my distaste for everything having to do with steam engines, my precious new wealth was committed to both. That being so, I was determined to commence our partnership on the right footing. No more would Oliver Jardine hear from me my inner disbelief in the merits of steam. If I was to be a full partner, and I was determined there should be no inequality there since my money would be at risk, I would be a partner in *fact*. I would become knowledgeable about steam engines and their application in order to protect my own interests. The very thought of forcing my unwilling mind to cope with so dull an undertaking was enough to send me to sleep. I was not always to find the subject so soporific, but I had no way of knowing that then.

CHAPTER 14

Oliver terminated his studies at the university of Glasgow, assuring me that he had learned all that they could teach him of steam engineering. Now it was only in practice that he could prove his theories. He was in a fever of suppressed excitement, full of plans and progress, sure that with his knowledge and my money, we could secure the additional financial backing we would need. He would try first in Liverpool, and was full of confidence that he would find no shortage of other men with vision, eager to share in the venture.

We were in the sitting room of my cottage on a pleasant July day when I reminded him that if we were to be partners we would need an agreement drawn up and signed.

Oliver threw back his head and laughed. "Margaret, Margaret! Surely we know each other too well to need solicitors to regulate our private affairs."

He took both of my hands in his and drew me closer to him on the sofa.

"Of course we are partners, child. But the very nature of our undertaking puts the burden of decision on my shoulders. That is as it should be, I think."

"But we will need further capital, Oliver, and you will expect to give some sort of legal assurance to partners who contribute it. Why make a distinction in my case?"

He pulled me onto his knees, a little girl to be dandled and cajoled. "We are the principals, Margaret. You and I together. You with the wealth to put my ideas into practice, I with the knowledge and acumen to make our venture prosper."

I ran a finger along his cheek, smiling. "I have great faith in you, Oliver. Otherwise I should scarcely entrust my fortune to you. But I wish to be treated as any other investor."

"Don't trouble your head with such dull matters, poppet.

The intricacies of finance are scarcely within the feminine province—and you are very feminine, my sweet." He nuzzled my neck. "I'll look after your interests, never fear."

"I have no doubt of that." I pulled away, for he was arousing sensations in me that I could not allow myself to feel just then. "All the same, I should like some paper to show the extent of my contribution. Otherwise, these investors who will join us are sure to feel themselves more important than a mere woman. They will pat me on the head but ignore my opinion, if I am so bold as to venture it."

I smiled, holding his eyes with mine. "I would not care for that, Oliver. Particularly if they had far less at risk than I, which is sure to be the case."

Oliver set me on my feet unceremoniously. Frowning, he began to pace the length of the room. "I see. You wish to play at being a woman of affairs, is that it? But I must tell you, Margaret, it will be thought most unseemly. You will be gossiped about, and I don't think you will enjoy that."

"Oh, pooh, what do I care for gossip? Better to be gossiped about than ignored or patronized. No, on the whole I think it will be more satisfactory if you ask your solicitor to prepare the papers as quickly as possible, so that I may turn the money over to you as soon as they're signed."

Oliver's face grew darker as I spoke, but I pretended not to notice. This was a battle that would decide my future. I did not intend to lose it.

"At least I was clever enough not to consult Mr. Robinson on the matter," I told Oliver. "His allegiance is undoubtedly to my mother. Or more correctly, to himself first, and then to my mother. . . ."

"My God, I would hope not," Oliver interrupted, the angry flush that suffused his face almost hiding his freckles.

"The estate agent who found this house for me is now looking for a larger house in Liverpool, where I will be handier to the center of our operation. He was kind enough to recommend reliable solicitors, the firm of Braithewaite and Cecil. Mr. Richard Cecil was most helpful when I called on him, and will be pleased to consider the document as soon as your solicitor presents it."

Oliver argued and ranted, declaring he would never agree to such an arrangement, that he could not conceive of my consulting a solicitor for such a purpose. But I reminded him that if he were doing business with my father, he would have no objection. In fact, he would expect nothing less.

When he found he couldn't move me, Oliver stormed out of the house in a ferocious temper. I heard him crashing along the path toward Greystones, where he had left the horse and new fast phaeton in Ned's care. No doubt the phaeton had been purchased on the strength of my money. I barred the door behind him. No matter how nonsensical my proposal seemed to him, he would be back. If not next day, the day after. He had little choice.

So it proved. Two days went by and Oliver returned in a cheerful mood, bringing with him a fine new bonnet of peacock shot silk and a cloak of soft gray fur which suited me admirably. As I paraded before him, displaying my finery, he grabbed me, and I only just saved my new cloak from the floor before he had carried me to the bed.

Perhaps there is a special joy in choosing to be foolish, for I truly felt that for once I was choosing when I responded to his ardor. Nothing within my mind had changed, for I respected Oliver Jardine's intelligence and feared his cunning. Yet I managed to forget my distrust of his motives as I listened to his blandishments.

"What flesh you have, my adorable Margaret. Glowing like a pearl, all roundness and sheen, yet so warm, so soft to my touch."

His words, like a litany, seduced my mind, stirring my innermost depths. I felt myself to be at once Eve and Delilah, giving myself up to passion, allowing him every license with my yearning body.

I was lying close against him, drowsy with love, when the words I had once wanted to hear more than any others sounded a tiny bell of warning in my mind.

". . . this talk of our being partners has made me realize it. I do indeed want you for my partner, Margaret. In every way, and for the rest of my life. Apparently I cannot exist without you. I want to marry you, my darling."

There was an air of benign confidence in the smile that Oliver turned on me then, but if my blood cooled rapidly, I regained my presence of mind. I propped myself on one elbow, to gaze adoringly into his eyes.

"Darling Oliver, what an honor you do me. And how willingly I would agree. But surely, love, you realize that I cannot marry quite yet, with poor Papa scarcely in his grave?"

His face darkened, and he pulled away an almost-imperceptible inch. Emotionally, it might as well have been a mile, for I was sure he never had considered for a moment that I might refuse him. We debated the matter. Oliver insisted that I was in need of a protector. If my father were alive, he would be overjoyed to have me safely married.

I shook my head with sweet feminine obstinancy and assured Oliver that nothing would persuade me to marry before a year of mourning had elapsed. But between us was the unspoken knowledge that if I was to marry him, he would have control of my property, as well as my person.

Once again Oliver Jardine left my house bitterly disappointed. This time he masked it with cool courtesy, as he assured me he would have the partnership agreement prepared without delay. I merely nodded. I had seen the shutters close behind his eyes when he realized that I was not to be persuaded into a marriage that would make us partners in every way—but unequal partners, to my detriment. It was not a role I was inclined to play. There would be no further talk of marriage.

I felt a twinge of regret for how it might have been, but I smothered it quickly, arguing the case in my mind, as usual.

"If you are to be a successful businesswoman—you are determined on that, Margaret?—very well, then, you will need to root out all such feminine vaporings. What manner you present to the world will depend upon expediency. But *within*, make no mistake about it, you will need to think like a man!"

I saw little of Oliver Jardine in the two months that followed, but scarcely had time to notice, for the weeks flew by in a welter of activity. The partnership agreement was prepared and signed. Oliver had taken premises for our new company, the Blue Funnel Steam and Navigation Company, Ltd., as it was called, and was fully occupied in finding additional financing. I was content to let him go about his business without question from me, for the moment.

The estate agent had found me a fine house of light-colored stone—Calcutta House—on Abercromby Square, a fashionable area of Liverpool. There was a restrained grace about its slender-columned doorways and tall windows that pleased my eye. Happily, it was fitted with two water closets accommodating commodes, a luxury I was determined not to forgo, as I had been accustomed to such refinements both at Greystones and at Berri. My faithful Ned and Emily moved in with me. While I was engaged in furnishing Calcutta House to my taste, Emily, who insisted she would serve as

my personal maid and housekeeper, engaged a cook, two un-
derhousemaids, and a scullery girl. I was eager to have everything in order as quickly as possible so that I might be free to
take more interest in our steam venture.

My stepmother and Commander Jardine had married.
Needless to say, neither Oliver nor I was invited to the nup-
tials, for Oliver was scarcely more popular with his father
than I with my stepmother. There had been a furious row
when he left the university and declined to join his father in
Jardine and Son. If Commander Jardine had little stomach for
steamers, he considered Oliver's dream of steam vessels to
trade with America rather than with the East nothing short of
idiocy. He and Oliver had quarreled irreparably, with insults
hurled from both sides. Oliver had explained my role as his
partner in the venture by the simple expedient of telling his
father our financial backing had come from my French relatives, the Cherbiers.

No doubt the commander was aware of every move Oliver
was making through his own contacts in the shipping circles
of Liverpool. He would do his best to ridicule his son's plans
to anyone who would listen, I felt sure, but Oliver was confident he could do no real harm. I was content to have no part
in the matter.

And then, one unseasonably cool afternoon in late September, Emily hurried to my sitting room to summon me.

" 'Tis yer mother and a man I take to be Commander
Jardine, mum. They arrived in one of them fine new closed
broughams. I put them in the drawin' room, fer they scarcely
waited to be asked in, mum, yer mother leadin' the
way. . . ."

Pushing down a surge of panic and loathing, I stiffened my
back and went to meet them. Had my mother found her
empty trunk at last? The probate of my father's estate had
been completed a fortnight earlier and Ned, on a final visit to
Greystones, had seen my mother and her new husband at the
ruined house. They had appeared to be searching diligently,
in company with a rough-looking man who dug in all manner
of strange places at my mother's behest.

Despite her unwieldy burden, soon to be delivered judging
from her appearance, my mother was as coldly composed as
always. Commander Jardine, of whom I had heard much but
never met, appeared a very different figure from his son, yet
uncannily like him, too. He was a broad, hulking man with
an oversized leonine head, and a rolling gait that testified to

his many years on the seas. Whereas Oliver's hair was a fiery red, Matthew Jardine's had faded to a coarse, curly thatch of ginger-gray.

Still, he was a commanding figure in closely fitted trousers and a braid-trimmed frock coat of the finest wool. His maroon waistcoat was of lavishly embroidered satin, festooned with a massive gold watch chain. If he did not look the gentleman that my father had, he projected an aura of power and wealth.

"Margaret." My mother greeted me with an infinitesimal nod of her head. "My husband, Commander Matthew Jardine."

He bowed over my hand while I murmured the usual "Delighted to make your acquaintance, Commander Jardine." The truth, for it is always well to know your enemies.

I managed the civilities—saw them comfortably seated and rang for sherry. But I recognized in my mother's assessing eyes cold anger restrained only by iron will. It was not long in slipping the bonds.

"I see that you are comfortably situated here, Margaret. You have come up rapidly in the world in only four months."

I cast my eyes down and looked demure. "I am fortunate that the Cherbiers are generous—and have affection for me."

"A preposterous amount, it would seem." Her voice was caustic. "At least, if the story Oliver tells is true and they have also supplied the money for this ridiculous venture you are undertaking."

"The Blue Funnel Steam and Navigation Company? Scarcely 'ridiculous,' surely?"

"Pah! Idiotic is more like it." Commander Jardine leaned forward, his face reddening. "Iron vessels. Steam vessels. On the Atlantic! Oliver's a fool. I offered him a chance to design and build proper wooden ships, clippers that will beat anything on the seas, and we'd trade where the future is. Out East. But no, not Oliver! All he can think of is that harebrained scheme of his, throwing good money away on a half-baked dream!"

"And the Cherbiers are a party to it?" My mother's scorn was immense, propelled by simmering rage. "I do not believe a word of it. The Cherbiers are not fools, to waste their hard-earned money on chimeras."

I shrugged and remained silent.

"Liar! Thief!"

The words burst from her, shocking in their venom. My mother was on her feet, her eyes glittering with fury. Despite her ungainly figure, there was nothing ridiculous in her appearance. Gone was the tight control that had restrained her rage.

"Helen! Take care," Commander Jardine too was on his feet, his earlier anger subdued by the need to control his wife. But she shoved a hand against his chest and advanced on me.

"Did you think you would get away with it? The empty chest, rifled and buried, all of my treasure gone! Wipe that smarmy innocence off your face, miss, or I'll—"

Only Matthew Jardine's strength restrained her then from attacking me. "Helen, come now, you will do yourself a damage."

"But it's true, Matthew! Look at her and you will see it's true. She found it, just as I feared. . . ." Her voice rose hysterically. "But she shan't keep it, it's mine. . . ."

Matthew Jardine stood before his wife, facing me. I had left my chair and edged behind it out of sheer terror, for the woman was capable of anything at that moment. Didn't I know what she had done to my father? Yet that memory, if anything, made me as strong as she was, and determined to thwart her. Silently I faced the pair of them.

"Margaret," Matthew Jardine began in a voice so reasonable after my mother's screaming that it sounded like a benediction, "you must see what you have done. You cannot drive your mother to the brink of madness, Margaret, you must return her rightful property—"

"Rightful!" I interrupted. "Perhaps, sir, you had better review your thinking, for 'rightful' is surely not the word you seek."

He waved away such semantics. "Your mother's property, Margaret, however you wish to designate it. Come now, you are a fine young woman, and no doubt you didn't think of it as thievery, simply as found treasure. But you see now that the matter is quite different from how it may have appeared to you at first. You must give it back, Margaret. Oh, not all of it, we are prepared to allow you to keep—" He hesitated, caught between cupidity and the need to convince me. "Yes, you may keep a tenth of it, enough to assure you of a comfortable income, wisely invested. . . ."

I laughed. "What generosity! How greathearted you are,

Commander Jardine. How can I possibly refuse so lavish an offer?"

His face flushed deeply, and fleetingly I thought how well suited they were, he and this woman I had thought my mother for more than sixteen years. But my purpose was unwavering. "What I have I will keep," I assured them, "for it is mine. Neither my mother's money nor ours, but *mine*."

They stood there facing me and I knew that if killing me would give them back their wealth, I would be dead within minutes. But Emily, white-faced and rigid, opened the door and walked into the room, her dark eyes black as pitch with fear and resolution.

"Did I hear the bell, mum. . . ?"

For a moment there was utter silence in the room. Then, in a voice that wavered despite my best efforts, I said, "My guests are just leaving, Emily. Will you fetch my mother's wrap, please?"

"Yes, mum." Emily trotted off hurriedly and was back in moments with my mother's moleskin cape. But not before an enraged Commander Jardine had time to voice the threat that was to haunt my future life.

"You think you have won, Miss Millbrook?" He shook his massive head and his eyes bored into mine. "Not so. But you have made a powerful enemy. I will hound you down the years for as long as I live. You will have no peace and no prosperity from your ill-gotten wealth. I will ruin you and I will ruin my son as well, for he is a partner in this thievery. Before I am through you will pay for every sou you have stolen, many times over."

When they had gone I sank onto a chair and struggled to regain my composure, for such was Matthew Jardine's aura of power that his oath of vengeance had terrified me far more than I had let him see. But when the hovering Emily bustled in and made me have another glass of sherry—"Ye need it, mum, fer truly ye're white as a sheet"—I slowly recovered my wits.

I had, by inference if not in words, admitted that I had found my mother's treasure chest and emptied it. But I had kept my own counsel about my father's letter. I wondered why. Not to protect my mother's unborn child nor even my own name as her daughter. Some other new wariness in me, then? The sense that weapons were made to be used to best advantage?

I wanted to believe that. Perhaps, partially, it was true, and yet—I felt a grue of cold horror as the truth loomed in my mind. It was more, much more than any of that. This woman who was now the new Mrs. Jardine was not my mother. No love existed between us or ever had. But something else did. I had longed to please her for fourteen years, without success, and the grip of those years was strong. I hated her, yes, but the force of her personality had marked mine, perhaps irrevocably. She was stronger than I still—at least, down deep in my heart, where the child in me existed.

I had defied her successfully for her treasure. I surely thirsted for vengeance when I thought of my father, that good man, being slowly prepared for death by her potions, and finally murdered by the most awful means. But when she had sat in my drawing room judging me with those cold eyes, even when she had terrified me in her wish to attack me, I knew beyond doubt that I had not yet thrown off the past. Something within me cowered and fled before her.

In spite of Emily's restorative sherry, I started to shiver and shudder, unable to free my mind of the horrible pictures it conjured up. Very near to physical illness, I went to my bedroom and sought the release of slumber. But my imagination would not be so easily deprived of its entertainment, for I dreamed horrible dreams. Of my stepmother standing on the scaffold, holding her weeping infant who, in my dreams, was me. Of my stepmother dangling from the rope, her dead, empurpled face still turned to me, mouthing the words, "The Curse, the Curse of the Flowers, is now on you!"

I woke to the chilly first light of another rainy September dawn and lay there under the eiderdown, caught in the terror of that dreadful dream. The Curse of the Flowers. My father had spoken of it as if it were real. As if he half feared that he was passing it on to me, along with the precious metal that was its source. I had discounted his words in my eagerness to have the treasure. An old wives' tale of no account in comparison to the bliss of having wealth of my own, at last. I had felt no evil emanations, nothing but joy, when I plunged my arms into the pile of gold. But perhaps the Curse took time to fulfill itself? To visit, as my father said, the sins of the fathers on the children?

No! I was a modern woman. I refused to believe such nonsense. I had had a fearful nightmare; to make more of it than that was sheer madness. I turned over in bed and told myself that at any rate I was probably safe for the present, for as long as my stepmother lived. I fell asleep again smiling at my own frivolity, for that was how I thought of it. Not that I was mocking God.

Howard Allison Jardine was born two days later, on September 30, 1842. In due course I learned of the birth through Emily's aunt who was in service with Mr. Robinson. She told Emily that the infant was reputed to be a large and lusty baby of excellent voice, but that my mother had suffered a difficult *accouchement* and Commander Jardine was worried for her recovery.

~~~~~~

CHAPTER 15

~~~~~~

I put all thought of my mother and Commander Jardine out of mind by the simple expedient of immersing myself in the mysteries of steam engineering and its use at sea. I had been grandiose in stating my intentions, as Oliver had pointed out, overbluntly, once our partnership agreement was signed and sealed. I would have been surprised if he hadn't. No one realized more fully than I how much my ambition overreached my present knowledge, but I had felt it necessary to take so outrageous a stand from the beginning. Unless I could manage at least a superficial understanding of our new venture, I would soon find myself on the fringes, thrown tidbits of information only when Oliver chose to indulge me.

My seventeenth birthday came and went, and I scarcely marked it. I had embarked on a program of investigation, searching out such information as I could find. I found nothing to encourage me. While steam vessels enjoyed considerable success on the Irish Sea and Channel crossings, their use on longer voyages seemed fraught with problems impossible to solve.

Oliver had company in his determination to conquer the Atlantic with his horrible, smoke-belching machines, but I was inclined to discount the dreams of such men as Isambard Brunel and Junius Smith, and agree with the Reverend Dionysius Lardner. Dr. Lardner, after all, was a prominent member of the British Association for the Advancement of Science, and had written a well-received book on steam engines. He sounded entirely reasonable in declaring that steam vessels could scarcely hope for successful voyages of even 2,550 miles; and as for crossing from Liverpool to New York, men might as well aspire to a steam voyage to the moon.

Yet Oliver was obsessed, and steamships did make the crossing, though the achievement always seemed to fall far short of the promise. Mr. Samuel Cunard was enjoying some success with his steamers in the mail service, running between Liverpool and Pictou, in Nova Scotia, Canada. The *Sirius* and the *Great Western* had made several trips back and forth, but after their much-heralded first race, a frivolity in my opinion, every voyage seemed beset with catastrophes and endless, costly repairs. No doubt, I reasoned, their engines were a help when there was no wind, but I felt convinced that for most of their crossing they were under sail.

My reading convinced me of one thing; Oliver had been correct when he told me that, as a nation, we British were not the triumphant natural masters of the sea that I had believed us to be. At best, we were following the lead of other, earlier seafarers. With my father in the Channel trade, and living so near to Liverpool, I had assumed that we had always led the parade. It was humbling to learn that not only the Vikings, but also the Irish, Portuguese, Genoese, Spanish, and certainly the Dutch, had been far more adventurous and sophisticated than we. Only the East India Company, protected by royal charter that prevented competition from free traders, accounted for our reputation as a trading force. Our Navy—that, at least, was the greatest in the world—had developed to protect the Honourable Company's trading empire and its handsome but slow East Indiamen.

Now that the East India Company no longer enjoyed a trade monopoly, everyone who could find the price to put a ship on the water saw a fortune to be made in marketing the goods spewing out of England's new manufactories. I had no doubt that Oliver was right in believing that that was where the new fortunes would be made. But why could he not seek to make our fortune by sail and forget about costly, dangerous steam vessels?

The first lines of our new vessel were laid down in the drawing office of John Clemson and Sons, Ltd., Clydebank. At Oliver's suggestion, she was to be named the *Lady Margaret*, perhaps to engender in me some fondness for her, for we had fought bitterly over specifications.

"Three hundred and forty five feet, Oliver, is a ridiculous length. *No* vessel is that huge, or needs to be," I declared, fortified by my neat assemblage of facts, gleaned from reading and one trip to the Clydeside to talk with ship builders there.

Oliver, his face set in the stubbornness I was coming to recognize, paced my drawing room. "I will not take direction from you on such matters, Margaret."

"Nor advice! On that or any other thing. And iron! At least if it were of wood, wood can be counted on to float. Iron can be counted on to sink like a stone, and *that* much iron is the very extreme of folly."

He whirled about and seized me by both hands, drawing me to a couch.

"Come. Sit here and listen, please, for I see that you have managed to learn a little bit about these matters, but *only* a little bit. We are in danger of foundering at the very outset if you persist in believing that what *you* know is all there is to know."

When I opened my mouth to speak, he laid a gentle finger across my lips and smiled, though I suspected from his eyes that he would far rather have slapped me and stalked from the room.

"Iron, Margaret, I am fully aware, has a greater specific gravity than wood. Still, you must take my word for it that a ship built of metal will be about one-quarter lighter than the same tonnage built of wood, because the framing of metal bars will be considerably smaller than wooden structural members would need to be. There will be more open space within, and therefore more cargo capacity—"

"But it will come apart—"

"It will *not* come apart."

"Who will trust us with cargo? Even the Postal Service won't allow the mails to be carried in iron ships."

"Granted, there is much ignorance in the field. But no reason to abide by it. A ship does not float or sink because of construction material but because of construction principles. Buoyancy, trapped air, that is what keeps it afloat. I imagine you will allow that I am more knowledgeable than you on that subject?"

"The Navy has no iron ships," I persisted. "Surely if iron were superior the Navy would be the first—"

"They will be the last, I have no doubt," Oliver declared, "but they will come to it, all the same, if for no other reason than that our hardwood is gone, felled to build their great sail armadas. But if England lacks hardwood, she has iron aplenty.

At the moment I am not concerned about the Navy, I am concerned about being first on the Atlantic with an iron ship. Moreover, the first iron ship to be driven by a screw propeller."

I clutched my head in desperation, but Oliver would hear none of my fears. No doubt he had heard everything on the subject from many another, but he was determined to follow his own lead.

I was forced to sit with my hands folded in my lap while he trod back and forth the length of my drawing room, extolling the merits of the screw propeller.

"Paddle wheels work well enough in calm waters. In America they are said to be successful on the Great Lakes and on the Mississippi. Here, they have proved themselves on the Irish Sea, but not so well on the rougher Channel. On the Atlantic, my dear Margaret, I assure you, paddle wheels spend more time out of the water than in it. The screw propeller not only remains in the water, which you must admit is vital to our case, but also is far more efficient hydrodynamically than paddle wheels. If you need further convincing, the use of a screw propeller allows the engine to be placed further aft, so again we will gain more cargo space."

"More cargo space! Is that all you can speak of?" I demanded, exasperated beyond bearing. "Who will consign cargo to an iron ship with only some strange whirring device to propel it? You are asking too much of both the owners of cargo and their insurers, Oliver! The risks of fire and explosion are already more than they can accept!"

"Ah, well. So long as the debate goes on, of course sailship owners will try to present bogeys to frighten away custom. But just wait, Margaret. Before long everything will depend on speed, on direct-course voyaging. . . ."

Of course, Oliver had his way. He would hear nothing I had to say, so I would keep my counsel for the time being. The engine for the *Lady Margaret* was ordered to Oliver's specifications from John Napier and Sons, Clydebank. I had to content myself with prayers that Oliver Jardine's stubbornness would not land us in bankruptcy. But I feared there would be far more cargo owners who shared my views than Oliver's.

I saw little of Oliver during these months and perhaps it was as well, for we were no longer lovers. Our partnership had become exclusively a business relationship. It was clear that Oliver Jardine would not accept me in the dual role of

sweetheart and business partner. If one part of my nature regretted that, another wiser part accepted it willingly. We were
both fully occupied with the pursuit of Oliver's dream, and
whatever the future might hold, for the present that was
enough. I loved and wanted Oliver still, but not at the price
of giving up my fortune and my independence to buy second
place in his life.

I, who had always taken my father's lucrative shipping
trade for granted, was freshly astonished each week at the
difficulties involved in monetary dealings. Oliver, in addition
to overseeing the work progressing on the Clydeside, was continually in an upset over obstacles on the financial path. In
Liverpool he had appointed a banker, solicitors, and auditors
without difficulty, but finding directors for our new company
proved a trickier undertaking than he had thought. The men
with whom he wished to be associated were already overex-
tended, both in time and money. Many disagreed with him
on principle, and those who professed to agree pleaded prior
commitments. In short, although raising 100,000 pounds was
not difficult for some projects, ours was not a conventional
project.

In the end, Oliver got what he wanted: three men of substance with venture capital to risk and prepared to risk it, for
a time at least, in the hope of substantial profit. It was not as
much as Oliver had hoped for—a total of 90,000 pounds in
all, 30,000 pounds from each man—but it was enough.

No doubt it was a cold and mercenary interval in my life,
but at the time I was content, for it was new to me. I was
like a child with a complicated and expensive new toy, not
sure quite what to make of it, but willing to forgo more
familiar pleasures while exploring the new possibilities. Then,
without warning, I was plunged into a nightmare that was to
haunt me for many years to come.

CHAPTER 16

Holylake on my second visit appeared no more prepossessing
than on my first, and if it had been daylight, with a hot sun
in the sky, it would have made no difference. The February

moon that rode high in the clouds outside the carriage window was bright enough to show me all I cared to see. It cast a cold, silver patina over the wet gray rocks sweeping upward toward the turreted house, turned the chipped unicorns on the gate lodge to prancing gargoyles, leering at me, warning me that worse lay ahead.

We had come at breakneck speed from my warm and pleasant house in Liverpool to this cheerless place, and I could only wonder what Commander Jardine had told the driver to make him so reckless of his own neck, if not of mine. No doubt it had to do with money and dire results if he took a slower course. My own motives were more obscure.

I had no affection for my stepmother, only fear and loathing. Much as I had delved in my mind on the long and frightening drive to Holylake, I had been able to find no trace of latent love, no childhood memory plucking at my heart. I saw her always as cold and forbidding; except for that other vision that lived within me, of the virago with the candle in her hand, setting fire to bed curtains and draperies as she fled from Greystones, leaving my father to burn.

Only civilization's hold on me could account for my answering Commander Jardine's urgent summons. The woman I had known as "mother" all of my life was dying and she wished to see me. Somewhere inside me the child I used to be stirred restively in the old pattern, anxious to please. Perhaps *this* time, if I were very good. . . I caught myself up short and tightened my grip on reality. She was not my mother. And if she was dying, she would die, but she would not change.

The gates to Holylake were opened and we went up the last steep length of drive to the ancient fortress-priory that was Matthew Jardine's home. He was at the massive oak door awaiting my arrival, and suddenly the long journey was not long enough. I gathered my unwilling limbs beneath me and descended from the carriage.

"Ah, Margaret, thank God you've come. She has done nothing but ask for you for hours. . . ." Commander Jardine, that bluff, bold-eyed man who had threatened me with vengeance five months earlier, seemed to have shrunk in on himself. To my dismay, I found him clutching my arm as if for assurance.

"But what *is* it, what's the nature of Mother's illness?"

Commander Jardine shook his head wearily, and shrugged.

"Consumption, so the doctors say. She never recovered her strength after the birth, you know. Lay there in her bed most of the time, and—"

Again the massive head wagged in helpless bewilderment, as he led the way across the chilly hall and up the darkened staircase. We seemed to traverse endless damp corridors before we entered a dimly lighted suite of rooms that faced on the sea. Even the fire in the bedroom grate couldn't obliterate the damp sea smell that must seep through the walls of Holylake. A woman would need to be in robust health indeed to endure here, I thought. I hoped that they kept the child well swaddled in warm flannel.

My mother lay in a vast mahogany bed with scarlet silk curtains drawn back on either side. Under the expanse of smooth coverlet she seemed to take no space, as if she had already gone, leaving only a wraith behind.

"Mother." In spite of myself, pity forced me close to the bed and I bent to slip my hand under hers, lying thin and waxen on the coverlet.

Her eyes opened and, indeed, my mother still lived within that fragile body, for they fastened on me in quite the old way; feverish now, but still—measuring.

"Margaret, I wished to speak with you one last time. I am leaving you a legacy."

"No, Mother . . ." I could scarcely speak as emotion overwhelmed me. I wanted no legacy from this woman who had killed my father and renounced me. Did she think to make amends *now*, on her deathbed?

"Oh, yes, Margaret. When one dies, one dispenses of worldly possessions. . . ." The words came thin and fast, as if she feared her strength would fail too soon. "To you, Margaret, I bequeath the Curse of the Flowers, for as long as you live . . . to follow you . . ."

Horrified at the sudden malevolence in the eyes that held mine, I tried to pull away, but her thin hand tightened on mine with inhuman strength.

". . . to exact its price from you and yours, from everyone you hold dear, for as long as you live . . . and afterward. . . ."

"Mother . . . *no* . . ."

"*Yessss.*" It was long-drawn, sibilant, unrelenting. The last word she spoke. Her hand released mine, her eyes closed, and though I learned long afterward that she lived for another hour, I knew she had died at that moment in every way that mattered, for she had achieved the last and only thing she had wanted.

The attendant stepped forward swiftly, her face impassive. Matthew Jardine, after a moment's hesitation, followed me as I ran from that room, along the corridors and down the stairs. He shouted up the coachman, patted me awkwardly, and rushed back up the stairs to his wife's bedside. On the endless drive back to Liverpool I had a fleeting memory of his face, reflecting my own sick horror, but it was a mere shadow in my mind.

The Curse of the Flowers. It never occurred to me to doubt that such a thing existed. That it was my mother's to dispense. That I was now possessed of it forever. She had known that I had her treasure, and she had given me its accouterment, the evil that went with it. I felt it, the Curse of the Flowers, a specter there with me in the coach as we jounced the long way to Liverpool. It followed me up the broad slate steps of Calcutta House, in through the front door and across the foyer. In the lighted house I was afraid to look over my shoulder, for fear I would see it grinning at me, obscenely clutching, welcoming me to its breast.

Emily found me unconscious on the marble floor of the foyer and with Ned's help got me to my bed. When I revived I screamed until my throat was hoarse. I was sure the Curse was there in the room, behind the door, under the bed, within the tall wardrobe, peering out to grin at me when Emily's back was turned. In the end, Ned fetched the doctor, who administered an opiate that wiped out my fears with oblivion.

Perhaps that sealed the bequest. Perhaps I was like Proserpine. For her, the single pomegranate seed that consigned her to six months in Hades every year. For me, a taste of the poppy, and the bargain was completed. I pleaded with God to let me, like Proserpine, live in hell only six months of every year.

At the end of a week I was well enough to go downstairs once again. But not before I had Emily remove every flower in the house, and Ned spade up, cut down, dig out, every flower on the grounds. I considered the bushes and shrubs and allowed them to remain. But never again would I wear, own, or allow to grow on my property *any* kind of flower.

I did not attend my mother's funeral.

CHAPTER 17

Oliver Jardine had been around to visit me several times while I was ill, so Emily told me. I had a vague memory of his presence at my bedside once, but my grasp of reality had been so weakened that it could have been merely a figment of my fevered dreams.

"Awful worried about ye, mum," Emily said, tucking a blanket around me in my chair, my first day downstairs. "Brought ye some fine roses too, but I made 'im take them away, much as I hated to."

I shuddered. "Just don't make any mistakes about that order, Emily. *No* flowers, in the house or on the property."

Emily sighed heavily, and gave me a sideways glance. "Well, I'm sure ye have yer reasons, mum."

"Good reasons," I assured her, but didn't explain. I couldn't bear to think of the Curse, let alone confide to Emily where and why it had come to me.

Oliver did pay me a call two days later, and managed to make me smile, flirted with me shamelessly, and listened with deep sympathy when I confessed to him the cause of my illness.

"It's a tale, Margaret, nothing more. Put it out of mind," he advised, taking one of my hands in his. He studied me and shook his head. "Look at you, a modern woman of affairs, and here you are, making yourself ill with fear over some foolish superstition!"

He leaned back and grinned at me indulgently. "I expected better than that of you, Margaret."

I was pathetically eager to believe him. "You don't think because I got the money, she was . . . was justified?"

Oliver gave a shout of laughter. "Justified! I think justice has little to do with this whole matter. And if your mother had got 'justice,' she wouldn't have died in her own bed! More likely at the hands of the hangman, if Laurie Oatway was to be believed."

I smiled wanly, wishing I could believe the Curse of the Flowers to be nonsense, as Oliver did. But I was heir to it; he wasn't, as long as his father lived. Still, when Oliver left, I felt as if I was on the road to recovery.

For several weeks I drifted, feeling secure in my mind that Oliver had given me much news of our progress—though when I tried to remember what he had said, there seemed to be little substance. I roused from the lethargy that had claimed me after my illness on the day I first realized that he was going ahead with our venture as if I no longer existed. I decided I had better look to my future, and quickly, or I should have no future!

Once again alert, I was no longer content to move from the shelter of my boudoir to the shelter of my sitting room, eating when Emily insisted, but refusing to dress or go out of the house. Hurriedly I wrote to Mr. Richard Cecil, the solicitor who had worked on my behalf when the papers for our company were being prepared, and entrusted to him a commission I could not perform for myself. Over the ensuing months he obtained for me every piece of information, every book and treatise and report that he could lay hand to, dealing with the use of steam engines in the civilized world, and their application to shipping. Apart from an occasional businesslike visit from Oliver when he was in Liverpool and could spare the time from his feverish activities, the information supplied to me by Mr. Cecil was my only contact with the outside world.

Those months of 1843 were odd, solitary months, but not unhappy ones, for I was immersed in a new world. Spring turned to summer and I scarcely noticed. I woke, I ate, I read, and I slept. The strange interlude ended one day in August when I stirred and stretched and my mind came to attention, crammed with a plethora of facts which suddenly fell into place.

Immediately I set up an office for myself in the library of Calcutta House and wrote out for my own perusal the conclusions I had reached. They were not, perhaps, earth-shakingly original, but neither were they commonly accepted theories. At least, not in England.

My father had been in the shipping business for much of his life. His philosophy, and that of other men similarly engaged, was that shipping was merely a corollary of his main purpose—the transport of wine and brandy from vineyards and an assured market for it in England. There was water between, therefore he had ships. In order that his ships should not travel to France empty, he carried coal on the outward

trip across the Channel. But the cargo of coal and the ships
themselves were incidental to his primary concern—the im-
porting of French brandy and wine to England.

At some time during my months of voracious study, I had
realized that American shipowners saw the matter rather differently. Their primary business was marine transport. The
goods that they transported could belong to anyone who had
the price of cargo space. The owners of the goods transported
worried about their own markets, their investment, their de-
livery dates. The carriers worried only about having a full
hold at the time of sailing. They comprised something that
England did not have: a merchant marine.

No doubt there was merit in both philosophies. But I, Margaret Millbrook, was apparently in the shipping business because Oliver Jardine was determined to put steamers on the
Atlantic on a regular schedule, as an end in itself, rather than
to transport goods which our firm controlled. That put us
squarely in the camp of the Americans. It also meant that we
had no assured cargoes for our new vessel, for we were neither importers nor exporters.

It should have been obvious to me earlier, but I was
steeped in the traditions of my father's firm. No doubt Oliver
believed that cargoes would materialize from somewhere
when his marvelous vessel was ready to carry them. His
whole attention was given to the mechanics of steamers. He
would not, I felt sure, change. If the *Lady Margaret* was to
show a profit, I would have to see to filling the hold with
merchandise traveling in both directions. I found that thought
exhilarating and made up my mind to set about it without
delay.

There was one other consideration. Steamers burned a pro-
digious amount of coal in transit. The space needed to carry
the coal was alarming, in proportion to the overall space for
cargo. Equally alarming was the price of the coal required. If
we were to be successful we would need to secure profitable
cargoes and a relatively inexpensive source of fuel.

The first time I left Calcutta House in the months after my
mother's death was to inquire into the matter of where and
how to obtain a sure supply of coal at a price I considered
economic.

It took a deal of time and effort, along with a few rebuffs
from coal brokers who considered the subject no business of
a lady. However, money is a powerful equalizer of the sexes.
Eventually I happened on a broker who, perhaps for the nov-

elty of the situation, was willing to tell me much about the business.

"Yuh see, mum, the problem of coal brokering is reaching the sea lines. Yuh have to have a right-of-way. That tally ups the price. Now you take the Rancorne Mine Number Two, for instance. They hit a fine seam over in north Lancashire, but they have no way rights overland to the coaling port."

"Really? Now why is that?"

"Simple, mum. The surrounding land is owned by Lord Netherson, who's sunk five or six shafts on his own. What man in his right mind is going to allow a competitor's coal to move over his land?"

I thought carefully on the matter for several days, studying a map of the area. Then I had Ned drive me to the pithead of the Rancorne Mine, some fifty-one miles north of Liverpool on the Ribble estuary. Once there, I saw for myself that what my informant had told me was true. Barges from the Rancorne Mine had to be horse-drawn down the river to where the coal was rehandled onto oceangoing colliery brigs. Competing mines, the coal broker had said, used a narrow-gauge railroad, at far less cost, to transfer their coal.

While I took my ease at a local coaching inn, Ned visited the waterfront to inquire about controlling depths of the river.

"Twenty-one feet at high tide, mum, and you can take that as a fact," Ned assured me.

I did, and gladly, for it meant that the *Lady Margaret* could navigate right up to the Rancorne pithead. But I was unsure of how the coal could be loaded, and Ned was a weak reed to lean on in so important a matter. We went back to Liverpool.

If I was going to surprise Oliver with a *fait accompli*, which I very much desired to do, I would have to garner more information. Rather than confide too much in the helpful but beady-eyed coal broker who had told me of the Rancorne Mine, I again started on my rounds, this time more knowledgeable in my questions.

In all, it took several more weeks, with five trips to the pithead and two to Preston, where the mine owner, an elderly gentleman named John Cooper, lived. But in the end I knew that the coal could be gravity-loaded onto the *Lady Margaret*. And I knew that it was worth doing, for I had engaged a mining expert and a navigation pilot to render a report on the potential of the Rancorne veins and the rate of silting in the river.

My first call upon John Cooper had begun inauspiciously, for he had been wary at the outset. He viewed dealing with a woman unfavorably and had never considered the possibility of selling the mine.

"I'll be passing the colliery down to me sons," he had informed me.

But if he was plainly out of countenance at dealing with me, he was just as plainly beaten by his competitor.

"What if I offered to buy three-quarters of your interest?"

"Huh! What would that nuckle for me?"

"Money. You would sell more coal and have a way of getting it directly to sea without transfer. Even your competitor must transfer from rail to ships. If my company were to buy three-quarters of your mine, it would cut the cost of trans-shipment for us. And it would guarantee you a sure sale of so many tons a month."

Cantankerous though he was, John Cooper was no fool, and I saw his interest quicken as he thought it through. Before I left, he gave me several samples of his production, hacked from a new seam.

"That's good burnin' stock, mum. Hard English steamin' coal. It'll suit, that I guarantee."

"What are your reserves?"

"The surveyors say the vein, at two hundred tons a day production, will last ten years. With maybe two more veins deeper down."

We settled on a tentative price that first day and agreed upon it at our second meeting, after I had checked it with the Liverpool brokers and been advised by my hired mining expert that production and potential were as Mr. Cooper had informed me.

Within a month of commencing my initial investigation of coal sources, I requested Liddiard and Rhye, our company's solicitors, to work out the terms of the sale and prepare the papers. I was determined to control this transaction as completely as possible.

Oliver's view of me, essentially cool and detached since my insistence on our partnership, had not warmed. For a time I told myself that I didn't care, I was an independent woman now and had no need of him as a lover. And for a time I had managed to believe it. That had changed and I seemed lately to be filled with a yearning that tormented me day and night. It would have been easy enough to find other men, but I did not want other men—I wanted Oliver Jardine, damn him.

Though I was now close to my eighteenth birthday, Oliver still viewed me as little more than a child. An enchanting child in the early months of our relationship; now an unreasonable, irritating one, hampering his efforts with my doubts and objections. As long as he persisted in that view, how could I go about winning him back? It would mean playing at being a good child to suit his whims, putting aside all of my hard-earned new knowledge and letting him run our venture, while I looked on and smiled.

I couldn't do it. No matter how I twisted and turned the matter in my head, I found that price too high. Oliver must be brought to realize that I was a full managing partner and a knowledgeable woman of commerce. Surely this mine I had arranged to purchase—and the reasoning behind it—would convince him I was deserving of equal status in our venture. He would accept me as a colleague and as a woman, and we would again become lovers. When all was ready, I set out for the Clydebank aboard the newly opened trunk-line railway, full of hopes and dreams.

The sooty, noisy railway did not, as many had feared, frighten cattle to madness, set fire to the fields, or cause mares to abort, but it was far from pleasant. The first-class carriage in which I rode accommodated six of us, with our luggage stowed on racks overhead. I was grateful that I had worn a warm wool travel cloak, as there was no heat save a foot warmer and no way to move about except when we stopped at a depot; the conveyance was designed like a horse-drawn carriage with a door on each side for entrance and egress to a depot platform, but no way of moving from one coach to another. I was the only woman in the carriage, along with five men. Several of them engaged in desultory conversation, but I sat by a window and watched the countryside flash by, as we roared and clacked our way northward. And when I wearied of that, I closed my eyes and dreamed of Oliver.

Perhaps it was the rhythm of the swaying vehicle, or the knowledge that I was traveling in the wake of one of Oliver's beloved steam engines. For whatever reason, I found myself lulled into a dream of perfect partnership with him—in business and in our private lives as well. Hour after hour, suspended from reality in a world of noise and motion, I let my mind dwell on the strength of Oliver, the feel of his arms around me, his lips on mine, and the quicksilver eyes shining down on me as I gave myself to him in love. By the time I arrived at Glasgow, weary and aware of a layer of gritty soot that seemed embedded in my clothing, I had almost convinced myself that my dreaming was reality. When I saw Oliver Jardine standing on the platform awaiting my arrival, vibrantly masculine in the chill Scottish drizzle, I was ready to throw myself into his arms and cling to him forever.

The reality was quite different. Oliver smiled at me like a fond uncle.

"Margaret, my dear, you enjoyed a comfortable journey, I trust? At last you've had the opportunity to discover that steam engines are somewhat more than a red glow in a Lancashire sky. . . ."

He handed me into the fast phaeton that was his pride and joy, secured my traveling bags, and we were off.

"Wait until you see your namesake, Margaret. A beauty, a fine piece of work, and very nearly completed. Eleven months, think of it! John Napier and Sons delivered the engine yesterday and it looks to be everything I had hoped."

Oliver talked on, as full of his handiwork as if he had crafted every inch of the *Lady Margaret* and her engine personally. The rain continued to fall, and my spirits with it.

Yet for all my dismal turn of mind, when I entered the shipyard and saw that structure upright, graceful of line despite its enormous weight, I felt a thrill of excitement along my spine. Pride of ownership was part of it certainly, but there was something more. We were explorers of new territory, the *avant garde* of a new species of transport; I, admittedly, a reluctant participant, but a participant all the same.

The *Lady Margaret* was three hundred and forty-five feet in length, as I well knew, remembering my unavailing protests that no ship needed to be so huge.

"The largest ever laid in iron, Margaret. She'll carry one hundred passengers and a crew of sixty." Oliver beamed proudly, not on me but on the vessel.

"And cargo, I suppose?" I asked, unable to keep a waspish note from my voice.

"Fourteen hundred and fifty tons, in three holds."

I didn't know whether that included the coal it would take to propel her, but I said no more. Truly, she was a magnificent sight, with three masts to carry the sails, three decks, and a long deckhouse which Oliver said would hold the main saloon and the galley.

"The ship's machinery will go aft, the boiler and steam engine where the flanks of the ship narrow. Come aboard, Margaret. . . ."

But I declined, for I was tired and gritty. I would wait until the *Lady Margaret* was completed to make my tour of inspection.

Oliver had booked rooms for me at the Duke of Cranford Hotel, where we had first become lovers. This time, as we enjoyed our leisurely dinner in a private alcove off the hotel dining room, there was no mention of that previous occasion. And despite my longing, no feeling of intimacy between us. Oliver was delightful company, full of talk of the adventures and misadventures that had attended the building of the *Lady Margaret,* but his manner remained as courteously impersonal as that of my solicitor, Mr. Richard Cecil.

When we had finished our dinner, I could no longer postpone broaching the subject that had brought me to Glasgow. But I refused to deal with it in the dining room of the Duke of Cranford Hotel. Pleading, as I had done one other time, that I must loosen my hair and make myself comfortable after my long journey, I asked Oliver to come with me to my rooms, for I had an important matter to discuss with him.

When I joined him in my sitting room wearing my most fetching negligee, my hair cascading in a way that used to drive him wild, I saw Oliver's cool reserve falter. There was a glint in his eyes; a flicker of emotion crossed his face that made my heart begin to pound. For a long moment the room seemed to vibrate with passion. Then the hand that had started to reach out for me drew back. Oliver's face was again composed, polite, waiting. I had no choice but to proceed with business matters. He listened calmly, nodding appreciation as I explained my reasoning.

"What a clever business partner you have become, Margaret." He smiled, leaning back to survey me as if I were his prize pupil. "I know nothing of such matters, having never so much as seen a coal mine. . . ."

"Nor had I. . . ."

"Ah, but you have studied our position to good advantage and that is what matters. My congratulations on a fine piece of work."

With a flourish, he signed the papers authorizing the purchase of the Rancorne Mine, which I had had the solicitors prepare. At once he drew a gold watch from his waistcoat pocket.

"After eleven!" He got to his feet with an air of affability. "I must let you get your rest, my dear. Tomorrow the installation of the engine is scheduled to begin and I wish to oversee the work myself. I am afraid you would find that tedious to watch, but of course you would be most welcome. . . ."

We arranged that Oliver would make himself available, despite his business, to drive me to the train returning to Liverpool. He clasped my hand, meaning it to be a hearty, impersonal kind of gesture, but he had not figured on the current of emotion that leaped between us. Once again we were within an ace of being in each other's arms. And once again Oliver Jardine, obeying some inner resolve, withdrew behind a polite smile. A moment later he was gone, and I was left standing, empty-armed, my head and my heart in a turmoil.

Outraged, bereft, scarcely able to bear the pain that filled me, I indulged in a temper tantrum like no other in my life—for it was necessarily silent. I flung clothes about the sitting room with a passion and stamped on them. I ripped to shreds the new negligee I had hoped would entice Oliver, and only stopped myself in time from smashing my bottle of French scent in the fireplace, for I knew I should be ill if I had to breathe that sickly stuff all of the night.

In my lonely bed, I muffled my sobs in the pillow and wept until my head pounded. That ache was as nothing compared to the ache in my heart. For eleven months the *Lady Margaret* had been in the building. For a full year Oliver Jardine and I had been business allies, but no more than that. A *year* since he had held me close and whispered of love. Seeing him again had made it all worse, much worse. When I closed my eyes all I could see was the warm vital maleness of him, striding about with his proud red head high and his face full of admiration—for his damned ship! I wanted those gray eyes to smile on me. I wanted him here, close beside me and the feel of him under my hands and against my breasts. I wanted *him*. And there had been nothing I could do against that solid wall of civility he had erected between us.

I wondered if he had a new love, and fell asleep still weeping.

CHAPTER 18

The *Lady Margaret,* after many delays, was launched on March 14, 1844. She had been sixteen months in the building and I was convinced she had cost considerably more than the original estimate. Oliver was suspiciously vague on that subject, but no doubt I would see the bills soon enough. I would worry then, if necessary.

I journeyed to Glasgow for the gala event, this time by coach. I had a striking new gown of ice-green satin, caught up to show an underskirt of ruffled silver lace. More narrow ruffles of the lace bordered the décolletage. With it I wore no jewelry except for diamond drop earrings. When I modeled the gown for Emily, together with a long cape of white fur lined in the same green satin, she assured me I was as fine as any princess.

I was scarcely more splendid than the wives of our company's directors, all of whom attended the great event. No doubt those women, and their men, too, thought me a strange creature. Unmarried, a managing partner in so grand a venture, and with a huge modern vessel named for me. For the first time I was triumphantly conscious of my growing reputation as an astute businesswoman. If that made me a matter of speculation, I found the attention not displeasing. I was eighteen and already a woman of note!

When the great iron vessel slid slowly off her greased stocks into the sluggish waters of the Clyde, the cheers could be heard for miles.

Ten thousand proud Scotsmen and many from the Liverpool and London shipping establishments jammed the Clydebank. I saw hard-bitten faces streaming with tears when finally the *Lady Margaret,* product of Scottish skill and talent, rode proudly in the water. Flags were flying from her bow and three masts, and her brightwork glittered in the thin spring sunlight. Beside me, Oliver Jardine stood with his head high and shoulders back, his eyes exultant.

It was a time of triumph, and our jubilation ran high, long into the night. Once again I had dreamed that on this occa-

sion Oliver and I would return to our old intimacy and once
again the dream had foundered. The Duke of Cranford Hotel
was overrun with our business associates. Oliver and I were
made much of by all the assembly, but even I, never the soul
of discretion, could not conceive of giving those watchful
eyes and ready tongues cause for scandalous gossip. I had far
too much to lose. I resigned myself once again to awaiting a
more auspicious occasion.

Nine weeks later the *Lady Margaret* had been outfitted and
moved down the Clyde for her acceptance trials. The reporter
from the *Glasgow Times Union* waxed eloquent:

20th June, 1844
Glasgow Times Union

IRON STEAMER, LADY MARGARET, COMPLETES AC-
CEPTANCE TRIALS IN FIRTH OF CLYDE. UNUSUAL
SPEED OF 11.5 KNOTS ATTAINED ON MEASURED-
MILE COURSE. VESSEL TO COMMENCE LIVERPOOL-
AMERICAN PACKET SERVICE IN EARLY AUTUMN.
345-FOOT STEAMER IS LARGEST VESSEL EVER
LAUNCHED ON THE CLYDE SIDE. REVOLUTIONARY
SHIP EMPLOYING NEW TYPE OF SCREW PROPEL-
LER HAILED BY BRITISH SHIPPING EXPERTS. ROYAL
NAVY EXPRESSES INTEREST. GALA PARTY HELD
ABOARD VESSEL DURING TRIALS. FIRST SEALORD
AND THE LORD CHANCELLOR REPRESENTED HER
MAJESTY, THE QUEEN. LORDS PEEL AND ABER-
DEEN ABOARD.

An event of worthiness took place upon the sparkling
waters of the Firth of Clyde when the iron steamer,
Lady Margaret, headed out of the river into open water
to begin her acceptance trials last Tuesday morning. An
armada of small craft accompanied the remarkable
steamer, whose engine of 1,750 horsepower was constructed by the Scottish firm of John Napier and Sons,
Clydebank. The screw steamer was launched from the
stocks of John Clemson and Sons on 14th March, 1844,
built to the order of the Liverpool-based firm, the Blue
Funnel Steam and Navigation Company, Ltd.

The freshly delivered vessel was hailed as a triumph.
In a special statement released to this reporter, Miss
Margaret Millbrook, co-managing partner of the new
Liverpool shipping firm, said:

"The advanced construction of the new steamer must be credited to the foresight of my partner, Mr. Oliver Jardine, whose decision it was to undertake the creation of a vessel employing iron as the building material and the newest design screw propeller."

The *Lady Margaret*, this reporter learned, will carry one hundred passengers and provide the finest food service available when she is put into service on the Atlantic run. Judging from the wines and brandies and the light meal served aboard the Blue Funnel vessel during her trials, opinion was unanimous that the proposed service should be extraordinary.

Mr. Oliver Jardine, innovative newcomer to the British shipping industry and responsible for the revolutionary design of the *Lady Margaret*, took the occasion to announce to his guests and the shipping world at large that construction of a sister ship to the *Lady Margaret*, the *Jardine*, is already underway.

The *Lady Margaret* was officially accepted by the owners in a signing ceremony on her way up the River Clyde. She arrived at her berth and was docked by two paddle tugs at 7:18 in the evening.

It was a landmark occasion in British shipping.

The following day, Oliver and I returned by train to Liverpool, for there was immediate business he needed to attend to there. Oliver was jubilant at the admiration our Blue Funnel liner had received from the shipping community, and in no way embarrassed at having publicly announced that he had commissioned the construction of another vessel without consulting with me or our financial partners.

"You worry too much, Margaret," he informed me, expansive in his confidence. "Two such ships will give the Blue Funnel Steam and Navigation Company a lead position on the Atlantic."

He leaned back contentedly against the blue plush of the first-class carriage, his stalwart shoulders and confident manner dominating the confined space. Dusty sunlight slanting through the sooty windows cast a golden mantle over him, master of all he surveyed in that dream behind his eyes. I, too, had a dream, as we swayed our way toward Liverpool. I savored it, watching Oliver Jardine from behind lowered lashes.

"Modernity, speed, reliable service on schedule," Oliver

continued. "The Blue Funnel Line will set a smart pace for the competition, such as it is. Let it wallow along in our wake."

"Mightn't it have been more circumspect to discuss the matter beforehand, Oliver? Out of courtesy to our other directors? Most especially our bankers."

"Pah! A bunch of cravens with no vision." He fixed me with an assessing eye. "There can be only one master at the helm of any vessel. Courage and foresight are not notable virtues in our confreres. We cannot allow ourselves to be hampered by their limitations."

At least he was classing me with himself and not with the cravens. I decided on the instant to put no new obstacles in my own path. I contented myself with a demure "Yes, Oliver," and continued to gaze at him with half-veiled admiration.

I received my reward. Instead of leaving me at the door of Calcutta House, Oliver accepted my invitation for a late supper within. Over excellent Melton Mowbray pie and champagne, we became quite merry in a private celebration of our triumph. We sat long over the table, sharing another bottle of champagne, recollecting past fears and reveling in our present success. The sense of intimacy between us deepened by the moment. At last Oliver tossed aside his table napkin and leaned close to me, his eyes gleaming in a way I had long missed.

"I have never seen the private regions of your new home, Margaret, but it's certainly far grander than the cottage. Can you find a comfortable bed for me tonight?"

I pretended to consider the matter. "It is scarcely so grand as Greystones, Oliver, but it is true that I have beds aplenty." My heart pounding, I lowered my eyes demurely. "Perhaps if we looked at them together, you might find a bed to please you?"

Oliver nodded with great solemnity. "That seems a capital idea. It would be best to test them, I think, to find the most comfortable, for I am so elated still that no doubt I will find it difficult to sleep tonight."

"Oh, but in that case, I shall have the Green Room prepared for you, for it is on the quiet side of the house, as are my own quarters. The bed in the Green Room is excellent, I believe."

In that sportive mood we mounted the stairs together, as soon as the rooms were prepared for the night. At Oliver's insistence, I agreed to show him each bedroom, that he might "judge the beds on their merit," he said, laughing. The undercurrent of our emotion was gathering headlong speed.

For want of inventiveness on my part, each of the bedchambers was called by the color that dominated its hangings. Oliver made much of the decor in the Rose Room, the first that we entered.

"Ah, here we have a rosy view of life, certainly. A place for sweet dreams, no doubt, but . . . a shade too feminine, perhaps. . . ?"

Solemnly I agreed that perhaps the Rose Room was more suited to a feminine guest and, hand in hand now, we entered the Blue Room. There, Oliver professed that all seemed perfect. Except the bed, on which first he bounced, then lay back, spread-eagled.

"Ummm. No, I think not. A mite too soft, somehow." He rolled over and propped himself on one elbow. "But come, Margaret. Perhaps I am being too finicky. Tell me what you think."

With a bound, he was off the bed and propelling me onto it. "Now. Lie as I did. Bounce. Come now, you must. . . ."

Giggling, I did as he instructed. Leaning over me, solemn-faced, he peered down at me, one hand under my skirts tickling me in a most undignified manner. "No, no, you must *bounce*, Margaret, or how can you judge?"

When finally he allowed me to rise, breathless with laughter and aroused passion, I agreed with him that one could never hope to sleep well on such a bed.

We discovered in the same manner that the bed in the Yellow Room was too firm. But when we arrived at the Green Room, Oliver positioned himself first on the left side, then the right, and finally in the middle of the bed. He lay there on his back, staring thoughtfully at the ceiling.

"Ye-es, it is just possible that this one will do. But I feel that I would benefit from your expert opinion."

He stretched out a hand to me and, my heart beating violently, I allowed myself to be drawn down beside him. With an arm under me, he urged me first to one side of the bed and then to the other, my skirts hiking up every which way.

"What do you think? Not quite . . . would you say? But perhaps just here. . ."

And—here—in the center of the bed in the Green Room, it was. Our play had gone on long enough so that our necessity was immediate and pressing. For the first time in my life I was made love to while wearing white kid boots.

That was convenient, Oliver pointed out afterward, because to walk along the corridor to my own rooms barefoot would scarcely have suited the dignity of a woman of affairs.

"The bed has been conveniently tossed, I will leave my clothing disposed in an orderly manner for propriety and the servants in the morning—and I will join you in short order."

Oliver was as good as his word. I had barely time to ready myself for bed, with the door ajar and one lamp burning across the room, when he entered my bedchamber. However he had stilled his passions during our long abstinence from each other, he had not been oversated, for his nightshirt scarcely disguised his eagerness for me.

"Ah, Margaret, Margaret, I've missed you badly these long months; there will be no more such separations," he murmured, and it was music to my ears. Our lovemaking this time was more leisurely, and if it lacked the driving need we had experienced in the Green Room, it was the sweeter for its tenderness and the time it gave us for every variation of our passion.

All the night we slept close and warm. When I woke, as I did often, being unused now to sleeping next to a man, I could feel the steady rhythm of his heart, close to mine. I would run my hand along that hard-muscled body, rub my face in the rough curled hair of his chest, and sighing with contentment that it was Oliver, Oliver lying close against me, fall back to sleep.

Although he kept rooms in Winchester Street, the five days that Oliver remained in Liverpool he slept at Calcutta House with me. During those five days it became increasingly evident, to my great joy, that there were new depths to Oliver's feelings for me. Often I found him gazing at me with pride and delight, and on several occasions he made reference, the intentness of his look belying the lightness of his tone, to the subject of marriage. I no longer feared that Oliver would use the marriage contract as a means to shut me out of our shipping venture; and I was elated at the prospect of having all I had yearned for—that perfect partnership with Oliver in business and in love—at last come to pass. But I did not press the matter. Better to let it reach fruition in his own mind first.

Unfortunately, a problem arose that left Oliver with no time for any thoughts save those of finding a solution. Our

brief idyll ended abruptly when he returned to Glasgow and
the *Lady Margaret* began her test runs. She was a hard-luck
ship, I soon heard it said in shipping circles. She twice ran
aground on the test runs in and out of the River Clyde. A
seaman fell from her topgallant yard and was crushed to
death on the deck. There was a rupture in the high-pressure
steam line which scalded one coal heaver and there were constant problems of propeller vibration and cavitation.

"We had her up on the stocks and bolted additional stiffen-
ers in the stern flanks," Oliver informed me on one of his
fleeting trips to Liverpool. "When we launched her again, the
vibration was corrected, but the propeller cavitation responds
to nothing!"

He strode about my drawing room, pounding one fist in his
palm, cursing under his breath. Despite his anger at fate and
his own position, for the first time I saw a dejected droop to
the wide shoulders, and the worried frown of self-doubt.

"Cavitation? Does it matter so much, Oliver? Oh, I'm sure
it must," I added swiftly when he flung me a look of disbelief, "if it upsets you so."

"*Upsets* me? Yes, you could fairly say it upsets me. I see
the old hands walking around shaking their heads, muttering
that we should have stuck to the paddles. We've had engineers from the Screw Propeller Company of London, who
forged the damned thing, up to the Clydebank on three occasions, and they know no more than I do!"

Abruptly he stopped his pacing and flung himself down in
a chair facing me. "It's the speed of the shaft, that and the
pitch of the blades. I *know* it, but I don't know why. Or how
to correct it. There's a vacuum forms around the propeller,
but why does that make a difference, Margaret? Why?"

I could be of no help, and even my efforts at comfort, loving him through the nights when he rolled and tossed about
the bed, unable to sleep for worrying at the problem, seemed
of little avail. But over the ensuing months, I learned a great
deal about cavitation.

The "vacuum" Oliver spoke of dropped the ship's cruising
speed of about 9.5 to 4.6. At that speed there would no longer be any advantage of steam over sail. For some reason, at
full speed, 11.2 knots, there was no cavitation. But John
Napier informed Oliver that if he pushed his engine at those
pressures day after day, it would not last six months.

The scheduled date for the maiden voyage of the *Lady
Margaret* came and went; the vessel had not even arrived in

Liverpool and Oliver's frustration knew no bounds. There was much skepticism now among the very people who had been most enthused when the *Lady Margaret* was first launched. The financial partners who had invested in the Blue Funnel Steam and Navigation Company in the hope of swift profits were at first impatient, then skeptical, and had now become sullen. Day by day, the coal at Rancorne Mine was heaped higher and higher, until the piles blocked out the horizon.

Production on the second vessel which Oliver had ordered was stopped, but the termination of that expense would not be enough to save us. Lloyds Bank, at first sympathetic, issued a date at which time they would have to call their loans and move against the pledged properties—both my home, Calcutta House, and the Rancorne Mine. Despite Oliver's frantic efforts, we could raise no more capital.

The Screw Propeller Company of London forged a new wheel with a more pitched blade angle, and Oliver was filled with hope. But the cavitation continued and, in the end, the propeller broke. The *Lady Margaret,* no more than a lifeless hulk, had to be towed back to her berth by the Clydeside.

That was bad enough, but I knew that even if by some miracle the cavitation problem was solved and the *Lady Margaret* was put into service, we would be hard pressed to find cargoes to fill her hold. A "hard-luck ship"; that was the reputation she now enjoyed. In desperation, Oliver called together every expert in England who had experimented with the screw propeller. For his trouble, he soon had as many theories as he had experts.

"And they're only guessing, that's what it amounts to. Well, I can guess too, but I'll do it in a way that offers at least some chances of success. It's something to do with the hull, Margaret, I'm sure of that. Wave action and the relationship of the propeller to the hull."

And so he ordered a small model of the *Lady Margaret*'s stern to be built in Glasgow, along with a series of miniature propellers, each with a different blade configuration.

"Once I see them tested in a tank, see the water forced past the hull section and how the bubbles form, maybe I'll know."

It was in the middle of this tangle of ill luck and forlorn hopes that Adriana Rantana wrote that she had recently taken a house in London and wished to see me again. She would arrive in August. Her letter was as nonchalant as Adriana herself, skimming lightly over the boredom of her recent life in Rome that had led to her decision to spend some months in London. She touched fleetingly on a marriage and its subsequent annulment, leaving me to wonder whether her sexual appetites had changed. They could scarcely have broadened. I felt that I had no choice but to invite her to visit me.

I lay awake all of the night before she was to arrive, thinking of my mother and her legacy to me. If I had thought that our misfortunes with the *Lady Margaret* were evidence that the Curse of the Flowers was manipulating my fate, I now felt certain that worse was to come.

CHAPTER 19

Adriana Rantana, tall and willowy in a brandy-colored travel suit, swept from her carriage and enveloped me in a cloud of French perfume.

"Darling Margaret, how wonderful to see you again. Three long years, *chérie*, since we parted. Ah, but I have thought of you often. Too often. . ."

Adriana's long, feline eyes glinted at me with all of their old daring as she linked her arm in mine. "We have so much to talk of, Margaret. The adventures I have lived—" She broke off to laugh. "Oh, poof, they were boring, I admit it. And the marriage to escape such boredom proved most boring of all. But first you must tell me how your life has fared."

Graceful as always, Adriana halted and stepped back, tipping her head on its flower-stem neck, surveying me. "Ah, yes. More beautiful than ever, my little friend. So . . ." Her hands outlined my body, almost but not quite touching me. "So much promise fulfilled." One slim finger traced my lips. "But the mouth, Margaret. So firm and controlled! I think you do not laugh enough these days, *chérie*. No matter, we will change that."

Despite my misgivings, and an ardent desire that Adriana Rantana would do nothing to disturb my new life, I found myself laughing with her, caught up by the arrogant charm, as of old.

"Dear Adriana. I hadn't realized how much I had missed you," I admitted as we dined together later that evening. Her polished aquiline beauty glowed tawny-gold in the candlelight, as exotic as some goddess idol from a Roman temple. "You are quite ravishing, Adriana, and I must show you off here in Liverpool. But I have so little social life now, no brilliant friends to produce for your amusement."

"No? That is sad for you, Margaret, but I realize that now you are a successful businesswoman with little time for frivolity. Oh, yes, your fame has reached London, I assure you. To speak of you was my one pleasure in that bourgeois city. One has only to mention the name of Margaret Millbrook—"

"And tongues begin to wag," I interrupted, laughing. "No, don't bother to deny that, Adriana. I know that it is true and I don't care. Truly. I like what I'm doing."

I stopped, dismayed, for one of Adriana's eyebrows had lifted that trifle that discounted what I said. "Of course, *chérie*," she soothed in a voice one adopts with a child. "It is just that you needn't pretend with me. I have heard rumors of the difficulties you are undergoing with that troublesome ship. It must be very wearing for you. But as for arranging social pleasures for my amusement, you needn't bother. It is to escape such activities that I have taken shelter with you in Liverpool."

She tilted her head, the heavy-lidded eyes glinting. "No, Margaret. Let us spend our time together renewing our friendship. Such rare affection should be tended as lovingly as a garden, do you not agree?"

I had had the Blue Room prepared for Adriana's visit. It was furthest from my own rooms, which seemed a sensible precaution. But I had had no occasion to enter it since that night when Oliver and I had amused ourselves testing its bed. Memory came flooding back, filling me with desire for him, as fresh and strong as it had been on that auspicious occasion. I was willing that my friendship with Adriana Rantana be renewed, yes, if she wished; but she must be made to understand that it would be within the bounds of convention. No more than that. Yet how was I to convey, in subtleties, the immense and permanent change that had occurred in my life during the years since I had last seen her? And how did I know so surely, as I did at that instant, that Adriana had not changed? Determinedly, I pushed down my misgivings and set about playing friend and hostess with all the aplomb I had developed in dealing with bankers and coal brokers.

Adriana and I passed two days in lighthearted chatter, falling easily into laughter as we reminded each other of some giddy episode during our school days at Berri. If Adriana touched my hand or my arm more often than I wished, I chattered the more until the moment passed. We caught up on all of the news she had to impart of her own life and that of mutual friends. She inquired delicately of my relationship with Oliver and of our problems with the Blue Funnel Steam and Navigation Company. I made no effort to hide behind a facade of either propriety or wealth.

Of Oliver she said merely, "How delightful he sounds, Margaret. I am happy for you. A man at once handsome, entertaining, and full of strength. If only Marcus had been strong."

Marcus was the discarded husband. I had no way of judging how strong he had been but, for Adriana, he would need to have been very strong indeed.

As for my present precarious financial situation, Adriana showed both interest and an excellent grasp of our difficulties.

"Money. Yes, it always comes down to money, does it not? The bank pressing you—Lloyds, did you say?—that is bad enough. And then the investors in your firm, who have lost confidence. The rumors of your financial situation must be stilled. You must have more capital. . . ."

She turned on me a long, slow look that made me uncomfortable.

"A beautiful woman should never lack for anything, Margaret. Have you not learned that lesson yet? But no, I see that you have not. I remember you when you first came to Berri. An innocent. I fear that perhaps you have not changed despite . . . everything."

She fell silent and the quality of the silence added to my nervousness. I made myself busy at small things, pouring her another cup of tea, waving away a bee that wished to sample one of the sweets on the tea table on the lawn, where we were enjoying the late-afternoon sunshine.

Then Adriana laughed, that throaty chuckle I remembered so vividly, and helped herself to another *petit four*. "Put away your cares, Margaret. I am sure these matters can be arranged between us."

Adriana, for all the casual confidence that her considerable wealth engendered, treated everything concerning money as a serious matter, and I felt hope stir within me. Immediately she changed the subject, leaving me to ponder on her words, torn between the desire for Adriana's help and the nagging unease she created in me.

In its own way the English weather conspired to hasten the crisis I had sensed approaching. As if to impress a foreign visitor, the next day was warm and soft in the way that only an English summer day can be—and seldom was now, in gray Liverpool. The sun was hot, and for once a warm breeze dispelled the sooty Lancashire clouds that usually hid it from our gaze. Adriana and I lazed in the garden below the terrace, enclosed within tall boxwood hedges. I was content to be peaceful and let the world continue on its way, until Adriana commented on the lack of flowers.

"I thought all of the English had fine roses everywhere. And the tall blue spikes, delphinium, is it? But here—nothing! Do not tell me, Margaret, that you employ a gardener with the evil eye?"

I could not join in Adriana's laughter. Though I had determined that I would keep the matter to myself, I was soon confiding to her the dreadful Curse of the Flowers, never far from my thoughts.

Perhaps because she had the medieval strain of mystic credulity that characterizes many Latins, Adriana Rantana listened in solemn silence. When I had finished she nodded.

"Yes. I see. The poppy. One would not . . . care . . . to have flowers."

She shivered in the warm sunlight and put out a hand to mine, offering that comfort, for she could not bring herself to pretend she did not believe that my dilemma was horrifyingly real. We sat in silence, wrapped in our own thoughts. Adriana roused herself first and stood up.

"Let us go inside, Margaret. Here we are caught in a melancholy mood, I fear. We must try to throw it off. It is . . . unhealthy. . . ."

I nodded, too distraught with my own morbid imaginings to speak. Wordlessly we went into the house and mounted the grand staircase. I wished only the solace of my own rooms, for I had learned by now that sleep was the best remedy when this fearfulness overwhelmed me.

"No, no," Adriana protested when I was about to leave her at the door of the Blue Room. "You must come in, we need to talk."

Reluctantly, I followed her into the room and seated myself in one of the blue velvet chairs before the bow windows.

Adriana, as lithe and swift-moving as in our school days,

plopped herself in the middle of the large bed, kicked off her slippers, and crossed slim legs, tailor-fashion, under her wide poplin skirt.

"I cannot bear to see you so troubled, Margaret. It will quite change your appearance if you allow it to continue." She gazed thoughtfully at me across the shadowed bedroom. "This Curse that haunts you"—she shrugged—"who knows, perhaps I will discover a way to lift it. In Tuscany there are many old women who are wise in such matters, and one can purchase their knowledge. But first there is the problem of your steamship company. As you know, money is no problem in my life. Nor will it ever be."

I could only marvel at the assurance that great wealth engenders. How would it feel if one no longer had to worry about money, ever again? Would one then find some other basis for fear? Ill health, or the death of a loved one? There seemed so few things money would not buy.

"Please tell me the sum that will solve your difficulties for the next six months, darling, and I will have my banker prepare the draft."

"Adriana! You cannot possibly—"

"Oh, but I can," she assured me airily. "I am determined to have a share in this great venture that you have undertaken. Can you not see that I envy you the excitement?" She laughed, shaking her head at me. "What a little goose you are, *chérie*."

My sense of foreboding deepened, for I knew Adriana, and her interest was not in steamships, but in me.

"You need a protector, darling, and your Oliver is not in a position to help you at the moment, whereas I am."

She lay back lazily, propped against the bolsters at the head of the bed. "Come over here, Margaret."

I wanted her help so desperately—but not at her price. When I sat unmoving, Adriana waved an impatient hand. "Margaret, do not frown so. Are we not old friends? Come, *chérie*. . . ." She stretched out one languid hand toward me. "I do not wish to shout across the room."

Hesitantly, I crossed to the bed and perched on the edge of it, facing her. Taking one of my hands in hers, Adriana turned it over, stroking my palm, smiling dreamily.

"Do you remember that summer together at my family's villa, Margaret? Have you ever had anything so wonderful since, darling?" She watched me from behind lowered eyelids. "How we loved each other, Margaret."

I nodded. "I remember."

Adriana laughed—that fond, throaty chuckle. "What children we were. I told you I loved you, that we would never be parted for all of our lives. I never told anyone else that, darling Margaret. I made a vow—"

"Adriana, don't! That was so long ago, we were very young—"

"Hah!" It was a shout of Adriana-laughter. "But hardly innocent, you'll admit, darling?" She cocked her head to one side, studying me through amused eyes. "Though of course you looked it. That was half the fun. You still look it—the little white and gold angel with green devil eyes! Do you remember how we would laugh about that?"

"Those memories are better left buried, Adriana. I have put that life far behind me now."

"And I, too, Margaret," she agreed swiftly. "I have tried many things." Again she tilted her head, considering. "I have tried everything, I think. And finally it is all so terribly dull, darling." She leaned forward, her hand moving upward on my bare arm, caressing, coaxing. "Except you. You were never dull, you were only . . . wonderful."

I looked at her mutely, longing to escape and yet mesmerized by those confident amber eyes that would not let me go.

"I vowed that we would be together always, darling," Adriana Rantana whispered, on her knees now on the bed beside me, sliding a hand up the back of my neck under my hair, her breath warm against my cheek. "Margaret—"

I tore myself away from her hands and jumped to my feet so abruptly that she lost her balance and tumbled sideways on the bed.

"Things are different, Adriana. You must make yourself understand that. I am fond of you, quite as much as ever—but differently now. I cannot go back."

"It's Oliver," Adriana stated, her voice flat, her eyes studying me.

"Yes, it's Oliver. But not *only* Oliver, Adriana. That other, that was schoolgirl . . . adventure. Oh, more than that, I know," I added hastily, alarmed by the expression I saw coming over her face, "but I can't go back! Ever."

Adriana's smile mocked my sincerity. "Oh, my poor Margaret, how utterly provincial you have become. Is this what your precious Oliver has done to you? Turned you into a proper little madam? But no, I don't believe it."

I shook my head, despairing of ever making her understand.

She was still smiling. "Oh, well, don't fret, Margaret. Keep Oliver, of course, if you want him. Or share him with me, what difference—"

"Adriana, will you *listen?* All of this is impossible! Oliver has no idea . . . he thinks me to be—"

"Oh, don't tell me, darling! He believes in that dear, innocent little face of yours?" She giggled as heartlessly as ever we had done as schoolgirls. "All the better. We won't tell him. What can it matter, anyway? Darling Margaret, we will spend tonight together, here in this bed, and then let us see in the morning if you feel as you say you do now."

"No, Adriana!" I knelt on the floor beside the bed and took both of her hands. "I know now what it is to love a man—and I do truly love Oliver. I often wish it weren't so, I assure you. Love can be so difficult. But that doesn't seem to matter."

I was near to tears, but when Adriana reached out a hand and stroked my hair, even that was enough to bring me to my feet again.

For a timeless moment Adriana Rantana looked at me through those knowing amber eyes, as if reading my soul. Then she rose from the bed. Slowly she smoothed her tight-fitting bodice with a strumpet's gesture of sensual preening in front of a rival, as blatant as if she had spit on the floor at my feet.

"So. You love this Oliver. And he loves you?"

"Yes." It came out a whisper and I said it again strongly. "Yes, he does," wishing I were as sure as I sounded.

"Good." Adriana tilted her patrician head back and gave me an amused look down her slender nose. "He will need to, won't he, when he learns how thoroughly you have deceived him all of this time? I can imagine his reaction. His beautiful little innocent, not quite so innocent as she has pretended—"

"What are you talking about? You can't—Adriana, you can't tell Oliver!"

"And this honorable man, oh, yes, I feel sure he must have been blaming himself for corrupting you. No doubt he believes he has taught you all of your pretty tricks, darling?"

She began to laugh, flinging herself into the blue velvet chair, throwing back her head, laughing with a wild abandon I had never seen in her before.

I pleaded with her, weeping, but she merely stared at me coldly and shrugged in the Italian fashion.

"I will think about it."

That did nothing to melt the icy fear in my heart. I had no illusions about Adriana. At the moment she was tormenting me, a tiger with a helpless victim. She might stalk away if she grew weary of the game; or she might play it out to the end. I believe, if I could have brought myself to resume our old relationship I would have done so gladly. But too many obstacles blocked my mind. My love for Oliver. My determination to become the woman my father had believed me to be. And the constant fear of the Curse I carried with me. I could not envision tempting God or fate by consigning myself to further vice. Especially when it would be vice without pleasure, without desire, partaken of with cold calculation only to save myself.

At Adriana's request, I had Ned engage a carriage for her return trip to London. I did not urge her to stay, I could not have borne it if she had. The following morning she departed with a final flourish of Italian charm; and behind the dip of her heavy eyelids, the gleam of simmering anger. Nothing I said had in any way placated her. I had made a dangerous enemy.

Still, fate was with me, for Adriana was safely away, well on the road to London, when Oliver arrived unexpectedly at Calcutta House. When I heard his arrival I ran to greet him and threw myself into his arms. He held me close and kissed me, while Emily frowned at our unseemly behavior, trying not to betray her disapproving fondness for him with an unwilling smile.

Oliver was hungry and weary after his journey, but he said that we had made some real progress at last. Hugging him, I begged him to tell me all.

"Certainly not under Emily's disapproving eyes," he said with mock severity. "You will hear it in good time, but we mustn't disturb Emily's sense of propriety further, eh, Emily?"

Emily produced a veal pie and pear chutney from the larder and we gave Oliver a late supper. Leaning my elbows on the table, my chin in my hands, I devoured him with my eyes as he ate and talked.

"You know that I have been experimenting with various propeller designs on a model of the *Lady Margaret*." He gave me a twisted smile. "Bubbles! I have seen so many bubbles on propellers that I may never again enjoy champagne."

At my frown of puzzlement he said impatiently, "That's what cavitation *is*. Air bubbles that form along the blades of the propeller. No matter, the important thing is that I thought I saw an answer. Instinct, intuition, whatever it was, I became convinced that a smaller propeller with extra blades would eliminate the cavitation. And it did!"

"Oliver!" I picked up my skirts and rounded the table to fling myself upon him. "Darling, clever Oliver."

He settled me on his knees and smiled at my excitement. "Well, perhaps I oversimplified. Actually it took two tries, adding an extra blade each time and reducing the diameter."

"Now don't pretend to be humble, for I know you're not. Nor should you be. Two tries or ten, what difference, if you've succeeded. Oh, darling Oliver, you are brilliant. I always knew it!"

Oliver frowned. "Yes, well, brilliance costs dear. I've ordered the Screw Propeller Company to forge a new five-bladed wheel, and Lloyds Bank is pressing me hard. All of this experimentation—these fool bankers are of the opinion that model ships in a tank are mere toys and prove nothing."

"Then they are wrong," I declared stoutly. "You must make them see that you have solved the problem, Oliver."

My assurances did nothing to lighten his deepening gloom. "We have to have more money, Margaret, and swiftly. Lloyds refuses to extend our credit one day past the call date. I need more time than that."

I removed myself from his lap and he went back to his supper, but a pall had fallen across the evening, for it seemed we had no sooner solved one problem than another arose.

Adriana would have supplied the money Oliver needed so desperately. Was I selfish to let him bear this burden without aid that I could give him—through Adriana? If I really loved him, would I see him lack for aught that I could supply? No, surely that was sophistry, a very Adriana-like argument. Anyway, none of it applied, for a bargain that might seem almost possible in Adriana's presence was clearly impossible even to consider when I sat across the table from Oliver Jardine.

Oliver came to my room later, and our lovemaking had a desperate intensity that sought to close out the world and impending disaster. We didn't talk afterward. Perhaps there was nothing to say, for our separate difficulties were not ones that would yield to conversation. I was a long time falling asleep and I knew that Oliver, still and silent beside me, stared at the ceiling, facing the collapse of all of his dreams for the Blue Funnel line.

At some point before morning I sensed that Oliver was leaving my bed to return to the Green Room. It was a charade we played for the benefit of the servants each time he stayed at Calcutta House. But this time, caught between fearful reality and nightmare, I thought Oliver was leaving me forever. That Adriana had made good her threat to tell him of my shameful past, and he had turned on me with all of my mother's scorn and contempt.

I woke to find my face wet with tears, enveloped by a sense of doom that choked my throat. At that moment I longed to be *old*. Old and peaceful and with my battles fought—not forever striving and plotting, unsure of every decision, loving Oliver more than was wise, and now doubly vulnerable because of Adriana. So many fears—but the greatest was of Adriana.

CHAPTER 20

The weeks that followed were a period of relentless torment, for I knew Oliver's desperation when he returned to Glasgow. He had been unable to raise the capital we needed in Liverpool or London; everything we owned was mortgaged to the hilt, and he was reduced to staving off creditors as best he could, while waiting for the final blow when Lloyd's would call our huge outstanding debt.

Always in my mind was Adriana. If I had Ned drive me to London, I could persuade her that I bitterly regretted my decision. That my new morality had proved unequal to my great need for her and I now begged to have her back. It would be highly dramatic, laden with tears and passion, and in the end I would have the two things I needed: money to save our foundering company and the assurance that she would not betray me to Oliver. Adriana would then be, as she wished, linked to Oliver as well as to me, and to the Blue Funnel Steam and Navigation Company. She would have everything she wanted. And I would be bound to her beyond recall.

Instead, I let the days go by, one after another, doing nothing. To go to London, to make my peace with Adriana, entailed a decision I found myself powerless to make. So I drifted, hoping that somehow Oliver would find the money and we would be saved. Hoping that Adriana would find a new love, or at least a diverting interest, and not pursue the vengeance she had planned. They were forlorn hopes and I knew it, but I felt helpless, caught up in a dream where will and effort counted for nothing and events proceeded of their own volition.

Yet when almost three weeks had passed and the blow had not fallen, I began to allow myself to believe that Adriana had softened. That illusion ended with Oliver's arrival from Glasgow late one September night when I was already abed. I had no idea he was coming to Liverpool, and I descended the great stairs to greet him. One look at him and I knew the death of my hopes, knew that I was finally come face-to-face with the rage I had sensed him capable of since that first night in Glasgow.

Oliver Jardine stood at the foot of the staircase, his small portmanteau in one hand. His eyes raked me from head to foot; his mouth curled in contempt. Without saying a word, he seized my arm with his free hand and half dragged me up the stairs to my sitting room. He thrust me roughly into a chair and sat down opposite me. When at last he spoke, his voice was very quiet, very controlled.

"I have found the money we need, Margaret. I received a visit from a wealthy new investor. A Miss Adriana Rantana."

He folded his arms across his chest and surveyed me with a hard grin that was more grimace than smile. "Well, Margaret? Are you not pleased that Miss Rantana has come to our rescue?"

His false composure broke. He leaped from his chair and towered over me. One cruel hand grasped my chin like a vise and turned my face up to his.

"She tells me that you two were great friends at that French academy you attended. That you shared many exciting adventures together."

Panic flooded through me. What had she told him? What should I say? I felt my face aflame and my head as thick as a ball of cotton, without wit or words.

Oliver released me abruptly and delved into his portmanteau, producing a bottle. "Look what I've brought you," he said. "Vodka, that elixir so dear to the Russians." Grasping the bottle by the neck, he sloshed liquid into two glasses sitting on the small table between our chairs.

"Come, Margaret, let's drink to your old friend—and my new benefactor."

I looked up sharply. "Adriana Rantana is no friend of mine. A dreadful creature I was careful to avoid at school. A liar and profligate. . ."

Oliver laughed, his eyes mocking me over the top of his glass. "Indeed? She spoke most glowingly of *you*. Your accomplishments in a number of fields. Why, Adriana tells me that your capacity for vodka was legendary. And here you are, not touching the treat that I brought you. Come now, down it! You must have that and more, to satisfy that famous thirst."

"Oliver, stop this nonsense. The woman is a jealous, demented type who—*no*, Oliver!" My voice and my hand, too, shook, spilling vodka down the front of my negligee as Oliver Jardine's hand closed around mine, forcing my glass to my lips, until I choked and sputtered.

"*Voilà*, my little French strumpet. See how easy it is, once you drop your pretenses? Tonight, I promise, you shall have your fill."

Again he seized my glass, pouring vodka into it until it spilled over onto the carpet. "There you go, my beautiful little slut, down that and then let us see what else you were famous for with your degenerate friends."

I started to cry. "Oh, Oliver, how can you speak to me so? How can you believe that horrible woman's lies and slanders when you know me so well? Have you no trust?"

"Ah! Trust." He nodded, mocking an air of judicious wisdom. "You wish to assure me that you were an innocent virgin when we met? But was there not a lecherous old count, the one with the gray goatee, and his handsome young buck of a son? A devoted pair who could only enjoy a woman while sharing her? Their affection for you was quite touching, if Adriana is to be believed. And were there not others? Was there not. . ."

His voice went on and on, cataloging Adriana's list of my misdeeds, such a skillful blend of truth and lie that I myself could scarcely distinguish the one from the other. All the while those quicksilver eyes were fixed on me with the full force of his scorn.

Suddenly all of the fear and misery I had lived with these past weeks boiled up inside me.

"Damn you!" I flung the vodka in his face and slammed the glass into the fireplace. "And damn Adriana Rantana! What a fine pair you make! A sanctimonious blackguard and a lying slut."

Shaking vodka from his hair like a dog coming out of the water, Oliver Jardine laughed, and it was not a pretty sound to hear. "Ah, what righteous wrath from the little white and gold angel. Isn't that what they called you at that school? And what I myself, fool that I am, have on occasion named you? How amused you must have been at my contrition over the seduction of an innocent!"

He seized me by a wrist and jerked me to him. Holding me fast, half between his legs, he shifted his hands to clutch my hair so I could move my head neither to the left nor the right.

"Look at me, damn you!" He peered down into my eyes. "Ah, yes. Yes, indeed. I see right into your corrupt little soul. The soul of a whore, cavorting about like a bitch in heat, behind the mask of sweet innocence!"

With a thrust, he sent me flying backward, crashing into a chair that only partially broke my fall. At that moment I knew total rage. Oliver Jardine's hateful face leered at me from beyond a red mist. Humiliation, worse than I had ever dreamed it, bathed me in waves of feverish heat. With no thought of the consequences, I launched myself at him, hungering to rake my fingernails down his detestable face.

I succeeded. Though he twisted and pulled back, I had the blood I longed for, long streaks of it like thin red rivers welling the length of his cheek from eye to chin. And then he caught me by my hair, tugging it loose from its pins, holding a fistful high above my head so that no matter how I twisted, I was forced to follow when he yanked me along into the bedchamber. There, with his fist still locked in my hair, Oliver Jardine shook me into position before the long pier glass. With his free hand he wrenched my negligee and nightgown from me, so that I stood shivering in my nakedness and fury, forced to face the pier glass as Oliver set about tormenting me like some lascivious auctioneer with a slave on the block.

"Now, gentlemen, what am I bid for this tender young creature, this succulent armful of endless delight? Note the smooth, high curve of the cheek, the vulnerability of the girlish chin, the innocence of that wide-eyed gaze. What's that?

Well, perhaps not precisely a virgin, sir, but what she lacks in virginity, she more than makes up in accomplishment. What you might call a professional innocent. And very provocative you'll find it, I guarantee."

He smiled at me in the mirror, that frightening tiger smile. Standing close against me, he fondled my breasts, cupping them in a hand, bending to flick them with his tongue. When I twisted to escape him, the tiger smile broadened.

"A wondrously agile creature, is she not, gentlemen? A lustful little beauty who developed her admirable talents springing in and out of Continental beds. Absolutely guaranteed to spread those deliciously rounded thighs without a moment's hesitation. The delight of lecher and voyeur alike—for rumor has it she prefers her lovers in pairs. . . ."

"Oh, that lying bitch, that lying bitch. . ." I was sobbing it like a litany.

With a final shake, Oliver released me. I stumbled to the bed to snatch up a coverlet and wrap myself from his sight. Covered again and sick with loathing, I turned to defy him.

"You have had your sport, now get out of my home! And I wish you much joy of Adriana Rantana. No doubt you've bedded her, for she has the roundest heels in creation. May you enjoy your bedfellows. All of them!"

"It's true that she, at least, is honest. She doesn't seek to conceal her licentiousness behind a white and gold mask. Still, why would I want another libertine, beautiful Margaret? When I have you."

It took a moment for his meaning to penetrate my fury. A moment before I recognized that heavy-eyed look of purposeful lust.

"Don't you dare to touch me!"

Oliver Jardine stood foursquare between me and escape, huge and formidable in the lamplight, his eyes holding mine as he slowly stripped off his clothing and tossed it into a heap on a chair.

"Surely you know that the auctioneer, like the *seigneur*, enjoys first rights?"

As he reached for me, I made a frantic effort to dodge around him and tripped on a trailing end of my coverlet. He snatched me up like a quilt-wrapped package and tossed me onto the bed.

At that moment I hated him with such a passion that I was determined to die rather than submit to him. But in the end, though I cried and fought, sheer male strength and body weight defeated me, and he took me with slow, hateful leisure. For once, I was in no danger of falling prey to my own responses. I lay like a stone, willing my flesh to be as cold and hard as marble.

When he took his leave, I kept my eyes closed, my face carefully blank, for I would not grant him any further response except total indifference.

As for Adriana Rantana, I realized later during that sleepless night that she had apparently told Oliver nothing of the relationship that had existed between us. Perhaps that was because she had wanted to have a further dagger to hold to my throat. Much good it would do her now! So far as I was concerned, Oliver Jardine as a man no longer existed. She could tell him whatever she chose. It would never matter to me again.

CHAPTER 21

The permanent severing of all links with Oliver Jardine was one thing; but everything I owned in the world was linked to him through the Blue Funnel Steam and Navigation Company. Moreover, Adriana Rantana now had a large stake in that venture. No doubt Oliver divided his contempt between us equally—the two libertines from the Berri Academy! Nonetheless, Adriana was a forceful woman and I had no intention of allowing her to usurp my place within the company. I might want never to see or hear of Oliver Jardine again, but it was a luxury I was not going to be able to afford. I was far too proud of my role as a successful businesswoman to relinquish it. Yet Oliver, I was sure, would now try to close me out of all active participation in the business venture that my fortune had founded. Against that threat, I had to look to my own survival. In the back of my mind grew a plan that might ensure it.

Oliver had one goal: the creation of steamships to plow the Atlantic Ocean in both directions. No doubt he envisioned them laden with cargoes, making enormous profits—more money to build more ships, in accordance with his progressive theories. But none of our setbacks had impressed upon him the view that potential shippers might now take of entrusting their merchandise to a hard-luck ship like the *Lady Margaret*.

Once again I enlisted the help of clever, patient Richard Cecil.

"I know too little about the commodities we ship abroad," I informed him. "What, precisely, are the products of those forges and mills that blacken our Lancashire skies? Wool and cotton stuff by the bolt? Stockings and vests? Plows, furniture, bullets? What do we sell to America that they must have and can obtain from us? Or obtain from us most advantageously? And what can we carry as return cargo from America to Liverpool?"

Richard Cecil smiled with that quick warmth that had originally persuaded me to employ his services. "I will begin inquiries immediately, Miss Millbrook."

Over a glass of sherry in the library of Calcutta House, Mr. Cecil spoke of visiting the Liverpool office of the Collector of Port Dues and Customs, to see what he could learn of inbound cargoes from American cities.

"Also, there are the buyers of the commodity groups in the various cities in the Midlands. But for outbound cargoes—" He hesitated and sipped thoughtfully at his sherry. "I have heard of a man whom it might be useful for you to meet. An American, Mr. George Gore of Edisto Island, South Carolina. Our firm has done some business for him. He is coming to Liverpool within the month, I believe."

"Oh? An American. What does he import from this country, Mr. Cecil?"

"I believe in the past his interest has been primarily concerned with export, Miss Millbrook. He is the representative of the powerful Edisto Island Planters Association and is himself the owner of a large Edisto plantation. Long-staple cotton for the Lancashire mills."

"Interesting, certainly. But you mentioned outbound cargoes?"

He would not be drawn. "Allow me to see what I can learn, madam. Perhaps it will come to nothing, but I am of the opinion that Mr. Gore can provide insight as to what the Americans, most especially Americans in the southern states, feel that they need."

"Yes, that might prove quite helpful. Please do what you can, Mr. Cecil. I have had a report that the *Lady Margaret*'s cavitation problem has been solved with the installation of a new propeller. Smaller in diameter and with five blades. It has yet to be tested, but—well, I am sure you understand the need for all possible haste with regard to forward contracts."

A week after my talk with Richard Cecil, the *Lady Margaret* put to sea for the seventh time. Over the measured-mile course, she achieved a full eleven knots at 80 percent horsepower. On receipt of that information, I could no longer put off a business conference with Oliver Jardine. As distasteful as the prospect was, I decided that I would not settle for half measures but would journey to Glasgow myself, thereby making my presence felt and at the same time assuring myself that I could now promise potential shippers that the *Lady Margaret* would make her maiden voyage within three months.

I had had no correspondence with Oliver since our parting as enemies. What news I had had of the progress in Glasgow had come through our firm's offices in Liverpool. I had no intention of allowing that situation to continue. No doubt it would suit Oliver admirably, but it would work to my detriment, and while he might be strong enough physically to rape me, he would soon learn that besting me in business matters was of quite a different order.

I took a hansom cab from the railway depot to the Duke of Cranford Hotel to leave my luggage, and thence to the shipyard. Oliver was not there, but I learned that he had recently moved into new rooms in Glasgow and I would be likely to find him there, for it was near to the dinner hour. I hesitated, half tempted to look over the *Lady Margaret* while I was at the shipyard, but decided it would be wiser to deal with Oliver first.

The address I had been given by the foreman at the shipyard proved to be in a square, quadrangled by old Georgian rose-brick townhouses with plain facades and handsome fanlights. For a price that amounted to a bribe, the driver agreed to wait for as long as I wished. I mounted the marble steps to the front door and was about to crank the bell when the door suddenly opened. I found myself looking into the startled face of a woman in a tattered bonnet and threadbare cloak.

"Oh, mum, ye gave me a turn, bein' right there when I didn't hear the bell. The maister is nae at hoom."

I favored her with a lofty smile. "Mr. Jardine will be along in a few moments. I came on ahead. He said you needn't wait."

She hesitated, but I was at my most imposing, and no doubt she was anxious to get to her own home. "Well, mum . . . perhaps, if ye're sure. I've left a fine wee supper laid oot. . . ."

She wavered a moment longer but hadn't the courage to face me down, especially since I was already inside the house. With a final doubtful glance she gave up the struggle, ducked her head in parting, and scurried down the steps and along the street.

I was in Oliver's new abode, unexpected and uninvited, and I had no idea why I had done it, except for a prideful distaste at being found waiting on his doorstep. I had determined from the outset that this meeting would be entirely impersonal and that I would not be caught at a disadvantage. I would do better to wait within, cool and composed, and let Jardine be the one to be taken off stride.

I mounted the staircase to the drawing room and settled myself to wait. More properly, the room was a "parlor," small and not at all attractive. While I waited the Glasgow sun, never strong, surrendered into October twilight. I sat quietly in the darkening gloom, picturing the scene to come. Oliver Jardine lighting the gas globe, surprised and discomfited at finding me here. I, dignified and civil, if not friendly . . .

When I heard the key turn in the lock and the lower door open, I composed my face in a haughty expression, ready for the scene I had planned in my head. A moment later I was incapable of motion, for Oliver had not returned home alone. Through the darkness, I heard Adriana Rantana's low-pitched, unmistakable voice say something to Oliver, and his laughing reply. There was an intimacy in that laughter that I recognized. I sat as if bound to my chair, arms on the chair arms, feet on the floor, caught in a blind panic.

Instead of stopping at the small room where I sat, Oliver and Adriana, arms linked, and laughing—for I saw them, though they didn't see me—continued on up the staircase. In the space of a moment my head whirled in a red mist of shock and rage. I wanted to scream. I wanted to hurl myself after them. Oliver and Adriana—together! Intimate in tone, mounting the stairs to the bedrooms above without so much as stopping to eat the "wee supper" that woman had prepared for them.

I was shaking with mind-obliterating fury that needed no reason or justification. It was enough to know that that pair of treacherous conspirators was together and I might never have existed, for all I mattered now.

I had no idea how long I sat in that dark room while the depths of their duplicity crashed through my mind, reverberating like thunder in a canyon. Once again Oliver Jardine had got exactly what he had intended—new wealth—for which he would pay any price demanded. And Adriana, willing victim, had bought her revenge, and a lover!

Half blind with rage, I listened to the footsteps overhead, back and forth, back and forth, and then . . . no more. The creak of a bed, murmurs faintly heard, a peal of Adriana-laughter and a laughing, protesting shout from Oliver. By some inner volition that had nothing to do with conscious decision, I mounted the stairs in a stumbling run and flung myself through the doorway of a softly lighted bedroom where the traitors cavorted on a wide, tumbled bed.

It was a scene I felt I would never be able to wipe from my memory. Their startled faces lifted to stare at me, Adriana's lascivious mouth an O of surprise, her heavy-lidded eyes wide and blurred with passion. I stood there for an hour-long moment while Oliver struggled up to a sitting position. Around the curve of her tawny flanks, his eyes met mine.

Later, I remembered half falling down the flights of stairs, clutching the balustrade, crashing into the curving wall. I remembered my hands tugging at the silver knob of the outer door, and the feel of cold October rain on my face as I ran to the waiting carriage. I remembered an incoherent plea to the driver to take me to the Duke of Cranford Hotel.

It is three days hard-driving from Glasgow to Liverpool by coach. I believe I was on the road for some twenty hours. I paid enormous sums of money for coachmen willing to drive until they and their horses were exhausted—and then to pass me along, like an inanimate bundle, at the next coaching inn. There was always a coachman, reasonably sober and with fresh horses, willing to drive day and night for the money I offered. I didn't sleep or eat, but sat like a stone idol, clinging to the strap as we rocketed and hurtled over the road south. I had the wit to know that I had to get home. Beyond that, my mind did not function. Or if it did, I had no memory of it after. No memory but one—Oliver's eyes on mine. I arrived at my own door in thin morning sunlight; Calcutta House, with Emily clucking and solicitous. She and Ned carried me from the carriage up the grand staircase to my own room.

CHAPTER 22

I did not make a good recovery. Within a week I set about studying the thick sheaf of information which Richard Cecil gave me, but I continued to feel ill and frail. I could digest little and often had to lie down when sudden weariness overwhelmed me. Strangely enough, I scarcely thought of Oliver and Adriana. My mind had given up on that score, exhausted. I cared for nothing except assuring the success of the Blue Funnel Steam and Navigation Company—and thereby my own future.

Mr. George Gore arrived in Liverpool aboard the American sailing vessel *Virginian,* and true to his word, Richard Cecil arranged a meeting between us at Calcutta House. By chance, it fell on my nineteenth birthday. I determined to make it a date that would count for much in the year to come. In the material that Mr. Cecil had supplied to me, I had found the seed of inspiration. Ill or well, it dominated my mind. I had studied it from every vantage point and now I wished to test it on this American who came from the prosperous agricultural states of the South.

George Gore proved to be a rangy man of pleasant manner, with small, shrewd eyes under heavy gray brows. I did not know by what means Mr. Cecil persuaded him to consider talking business with a woman, but after the first awkward moments we fell easily into a lively discussion. Mr. Gore was clearly much entertained by the novelty of the situation, for I had made a full study of my subject and found it stimulating to match wits with him.

"We have heard considerable talk of your new steamship, ma'am. A hard-luck ship, so they say in Charleston. And in Liverpool."

"I cannot speak for Charleston, Mr. Gore, but in Liverpool no one is now scoffing at a vessel that has proved itself capable of eleven and a half knots over the measured mile—and that at only eighty percent of horsepower."

With an air of total confidence, I told Mr. Gore something

of our travails over the past months, all now completely resolved by my copartner, Oliver Jardine.

He was polite, if not entirely convinced, but I was content for the moment to let that matter rest.

"I have learned, Mr. Gore, that America is building some of the finest ships in the world. Both sailing ships, and paddle wheel steamers for your coastal trade."

"We like to think that's so, ma'am."

"But you buy our engines to install in your steamers. And also for your rail locomotives, I understand. It would seem to indicate admirable judgment, for if our ships are not in all respects the equal of yours, our steam engines are the finest in the world. But I fear, Mr. Gore, that Americans may not always get the excellent performance they are paying for."

The American's bushy gray eyebrows shot up. "Indeed, ma'am? You mean your country is selling us inferior engines?"

"Oh, not at all, Mr. Gore. I mean that British boilers are designed to burn British coal. It is not only the finest steaming coal available, but also costs less than American coal, even transported. It burns hotter and it prevents boiler breakdowns, because of the carbon composition."

Mr. Gore was prepared to argue the point, and he had every right to do so, for my sweeping statement was pure fakery. Or almost so. However, I made a great business of taking from my desk drawer the sample chunks of steaming coal I had obtained from Mr. John Cooper when we had first begun negotiations for the buying of three-quarters of the Rancorne Mine. Mr. Gore examined the samples with interest—there is something convincing about having in your hand possible evidence of what is otherwise merely theory—and I made it a point to show him also the assayer's report of the quality and production level of the Rancorne Mine.

I quoted prices, to prove that even with import duties we could guarantee a better burning coal at three shillings under the price of the American product. British coal stocks landed at Savannah and Charleston would supply the southern railroad, and the line linking Savannah with Atlanta. British coal could be used in the steamers which traded cotton up and down the coast.

"And then, Mr. Gore, you would be assured of getting the excellent performance for which British boilers are justly famous," I concluded.

"Interesting, Miss Millbrook. Worth careful consideration,

certainly." The shrewd eyes crinkled at their corners. "I wish I felt as confident of your new steamer as I do of your figures." He indicated the paper on which he had made notes of the information I had given him.

If Mr. Gore's eyes were shrewd, my own were guileless. "Perhaps, sir, you would feel more assured if you were to test the *Lady Margaret* for yourself? She will be making her initial voyage from Glasgow to Liverpool within the fortnight. Would you care to be aboard?"

It was not so great a gamble as it seemed, for if the vessel did not do well, the report would reach Mr. Gore's ears in any case, and I would have no hope of putting my plan into operation. As it was, he was more than eager to make the voyage to Liverpool aboard her. No matter what the outcome, he could be sure of dining out on that story back in Charleston where, it appeared, there was considerable interest in our venture.

I assured him that I would arrange for his passage, and that Mr. Richard Cecil would advise him of the sailing date. "After that, sir, if you find the *Lady Margaret* all that I say it to be, I would like to discuss the matter of transporting your fine Sea Island cotton to Liverpool on her return voyage."

The tall American looked thoughtful. "Miss Millbrook, I must tell you that I have had some negotiations with Commander Matthew Jardine on that matter already. He is the father of your partner, Oliver Jardine, I understand? Commander Jardine's two new clipper ships, just completed on the Chesapeake, promise great speed, and without the uncertainties of steam."

"No doubt, Mr. Gore. Great speed as compared with other sailing ships, that is to say. But hardly comparable to the speed of the *Lady Margaret*. And that, Mr. Gore, does not depend on whether or not the wind blows."

George Gore was amused. "You are an able debater, ma'am. Am I correct in deducing that there is some ill-feeling between Commander Jardine and his son? A falling-out over this matter of steam as opposed to sail?"

"A difference of opinion, sir. Commander Jardine is of the old school. His considerable experience has been with sail, so his view is understandable, if unprogressive. Mr. Oliver Jardine possesses genius, or something closely approaching it, where matters of steam propulsion are concerned. As I explained, it was his intuition and knowledge which solved the earlier problems of the *Lady Margaret*."

"Intuition is a problematical virtue, Miss Millbrook. Hardly to be considered the equal of experience, I would say."

"Perhaps so, Mr. Gore. But experience bows before it, for intuition linked to knowledge is the stuff of all true progress, do you not agree? Oliver Jardine combines those virtues to great advantage. He is not only an innovator, but also has been well trained in all aspects of steam engineering at Glasgow University." I shrugged. "I do not wish to disparage Commander Jardine's abilities, sir. I merely point out that he is following, very capably, no doubt, the method of shipping that has prevailed with little change for hundreds of years. His son is in the vanguard of progressive modern methods about to revolutionize the Atlantic trade. Where you choose to place your faith—in the vagaries of the Atlantic winds or with the science of steam—is a matter which only you can decide."

I had the satisfaction of seeing respect and admiration in the American's eyes, as he agreed to think further on the matter. Once I had his assurance that he would make no firm commitment elsewhere until he had had a chance to judge our vessel at firsthand, I turned the conversation to lighter matters, for I did not wish to press too forcefully.

Richard Cecil assured me that Mr. Gore had the authority to complete arrangements for the cargoes in both directions across the Atlantic. That was, in fact, the purpose of his visit to Liverpool, and the commercial paper would be issued through Lloyds Bank, if and when the arrangements were undertaken.

There were grave difficulties involved in carrying on a business relationship with a man whom you despised and had no wish to see. However, I refused to let such considerations hamper the progress I was now making. Pleading ill health, I employed Mr. Cecil to travel to Glasgow and arrange for George Gore's journey to Liverpool aboard the *Lady Margaret*. With him I sent a letter setting out my efforts to secure forward contracts for the Rancorne coal to Savannah and Charleston, and long-staple cotton on the return voyage to Liverpool.

For once, matters went my way. The long-awaited voyage took place on a clear, crisp day in December. It was a triumph, free of catastrophes and proving an average speed of over eleven knots for the entire course, despite the winter roughness of the Firth of Clyde. George Gore sent word by

Richard Cecil that he was mightily impressed. He wished to
do Commander Jardine the courtesy of speaking with him
again, but confidently expected that we would work out the
contracts for coal and cotton along the lines of our previous
discussion.

Though my excuse for sending Richard Cecil to Glasgow
in my stead had been ill health, I was in fact completely
recovered from my malaise, enjoying a ravenous appetite and
full of energy. The day that I received word that Mr. Gore
was almost certain to be the Blue Funnel Steam and Navigation Company's first client, I ate an enormous dinner
washed down with a glass of champagne, by way of celebration. At last, I thought, our success seemed assured and my
own self-esteem was restored. Oliver Jardine could do as he
pleased, for so long as he proved useful as a business partner.
That was the only way in which I had need of him, I told
myself, and I was secure there, for I had proved that he had
at least as great a need for my abilities. I could plan and
carry through a major financial undertaking, and I vowed
that my successful negotiations with Mr. Gore would be only
the first in a long line of successes.

My jubilation was not destined to last. Emily Carter
presented herself when I was ready to rise from the table.

"Could ye spare me a few minutes, Miss Margaret? Upstairs, if ye please, fer it's a matter of some privacy."

We repaired to my sitting room and Emily struggled to begin. It was evident that whatever she had to say was making
her ill at ease.

"Come, Emily," I said reassuringly. "I cannot think what is
making you so hesitant. Do we not know each other well
enough for you to feel free with me? You and Ned are all
the family I have now—"

"That's it, mum, that's the very point," Emily burst out.

"Emily, whatever are you talking about?"

"Yerself, Miss Margaret. And family—so to speak. Ye're
in the family way, mum, and me and Ned, we talked about it
and we think ye don't realize. Though how ye couldn't. . ."

I thought Emily had lost her mind. But flushed and defiant,
she could now scarcely control the flood of words that poured
forth.

"At first I told meself it was the upset ye'd had, whatever
that may have been, when ye came back from Glasgow so
sick and sorry. Scarcely able to keep a bite down for months.

Sick of a mornin' more often than not, and tired all of the time—"

"But that's all over, Emily. I feel quite well again," I protested.

"Yes, mum. Ye're past the first few months all right and now ye're hungry all the time. Eatin' for two."

"Oh, for heaven's sake! Am I not to be allowed to recover from an illness without you reading some mysterious meaning into it?"

"That's as may be, but there's no gainsayin' that ye've got the *look*. I'm not wrong about *that*, Miss Margaret!"

The first flicker of doubt crept into my mind. My clothing, just this past week or two, had been uncomfortably tight. I had missed several periods, but I had thought that, too, a symptom of the shock that had caused my malaise.

Emily would have none of it. "There's a look, Miss Margaret. Oh, it's not what ye'd notice, like as not, nor most others neither—yet. That'll come soon enough," she added darkly. "From the back, mum, that's where ye see it first, if ye've an eye fer it. There's yer waist a mite thicker at the sides, and—oh, mum, I'd never have spoken to ye if I wasn't sure!"

Emily fell silent, seeing the beginning of doubt overtaking me. She crept quietly from the room. Her backward glance of sympathy as she softly closed the door was as convincing as her words.

Panic came by slow stages as I faced my dilemma, beating my fists against circumstances, surrounded by slowly closing prison doors. I wouldn't put up with this! It was all a figment of Emily's countrywoman imagination! I would wake in the morning and laugh at this foolish nightmare. My menstrual period would start, if not the next day, surely the day after. Underlying all of my storming was the fear that if Emily was right this child I was carrying was conceived on the last night I had seen Oliver Jardine. The only night I had lain with him and truly hated him. A child born of rape!

I wept and shivered and gave vent to the fury that engulfed me. I pitched everything that came to hand against the walls. Then, shamed to the core of my being, I carefully repaired all the damage I had done, unwilling to let any servant know the depths of my despair and anger. When I finally slept it was from exhaustion, and I woke to the nightmare next morning.

There was no escape. I would have to cope with this evil as

I had with others. Start with the certainty that I would not bring into the world Oliver Jardine's hate-child and work from there. I would abort.

In the next week—Christmas week as it happened—I indulged in every form of violent exercise I could devise, and nothing availed. I flung myself down the last few steps of the staircase, spraining my wrist and causing a large blue bump on my brow that made my head ache abominably for several days. I examined my unclothed body every night and every morning and was horrified to see that my waist was inexorably thickening. With my bound wrist, I was obliged to demand Emily's aid in lacing myself more tightly, to hide my horrid secret.

As for Emily, I damned her night and day, vented my anger on her loyal head, and burst into tears on her shoulder. She watched my antics with a mixture of sympathy and disapproval, knowing full well what I was trying to achieve and torn between pity for me and the certainty that it would do no good.

"Tighter, Emily! *Pull,* damn you, or I will never be able to fasten the green dress."

"It will do no good, mum," she admonished, even while she tugged at the lacing. "Ye're too far along and ye're healthy. I don't say ye couldn't do the wee one a damage, though. Mayhap ye already have, poor little tyke," she muttered, as we managed to fasten the green dress one more time.

When I could no longer avoid having the seams of my dresses let out, I was obliged to accept the reality of my position. I would not permit a dressmaker to do the necessary work, and once again Emily proved her worth.

"They will do for another few weeks, Miss Margaret," she warned. "After that ye must resign yerself to giving up yer business ventures, for ye can scarcely appear in public in yer condition."

In January, we signed our contracts with Mr. George Gore. I presented myself at the headquarters of the Blue Funnel Steam and Navigation Company, assured by Emily as I left Calcutta House that while she could tell, none of the others would notice—yet. I prayed not, for I would be the only woman among that gathering of bankers, solicitors, and company directors, as well as Richard Cecil, present as my own assistant, and, of course, Oliver Jardine and George Gore.

All went well and I was greatly gratified when Mr. Gore commended me for my part in the transaction. Afterward we adjourned to a private dining room of the Admiral's Arms Hotel for a late luncheon. I had no doubt but that Oliver would have preferred that I excuse myself and allow the gentlemen to conduct the celebration without me. However, on the conviction that it is always wise to begin as you mean to go on, I took my rightful place with composure, for I had earned it.

As if matters were not sufficiently strained between us, I was obliged to tell Oliver that I wished to confer with him at Calcutta House when our business matters were concluded. He agreed reluctantly. I had had Ned wait for me with the carriage. If Oliver would have preferred to take a hansom cab, I gave him no opportunity. It was all very civil.

"You are looking exceptionally well, Margaret. Quite radiant, in fact."

"I am feeling well, thank you, Oliver."

"This sort of thing agrees with you, obviously."

"I suppose that success agrees with everyone, don't you think?"

"Ummm."

"Our new ship is progressing well, I trust?"

"Oh, yes. Quite. On schedule."

"How very gratifying for you."

"You said you wished to speak with me on a matter of importance?"

"It is personal in nature. I would prefer to wait until we are at Calcutta House. Will you pardon me if I rest for a moment? I found the excitement of our meeting quite wearing."

With that, I leaned my head back and closed my eyes, leaving him to fret.

Oliver seemed relieved that I conducted him to the library of Calcutta House rather than to my upstairs sitting room. His relief was short-lived. As for myself, I was quaking inside but determined not to allow it to show. Since it was a business matter we were to discuss, I seated myself behind the desk. After a startled glance, Oliver took the chair facing the desk.

"Oliver, I have a business proposition to present to you. I regret to tell you that as a result of the last night I lay with you—very unwillingly as you'll recall—I am going to have your child. . ."

"Christ! Margaret!"

". . . in approximately four months' time, as nearly as I can judge. I have seen a physician. A discreet one. He congratulates me on my excellent condition."

Oliver, on his feet and red of face, slammed a hand on the desk. "Stop it! My God, you make it sound so cut and dried! How can you sit there and calmly inform me—"

"I have had some time to accustom myself to the idea."

He sank back into the chair and buried his head in his hands. "Oh, Christ. Now what do we do?"

"I rather think we might marry, Oliver."

His head came up slowly and our eyes met.

"You don't care for that solution? No more do I. But I haven't been able to think of a more acceptable one."

"You could go away . . ." he suggested hesitantly, and then, gaining courage, "you could have it somewhere else, in the country, perhaps, and no one need know. If you need money—"

"No. I thought of that but discovered that I don't care for the idea. No, Oliver, I am going to have the child and the child is going to have your name. Jardine."

He sat mute, and I saw the redheaded Jardine stubbornness gathering on his face. I held up a silencing hand before he could say the words we would both have to live with for a lifetime.

"Oliver, I have felt the child move within me. Before that, I cared nothing for it, I wished only that it would leave me as swiftly as possible, leave me in peace to get on with the life I have chosen. I did not wish your child, nor did I wish to marry you. But I am prepared to compromise on that score now. At one time you coaxed and cajoled me to marry you."

He sat silent, scrambling in his mind, no doubt, for an alternative. God knows, I knew the feeling. But if my own sentiments counted for little, certainly his counted for less now.

Finally Oliver stood up, his hands jammed into his breeches pockets. He looked at me coolly. "I am sorry, Margaret, but we must settle on some other solution. I think you will agree that anything that existed between us is finished."

"Not quite everything, surely?"

"You will have to decide what is best for you—and the child, I suppose—short of marriage."

"I mentioned a business proposition. I think it would be well if you sat down and we discussed it, at least."

He sat down grudgingly. "I see. You want me to buy out

your share of the company? Perhaps it is not a bad solution, you would have money then to do as you choose—"

"But I'm doing as I choose, Oliver. I am co-manager of the Blue Funnel Steam and Navigation Company. I have equal authority with you. Unless, of course, I marry. English law is not overly generous to married women."

As he took the import of those words, Oliver Jardine went perfectly still.

"My husband would control my property, Oliver."

He laughed. "You're clever, Margaret. That is to be the deciding factor, is it? To prevent you from marrying anyone else, I am to marry you. To retain control of my own company. But perhaps I will quite like your new husband. Could you not choose a shipping man with advanced ideas, so that we could work amicably together?"

"A shipping man?" I pretended to consider it. "That is quite possible, isn't it? The only difficulty is that this child that I carry is a Jardine. I wish it to have the Jardine name."

I had led him to it carefully. I watched realization dawn.

"You bitch! You wouldn't—"

"I would, Oliver."

"My father? An old man! You'd look a fool."

"But not so great a fool as you! And he would do it, you know. I have just done him out of a profitable arrangement with the Americans, to transport their cotton here to Liverpool. I doubt that he has much love for either of us at the moment. But he is a man who knows where his own interest lies. How do you think he would respond to the offer of half control of the Blue Funnel Steam and Navigation Company?"

"Bitch! Conniving, treacherous—"

"You don't fancy me as a stepmother, Oliver?"

He got to his feet, face as black as a thundercloud, and loomed over me, his quicksilver eyes longing to see me hung by the hair. "And all of that performance today! George Gore eating out of your hand, quoting you as the authority on steaming coal—"

"But I *am*, Oliver. If only you knew a bit more about it yourself, you could appreciate—"

"I won't do it! God save me from a slippery eel of a woman, a traitorous Jezebel!" He leaned across my desk, his furious face close to mine. "I will not marry you. . . ."

CHAPTER 23

Oliver Jardine and I were married three weeks later, in February, 1845. He left immediately for Glasgow—and for Adriana Rantana, I had no doubt. That was of little concern to me—for the moment. I had what I wanted and Adriana would know that. If I knew her, she knew me equally well. She would soon grow bored with Oliver, now that her sport with me was finished. I was content to await the birth of my child and allow Oliver time to reconcile himself to his new role as husband and father, in the eyes of society.

The *Lady Margaret* sailed from Liverpool for Charleston, South Carolina on April 15th, carrying 1450 tons of the Rancorne Mine's finest steaming coal, and logged an east-west crossing speed of twelve days, a record that was not to be broken for six years. The reputation of the Blue Funnel Steam and Navigation Company, Ltd. was established, at least for the present, and Oliver Jardine's belief in the future of steamers for the Atlantic trade vindicated at last. I had no difficulty in obtaining forward contracts for both the east and west voyage of the *Jardine*, which was scheduled to enter service in mid-August, if all went according to the posted schedule.

I allowed myself to relax and enjoy the latter days of my pregnancy, resolutely putting out of mind what my future might be, with a child to care for and a husband in name only. One advantage of my temporary retirement from public appearance in shipping circles was that I ran no risk of encountering Commander Matthew Jardine. I had heard vivid accounts of his towering fury when he learned that we had deprived him of the lucrative trade with the Edisto Island cotton combine. I had no wish to experience that fury in person.

Charles Millbrook Jardine was born on May 24, 1845, a large, lusty boy of robust voice and well-formed features, at least to my adoring eyes. His fine head of peach fuzz was dark, but Emily assured me that was usual with newborn babes, and I amused myself by examining it in the sunlight for traces of red. My own hair, I had been happy to discover, had neither thinned nor darkened with childbirth. If Charles proved not to be a redhead, perhaps he would have pale gold hair like mine.

Oliver, whom I had not seen since the day of our marriage, made no acknowledgment of his son's birth. No matter. The date was memorable for me, and I had no doubt would prove easy for Oliver to remember, whether he wished to or not, for his son shared the birthday of the Queen herself.

Emily had engaged as wet nurse a young woman from the village near Greystones who had lost her own child at birth and her husband at sea, within months. The days passed pleasantly, one running into another, as I made the acquaintance of my fascinating small son. But my contentment lasted for scarcely more than a month after Charles's birth, and then uneasiness crept back. Fortune, if left unaided, has a way of changing rapidly for the worse, and as a woman alone with a son to provide for I could ill afford to drift and trust to fate.

I decided that I must reenter the business world as swiftly as possible. At the same time, I would strive to make the Jardines—Oliver, Charles, and myself—appear in every other respect to be a family conventional enough to gladden Queen Victoria's own heart. I could scarcely hope to enlist Oliver's support in that, but I would create the illusion of harmony as best I could, for the sake of my son.

Once I had made the decision, fortune presented the opportunity I needed. The *Jardine,* finally completed, would be leaving Glasgow for Liverpool within the fortnight. Before she was outfitted and ready to enter service, Oliver had arranged a gala weekend voyage from Liverpool to Cobh, on the Irish coast. Aboard would be a collection of notables from London, Liverpool, and Manchester—importers and exporters, buyers for the various commodity groups with whom we either had or hoped to have signed contracts for cargoes to be carried aboard the *Jardine* on her first voyage to New York.

Accordingly, I wrote to Oliver in Glasgow, informing him that I felt it would be excellent business practice for his wife and son to join the voyage to Cobh.

What better way to show the world our confidence in the safety of steam voyaging—and in the process to garner the greatest possible interest in the vessel itself? The

166 JANET GREGORY

Lady Margaret has established an impressive record. If we now demonstrate the *Jardine* to be her equal in all ways, most particularly for safety allied to speed, we will be well on the way to establishing a *tradition* of reliable performance for the Blue Funnel Steam and Navigation Company. Also, as the Jardines are historically a seagoing family, it will be well for Charles Jardine to take his place early amongst the august company of forebears.

Therefore, Oliver, will you please make arrangements for adequate accommodation for myself, Charles, and Mary Watson, the wet nurse who will accompany us. I feel sure you will agree that for so public an occasion—and with attention certain to be paid by the Palace itself—the Jardines should present the appearance of utmost respectability. I believe the occasion will create a most favorable impression and result in valuable publicity for our company, beneficial to our future success.

I had no way of knowing Oliver's reaction to this missive, nor did I wish to. I had given him ample time to see the reason of my suggestion and counted on self-interest to do the rest. In that much, at least, I was proved correct. Oliver was on hand to welcome us aboard the *Jardine*. A smiling, indulgent husband and father, he bent to kiss my forehead, then plucked Charles from his nurse's arms.

"Aha! Another seagoing Jardine. And redheaded to boot. Welcome aboard, Charles Jardine."

He surveyed his son with amused curiosity. Charles, gazing around bright-eyed, made small grabbing motions for his father's chin, and Oliver's superficial interest suddenly sharpened. He went quite still, studying Charles as if realizing finally that here was not, after all, merely a baby, but his own offspring, carrying Jardine blood and perhaps—he squinted at the small face—even resembling him.

"Humph! He looks to be a lively fellow. Let's hope he's a good sailor. Are you, boyo?"

He held the child aloft, at arm's length, and Charles, for the first time in his young life, crowed with laughter. Watty exclaimed over that, and Oliver's face was something to behold as delight and reluctant pride dawned.

But when he had handed Charles back to Watty and turned again to me, though he smiled for any onlookers, his eyes were once more chips of gray granite. No matter; what I sought was the appearance of family solidarity. Oliver's love,

I reflected bitterly, was bestowed only where it would work to his immediate advantage, and could be turned off at whim. An ill thing to win, and the present arrangement suited me far better.

I felt sure that young Watty, displaying Charles in her arms as proudly as if he were her son, saw nothing amiss. Nor would the rest of the company assembling aboard the *Jardine*, in readiness for the departure at dawn next morning. There would be thirty guests aboard, Oliver informed me. They were arriving up the gangplank in small, excited groups, the men looking very important and pleased to be included in the company, the women bedecked in their finery and calling gaily to acquaintances while watching to see that none of their luggage was left standing on the quay. I felt my own excitement mounting, for this was my first venture into society since my confinement.

As for the *Jardine*, my first glimpse of her in many months impressed me greatly. Looming huge, and glistening black against the muddy waters of the harbor, she was bedecked for the gala occasion with flags flying from every mast. Her bright blue funnels, like those of her sister ship, the *Lady Margaret*, seemed to proclaim to all the world that the Blue Funnel Steam and Navigation Company was a name to be reckoned with in the annals of British shipping. As I stood on the *Jardine*'s deck that warm midsummer eve, I had no difficulty in being generous in my praise.

"She is entirely beautiful, Oliver. I congratulate you, as I am sure all of our guests will, for certainly they haven't seen her equal. Like an enormous, glittering toy vessel, meant for some child giant's delight. As perfect as if she had just been unwrapped from a gift box and put to float here."

Oliver's eyebrows rose at such heights of whimsy, but his smile was pleased. "Her performance is finer than her appearance, as you will discover tomorrow. Come, let me show you around," he said impulsively.

Watty, with Charles, was in a cabin adjoining mine. Though not large, the cabins were adequate and well-appointed. Leaving Watty to settle us in when our luggage was aboard, I accompanied Oliver to the saloon, where I could hear champagne corks already beginning to pop.

He halted in the doorway and flung out one arm dramatically. "Well, Margaret, what do you say? Will it serve? Is there aught lacking?" he demanded, laughing at the expression of astonishment on my face.

The room that opened before us was large and opulent, gleaming with dark mahogany and shining brass and crystal. The guests who had already boarded moved about through the large room, their voices raised in excitement and gaiety, as they took in the luxury that surrounded them.

"It must have cost a fortune, Oliver!" I exclaimed, and then could have bitten my tongue, for I realized that it was Adriana Rantana's fortune that had footed the bill.

Oliver brushed the remark aside, as if determined to keep all smooth between us, on the surface at least. But as I sipped the first glass of champagne aboard the *Jardine*, I was doubly pleased that I had decided to make the voyage. Otherwise, Adriana Rantana would have been here in my stead. As it was, I reveled in the praise heaped on the vessel and on Oliver and myself, and I moved through the saloon at his side, in my rightful capacity as hostess of this important occasion.

Back in my cabin I dressed carefully for the late dinner to be served in the saloon. I had brought new gowns for the occasion and knew that I looked well in the ivory satin that I chose to wear that night. I fastened a long rope of pearls with a gold and green jade clasp around my neck, and matching teardrop pendants to my ears. Surveying myself in the mirrored door leading to Charles's and Watty's cabin, I was well content. The soft ivory of the gown gave my skin the luminosity of the pearls I wore. The green ostrich feathers of my fan exactly matched my eyes. Oliver might be no more pleased to have me for wife than I was to have him for husband; nonetheless, I would do him proud.

It was a glittering company that gathered beneath the crystal chandeliers of the saloon, and I was prepared to enjoy my role to the full until I saw Adriana Rantana enter the room as regally confident as any *principessa*. She was swathed in layers of some metallic gold fabric that gleamed and blended with her tawny skin to dazzling effect. I was so taken aback at Oliver's perfidy that when her arrogant eyes met mine I faltered, and was rewarded with a supercilious smile that angered me sufficiently to steel my courage.

From that moment, though we avoided each other assiduously, it was a contest as to which of us would win the greater admiration from the room at large. Oliver appeared to pay little attention to either of us as he held forth to our more business-minded guests on the merits of the *Jardine*. But when we sat down to dinner—he at one end of the long table, I at the other—I looked up to catch his sardonic eye.

It brought me back to my senses as effectively as a pitcher of cold water in the face. I managed, despite my inner rage, to laugh and sparkle throughout the Lucullan banquet that followed, but the spark of red fury burning within me forbade my remaining once dinner was through. I had been competing with Adriana Rantana, and honesty forced me to admit it.

Pleading concern for my son in strange surroundings, I made my apologies for quitting the festivities early and repaired to my own cabin in good order. But the moment I closed the door behind me, I was forced to bite my tongue to keep from a monumental demonstration of rage that shook me from head to toe. I took off the pale, soft satin gown and carefully crumpled it into a ball, threw it on the floor of the cabin, and trampled it. I flung myself onto the bed and pounded my fists and my feet into it—I did not dare to pound the wall for fear of waking Charles and Watty.

Lewd visions of Oliver and Adriana flooded my mind until there was room for nothing except screaming fury which I was obliged to choke down. Oliver and Adriana! He had the effrontery to have her here when I had thought to establish our position in the eyes of the business world. I cared little for the social world. The pressures of being a woman of business in the climate of England with Victoria reigning was enough to contend with. Did that assemblage of guests all know that Adriana was Oliver's mistress? Were they being only polite—and pitying—in the attentions they had paid to *me?*

"Poor little creature, married to him, you know, and with a young child, though the Italian woman is a beauty, isn't she? One can scarcely blame him, I suppose. . . ." I imagined I could hear them saying it and I writhed in humiliation. Pity! I wanted no one's pity. It was as hateful as the chilly lack of concern I had felt from the solicitor, Mr. Robinson, and from the clerk in my mother's apothecary shop when I approached them, penniless and alone. I had hated being poor and powerless in the world of men. Now I knew that I hated being pitied at least as much. What was the difference? Cool surveying eyes, amusement no doubt, though carefully concealed. It all diminished me, and I could not bear it!

I fell asleep sobbing, at first in hot grief and then, as rage subsided, in cold loneliness, which was worse, for it did not obscure the bleakness of my view. I had thought I was free of Oliver's emotional grip on my soul and I was wrong. Disappointment, humiliation, hurt pride—they were all a part of my unhappiness. But cowering behind it all was the lost-child knowledge that I still loved, and was not loved in return. And that I must live with it, for I couldn't change it. Adriana Rantana bought, manipulated, claimed love at will. And she had claimed Oliver.

CHAPTER 24

I arose late the next day, exhausted and depressed. We were moving. I had been vaguely aware of it for some time, but too preoccupied with my immediate problems to pay any heed. I could feel the vibration of the great engine on the floor under my feet, and the motion of the vessel through the water. Truly, she rode well and smoothly. I wondered where we were, for it was now close to one o'clock and we had been scheduled to depart from Liverpool at six that morning. Peering out of the porthole told me nothing, for within my view there was only the limitless swell of water to the horizon. Presumably Ireland lay to our right.

I passed a boring day and a dismal evening, keeping mostly to my cabin, for although I knew it was cowardly of me, I could not bear the prospect of another contest with Adriana under the fascinated gaze of the passengers. I pleaded illness to Watty and she relayed that story to Oliver. If he made any comment, Watty did not report it.

The *Jardine* steamed into the harbor at Cobh just after sundown. For a while after the engine fell silent, there were the usual shouts and general brouhaha of docking, but soon the only sounds were of distant conviviality as the party planned for the evening gained momentum. Its gaiety came to me in occasional bursts of merriment and the excited voices and hurrying footsteps that passed my cabin. Soon there was only the far-off murmur of laughter and chatter, the clinking of cutlery, and the music of the small orchestra performing for the festivities in the main saloon. I tormented myself with picturing all that I was missing, and Adriana Rantana queening it at Oliver's side, while I languished in seclusion. I fell asleep early, half waking from uneasy dreams as the muffled sounds of frolic continued on long into the night.

Shortly after dawn I woke to the boisterous clatter of casting off and the engine getting us underway once again. Weary to death of the confines of the narrow cabin and the dreariness of my own thoughts, I dressed rapidly, determined to go on deck.

A sharp wind struck me full in the face when I reached the upper deck, driving thin rain before it. I wrapped my scarf more closely about my head and stepped out smartly. Plumes of salt spray mingled with the rain to drench me.

Viewed at dockside in Liverpool, the *Jardine* had appeared huge; against the limitless expanse of heavy sea and leaden sky, the vessel looked no more substantial than a toy, plowing its way through mountainous, wind-driven waves. Under my feet the deck throbbed to the beat of the hardworking cylinders in the bowels of the vessel, great beasts driving us on our course.

The Irish coast behind us was invisible. The watery grayness suited my mood, and I was taking strength from it when I became aware of unusual activity some distance along the deck, where the lifeboats were suspended. I stood in the shelter of a mast and its lowered, shrouded sails, watching as two oilskinned crew members hauled a shivering hulk of a man from one of the lifeboats and along the deck to what I knew to be the captain's quarters. A stowaway? On a short pleasure cruise? It seemed unlikely, but no other interpretation came to mind. No doubt I would hear in good time.

At least my brisk walk had cleared the shadows from my mind. I decided that I would skulk in my cabin no longer; let the other passengers think what they wished. By eight o'clock I was ravenous. I took breakfast in the deserted dining saloon, savoring every bite and hoping the heavy seas and rolling decks would keep everyone but me abed for hours. It was not to be. I was halfway through my breakfast when Oliver appeared in the doorway. He was the last company I wished, but he joined me nonetheless.

"Good morning, Margaret. Recovered from your illness, I see. What a shame that you had to miss our successful evening."

If he felt any shame at having brought Adriana aboard it was not apparent. Nor did my coldness appear to penetrate. He enjoyed a large breakfast and insisted that I remain for another cup of tea. A further effort to humiliate me, but I would not give him the satisfaction of stalking out of the dining saloon, for I had no doubt he would laugh and think he had routed me. The silence between us grew unbearable.

As we were about to leave the table a ship's officer hurried into the dining saloon with a request that Oliver see Captain Craigh "on a matter of extreme urgency." Oliver, without so much as a farewell nod to me, hurried off. "A matter of extreme urgency"? Something that concerned the *Jardine,* and therefore me? On impulse I left the dining saloon in time to see Oliver disappear into Captain Craigh's quarters. Almost immediately the door opened again and both men rushed out and down the companionway, toward the bowels of the ship. I hesitated, tempted to follow, but in the end I gave up the idea and returned to my cabin, in order that Watty might breakfast while I tended to Charles. As a result, I learned of our disaster almost an hour later, along with the other passengers aboard the *Jardine.* Watty had returned from her breakfast and finished feeding Charles when a seaman came to my cabin door.

"Your pardon, mum, but the captain will be making an announcement in the main saloon and requests all passengers to go there immediately."

Alarmed, Watty and I bundled Charles well against the elements and hastened to the saloon. Captain Craigh stood at the head of the room, with Oliver at his side. Both men appeared to have wiped at grease and coal dust that begrimed their faces and hands, but telltale streaks remained and their clothes were dirty. Murmurs of alarm were everywhere in the large saloon, but I could see Oliver counting heads, and only when all were present did the captain speak.

"Ladies and gentlemen, there is no cause for alarm. We merely wish to put your minds at rest should you happen to see smoke in the deck area. There is nothing to fear, the source is a small fire in the coal bunkers, and we will have it extinguished within the hour. The hoses will be needed, and in the interest of general safety and to prevent your interfering with the work of the crew while the hoses are on deck, Mr. Jardine and I request that you remain in this saloon. The chef is preparing a buffet collation for your pleasure, and champagne will be served immediately and for the balance of the voyage. I suggest that you relax and pass this inclement day enjoying yourselves indoors. As soon as the hoses are no longer in use, I will join you in a toast to Mr. Jardine, our host, and to this fine vessel."

There was an immediate uproar, but Captain Craigh and Oliver Jardine moved among the guests, smiling and explaining further, making light of the temporary "difficulty," while champagne was brought around. The orchestra assembled in a corner of the saloon, and soon strains of music mingled with calmer voices, as the guests concluded that there was no real danger and they might as well enjoy themselves.

I could not share their relief, for I knew Oliver too well. Tension emanated from every inch of his body. My first reaction was fear for Charles, followed swiftly by fear for the vessel itself. Oliver made no effort to speak to me apart from the others, but I followed him from the saloon, determined not to be treated as merely another passenger. This was my concern as much as his.

"Oliver, I wish to know the truth."

He frowned, impatient to be on his way, free of me. "It is just as Captain Craigh said, a small fire in one of the coal bunkers. Nothing you need worry about. If you'll excuse me, I have to go below—"

"Fine. I'll come with you."

"Don't be a fool, Margaret. Down below is no place for a woman."

"No doubt. But for an owner of this vessel, it is the only place to be, at least long enough to learn what is going on."

"I forbid it, Margaret. And I have no time to stand arguing—"

"Then lead and I'll follow."

With an angry shrug, Oliver turned his back on me and loped off. I followed, and for the first time saw the *Jardine* as something more than merely a fine new addition to our shipping company.

Gathering my skirts close, I descended winding, open iron stairs leading into a subterranean territory that drove out all sense of being at sea. Halfway down, the heat and roar of it rose up to engulf me, and I clutched at the iron stair rail to steady myself against sudden dizziness. I seemed to be looking down into hell itself, hell smelling of hot oil and friction, pulsing with noise and life and the hiss of steam. In the glare of open furnace doors I recognized Mr. McConnish, our chief engineer, stripped to his waist, his barrel chest a forest of curly black hair. Oliver and Captain Craigh hung on his every word. Judging by his harsh frown and angry gestures, Mr. McConnish was far from reassuring.

Everywhere I looked were blackened, oily men laboring

grimly. Some crawled in and out of the machinery, squirting oil cans on flashing brass rods. Some, bare to the waist, with straining backs and shoulders, fed the stokeholes with great shovelfuls of coal, seemingly without cease. All of them stooped at their labor, muscles straining, the hair on their heads and bodies matted and soaked with steam and sweat. I seemed to touch nothing, yet my hands were grimy almost immediately, and soot and sweat stains appeared on my clothing. Although I strove to appear confident, I was secretly terrified to be in the bowels of this ship with fire burning somewhere out of sight, and all the fuel in the ship to feed it. Sooty black curls of smoke seeped from the bunkers into the boiler room. That, and the expression of grimness on the face of Mr. McConnish, was enough to convince me that I was right to be afraid.

Mr. McConnish spared me one surprised glance and a nod of recognition, then held out a wad of wet, oily rag to Oliver and the captain.

"Gie a look to this, gentlemen! Out o' the pocket o' that stowaway that boarded at Cobh. Drunk as a laird and snuffling in his sleep, or they'd never hae found him. Nae tell me, we've got a fire in the bunkers and a drunken lout wi' no business aboard and this in his pocket. What de ye deduce from a' that, I ask ye?"

Oliver took the filthy wad in his hand, his face frozen in disbelief that changed slowly to fury. "Where is he? I'll kill him!"

"We've no time for that, laddie," Mr. McConnish replied. "He's landed us with plenty tae do as it is." He looked at Captain Craigh. "A puir Irish sailor was he, wantin' to find work out o' Liverpool, and fortified against a cold night on the Irish Sea?"

"He'll find work in an English jail," Captain Craigh observed grimly.

"What does he have to say for himself?" Oliver demanded.

"Och, who's tae ken? He mumbles and blathers, and what it comes to is he did his work wi' a skinful of whusky in him and folded afore he could get off the ship, I've nae doubt."

He took the wad of cloth from Oliver and pitched it across the boiler room. "There'll be mair o' those tucked awa' in the bunkers to help along the burnin'. Naught to do now but kill the engine till we put it out."

"With the glass dropping steadily, Mr. McConnish?" Captain Craigh replied. "With no power we'll be in poor shape to take a storm."

"Aye. But nae doubt the fire's drawin' weel enou' as it is wi'out us fannin' it further, rushin' along, sir. We've got leetle choice, in my opinion, but tae drop anchor for a time, and the sooner the better, before the storm gets tae fierce. I'm not of a mind tae save her from fire and lose her tae the sea!"

Captain Craigh weighed the choice of evils and nodded his head. "Very well, Mr. McConnish, stop engine. We'll try to put out the fire before the storm hits, and mayhap we'll be lucky. I'll need all the men you can spare to help with the pumps and the hoses."

Mr. McConnish turned to his men and bellowed over the noise of the boiler room. "All right, lads, blow her off and let the fires die. I need eight strong fellas tae man the pump rails. . . ."

CHAPTER 25

With Oliver and Captain Craigh, I made my way back to the main saloon. Incredible as it seemed, the guests were still drinking champagne and stuffing themselves with food, as unconcerned as if they were in a Liverpool mansion. I saw Adriana Rantana try to draw Oliver's attention, but he brushed her off without a glance as he mounted a table at the front of the room to address the crowd.

At that moment the engine ceased. In the sudden quiet from the heart of the ship, the cessation of vibration underfoot, the room fell into shocked silence. I had found Watty sitting patiently in a corner, and squeezed her hand. Charles, bless him, was sleeping soundly beside her on a bundle of woolen blankets.

"Ladies and gentlemen, as you have just heard, we have stopped the engine temporarily. Captain Craigh wished me to inform you that it will aid in extinguishing the bunker fire swiftly. We may wallow a bit; there's a heavy sea running, and possibly a storm on the way, but there is no cause for worry. There is nothing wrong with the engine and we will be starting up again shortly. For your own safety, stay in the saloon so as not to interfere with the work on deck."

While Adriana was again clinging to Oliver's arm—little good it would do her, for Oliver had no patience for women when danger threatened his beloved steamship—I slipped quietly from the saloon and got my oilskins and a warm scarf from my cabin. It had begun to rain in earnest and there was a high wind and a lumpy, angry sea. The *Jardine,* without power or sail, wallowed and dipped like an old tub, at the mercy of every crashing wave.

I clung close to the side of the upper-deck cabins, seeking every handhold as I made my way over treacherous footing to where the two great flaxen hoses were being wrestled into position. While I watched, two of the coal-bunker hatches on the top deck were opened and seamen held a writhing hose at each of them, pouring water into the bunkers where telltale clouds of black smoke billowed outward. Thank God the other passengers hadn't seen that as yet. To hear of fire in the coal bunkers was terrifying enough; to see evidence of it would surely bring on panic. Four of Mr. McConnish's men manned the suction pump for each hose, two on either pump rail, drawing water up from the bottom sea cock in vast spurts.

The drunken stowaway, who had stuffed wet, oil-soaked rags into each of the bunker hatches and fired them, was in chains. If he was sober enough by now, no doubt he was terrified at finding himself still aboard, for his work had been done all too well. The *Jardine* had four suction-operated pumps and hoses, and a dozen would not have been too many. No sooner had the frantically working crew seemed to smother the fire deep in one hatch than 'telltale wisps would appear at another—and the pattern would repeat. In the smoldering depths of the bunker, despite the water, even one or two live coals dropping downward were enough to start others smoldering, so the fire spread, one coal to the next, laterally as well as downward, throughout the vessel. Though Captain Craigh had ordered the engine stopped so that the rush of our passage would not feed the fire, the high wind that drove rain and salt spray into the faces of the crew provided more than enough draft to fan the conflagration.

Oliver Jardine was everywhere, shouting encouragement, taking his turn at the backbreaking work at the pump rails with the rest, checking everywhere for I knew not what. All I could envision was the *Jardine* itself under attack by one enormous furnace of banked fire. At length, Oliver approached the vantage point from where I watched the unequal battle.

"The bulwarks may hold for another hour." He mopped his blackened, salt-encrusted face with a filthy sleeve. "Iron won't burn, but it will melt when the heat is great enough. There is a good chance the cabins will go—here or on the middle deck—or both. There's no way to know. Margaret, you will have to help with the passengers."

We looked deep into one another then. The antagonism was still there, no doubt, but something stronger overrode it. "What shall I do, Oliver?" I asked, suddenly quiet within, as if, despite the chaos all around us, together we made an entity, a solid center that would hold.

"Somehow we have to survive *aboard this vessel*. We're nearing the coast of Wales, an inhospitable place at the best of times, and in this weather, impossible. Any lifeboats that didn't capsize would be ground to pieces on those rocks and cliffs. No . . . for now, we—or rather *you*—must get the passengers on deck, as far away as possible from the most dangerous areas, and persuade them to endure." He peered down at me and then, incredibly, a grin split his dirty, salt-encrusted face. "You wanted to be an active partner? That entails good times and bad. Prove yourself now, woman, and shame me—if you can!"

He grabbed me by the wrist and led me back to the main saloon. I stood beside him as he instructed the now-silent, frightened passengers to go to their cabins and don warm clothing, take whatever valuables they had with them, and go swiftly to the afterdeck.

"Do not linger in your cabins. Don't bring more than you can carry easily on your person. Above all, don't get in the way of the crewmen. We are in an emergency situation. These instructions are for your own safety. I have to warn you that while you are not in immediate danger, you will have to endure considerable discomfort for several hours. My wife, Mrs. Jardine, will be with you to answer your questions and if necessary relay messages to me or Captain Craigh. If any of the men among you wish to help—you are needed on deck."

With that, Oliver Jardine was gone out of the saloon with eight of the younger men in his wake. I found myself facing a roomful of people watching me silently, willing me to save them. With no time to think I made what seemed the obvious suggestions.

"We will be on open deck, in heavy rain and with wind and salt spray driving into us every moment. It will be uncomfortable in the extreme, but it is the safest place to be, so we will have to endure it. You know, I think, that I have my young son with me. He is two months old, and if there were any safer alternative, I would not choose open deck in a storm. I stress this because you must protect yourselves as best you can against the elements. Put on your warmest woolens. Pin jewelry and other valuables to your person. Carry as little as possible, apart from the blankets and pillows from your cabin and a piece of luggage that will serve as a seat.

"Go two by two to your cabins, husbands and wives together, single men with a companion. Return here as swiftly as you can, within twenty minutes. Please hurry."

They bolted from the saloon in desperate haste, and Watty and I, with Charles sounding fretful, hurried in their wake. But not before I had snatched up the linen tablecloths from the depleted buffet table. Torn, they would serve Charles for diapers. Watty assured me that she had eaten well, important because she was Charles's source of nourishment—and I was determined that Charles should survive.

It was my good fortune that Watty had proved to be a natural follower, competent in all things but content to leave the worrying to me. If I pretended to more knowledge than I had, and all of it comforting, it was in a good cause. A fretful nurse would mean a fretful baby and I needed, at the moment, to concentrate on less maternal responsibilities.

There were many weeping women in the group that reassembled in the saloon, and I dreaded what was to come. I shook myself free of such forebodings, no matter how justified, and escorted my charges briskly to the afterdeck, where they settled in a huddle of sodden misery, under tarpaulins. Watty and I made a tent for Charles under a blanket and one of the tarpaulins to ward off the wind and driving, icy spray.

I don't know how long we sat there; perhaps two hours, for our fear had faded to apathy. The prospect of discomfort with no end in view wiped out all other thought. Suddenly, amidst the black smoke rolling and billowing about the upper deck of the *Jardine,* a lick of flame appeared. It was followed by another, and then a dozen hungry tongues of flame, spread by the wind. It was the dining saloon burning, encompassed by fire before our horrified eyes, and an omen of the end that could not be long in coming now.

Shouting and cursing, the weary crew flung themselves into the fight against this new threat, stretching the hoses further along the deck, mounting the roof of the main saloon to pour water across onto the dining saloon from above.

At that moment Adriana Rantana, whom I had always thought so brave, gave way to panic, shrieking through the noise of the storm and the chaos on deck.

"Oliver! Get me away while there's still time! I will buy you another vessel, I swear I will. Only let us leave now!"

He didn't hear her and would pay no attention if he did. But Adriana was past reason, wild-eyed as a mare seeing fire in the stables. She plunged down the deck, weaving through the crewmen at work, to fling herself on Oliver, tugging at him hysterically.

Watching, other women in our party began to weep and implore their husbands to get them off the burning *Jardine*. Before I knew it, everyone except Watty, Charles, and me seemed to be edging forward toward the lifeboats, all determined to be in the first one launched.

Seizing Adriana roughly by the wrist, Oliver dragged her aft, to meet the advancing horde, while she stormed and pleaded.

"You make him listen, Margaret! You have your child on board. Tell him, for the love of God—we must get away *now*, before it's too late!"

Several of the male passengers began to mutter, threatening to take matters into their own hands if Oliver Jardine and Captain Craigh refused to protect them, caring only for the vessel.

Oliver's voice rose over the roar of the waves. "Listen to me. Are your eyes good? Look over there—what do you see?"

As eager as the others, I peered into the distance, straining to see through the murky grayness where Oliver was pointing. The rain had suddenly slackened but twilight was near and—surely that was a tall headland off to the left? Excited talk broke out.

"Land. There's land! Thank God!"

"We're saved. Put us ashore!"

"Why have we been kept here all this time?"

But it was the women who were talking now. The men peered through the mist—and fell silent.

"We're drifting," Oliver stated bluntly. "The anchor won't hold in this sea. We've been drifting for the past hour. That's the coast of Wales. Can you see it? Sheer cliffs and an apron of rocks, with the sea pounding in on them. There's no man alive could take a lifeboat in there, and none on this ship fool enough to try!"

The men, if not the women, recognized the danger. "The sea will carry us. We'll go aground."

"We're putting up a small steadying sail immediately," Oliver stated, "and firing the boiler. But we have to keep the bunker fires under control or flames will sweep the whole vessel as soon as we get up speed. We need more hands." He looked over the pathetic assembly in front of him. "I suggest that you pray. And be ready to man the pumps."

Oliver turned and strode back along the deck to where he was needed, leaving consternation behind him.

"What did he mean—man the pumps?" one woman quavered. I had to look twice to be sure that it was Mrs. Hardesty, a darkly handsome, buxom woman ordinarily, but now almost unrecognizable in her haphazard layers of clothing. "John couldn't possibly . . . John, you aren't strong enough. . . ."

John Hardesty, short, overweight, and well past middle age but with heavy shoulders and arms, pulled himself up. "I would rather pump than drown, my dear."

Slowly, while we watched, the flames grew smaller and more scattered. Men, now atop the roof of the captain's cabin, three of them manning each heavy hose, directed broad streams of water onto the dining and main saloons. When the last spike of flame guttered and disappeared, a feeble cheer went up.

I considered my charges thoughtfully. Sixteen women, counting Adriana, Watty, and myself; six men, not including the eight who had left to help Oliver earlier. A poor lot, but all we had.

"Mr. Hardesty, can you help man the pumps? Are you able? It looks to be grim work."

John Hardesty, whom I knew only as a successful exporter of fine furniture to America, managed a wry grin. "I was raised on a farm, Mrs. Jardine. I know how to bend my back with the best of them. I don't know much about pumping, but I can adapt as need be."

Ignoring Mrs. Hardesty's wail of lament, I asked for other volunteers. The five men remaining spoke up hesitantly, for they doubted their own capabilities. They were relatively hale; not the stuff of heroes but with hands and backs and reason enough to pitch in.

"Very well, you men and all of the women who would prefer not to drown will help on deck. If we all work, we can spell each other every few minutes. At the hoses—and pumping water . . ."

Adriana Rantana looked at me as if I had lost my mind. "You expect *me* to lift a hose? You are absurd, Margaret, women cannot do such work. Furthermore, I am not a slavey!"

"Slavin' is better than drownin'," Watty observed to the group in general. "I've no wish to see Wales from the bottom of that cliff."

But Adriana's closed face rejected my appeal. Mrs. Hardesty fluttered a good deal and moaned that she was not a strong woman, she could do no more, after enduring this dreadful ordeal. She and Adriana moved closer together, but the rest of the women agreed to do whatever work they could.

If we were a forlorn lot as we presented ourselves to Captain Craigh, it was a measure of his need that he accepted our offer to help without delay. Mrs. Hardesty and Adriana had agreed, somewhat reluctantly, to guard Charles while Watty worked with the rest of us. What we lacked in strength we made up in numbers, and courage born of fear.

It had grown dark and the storm had abated somewhat, but the sound of the breakers striking the cliffs of Wales lent purpose to our efforts. In the blackness of the night, lighted fitfully by the ship's lanterns, we were deployed to our stations. A line of striving women handled each hose, lifting, dragging, supporting the nozzles and directing them once again into the coal-bunker hatches. It was an eerie scene. When one woman was exhausted, another took her place, laboring under her burden like a rag doll, with bent knees and crooked body, staggering in place, but striving to *last*. All the male passengers who could be spared from elsewhere on the vessel applied themselves to the pump rails by turns, for none of them could last more than a very short stretch of time.

Everywhere, sweating men and women struggled at tasks beyond their strength, knowing that their lives were at stake. Around us the crew was putting up sail, and when at last the wind caught, my feeble crew on the deck, with little to cheer, at least took heart.

Slowly the *Jardine* came around. In the darkness we had been unable to see the rocks and cliffs waiting to claim us, but once we moved under sail, their oppressive presence withdrew. The *Jardine* wallowed out into the Irish Sea and began to claw her way north, toward Liverpool.

I took my turn at the pump rails, for that was the hardest work and none could last for long. I could scarcely believe the effort it took for one plunge downward, one after another, until my leaden arms trembled and refused to move. Another woman took my place; when she failed, yet another was there. When it was my turn again, from somewhere came the strength for a few minutes more of lung-searing labor. We worked in a state of mindless despair, hands blistered, blinded by tears, but obliged to go on until, one by one, we dropped and crept away to lie, like sacks of sodden rags, in whatever corner we could find.

Perhaps at last God was with us. When my sorry band could do no more, some of the engine-room crew again took over, for the bunker fires still burned and only constant effort could keep them under control. Watty brought me water from somewhere; someone gave me bread and cheese that I swallowed without chewing. I wept then, wept for want of the strength of Oliver's presence and for poor innocent Charles, who I felt certain would never see land again. I heard a crew member say that we were making for Caernarvon Bay and started to pray that we might make it to that haven. My prayer went unsaid, for sleep overwhelmed me where I lay.

Perhaps I slept for as long as an hour, though it felt no more than a few minutes. I was woken by Watty, shaking me and weeping.

"Mum, mum, ye must wake up. Ye're needed, mum. It's Mr. Jardine."

I struggled through layers of exhaustion and bewilderment. I had been lying in a sheltered corner of the deck, oblivious to the dampness beneath me and the force of the wind that was now whipping the ends of my scarf across my face, stinging me to wakefulness. The import of Watty's words finally struck home and I began to shiver uncontrollably.

"What's happened? Where is Oliver? Watty! He's not dead?"

"No, mum, but hurt bad, they say. There's one dead, or near to, and Mr. Jardine burned from the steam. They're bringin' him up, mum, and ye're to come quick!"

Watty had Charles in her arms, bundled in blankets and crying. I staggered to my feet and stumbled beside her, my heart a sick thing beating in my throat. Oliver! Oh, God, everything I touched, everyone I loved . . .

But I had no time for more than muddled fear, for Watty led me to a cabin on the deck below, where two grimy stokers had placed my husband face down on the bed. He was unconscious and moaning, and his clothing, soaked and filthy, clung to his body.

"Ye'll need to cut his clothes off, missus. Careful-like," one of the black-visaged men advised, not meeting my eyes. "The captain is giving him opium."

A moment later I was left alone with Watty and the knowledge that I had no idea of what to do next.

"There's sewin' scissors in me cabin, mum. I'll just fetch 'em."

I took Charles, who was still crying, from her, and knelt by my husband's bed. I prayed then, for I had need of help and it was not going to be forthcoming from anyone aboard the *Jardine*. If God could hear me, if all of my wickedness of the past, and the Curse that smothered my every endeavor, did not block me off completely from Him, surely he would help me now!

When Watty returned with the scissors and, incredibly, a box of tea and a bucket of water, I was ready.

"We've got nothin' else, mum, and tea's the best anyway for burns, my granny always said." She poured the tea leaves into the bucket of cold water and stirred it. "Not fit to drink, but the good is in it all the same. And cold is best fer bathin' burns."

I steeled myself to cut away Oliver's clothing with a pair of embroidery scissors, but when I had slit one sleeve and eased it away from his arm, I knew how ill prepared I was for such horror. I gazed at that raw, red flesh and the cabin darkened and tilted dangerously.

Watty, who must have known better than I what to expect, shoved a glass of whiskey against my lips and forced me to swallow. I sat on a chair with my head on my knees until the faintness passed. And then I returned to my duty, for there was only Watty and me, and if ever a man needed help, Oliver Jardine was that man. I tried to pretend to myself that it wasn't Oliver, that it was just someone, a stranger needing help, for when I let my mind look at this man whom I loved—yes, *loved*, despite everything—tears blinded me, and

I could afford no such luxuries of emotion if I was to help him now.

Watty did what she could, bringing sheets from our cabin and tearing them into squares, and keeping a glass of whiskey and water at my elbow. For what I was doing, only numbness of mind could prevent hysterical abandon. She fed poor little Charles and changed him, while I wrung out the pieces of torn sheet in cold tea and laid them gently on angry, blistered flesh as I uncovered it.

Oliver's left arm had escaped, and his left side from the waist down. But his right arm, buttock, and leg almost to the knee, and all of his back, were a mass of oozing, half-cooked flesh. His beloved steam had done this to him, and I cursed it with a passion.

"Ye have to keep the cloths wet all the time, mum, so they don't stick. They keep the air off, and somethin' in the tea soothes the burnin'."

She looked at Oliver doubtfully. Neither of us could believe that anything we put on those burns could possibly be said to soothe.

"He needs to drink liquids, too," Watty advised, out of some lore from her past experience. "Though how he'll be able to swallow lying on his front like that I don't see."

Nor did I, and there was no other way he could lie. Though he was not conscious, he was crying out from the hell he inhabited, and my own flesh crawled in sympathy with that tortured moaning. When his eyes flickered open there was no recognition in them; he had room for nothing but the all-enveloping torment of his wounds.

The balance of that trip was a nightmare within a nightmare. My mind was prey to every imagining, and all of them were beyond rational contemplation. When Oliver regained consciousness, Captain Craigh administered another draft of opium, which he swallowed with great difficulty. I had never thought to be grateful to God for opium in any form or for any purpose, but the Curse of the Flowers was suddenly a priceless blessing as I saw Oliver again sink into the troubled stupor that was his only relief from agony.

"What of the other man who was scalded, Captain Craigh? Is he. . . ?" I couldn't bring out the dread words with Oliver before my eyes.

"Gone to his rest, God save his soul."

"Poor man, poor man . . ."

"Aye, he took the worst of it." Captain Craigh looked at

Oliver from beneath brooding brows. "Mayhap he's the luckier."

"No!" I struggled to my feet. "Oliver will recover. But we must get him to the infirmary without delay. How long before we make port, Captain?"

"God willing, we'll be in Caernarvon in two hours. In my opinion, Mr. Jardine would be best off in Glasgow, for they've fine doctors at the infirmary there—"

"Glasgow! Are you mad? I pray he will last long enough to reach the Royal Infirmary at Liverpool!" I was past all pretense of polite conversation. I knew only that Oliver must have medical attention as quickly as possible and it was my duty to see that he got it. "Must we stop at Caernarvon? Can we not go direct to Liverpool?"

"We can't hope for that, ma'am, or we'll all go down together, Mr. Jardine included. The bunkers are still burning, and my men are that weary it's a wonder if they last till we reach the bay."

"Then we must find other means of reaching Liverpool swiftly, and by water, Captain Craigh. Mr. Jardine will never survive the trip by coach. Is there a signal station at Caernarvon, or Holyhead? Ask them to have a fast coastal steamer stand by."

Captain Craigh looked doubtful. "Not likely there's anything suitable on the spot, ma'am. But mayhap the Irish mail, now—it's fast, and there's twice-a-day service. . . ."

"The Dublin-Liverpool packet? Yes! It would be scarcely off their route, surely. Signal the Lloyd's station, ask them to relay, tell them I'll pay whatever is demanded—anything. . . ."

"As soon as we're near enough, ma'am," Captain Craigh replied, a gleam of satisfaction in his eyes despite his weariness. "Aye, that's an answer, all right—a fast five-wheeler. . . ."

The Irish mail, when the signal was relayed from the Lloyd's station at Holyhead, made the necessary detour to Caernarvon Bay. No doubt it took a deal of persuasion, but of that I knew nothing. Once assured of Captain Craigh's cooperation, I slept.

It was Adriana Rantana who wrung cloths in cold tea and placed them on Oliver's burns, while I lay on the floor near the bed for an hour or better. She was the one among us who had done the least, and so was physically capable of staying

awake to be sure the cloths were kept wet. For that alone, I
decided, I would forgive her for past wrongs.

Five of us boarded the mail packet: Oliver, Watty with
Charles, Adriana and myself. The other passengers would
make their way back to Liverpool as best they could. With
the help of opium, Oliver survived the trip to Liverpool and
transference from the mail packet to the Royal Infirmary by
means of a wain, a large open farm wagon on which he
could be placed flat on his front. Adriana and I accompanied
him, while Watty took Charles home by hansom cab to Calcutta House.

In later years I was to hear the expression "politics makes
strange bedfellows," and immediately recall that journey to
the Royal Liverpool Infirmary with Adriana by my side. In
our misery we made common cause, holding hands tightly for
courage as the wagon bounced and swayed through the night
streets of Liverpool. With a lantern swinging perilously from
the pole behind the driver's head, and the two of us, grimy
tatterdemalions, crouched over Oliver, we made slow progress
amidst vehicles of every description. Ragged wretches jeered
at us on our tumbrel, and darted almost under the hooves of
the horses. Impatient drivers of fine carriages shouted abuse as
they tried to crowd before us or, failing that, drive through us.

At the infirmary we hovered like two bedraggled witches as
the physicians I had sent for tutted over Oliver's condition
and looked with distaste at our dishabille. Their manner
changed quickly when Adriana roused herself to arrogance
that matched their own and made our identity known.

Only when Oliver was safely abed in an opium-induced
sleep, and silver coins, with the promise of more to come,
had ensured the attentions of an attendant for the night, did
the two of us withdraw. Without need for discussion we repaired to Calcutta House, and blessed sleep.

CHAPTER 26

The Royal Infirmary was an elderly stone building erected in
1745, and a century of Liverpool grime was everywhere evident. Oliver lay in a narrow bed, one of a row of like beds in

the long room where critical cases were kept. There was no privacy and little air, for the windows were high and were never opened. The walls had been whitewashed, though obviously not for some time, and there was every sort of accumulated dirt in the corners and under the beds. It was dismal in the extreme, filled with the sound of moaning cries and desperation. Pervading all was the smell of vinegar, sprinkled on the floor to keep the dust down and, I had no doubt, to dilute more offensive odors. Most of the patients were attended by a family member or friend; few of them could afford the expense of trained attendants. I had a folding screen brought from my home to shelter Oliver's bed, but found that it cut off what little air circulated within the room, and in the end I had to forgo the blessed privacy it afforded.

Oliver's condition was pitiable, and Dr. Virgil Beck, in whom I had placed what faith I could muster, offered little encouragement.

"His chances, madam, rest with God. We will do what we can, but . . ." Dr. Beck pressed his lips together as if he could spare no further word of hope. However, Dr. Beck, as I was to learn, was an incurable optimist—perhaps a good thing in a doctor—and he relented. "Mr. Jardine is a strong-bodied man. He has lasted this long, and that augurs well. . . ."

With that crumb I had to be content. I longed to do something useful, to make some miraculous difference through my own efforts, but there was nothing. I could only watch and wait, trying to see some sign of healing in that raw, red flesh. Truth to tell, there was little anyone, including the doctors, could do apart from dressing Oliver's wounds, administering the opium that enabled him to endure, and urging him to swallow what liquid was possible through an ingenious arrangement of curved glass tubes.

Either Adriana or I was always at Oliver's bedside, except for a few hours during the night. In addition, I employed trained attendants around the clock, for I had no faith whatever in the "nurses" who came in at night to attend to the patients. They were the commonest of street women, and from all reports serviced the interns far more assiduously than the ill.

Commander Matthew Jardine called on two occasions to visit his son when I was present. The stalwart, blustering man I had known seemed strangely meek, acknowledging my presence with an old-fashioned bow and staring down at Oliver with an unreadable expression. On both occasions Commander Jardine stayed but a few minutes and uttered not a word. Oliver, in his opium-induced slumber, remained unaware.

Perhaps I should have been grateful for Adriana's presence in those early weeks when Oliver hovered between life and death—but her manner made that impossible. In every word, in every attitude, she made it clear that she took precedence over me—at Oliver's side and even in my own home. She engaged a personal maid, a lynx-eyed Frenchwoman named Janine Brosse, and settled in as if she intended to remain at Calcutta House forever.

When I allowed myself to think about it, resentment threatened to choke me. But I had too many duties and responsibilities to permit the luxury of quarreling with Adriana. I had only a great longing that she would eventually become bored with her self-appointed role and leave us in peace. It seemed a reasonable hope, but I had misjudged the depth of her enmity for me.

I had many matters to worry me. First and foremost was Oliver's precarious state. In addition, I was forced to deal with our finances. Besides the salvage and repair of the *Jardine* there was the problem of obtaining the insurance money; Lloyd's was showing great reluctance to honor our claim. As for the shipping world, it showed a steadfast refusal to believe that the *Jardine* had been sabotaged, preferring to believe the vessel itself at fault.

In the midst of these conflicts Adriana, sensing my weariness and vulnerability, chose to deliver her *coup de grace*. It was the day after I had noted some slight improvement in Oliver's condition. Most of the oozing of raw, burned flesh had stopped. Under the ointment, a paper-thin layer of dry surface could be detected over much of the scalded area—the start of healing. I was jubilant; for the first time, here was some encouraging evidence to support my faith that Oliver would recover! The following morning I was eager to get to the infirmary, full of hope and humming to myself when Adriana entered my rooms without knocking. She was dressed to go out, in a silver-blue skirt and deeper blue Zouave jacket with silver buttons.

"You needn't bother to visit Oliver today, Margaret. I am going to the infirmary and it serves no purpose for both of us to be there."

I stared at her, dumbfounded. "Of course I am going. Why would I not?"

The tawny eyes measured me. "Because your time could be put to better use. I have heard—endlessly, it seems—of your prowess as a businesswoman. Perhaps if you were to devote more of your attention in that direction, we would enjoy more success. Your true concern is with the Blue Funnel Company, is it not?"

"My 'true concern' is with Oliver, above all!"

"You wish to keep up appearances as his wife? Surely you have done that adequately. I would prefer that you have the decency to subjugate that role from now on. In view of the circumstances."

"*You* would prefer? And *what* circumstances, pray?"

"Please, Margaret"—Adriana's voice was unutterably weary—"let us have no pretense within these walls, at least. We both know that Oliver is no longer a part of your life—"

"Are you mad?" My heart was pounding. "Oliver *is* my life!"

"Perhaps I should have phrased it differently. My natural wish to spare you offense." Nothing could have been more purposely offensive than Adriana's voice. "If you prefer—you are no longer a part of Oliver's life."

"I am married to him."

She spared me a cool smile. "Yes. You handled that cleverly. Has it afforded you much pleasure, knowing that he came immediately to *my* bed?"

"And stayed there, Adriana?" It came out so softly, the devil's own inspiration, for it sounded convincing even to me.

I had the satisfaction of seeing her eyes go blank, considering. Business matters had required Oliver's presence in Liverpool during recent months. She could not be sure he hadn't been with me.

She flung herself onto my chaise longue and swung her legs up, affecting an easy laugh. "Dear Margaret! You would be amusing if you were not so obvious. I am to look to my laurels, is that it? You propose doing battle for this devoted husband of yours?"

"The battle has been fought—and won. Oliver and I effected a reconciliation aboard the *Jardine*." I returned the pitying smile she had earlier turned on me. "Oliver seems to fancy the idea of being a father—and the founder of a new dynasty."

Adriana no longer sprawled on the chaise longue. Leaping to her feet she faced me, hands on her hips, her head arched back on that slim neck so that I was reminded of a snake about to strike.

"Liar!"

I shook my head slowly, holding her eyes with my own. "He planned to tell you once the *Jardine* was back in port and our guests safely away."

There was dead silence while Adriana measured my lie. I thought I had won. I should have known better—she was merely realigning her weapons. Animosity vanished and sweet reason flooded her face.

"Margaret, let us sit down and talk together sensibly. As women of the world."

Determined to match her in coolness, I moved to one of the blue velvet chairs as she took the other.

"It seems I must be cruel." Adriana sighed. "There is no assessing the unreality of a woman's self-delusion. Perhaps you truly believe you have some hope of regaining Oliver Jardine. But Oliver is an expensive luxury to maintain. He has used up your wealth—but he has not used up mine." Her amber eyes glinted under the arrogant arch of brows. "So you see, darling Margaret, waving Charles before his eyes will scarcely change the important things. Who knows, I may yet give him a son myself. . . ."

I felt the bile rise in my throat as I leaped to my feet. "You patronizing slut! Do you think I'm still that credulous schoolgirl you met at Berri? To be twisted any way you choose? I am to *give* Oliver over to you?"

Adriana Rantana's composure evanesced into blazing fury. She pushed her tight-jawed face to within inches of mine.

"You will do as I tell you to do! You will leave Oliver Jardine to *me*—and concern yourself with your precious steamship company, or I will call every sou's worth of paper I hold on your venture and dump you in the dirt! Do you understand now? Finally? You will have neither Oliver nor your vaunted position, nor even a roof for yourself and your brat! Is that clear enough for you, poor *salope*? Oliver Jardine is *mine*."

She breathed deeply—and smiled a slow, hot smile. "I can afford him. If I choose."

With that, Adriana stalked out of my rooms. Winner takes all.

My knees folded under me and I sank onto the bed. Anger roiled inside me, but my mind turned over almost idly, holding my fury at a careful distance.

Adriana Rantana. My continuing nemesis. She would have been at home as an Inquisitor, turning the screw slowly. Finding the greenest boughs for the slow-roasting fire. And she had won. She would stay in my house for as long as she pleased. No doubt she held paper on that, along with all else. She would nurse Oliver and be there at his side as he recovered. While I was off tending to the business. I wondered bitterly if poor biblical Martha had chosen to do the housework while her sister Mary sat at Jesus's feet. Or had she, like me, been warned off? No matter, I was neither a Martha nor of biblical meekness.

I moved from the bed to face a tall pier glass that stood between the windows. Flushed and disheveled, striving for calm, I gazed back at myself. Once again Adriana had threatened to destroy me. But this time she had not used her former threat, that she would tell Oliver about our relationship at Berri. That would destroy her, too, in his eyes. Instead, she would bring me to my knees financially. But *could* she do it? Pull down our perilous paper kingdom without destroying Oilver's infatuation with her? I knew she would take the chance, to spite me.

The following day I journeyed by railway to Glasgow. I needed to see for myself the condition of the *Jardine*. Captain Craigh met me aboard and we picked our way through workmen clearing away charred debris.

"Aye, a fine mess it is, ma'am, above *and* below. To put out the fires we had to open the sea cocks and flood the bunkers. Half sink her and pump her out again."

I looked around in dismay. Even the fresh wind off the Firth could not blow away the acrid stink of wet, fire-blackened wood. I was reminded again of Greystones and the countless hours I had spent there, searching for the wealth that had paid for *this*!

"How long will it take to put her in commission again?"

Captain Craigh shrugged. "Three months at the least. Thank God she's iron, or there'd be naught left to do but start all over." He looked around with measuring eyes. "Mayhap it's not so bad as it looks at the moment, ma'am. There's a deal of work to be done, and some of it in the engine room, needless to say. But it's mainly the saloon and the cabins."

"You've talked to the Lloyd's man? He's been over it?"

"Aye, and a glummer face I've seldom seen." Captain Craigh chuckled. "He was not a happy man. Apart from all else, there's the expense of all the folderol, the great crystal chandelier and the fine fittings."

"But they are going to pay? We've had no report at the offices in Liverpool as yet."

"Aye, they'll pay right enough. Act of God or act of man, they're liable." He grimaced. "That lout that started it all won't see Ireland again for a while, though there's little comfort in that for us."

" 'Sure and 'twas the fault o' the poteen, Yer Lordship,' " I mimicked viciously. "How fortunate that he happened to have a sack of oil-soaked rags at hand!"

"Aye, they're not overfond o' the English. No doubt he'll be happy enough in an English jail, all the same, for he'll eat, which is more than he'd do at home right now."

I spent two days in Glasgow, for there was much to see to. But at least I would be able to tell Oliver that the *Jardine* would be ready for outfitting in three months, if all went well. I had been away from home for four days in all. Four days with no word of Oliver's progress, four days away from Charles! Ned was waiting for me at the railway depot with the carriage when I arrived back in Liverpool. When I asked how Oliver was, his honest Lancashire face remained impassive.

" 'As good as can be expected,' mum. Or, 'much the same.' Them's Miss Rantana's words when we ask, Emily and me." He shot me a reproachful look. "It's not like we aren't family, Miss Margaret."

"I know, Ned." I sighed. "Miss Rantana doesn't understand these things."

He nodded, and a sly smile wrinkled his brown face. "That's so, mum. So I went m'self to see what was what, last night late, when I was sure she was safe in fer the night."

Ned stowed my bag, and me, inside the carriage and looked me in the eye. "He's doin' much better, mum. Knew me, he did, and asked where you was. I took the liberty o' tellin' him you was in Glasgow lookin' after business. Better 'n him thinkin' you didn't bother about him, in my view." He gave me a dark look with knowledge behind it. "I had more than enough o' that with yer father."

Embarrassed, or perhaps worried that I might take offense, he got swiftly on the box. But I stuck my head out the window. "Thank you, Ned."

He nodded, satisfied, and we were off. I relaxed against the velvet upholstery of the carriage. It was good to be home again. In the morning I would help Watty give Charles his bath. And then I would visit Oliver. Adriana could go to hell. From whence, I had no doubt, she came originally.

The weeks that followed had a nightmare quality about them. Everything I attempted progressed as if mired in quicksand. My only comforts were Emily's bustling good nature and dear little Charles. So I soldiered on, scrupulously civil to Adriana and smiling but adamant in all of my business dealings with Lloyd's, who showed a disposition to withhold monies due on our insurance claims. Where and when I could, I endeavored to persuade bankers and exporters that steam vessels were not fire hazards, as they seemed determined to believe.

I visited Oliver every day, despite Adriana's edict. It was a compromise, of sorts. I called at the infirmary each afternoon and stayed but fifteen minutes, smiling determinedly and making no claims on Oliver's small, returning strength. Adriana was not pleased, but so long as I was not a threat—she clearly felt I was not—she seemed disposed to consider that she had won her victory.

God knows, she had no reason to be jealous. At first, when Oliver began to mend noticeably and was aware a part of every day, I was sure he welcomed my visits. His face seemed to lighten; once he extended a hand and I felt his fingers tighten over mine. But as days went by—as if more recent memories had returned to haunt him—that changed. He was not pleased to see me, nor had he any words to exchange with me when I tried to speak with him of business matters. I found the visits emotionally exhausting, as if I were trying to scale a high wall and falling back long before I neared the top. As for Adriana, she maintained a smiling silence and never left us alone for a moment. Day by day, while I struggled to maintain my outward calm, I was forced to acknowledge that I was defeated.

Then fate took a hand in the strange charade. Adriana fell ill with an indisposition of the stomach. She accused me of poisoning her and sent her maid, Janine Brosse, to fetch Dr. Beck. I could spare no time for her foolishness and Emily would not.

"Let her fine French slavey tend to her." Emily declared, a wealth of resentment in her voice. "We owe her nowt, mum. Or nowt that she'd welcome!"

Dr. Beck prescribed a stomach powder and spared me a glance of sympathy as he left my home. Perhaps he read the situation correctly, for he had seen Adriana often at Oliver's bedside.

Adriana's malaise gave me the opportunity I needed. Let the Blue Funnel Steam and Navigation Company fend for itself—I would pay a call on Oliver, and of more than a few minutes' duration.

He lay on his side, the side that had suffered less from the scalding and was thus healing more swiftly. One of the attendents had cut his thick red hair to a reasonable length, and although it was a haphazard piece of work, he looked the better for it.

"Adriana is ill today, a disorder of the stomach." I smiled. "She professes to believe that I poisoned her."

Oliver lifted a laconic eyebrow. "And did you?"

"Not unless wishing works such wonders. God knows, I've wished her ill enough."

"No doubt." He studied me with eyes as cold as his voice. "But you mustn't waste your valuable time here, doing penance. I'm sure the Blue Funnel Company cannot survive without your aid. I can."

I drew a deep breath, determined to keep my temper. One cannot fight with a man on a sickbed, no matter how avidly he invites it.

"Oliver, let us not quarrel over Adriana or any other matter. I have been sick enough at heart these long weeks, watching you suffer. I have done all I could to protect our future. If you feel that I was overly bold, you have only to say so. I saw no alternative. As for spending my time here, nothing could make me happier. Adriana stopped me by threatening to call all loans against the company unless I did as she said and stayed away."

"Can you never leave off about Adriana? She has been more than generous to you. Far too generous. Making excuses for you, professing to believe the line would be ruined if charges were pressed."

"Charges? What are you saying?" Foreboding rushed over me in waves. What new mischief had that she-devil devised this time?

Oliver shifted position and winced with pain. It lent savagery to his voice. "Little Miss Innocence still, I see. How proud I was of you during the fire! Once again I was credulous enough to accept your mask as truth. Always, always hiding behind the mask! How I would love to see it stripped away! See you in court with the evidence confronting you. Even your angelic airs would do you no good there!"

"Oliver, are you mad? I don't know what you're talking about."

"The *Jardine*! Demented female jealousy! Oh, God, if only *you* could have spent one hour of the agony—but the devil looks after his own, eh, Margaret?"

"Oliver—" I was sobbing under the force of his fury. "What are you saying? You cannot believe that I had anything to do with the fire. . . ."

He raised himself on one elbow, his eyes that terrifying quicksilver gray. "You were right about one thing, Margaret. The Curse of the Flowers. You inherited it along with your mother's legacy. Mayhap with your mother's milk, for your deviltry goes far back."

I tried to speak past the pain in my throat, but he held up one bandaged hand. "No! Spare me more of your pretty lies. Adriana employed investigators. You had some Irish ne'er-do-well fire the *Jardine*'s bunkers out of spite—"

"No, Oliver!"

Laboriously, he turned onto his stomach, his face in the pillow. "I have seen the proof."

Though I stood by the bed and wept and pleaded, he gave no sign of hearing me further. I became aware that around us curious faces watched with rapt attention. Hiding my face in my kerchief, I half ran from the room. I wanted air. Even the sooty air of Liverpool was preferable to that of the room where Oliver lay, for to me it smelled of brimstone, of Adriana—devil-spawn. . . .

I collided with a large man in the outer doorway, and when I made to pass him, he seized me by the arm.

"Margaret! What's wrong? My God, woman—is it Oliver?"

I looked up into the florid face of Commander Jardine, his eyes wide with frightened surmise.

"No, no, Oliver is much better. It's—nothing." I tried to extricate my arm from his grasp, but he turned with me and led me down the front steps of the infirmary to where his carriage waited. Bundling me in unceremoniously, he told the driver to go to the park.

"Now, madam"—he handed me a large handkerchief—"let's hear what is amiss. That Italian woman, I'll be bound. Always there when I've looked in on Oliver, smiling like some damned Medusa."

I felt a stirring of fondness for Matthew Jardine. Thank

God someone could see what Adriana was. I despaired that Oliver ever would. But I knew better than to put my faith in this elderly rogue. Matthew Jardine was accountable for my father's misfortunes and death. No matter what he might pretend now, with his fleeting visits to the infirmary, he was still Oliver's avowed enemy, a purveyor of drugs, and a scurrilous old reprobate who would never be trustworthy unless he saw a profit it in for himself.

No doubt he watched the emotions racing across my face, for he put out one large, freckled hand and seized my chin, turning it so I was forced to look into his eyes.

"Don't be a fool, Margaret! Oliver is my son. You have a son of your own and enough wits to put yourself in my boots now. Past anger counts for naught when it's your own flesh and blood that's hurting. Talk, woman!"

It poured out of me like wine from an upended bottle, beginning with when I found I was to have Oliver's child. He interrupted only once, when I explained how I had forced Oliver to wed me.

"Aye, you were right enough on that score, my girl." He grinned at me. "I'd have wed you fast enough and counted myself a lucky man." His face sobered. "And I wouldn't have scoffed at the chance of a share of the Blue Funnel Company."

By the time I had finished recounting Adriana's lies and Oliver's belief in my duplicity, Commander Jardine had given up even the snorts of anger that had punctuated his listening at the start. He sat slumped in a corner of the carriage, his eyes closed and his head turning from side to side against the back cushion, as if in pain.

Just as I decided he was having a seizure of some sort, Commander Jardine sat up suddenly, pounding one clenched fist into his other hand.

"Damn me! It's a wicked old world. And worse for some of us, meant to live in other times, I've no doubt. You get soft here in England—once you're too long away from the places where anything goes. You think you won't, but you do. And once you're softened up, there's no going back. England's grip is on you again. Morality! Phaaaah!"

He shoved his head out the window of the carriage and shouted to his driver. "Potter! Back to the infirmary!"

He looked at me. "You'll come in with me."

"No. Oliver has no need of me. And I cannot abide any more."

"You'll come in with me. I have things to say and I'll say them once."

Mathew Jardine had not lost the habit of command. I could see no purpose in accompanying him, but I found myself trotting along meekly in his wake.

Oliver regarded us with narrowed eyes and closed face. His father hauled a straight chair into position beside him, and straddled it. Resting his arms on the back, and his chin on his arms, he stared into Oliver's eyes.

"I have something to say. I don't want to be interrupted—no, don't look away," he ordered, as Oliver prepared to pretend we weren't there. "This is not some paltry dispute in a tavern that exists between us. You and I are very different men, Oliver." He gave a sharp bark of laughter. "I'd never pass up Margaret, here, for the Italian woman. You lack your father's eye. Ah, well, I didn't come here to talk of women but of ships. We both know where we stand on that matter. I've not changed my mind, and nor have you."

He paused and drew a large hand down over his face, hesitating, studying Oliver, suddenly reluctant. "I have been feeling old, of late. Now and again a doubt has crept in. We never welcome changes, you know—not once past a certain age. I knew you were wrong about steam—but what if you were right? I am committed to sailing vessels. Moreover, I am a man who likes to be right."

Commander Matthew Jardine expelled a gusty breath. "And so I decided to hedge my bets."

He had no need to ask for Oliver's attention now, nor mine. We were scarcely breathing for hanging on his words.

"To hire a blackguard is an easy thing. To decide to do the deed is considerably harder." Again the short bark of laughter. "Mayhap my heart wasn't in it, for I hired a knave who needed liquor to fuel his wickedness. But who am I to call him a knave? The deed was mine, all right, and it cost heavier than I knew. For I wanted an embarrassment, Oliver, not a tragedy."

Suddenly Commander Jardine's stolid face dissolved into a mask of grief. "You don't walk away from tragedy. Not when it strikes your son."

The big head went down for a moment and then rose again, as if he refused to take refuge from our eyes. There was silence throughout the entire room, though I only realized that afterward.

"*You?*"

The single word dropped like a stone into a pool and the eddies spread silently in my mind. The terror and ruin aboard the *Jardine*. Oliver's suffering and the death of the assistant engineer. The renewed fear of steam vessels that now threatened the survival of our line. And Oliver's belief in my perfidy. All because an old man wanted to win.

Blood-red rage exploded in my head. At that moment I could have seen Matthew Jardine drawn and quartered. But the rage ebbed away as I faced the reality: an arrogant old sealord brought down by his own vainglorious pride. Facing his son, his brash blue eyes awash with tears—perhaps of self-pity, who could know? But of sorrow, too.

Oliver inched himself laboriously to a semi-upright position. The copper freckles stood out across a face white with effort. I longed to help him—but what would help and what would hurt? He motioned me toward him.

"Take the bandages off, Margaret!"

"No!"

"Damn you! Take them off, I tell you."

I looked around in desperation for an attendant, or better, Dr. Beck. But no help was forthcoming.

Oliver called out to the ever-present audience in that room.

"Who'll help me? Come, any one of you, a purse of guineas for two minutes' work."

There was a breathy stirring among the other patients and the friends or family attending them; but at the sight of Commander Jardine's face, no one dared come forward.

"Damn you all, then. I'll do it myself!"

He couldn't have, but his frustration and fury were such that he would have done himself a damage. While I havered, Matthew Jardine got to his feet.

"There's no need, Oliver."

"There is every need. You can't see Shand, the man who took the worst of the steam. He's in his grave. But you'll see me, damn you. Come, you want to admire your handiwork, don't you?"

Silently Matthew Jardine, his big, freckled hands trembling, striving to be gentle, unwound and stripped away the bandages, one by one. Oliver lay silent and without wincing, but his teeth drew blood from his lower lip and tears coursed slowly down his white face.

When at last he lay exposed, the thin, soft scab with its angry red edges covering most of his back and legs, there was silence in the room. I thought Oliver had fainted until he spoke.

"A handsome piece of work. Even finer viewed from within, I assure you."

Matthew Jardine knelt by his son's bed, his hand on Oliver's head.

"God forgive me, Oliver. I don't expect you to."

"It's done. There's no going back."

The old commander bowed his head. "I'll mend what I can. I'll go before the Board of Trade and tell the story, vindicate the *Jardine*. They'll know it wasn't the vessel at fault—"

"No! They'll prosecute. A man died. The insurance money will be withheld if there's an inquiry. Two of us ruined will cure nothing."

At that moment an intern, summoned no doubt by one of the onlookers, hurried to Oliver's side. A great foofaraw ensued. Oliver was given a draft of opium and his burns were redressed. Commander Jardine and I were castigated and invited to allow the patient to rest.

But Oliver, before the opium removed him from the present, stretched out a hand to clutch his father's wrist. "Help Margaret . . . and Charles. It's too much for one woman. Watch out for . . . the Italian woman, as you call her. She lied to me . . . to do Margaret harm."

Commander Jardine left and I watched by Oliver's bedside as he slept. I was grateful to be there, to be vindicated, to savor over and over the knowledge that he did care about me and about our son. And that, finally, he knew Adriana for the traitor she was.

As for Commander Jardine's assistance, that I put out of mind immediately. It would not be forthcoming, and if it were, a dubious benefit at best.

CHAPTER 27

In the months of struggle that followed I fretted and fumed over Oliver's refusal to allow his father to go to the Board of Trade and make his confession. Things could scarcely be

worse for us. If Matthew Jardine had to pay the price for
sending us to ruin, I considered that to be no more than he
deserved. Yet Oliver would countenance no opinion but his
own. The name Jardine was not to be brought low, no matter
what the cost. We had a son to consider and we would solve
our difficulties as a family or not at all.

His references to us as a family were balm to my heart.
And perhaps secretly I admired Oliver for his stand. It was
one my father would have understood. Honor was all-impor-
tant, it came first. After that, one did what one could. My
complaint was that the difficulties did not abate as a reward
for virtuous sentiment. Despite all my efforts, faith in the
iron steamer had vanished. It had never been a sturdy conviction at the best of times—more a question of theoretical
debate and a sporting willingness on the part of more
adventurous firms to indulge their optimism, in the hope that
they were moving with the tide of progress. After all, steam
was the foundation of England's present prosperity, the *raison
d'être* for her domination of steadily enlarging markets
throughout Europe and America. But the forward-looking
men—and they had never been in the majority—no longer
looked on steam vessels as the wave of the future. It had
been a gamble, a fine dream that had come to nothing. Or
worse, had come to disaster. Nothing I could say or do
changed that view, and our financial ruin came closer with
every week that passed.

Oliver came home to Calcutta House from the infirmary. I
would have rejoiced in this further indication that he now
had truly linked his life with mine and Charles's, save that he
seemed so detached and indifferent. His physical condition
continued to improve, but he was lacking in energy—or perhaps concentration. He seemed untroubled by the desperate
straits we were in, and told me that I should relax more.
How could I relax? No one would ship by the Blue Funnel
line. No one would even discuss the matter—their opinions
were formed and there was no leverage I could use to influence them.

The *Lady Margaret*, thank God, was still in successful operation, though it profited us little. George Gore and his
Edisto Island cooperative were quick to take full advantage
of our difficulties. The *Lady Margaret* had made two
crossings east and west, and had lived up to my promises in
every respect. But Mr. Gore comprehended our dilemma and
altered his terms accordingly. I was forced to give him a

preferential price on the Rancorne coal shipped to Charleston and lower freighting charges on Sea Island cotton shipped to Liverpool—in view, he said, of "the increased risk" he was incurring, and his higher insurance rates as a result of shipping by steam vessel. In short, though our heads were above water, we were in danger of foundering financially at a moment's notice.

As for Adriana, she had made several trips to London but had left me in no doubt about her intention to reside at Calcutta House. She had had her possessions sent from Glasgow, kept her own carriage and horses in my stable, and treated my home as if it were her own and I the tolerated guest. Moreover, while I was occupied with seeing to the repairing and refitting of the *Jardine*, trying every way to drum up cargoes for both vessels, and staving off financial ruin month by month, Adriana spent her time with Oliver. Yet I dared say nothing. No matter how much I wanted her out of my house, I could not afford to put her threat to ruin us to the test. Besides, I noticed that Oliver showed no more interest in her than in anyone or anything else about him.

There were several weeks of respite from Adriana during the Christmas season. Perhaps the pleasure of tormenting me with her insolence seemed too tame—or Oliver too preoccupied and our household too isolated from holiday gaiety—in any event, she went off to Italy. I enjoyed the first truly happy time I had known in Calcutta House, for I had Oliver and Charles—and temporary peace of mind at last.

Despite his puzzling remoteness, and an occasional sudden show of irritability, Oliver was for the most part smiling and placid, agreeable to all that I suggested. He appeared to be almost well again, for all that he was pale and thin and slept a great deal. He took to visiting Charles in the nursery and the two would hold long, leisurely conversations, to which Charles contributed gurgles and assorted noises which Oliver could interpret as he pleased. Watty assured me that he told Charles "wonderful stories, mum. He should write them down, fer they're as good as that Mr. Dickens makes up, I'm sure."

With Adriana out of the way, I turned my mind to the holidays, determined that the Christmas of 1845 should be a happy one, in spite of our precarious position. I had a tall hemlock brought into the house and set up in the library. Emily and I girded it with beautiful garlands and dozens of candles, and strung holly and mistletoe throughout the house.

Together, she and I planned the Christmas feast. There was much evidence in Liverpool that great numbers of our people suffered severe privation in the midst of plenty. These were the "hungry forties." England's vaunted industrial prosperity filled the pockets of the very few at the top, while the rank and file, for all their hard labor, went to bed hungry. Bread had climbed to a shocking price, and Sir Robert Peel, the Prime Minister, was urging the repeal of the Corn Laws.

Our government had imposed the Corn Laws in 1815, when the price of corn fell drastically after the Napoleonic wars. By keeping out European corn so that the price of English wheat would climb, the government most certainly aided the cause of the landowners—and obliged workingmen to spend most of their money for bread and little to go with it! This year things had become worse and much worse. Along with a bad harvest and widespread unemployment, we heard dreadful accounts of thousands starving to death in Ireland because the potato crop had failed.

But the wealthy and powerful men who sat in Parliament were the owners of mills and factories, and large landowners. They turned a deaf ear to all pleas. They knew where *their* bread was coming from, and their interest was in keeping it well buttered.

I made it clear to Emily that in our household, *all* were to enjoy a true Christmas feast. Not just their fill of meat and the staple foods, but also sweets and pastries and most especially a good, rich plum pudding. My mother had been niggardly in that regard. She maintained that it would be ruinous to feed the help what *we* ate, and if one made an exception at Christmas, they would develop tastes that would beggar us. There was no danger of that in her household, for she had a sharp eye for such matters. I despised that sort of penny-pinching, and it could make no difference anyway to our disastrous finances.

After giving the matter a great deal of consideration, I invited Commander Jardine and his three-year-old son to Calcutta House for Christmas Day. As I had thought, it seemed to please Oliver, and I felt that we appeared a quite ordinary and affectionate family. But it was on this occasion I realized more fully that all was not as it should be with Oliver, despite the progress he was making. He sat at the head of the table, smiled pleasantly, and was in good spirits, but once again he seemed dreamy and distant—and he ate virtually nothing. I would have to remind myself to speak of that to

Emily. Perhaps he fancied something special to tempt his appetite. We would devise something. But in the general excitement of the occasion I did not give the matter overmuch thought.

With Adriana's return to Calcutta House came the familiar sense of strain and turmoil barely below the surface. The time away had agreed with her, for she looked well and seemed filled with new energy—for mischief, I had no doubt. I was correct in that assumption, as I discovered one evening soon afterward.

I had retired to my sitting room to study the terms of an agreement I proposed offering to a leading commodity broker who represented a number of merchants throughout Lancashire. It contained enough advantages for his principals so that I was sure it would be appealing, but I needed assurance that the terms would not prove ruinous for us. It was of my own devising, for I was determined to fill the holds of the *Jardine* for at least two voyages to America and thus prove to the shipping world that it was not consigning goods to the ocean bottom by giving us custom. I wanted Oliver's opinion.

He was not in his bedchamber, nor was he in any of the downstairs rooms, for I peered into them all. If he had gone out, it would be the first time since his return from the infirmary. A suspicion sprang full-blown into my mind. He was with Adriana! I sped up the grand stairs in a frenzy of anger, jealousy, outrage—everything but sense. Adriana's bedchamber was furthest from my own, opening off the small hall at the western end of the long upper gallery. I flung open the door of her room with no thought of what I should say if she proved to be alone. She was not.

Adriana and Oliver lay on the wide bed in contented lassitude, their passion spent, obviously; their limbs still intertwined, and their faces—oh, God, their faces—sated with gratification. All . . . all . . . rose up to blind me with anguish. Oliver's contemptuous rejection of me, and the brutal rape. Memory of that other scene I had interrupted in Glasgow, memory of Adriana's too-familiar lasciviousness at the Villa Rantana. My own long abstinence from Oliver's bed while I had feared for his life and tended his pain. My dreams of a future built on new love and trust.

I moved toward them without knowing that I was doing so, stopping only when I felt the edge of the bed against my limbs. Then I stood motionless, staring down at them.

Adriana chuckled that low, lewd laugh I knew so well. Oliver smiled at me. I could not interpret the odd expression in his eyes, nor did I try to. I was overwhelmed with revulsion and a sense of final defeat.

"We were just speaking of you, darling," Adriana purred. "Oliver, did I not say how nice it would be if Margaret were with us? How selfish we were being to leave her out of our pleasures?"

Oliver's response was a soft moan. "My white and gold angel, still—always—beyond any that I dream . . ."

Adriana's long, curling fingers reached out and grasped my skirt, pulling me down toward the bed. Realization of what she was doing released me from paralysis. I pulled my skirt from her grasp and was out the door, running down the small hall, along the wide gallery, and into my own chambers. I slammed and locked the door, leaning against it heavily until my shaking limbs were steady enough to take me to a chair.

I sat like one dead until the chill of the room was deep in my bones. Or perhaps the chill came from within, for God knows my heart felt carved of ice. Whichever, I roused finally, and sought shelter in a woolen robe.

Was it for *this* I had suffered through so much guilt and pain about that summer in Italy? Did past sins exact a price forever? I would have been better to continue on my uncaring path to perdition. At least I would have been spared the self-hatred and the constant fear that each stranger I met would have heard of my shameful exploits.

I had been able to convince myself that the Curse of the Flowers had somehow departed from us. Despite the unceasing problems that beset the Blue Funnel Company, despite Adriana's presence and Oliver's suffering, I had *felt*, rather than thought, that my good intentions, Charles's birth, my devotion to duty, had earned me absolution. Here was conclusive proof that I was never to be free of it. Oliver, whom I had believed finally had come to love me, wanted only to possess us both! I had waited so patiently for him to get well and come to my room, become again my lover. To assume his place as husband and father. When he had more strength and more interest in life, I'd told myself; when he had regained his appetite and wits, and his passion for his once-loved steam vessels. None of it had happened the way I had planned! Oliver had become a different man. Corrupted by Adriana? Or by the Curse—that touched all that *I* touched?

On my feet, pacing my sitting room, I ranted and raved aloud, shaking my fist at God. I damned the Curse. I damned

Oliver for his faithless heart. I damned my mother and Matthew Jardine. And I damned Adriana Rantana. All of this wrath of God descending on my head— "Why only me? Why don't You punish Adriana? Make her pay, too!"

I refused to believe in the Curse! Poppies were only flowers, put on earth by God, not by me. Opium had *saved* Oliver! I seized on that and reasoned from there, if reason is the word. I would henceforth renounce all responsibility for my mother's—no, my stepmother's—sins. If I did not choose to believe in the Curse it ceased to exist. I defied God to prove otherwise. I flung myself on my bed and buried my face in a pillow, blotting it all out—Adriana, God, my stepmother, opium. Exhaustion finally provided relief and I fell into a troubled slumber.

When I woke I was cold but in a strangely luminous state of mind. My small Lancashire clock told me it was three in the morning. I had been dreaming, a languorous dream of Oliver and Adriana, hand in hand, in a garden of exotic flowers. While I watched, they drifted slowly into an embrace and as slowly drifted apart. Adriana appeared to speak but there were no words, only music, and she moved her head in time with it, as a snake does to the music of a lute. Oliver followed her every movement, in unison with her, to the strange music. I strove to run to them and tear them apart, but my feet were rooted; I was a small bush among many and powerless to move or speak.

Then Adriana was gone and my stepmother appeared, approaching Oliver, smiling, her hair decked with blood-red poppies. He looked at her with disdain, but she plucked a poppy from her hair and extended it to him, and he reached out and took it. I screamed a silent bush-scream that no one could hear, as he sniffed the poppy and reached for another. While I stood, immovable, screaming warnings that no one could hear, Oliver and my mother walked slowly off, arm in arm, while she plucked more of the red poppies from her hair and Oliver accepted them.

I got my feet on the floor and the woolen robe wrapped about me. Barefoot, I drifted into the sitting room and poured a generous dollop of cognac, moving as languorously as the people of my dream, for I was still a part of it and I knew where it was taking me.

How had I not seen it before?

Oliver was addicted to opium. The horror of it took time to seep into my consciousness, but the knowledge was born

full-grown, born of all of the small glimmers I had let slide
by my waking mind. His pallor and loss of appetite, the
changes of mood from restlessness and irritability to cheerful
animation, the absence of any real interest in anything. Poor
little Charles, recipient of so many lengthy monologues. Poor
me, for I had dreamed he would soon come around and
again be interested in his beloved steam vessels—and me.

Able at this point to view it more dispassionately, I realized that his behavior a few hours back had been still another
indication of his addiction. He had been so unlike his usual
self, so passive, as if he were only half there. And now I
recognized the look in his eyes—emptiness.

I thought of all the dreadful stories I had heard of opium
addiction—not the poor wretches to whom my mother and
Commander Jardine sold their wares, but people like Oliver
who had started taking opium for some malady of the stomach or joints on the advice of their physician—and found
they had a new affliction harnessed to the old.

What would I do? Hot on the heels of my fear for Oliver
came outrage. I was not so selfless, so charged with Christian
spirit, that I did not resent all of this. Oliver took his pleasure
with Adriana while I stood outside, starving for his arms, and
offered insult. Oliver sat about the house, untroubled by our
problems, while I struggled and worried and strove to solve
them. Yes, he suffered, but I hadn't caused the suffering.
Matthew Jardine had. *Yes*, God—I was sorry for Oliver, but
sorrier for myself. Oliver was comfortable in his opium-
induced nirvana—surely that was better than enduring the
horrid cold reality that I faced?

As for Adriana, I felt a new wave of hatred for her. The
memory of that bedroom scene poured back into my mind
with the rush of a sea tide up a narrow bore. She had known
all along! She had known before she left for the Continent
that Oliver was addicted and that I, poor goose, struggled on,
blind as always. She had made use of the lack of will engendered by his addiction to suit her own purposes.

For the second time that night I strode about my sitting
room in a passion of anger. Tomorrow Adriana would leave,
if I had to have Ned eject her bodily. I would endure no
more from her, no matter what the consequences. As for Oliver, I would present his problem to Commander Jardine.
Since he knew so much about opium, let him deal with it.
Full of bravado and resolve I went back to bed and to sleep.

Cognac in sufficient quantity has remarkable soporific power. Perhaps the equal of the hateful poppy.

I woke late next morning to a cold, blustery day with wind-driven sleet beating on my windowpane. Downstairs, I forced myself to eat a hearty breakfast for strength. I would need it to cope with Adriana, and I was determined to be rid of her before nightfall. But as is sometimes the case, once you make up your mind to deal with a problem, fate steps in and does it for you. I had just finished eating when Emily brought me the news, her face alight with ill-disguised glee.

"Miss Rantana, mum, she's been called back to Italy. A letter in this morning's post, all fancy stamps and sealing wax. Someone died, so she's off fer hóme with her la-di-da French maid. Fer good this time, by the looks of it, fer she's had Ned take all her trunks to her room. It's a great flutter up there. I keep out of it."

I felt an immense weight lift from my spirits. The day was going to go well, I knew it! "Has Mr. Oliver come down yet?"

"No, mum. Had his pot of tea in his room, like always." She looked at me with knowing brown eyes. "Mayhap he's helping Miss Rantana with her packing."

When I did not respond, Emily took herself off with an impatient flounce for my lack of spirit. I wondered how much she had observed in recent days that I had missed. No matter, I was full of resolve now, and I would waste none of it fretting about Adriana. She was leaving and that was all that mattered. With luck, I wouldn't have to see her at all before she left.

I should have known better. I had paid my respects to little Charles, in his bath, and told Ned to bring the carriage around in half an hour, for I was going to visit Commander Jardine. Then I went to my rooms to prepare for the journey. I had donned a red woolen dress and was getting my warmest travel cloak from the wardrobe when Adriana entered my sitting room, as self-possessed as if the previous night had never been.

"Dear Margaret, I've come to say good-bye." She extended both hands to me, her head tipped prettily to one side. "Duty calls me home."

I would as soon have clutched a snake as touch those hands. When I turned away and busied myself with my preparations, she dropped gracefully onto my chaise longue and smoothed her silk skirt demurely over her ankles.

"My poor grandfather, the patriarch of our family, has been called to God."

"Perhaps he will put in a good word for you."

She laughed, turning her head to admire her reflection in a nearby wall mirror. "Oh, he's done rather better than that. I was a great favorite of his. He admired women of spirit, and so I inherit a most impressive fortune. Are you not pleased for me, Margaret?"

"It requires that you return to Italy? Nothing could make me happier."

"Ah, well, don't fret, darling. I promise to return. Where else could I hope to find two such devoted friends as you and dear Oliver?"

I turned my back to her and stared out the window at the runnels of half-frozen rain inching down the panes. My heart and my voice were as icy.

"I suggest you try America. Or Russia. Anywhere, so long as it is a continent away."

"Margaret!" Adriana pretended to pout. "You don't mean that. After we have shared so much——"

"Most notably my husband."

"Darling! Surely you don't mind? I would share mine with you gladly, though at the moment I don't have one. But perhaps the next time I visit you—what a splendid idea, Margaret!"

I whirled to face her, unable to stand more of her insolence.

"Get out! You, your maid, everything—take your possessions and get out of my house!"

Adriana sat up in my chaise longue and arched her body in a leisurely stretch, laughing at me. "All of my possessions, Margaret? No, no, I'll leave Oliver with you. For the moment."

She got to her feet and surveyed me with eyes that belied the easy amusement of her taunts. There was no laughter in those gleaming amber depths, only implacable hate. Eyes that hunted me down to devour me, hungry to savor every misery she could inflict.

"Think of me while we're apart, darling Margaret, for I am bound to you by ties I couldn't loosen if I wished"—there was a fondness in her voice, a poisoned sweetness that made the hair at the nape of my neck prickle—"closer than a sister, more attentive than a lover. . . . You will never be alone while I live Margaret. Do you not understand that yet?"

With that, Adriana Rantana walked swiftly across my room and out of my life. She would be back one day, as she promised, and the thought filled me with unutterable weariness. I shook it off impatiently. I'd deal with that when it happened. Being rid of Adriana, even temporarily, was bliss. Snatching up my travel cloak and a cashmere shawl, I hurried down the grand stairs. Ned would have the carriage around by now.

CHAPTER 28

I had decided to use the lumbering old coach we now reserved for state occasions and long journeys. I would have preferred the faster new phaeton, with its light steel shafts and stripped-down elegance, but the coach would afford more protection if we were obliged to go all the way to Holylake. But first I ordered Ned to drive down Water Street to the Clarence docks, to the offices that had once been the headquarters of the Millbrook Line and now bore the insignia of Jardine and Company.

As I had feared, Commander Jardine was not there, nor expected. Neither was he at the rooms he kept in Ranclagh Street. There was nothing for it but to continue on to Holylake. Ned, up on the box, was bundled into his heaviest coat with thick caped shoulders. A woolen scarf, wound over his tall hat to hold it in place, was twisted and tied to cover most of his face, for there was a bitter wind.

The high wheels of the old coach splashed and churned over the roadway as we hurtled our way toward the Mersey, and the Liverpool-Birkenhead ferry. Ned brought the coach to a halt on the square deck of the ferry barge and I peered out through the curtains. Steam rising from the horses mingled with the pall of rain and fog that hung over the river. There was a small steamer alongside, linked to us by heavy, black-tarred hawsers, and aboard I could see two black-faced tenders stirring the flaming coal bank. As I watched, a cloud of sooty smoke broke from the steamer, its engine hissed and spat, and then, slowly, amidst much shouting and bustling about, it began to move out into the mud-colored river, towing our cumbersome bulk in its wake.

Once on the other side of the Mersey, we turned right, toward the Bootle Light. I braced my feet and clung to the hand strap to keep my balance as we swayed over the deep, half-frozen ruts of the King's Parade. The sleety rain continued unabated and I was grateful for the fur rug tucked around me. Across the top of the Wirral Peninsula the wind caught and tossed the downpour into frenzied whirls against the windows, so that half the time the coach seemed to be swimming through an eerie underwater world. As we progressed through that winter-bleak landscape, I felt my early-morning courage dissolve into amorphous fear and melancholy. The ghost of my stepmother's presence was close, and her Curse rode at my side in the coach. I seemed again to feel her thin hand fastening on my wrist, to hear her voice on the cold sea breath that coated the carriage windows with ice: *"To you, Margaret, I bequeath the Curse of the Flowers ..."* I saw her again in my night's dream, bedecked with the red poppies, leading Oliver off into some oblivion where he would be lost to me forever.

A fearful quaking began deep inside me, and I clasped my hands tightly together to stop their trembling. Beneath my fear seethed a rage that had been building within me for weeks, a rage born of helpless frustration in the face of this manipulation I endured at the hands of others—and of fate. By the time we reached the gatehouse that marked the outer boundary of the Holylake estate, my teeth were chattering and I was muttering French curses under my breath. The sea-borne chill had settled in my soul and I longed to be free of the imprisoning coach, to shriek defiance and demand of God that Adriana and my dead stepmother go back to whatever hell had spawned them and leave me in peace!

We rattled over the slippery cobbles and then, with much straining and churning of mud, lurched our way up the twisting road that climbed the mount. Stunted trees and shrubs, eternally blasted by the winds off the Irish Sea, looked like huddled gray gnomes, marking my progress with malicious amusement, jeering at the alien entering their domain. I shook my fist at them, and a moment later was glad there was no one to witness my folly. With an effort I wrenched my mind back to reality and my errand. Commander Matthew Jardine had grown sleek on the profits of his poisonous opium trafficking. Now he could cope with its less-pleasant manifestations within his own family.

We drew up in the courtyard before the heavy oak double

doors of the ancient priory. I was admitted to the drafty hall
by Meredith, the wizened old man who had opened the door
to me that first day, when I had come here seeking Oliver
and found, instead, my stepmother. Now, as then, the sound
of the sea breaking far below was a continual muffled thunder, beating its fists on the foundation of the fortress.

Commander Jardine came hurrying along an arched gothic
passageway into the vast, ill-lighted hall.

"Margaret! What brings you here on a day like this? You
look half frozen. Come back to my library, there's a good fire
there. You must have a hot drink to take away the chill.
Meredith, a hot rum for Mrs. Jardine."

The library proved habitable, though not proof against the
sound of that pounding surf. A wide fireplace housed a cheerful blaze, and heavy draperies of maroon velvet were drawn
close across the windows to ward off drafts. It was an old-
fashioned room, oak-paneled, with a high beamed ceiling and
a motley collection of books on two walls. There was an
enormous oil painting of a sea battle—Trafalgar, I
thought—on a wall behind Commander Jardine's heavy oak
desk. Near it hung a large, framed map of the East, with
dragons frolicking in its seas. I could imagine Commander
Jardine spending long hours gazing at that map and dreaming
of past glories, for the rest of the room reflected his many
journeys to the East. A weighty brass plaque featuring a
fierce, grimacing dragon hung between two windows. A red-
lacquered chest, with a Chinese scene picked out in gilt, held
an array of jade carvings and porcelain jars that looked to be
of great value. On the floor, Chinese rugs glowed with rich
color that breathed warmth and life into the room.

Commander Jardine, as if pleased to have an opportunity
to play host, ensconced me in a large chair, with my feet on a
stool and a mug of the promised hot rum in my hand.

"Now, Margaret," he beamed when I was settled to his satisfaction, "what brings you so far on this blustery day? Oliver
continues to mend, I trust?"

He was a disarming old rogue. If he had a weak spot, it
was his reluctant pride in Oliver, though he had been able to
sink it without a trace when it suited him—which appeared
to be most of the time. I wondered how young Howard
Jardine fared in this austere and elderly household. No doubt
as well as he would have had his mother lived, if my own experience proved anything.

"Oliver's burns are healed, though the scars are still livid.

They will fade with time, so Dr. Beck assures us. It is not Oliver's burns that bring me here, but Oliver's head."

"His head? Surely there was no injury to his head?"

The anger that had been simmering inside me erupted into frenzy. I was on my feet, shaking and screaming in blind fury.

"You poor fool! Don't you know what you've done? Oliver is addicted to opium! *Your* Curse—the biblical eye for an eye; only Oliver must bear it instead of you, who earned it! Do you enjoy the irony of that? Is it worth all your tainted money—your ridiculous swagger and stupid delusions of grandeur?"

I collapsed into a fit of weeping I could not control. I didn't want to cry, I wanted to pummel that arrogant, greedy old man until he cried out for mercy, and my helpless sobbing only fed the inner fury.

"Oliver. So strong and good and brave. And you brought him down, didn't you? The agony he has had to endure. And the foundering of our hopes, the success we've worked so hard to achieve. And now *this*!"

It was as if time stood still in that old-fashioned room, suspended in silence except for my rasping sobs and gasps for breath. For I was not crying prettily into a lace handkerchief, but from some depths within my soul that had stored up all of my grief and had now burst its bonds.

Eventually I looked up, sodden and snuffling. Commander Matthew Jardine was slumped in his chair as if struck by a fist. His ruddy color had paled to a sickly hue and my first thought was that he had been stricken with a heart attack. Or by God. As he deserved! But he stirred and then tugged at the bell rope nearby. Meredith appeared immediately, and I knew he had been listening outside the half-opened library door, for he was too feeble to have moved so swiftly from the back of the house.

"Cognac," Commander Jardine grated out in a voice rusty with contained emotion. "Two large ones, Meredith, and leave the bottle close at hand."

I accepted my cognac gratefully and Meredith placed the bottle on a tray near Commander Jardine.

"Close the door on your way out," Jardine growled in a voice intending offense which Meredith ignored. No doubt he was inured to it. Commander Jardine would not be an easy man to live with.

When the door had closed behind the old man, Matthew Jardine straightened in his chair. "How sure are you?"

"He takes no interest in our business venture—his beloved steam vessels. Or in anything else, for that matter. He shrugs off good news and bad, it's all one to him. He eats poorly and has a sickly pallor—"

"Damn me, Margaret, it's the dead of winter. When spring comes . . ."

". . . he will be worse! His progress is steadily downhill. I tell you, he cares for nothing! And he tells me—*me*—that I take too much care, that I should relax, life is meant to be tranquil."

I challenged that hateful old man to fob me off with some stupid sop of small talk.

But he didn't. "How much does he use?" Commander Jardine asked finally, his voice admitting the truth.

I shook my head. "I have no way of knowing. Until yesterday I didn't know he still relied on it. He mentions only that he takes a few drops at night, in milk. To make him sleep! Dear God, he never *wakes*—not truly, not the man within."

Again silence claimed the room. Commander Jardine was sunk in some dark-browed inner vision that admitted of no interruption. Despite the warmth of the cognac, ice was settling around my heart, for his fear seemed greater than mine. Unconsciously I had counted on his rising to the occasion, lifting the burden from me. Instead, I felt as if a new burden had been added. I had no idea what to do. My thoughts had taken me no further than my anger—to this man and his responsibility.

When I thought I would surely stand and scream, Matthew Jardine rose from his chair and, grasping the cognac bottle by its neck, refilled my glass and then his own. Meredith had given me a good portion and I had not noticed that it was gone. No matter, I welcomed it if it would only numb my aching mind. That realization made me cringe; I was like Oliver—seeking nepenthe! I shook myself free of the delusion. There was a difference of degree, if nothing else. Too much sympathy for Oliver would serve him badly. As self-pity would cripple me.

"Very well, Margaret. We will accept it as fact that my son Oliver has fallen prey to the damned poppy." He fixed me with those protuberant blue eyes and I saw there was strength within the man, behind all his bluster.

"Perhaps you are right in thinking there is a Curse and

that this is a manifestation of it. God knows, there are plenty out East who would agree with you. But that solves nothing. To cringe and cry and throw up our hands won't help Oliver."

"Indeed?" I muttered. "No doubt you will?"

"I will." He said it so staunchly that for a moment I felt a stir of hope. But Matthew Jardine was a braggart, an arrogant old fool who believed his own lies and embroidered his life with dreams. I refused to let him get away with cheap bravado.

"You will give up the opium trade, perhaps? Make a bargain with God? If I understood my stepmother correctly . . . your wife"—I gave him an insulting little bow of the head—"there is no bargaining that avails. The Curse is visited on the heads of those who are in the traffic and their kin, down through the generations. God knows, we have evidence to support the view. My father, my stepmother, the destruction of Greystones, the ruin of the *Jardine*—and now this! Oliver."

But Commander Jardine was on his feet, pacing the room with his glass left on a table and his hands clasped behind his back. The light blue eyes seemed to peer over some distant horizon, as if he were on board that Royal Navy ship of the line he had commanded for so long.

"Don't be a fool, Margaret." He flung the words at me over his shoulder. "What you are tallying up so sadly is *life*. Did you expect to go through unscathed, woman? There are deaths and disasters everywhere, you needn't deal in opium to discover them touching your life. *You're* alive, aren't you? And so is Oliver. As long as you're alive and kicking, you can still win!"

One half of my mind welcomed his words, for their hope. The other half resented his easy acceptance of troubles that were mine through no fault of my own.

"More talk, Commander Jardine—or are you prepared to make some sacrifice for your son?"

He wheeled around and the frosty eyes fixed on me. "Such as?"

"Give up the opium trade! Renounce it, and hope that God will know."

Matthew Jardine refilled his glass and resumed his chair. "I think more direct action is called for." He held up a restraining hand as I was about to burst forth again. "No, listen."

I remained silent as he settled in his chair.

"I served in Nelson's fleet. I was with him at Trafalgar, a line officer aboard the first-rater *Agamemnon*. And something of a hero, incidentally. My reward in peacetime was command of His Majesty's brig, the *McIntosh*, at the age of twenty-seven. On the Singapore station first, then Calcutta. It was as commander of the *McIntosh* that I became part of the 'old' trade. Authorized smuggling of opium."

"Authorized?" I sat up smartly. "By whom?"

He shrugged, a slight smile playing about his full lips. "The trade existed. Even the Honourable Company, the East India Company, traded in opium. And the Royal Navy protected their vessels. So they were more or less obliged to protect the vessels of other English merchants engaged in the lucrative trade. More than fifteen British firms in Calcutta traded opium, and others out of Singapore. A nefarious business, no doubt, but its practice was well known to the First Sea Lord and the Select Lords for Admiralty Affairs who sat in the Upper House."

"I don't believe it!"

Commander Jardine gave a shout of harsh laughter. "No? It shocks your delicate sensibilities? All the same, it's true. Many a 'tea wagon'—it's what we called the big, cumbersome East Indiamen—I've convoyed up to the Bocca Tigris, carrying four hundred or more chests of the best Malwa. Worth a hundred thousand quid, Margaret!"

Again he shrugged his powerful shoulders. "Oh, I don't say it was precisely approved. But it was tolerated, just as escorting slavers was tolerated before my time. Both trades, drugs and slaving, were sanctioned as suitably profitable for English owners and English tonnage." He leaned back and shot me a cynical look from under sandy brows. "We're a practical people, Margaret. Keep it in mind."

"Corrupt!"

He gave me a sour grin. "It didn't trouble my conscience. Why should it? It didn't bother England's."

"Perhaps you will see it somewhat differently now," I observed with an unpleasant smile of my own, "but frankly, I care very little for your conscience, Matthew Jardine. If it exists at all. I care only about Oliver."

He nodded his large, shaggy head. "The present. I agree, and so I propose to return to Liverpool with you and stay at Calcutta House, close to Oliver, for as long as necessary. You realize that Oliver will at first deny that he is addicted? And then fight to protect his addiction?"

I nodded. I had thought of trying to influence the granite-hard will within Oliver Jardine, but knew I was no match for that, reinforced with addiction.

"If I'm to cope with this matter," Matthew Jardine continued, "I want it clearly understood that I am in full charge. I will do the talking, I will make the proposals. Agreed?"

When I hesitated, every instinct within me unwilling to trust him so completely, he spoke brusquely. "You understand nothing of this. I do. And I understand my son. The man cannot be hag-ridden, pecked to death, or we'll lose him. My way will work. Make up your mind."

Reluctantly, I nodded. Trust him I did not, but his words conjured up an image of Oliver, his temper flaring, while I cajoled—and went down to defeat. Oliver was what mattered now.

Matthew Jardine got to his feet and pulled the tasseled bell rope near his chair. "Then that's settled. Now we will have tea, for we have a long drive ahead. And then we must be off. The problem won't improve for waiting."

It was on the road back to Liverpool, in the dim seclusion of the coach, that I at last gained some insight into the ambition that drove Matthew Jardine. Perhaps in no other milieu would he have so openly revealed the devil that rode him. But the coach that night was a world apart. The rain had ceased and even the wind had died to no more than an occasional gust. The coach rattled and bounced on that uneven roadway as Ned drove the horses to their utmost. But inside, we were isolated from what had gone before and what would come after. The hanging lamp swung and flickered; its fitful shadows created a mysterious ambience of hypnotic power, soothing us into an intimacy foreign to our normal view of each other.

Weary from an eventful day, I had fallen into the trancelike state that precedes sleep when Matthew Jardine began to speak.

"I will tell you a story, Margaret. I know you have never liked me, yet we are doubly related. Perhaps it is a duty to try to understand those whose lives fate has interlocked with yours, through no fault of your own."

I neither moved nor spoke, for there was no need. Somehow, I knew that what I was about to hear required nothing from me but my listening presence.

"Once there was a family who lived in an ancient, threadbare sort of castle. Or something resembling a castle, with turrets and a tower and a sea all around it. They were of high birth, linked by blood to a family some consider the highest in England—the Howards of Norfolk. Their lineage ran back to royalty—on *one* side of the family. But they were poor. Their land was not prosperous and they had no old wealth to draw on. Also, there was an ancient blot on their escutcheon, so though they were of noble birth, they were without title and privilege. With no other doors open to them, their sons, for generations, entered the Royal Navy. It was a way up. Though not as far as they longed for, and were born to.

"Eventually, a son of the family achieved notable distinction in a war, which proved fortuitous for him. When the war ended he was made a commander of a ship of the line. For the first time, a way began to open up. Perhaps it was the added opportunity—or it may have been the nature of the man himself, for he had always hungered for what had so long eluded his forebears. Whatever the reason, he determined that he would someday restore the family to its rightful place. I am that man . . . and I bided my time."

The swaying carriage lamp cast its light directly on Matthew Jardine's face. For a moment I saw written there the fierce singleness of purpose that would have accounted for his heroism long years ago at Trafalgar. Just so would he have looked swinging aboard an enemy vessel, slashing his way along a slippery deck, cutlass high and hacking a path before him. Nothing about him had mellowed with the years. He was still fighting to win.

"I was retired from command of the *McIntosh* in eighteen thirty-five, after more than thirty years' service in the Royal Navy. Fifty-four years old, and all I knew was the sea. There was Oliver to educate, Holylake to keep up—or to keep from falling down—and no money. A small pension from the Navy; England is not generous to her erstwhile heroes. Our Howard cousins provided a small honorarium, but withal there was not enough to go round. I made a decision to wait no longer. I would do what I knew best. Before I left the East I made arrangements.

"I had friends, masters of Royal Navy vessels that put in to Liverpool regularly. Opium smuggling was nothing new to

them, any more than it was to me. They were willing to bring
in supplies for me, for a share of the transaction. At first, I
told myself it was opium for medical purposes, to alleviate
suffering. I wanted to see how I would prosper, what the
danger might be on this end of the proceedings. There was
none, I soon discovered, and so I branched out quickly into
serving certain apothecaries where the drug was sold to mill
operatives. Comfort, Margaret, comfort for the oppressed."

At that note of irony, I knew I needed to say nothing.
He was fully aware of what he did.

"I met your mother, and we recognized each other as
kindred souls. By then I had a modest fortune and—well, you
know how we took over your father's shipping line."

He broke off his narrative abruptly, casting me a troubled
look. "Since your father's death there have been—rumors. I
don't know how much truth there is in them, but I swear to
you, whether you believe me or not, that at the time I
thought your father's illness a natural one and the fire an accident." He waited for me to respond, but I said nothing. After a long pause, he went on with his story.

"At last I had what I'd dreamed of, my own ships under
my own name! I was a man of property, commercial
property, and that was to be the apparent source of the fortune I intended to amass. The fortune I needed to make the
Howard relatives take proper notice of me and see that something was done about the peerage I was entitled to by birth;
and by dint of a distinguished career, first in the Royal Navy,
and then in commerce."

"Peerage?" I sat up abruptly. "You seriously intend to
achieve peerage through a fortune made in smuggling opium?
My God, Matthew, are you mad?"

An expression of incredible insolence settled over his heavy
features. "I want my birthright! Lord Jardine!" He stared at
that in his mind for a moment, his face beatific with the ring
of it in his ears. "Lord Jardine." He turned to me with an eager smile. "Think of what it will mean to you, Margaret, and
to Oliver. To your son!"

I waved away such vagaries. It was impossible. But all the
same, for one mad moment I entertained his dream, for
Charles's sake. No doubt Matthew watched the expression
flitting across my face, for he smiled and patted my hand.

"Oh, it's not the mad raving you think, my girl. It's solid
enough. I tell you, the Jardines are directly related to the
Norfolk Howards—to the Duke of Arundel, Surrey and Nor-

folk, the hereditary Earl Marshal of England! That's assurance enough of automatic peerage!"

It needed no thought on my part to recognize the truth of his words. But why, then, had it been denied?

Matthew watched me, a quizzical expression on his face now that he had secured his audience.

"I told you at the start of this story, Margaret, that we are linked to the Norfolk Howards on *one* side of the family. Now you had better hear of the other side—the Jardines. It was just after Elizabeth's time that one of the Howard daughters married a seaman. The seaman's name was Jardine. A rumor persisted that his time at sea was spent aboard a pirate vessel, and some of his booty came from British ships. That closed the royal door with a slam! Oh, the Howard marriage raised us in the world to a degree. The Jardine men, thereafter, served as officers in the British Navy for generations. The truth is that we're a hard lot. Sea lords, born sea fighters, with a native streak of brutality that's served us well in the past—and still appears now and again."

Matthew Jardine's face bore a smile of perverse self-satisfaction, for he knew himself to be a Jardine in every way and was proud of it. God knows, I had to agree that the streak of piracy existed in him. I was inclined to believe his protestations of innocence in regard to my father's illness and death, but I knew what he had done to the ships of the Millbrook Line and to the *Jardine*. And I had had glimmerings of that same ruthless streak in Oliver—a tough determination to have what he wanted, no matter what the price or who was to pay it. That blood ran in Charles, too, I realized with foreboding. But Matthew continued in his dream.

"I'm almost there, Margaret, almost there, after all these years. The Howards will have to take notice and do something about us; we're part of them, and the pirate forebear is ancient history now. It's the fortune that will make the difference. I've already spoken to Norfolk about returning the title that should be ours. He's a decent sort of fellow, he's as good as promised to speak to Her Majesty and the Lord Privy Seal on my behalf."

In spite of myself, I had started to believe him. "What title, Matthew?"

"Viscount Jardine of Birkenhead, in Cheshire." The words rolled off his tongue with the ease of practice, something he had savored over and over again in his reveries. "Matthew Howard Jardine, Eighth Viscount of Birkenhead."

A long silence fell in the old coach, broken only by the rumbling of the wheels over the metaled streets of Liverpool. Finally I roused and sighed.

"Matthew, the source of this fortune you talk of so glibly, what if it becomes known? Surely then there will be no peerage for you."

He turned on me with a low-throated growl. "It will not become known. It had better *not* become known, Margaret, through your efforts!"

I waved that away. "Don't be a fool. I share the Jardine name now, for better or worse. And I have a son to think of. But surely there is too much risk? Matthew"—I looked at him pleadingly—"this is the time to give up that evil trade. Before it brings your whole dream down in ruins."

He folded his arms across his massive chest and stared straight before him. His face, by the light of the swaying lamp, was a study in chiaroscuro. How like the gleaming granite rocks of Holylake the Jardine men could be, when faced with opinions contrary to their wishes!

"Later, Margaret. I cannot stop yet, for good and sufficient reasons which need not concern you."

"Greed!"

"Not greed. Business situations which you would not comprehend."

"Indeed, Matthew Jardine? I comprehend well enough that you're risking our good name to satisfy your own ambition and avarice! How can you tempt fate still further, after all the evil you've already created?"

But Matthew Jardine might as well have been deaf, for his face remained adamant. We rode the rest of the way to Calcutta House in angry silence.

CHAPTER 29

The week that followed Commander Jardine's joining of our household was one of chaos. I had promised that I would not interfere in his handling of his son, and I was content with that bargain, for Oliver's attitude proved to be all that I had feared, and more.

He accepted his father's "visit" with mildly pleased indifference. Like everything, now, it appeared to have little meaning for him. As for Matthew, he set about the business at hand with dispatch. He first called on Dr. Beck, to inform him of Oliver's addiction, and to make sure that no further supply of opium would be forthcoming from that quarter. He returned to Calcutta House in a temper.

"The man's a fool or a knave! Probably both. Greatly surprised at 'this disturbing news.' " Matthew's voice was heavy with sarcasm. "Then, damn me, he shrugged it off, easy as you please. Nothing to do with him, he had no idea of Oliver's 'unfortunate predilection'! He did allow that 'these things will happen sometimes.' Damned quack! I don't doubt he kills more patients than he cures."

Commander Jardine stamped off to the kitchens, where he called a meeting of the household staff. He spelled out the nature of our dilemma and threatened instant dismissal to any servant who pandered to Mr. Jardine's habit. I don't doubt that his stentorian voice and ferocious temper made his message abundantly clear. Later, while we were at dinner, Matthew left the table and investigated Oliver's rooms, commandeering a dozen bottles of the tincture of opium, secreted in a chest of drawers. He left the half bottle that stood on the bedside table.

After dinner, when the three of us sat in the drawing room, in the most matter-of-fact manner Matthew Jardine taxed his son with the fact of his addiction. He spoke of it as an understandable result of Oliver's illness and as if the necessity of effecting a cure immediately were obvious to all three of us. Oliver, far from flying into a rage, as I had expected, smiled indulgently.

"Nonsense. Addicted to opium?" He flicked the idea away. "I'm not one of those unfortunates who fill your pocket, sir. But no doubt you've steeped in the stuff so long that your own sensibilities are dulled to the proper use of opium in modern medicine."

He leaned back in his chair, unruffled in his humor, and nothing Matthew said, no accusation or dire warning, penetrated that amused indifference. Oliver was tolerant of his father's fanciful notion, but unconcerned. He refused to say how many drops of the tincture he used in a day. What we mistook for addiction, he insisted, was merely a normal medicinal reliance on the drug, quite justified by the pain it alleviated.

Oliver's very plausibility added to my horror, for it revealed the depths of his intent to deceive us—and himself. Next morning brought a very different reaction. Oliver had discovered the loss of his supply, and his good humor vanished abruptly. He complained bitterly of the pain he endured, the deserved relief he was deprived of, and lashed out at us with the fierce anger of those unjustly treated. He stormed and ranted in a towering rage; and then, as his meager strength was quickly spent, lapsed into a state of melancholy, shaking and weeping, his face clammy with cold sweat. Only then did Commander Jardine administer a few drops of the tincture he had taken from Oliver's rooms, for truly, Oliver was in a sorry state. Despite my own pity for this man whom I loved so dearly, I wondered at Matthew's knowledge. He obviously understood what he was about, and proceeded with calm self-assurance.

Our days were now filled with alternating storms of rage and fits of gloom. Oliver, obliged to wait for his next dole of medicine, suffered the torment of cramps, and a restlessness that gave him no peace. When he had worn himself out with ranting, he would sink into an apathy of misery. His hands shook abominably; he had fits of violent yawning and sneezing that left him exhausted and gasping for breath. He had no time for poor little Charles, and for me evinced only loathing, for I was party to this cruelty he was subjected to.

After several days of suffering through the reduced rations of his drug, Oliver came to see me privately. I was in the library, which served as my office, making a poor pretense at working, for I could think of nothing but Oliver and his misery.

"Margaret. Help me!" He was drawn and worn looking, his broad shoulders so hunched in dejection that he seemed shrunken in size. The hoarse, soft-spoken voice wrenched at my heart. "I can't fight that old fool. He maunders on about opium addiction while I suffer. Surely *you* know better than that, Margaret. I know that you love me, you can't want to see me in this hell of pain."

He held out his arms to me like a child and I flew from behind my desk to comfort him. He felt so thin, so spare and bony under my hands, that the fear of his addiction paled beside the sudden fear that I might lose him to death, after all he had suffered to escape it in the long months after the fire.

"Margaret, little Margaret, you will help me, won't you?"

His voice cajoled, and in that moment I felt I would do anything to save him this misery.

"You must go at once, my darling, to the apothecary in Castle Street. I'll give you a note to present to Mr. Harris, the chemist there—"

"No, Oliver!" It burst from me in an agony of fear and frustration. "You mustn't ask me that. Matthew is allowing you all that is reasonable; we want only to help you, darling—"

He shoved me from him so that I would have fallen if the desk had not been behind me. "Bitch! You'd side with him against your own husband? I tell you I must have it, I *must*—"

At that moment Matthew Jardine, who kept close watch on his son, entered the library and took in the situation at a glance.

"So, Oliver? You *must* have it? Would you care to tell me again that you are not addicted to opium? After you have tried to bribe Ned to run your errand, and little Jessie, the upstairs maid? And now Margaret? It would do you no good in any case. Neither Mr. Harris nor any other supplier will sell to you, for I've warned them. They value my services far higher than your custom. Why not admit that you are caught? Then perhaps we can make some progress."

Within minutes I was shaking as badly as poor Oliver, for much as I loved him I was seeing a different creature revealed. He pleaded and cajoled and wept. When that proved fruitless, he shouted imprecations on both of our heads, swept everything from my desk in a clatter of paper and broken glass, and snatched up a brass candlestick to swing at Matthew. He was far too weak, and no match against the brawny arms and shoulders of his father. Matthew caught and held him fast, like a child, while Oliver raved and wept.

At last he fell silent and Matthew Jardine lowered him into a chair. Oliver sat there, spent and gasping for breath, his once-proud head bowed; a man bereft of all hope and pride.

"All right," he whispered when he was able to speak. "All right, damn you! What does it matter? Call it anything you like. I *must have* the damned stuff, can you understand that?" He looked miserably up at his father, who stood with sturdy legs planted, arms folded across his barrel chest.

Commander Jardine nodded. "I understand. Better than you know. Oliver, do you want to be cured of this devil that drives you?"

"No." Oliver's voice was unutterably weary. "I want what I *want*. Anyway"—his words were so low we could barely hear them—"it's too late. I cannot be cured. I cannot *endure*—" He put his head in his shaking hands and wept.

My heart wept with and for him, but I made no move to comfort him. He needed strength to draw on, not weakness. Commander Jardine was made of sterner stuff. If Oliver's tears moved him, he gave no sign.

"You *can* endure, Oliver. And you will. I'll see to that. You will be cured. I won't lose another. . . ."

I dashed the tears from my eyes to stare at him. ". . . lose another?"

Matthew Jardine shook his head impatiently. "Dear God, did you think I was born knowing about this?" His hand indicated Oliver and his condition. "I lost a brother—Ronald Jardine—out East."

His words, or perhaps the bitterness behind them, penetrated Oliver's consciousness. "Uncle Ronald? He died of dysentery. On the Calcutta station."

"He died of opium in a stinking Calcutta alley! Pock-marked, hairless, white as milk and just as weak."

Commander Jardine paced the length of the library and returned to fix us with his prominent eyes. "Ronald started using opium on the Singapore station. A lot of Royal Navy officers smoked the water pipe, but Ronald couldn't manage it without going to excess."

Matthew's big, rusty-haired fists closed convulsively. "I daresay I spent years and a fortune trying to get him off the bloody stuff. Time and again I hauled him away from verminous pallets in stinking dens, cheek by jowl with the dregs of the Calcutta waterfront. No silken couches and perfumed houris to sweeten your pipe dreams in those hells, Oliver! You push your way in past greasy curtains, to the sound of that damned reedy music of theirs. Creaking punkahs barely stir the hot reek of the place. And there they slouch, dreaming over their water pipes, watching a few young girls dance and crawl about the floor, manipulating their bodies to pick up the tossed coins. And there would lie Ronald—among the Malays and the lascars—no different from the rest."

Commander Jardine's harsh voice broke. When he spoke again his tone was no longer angry, but infinitely sad.

"He was the handsome one, I was the rough-looking brute. I remember him as a boy, laughing and easy to like, full of promise and ready for anything. But there was something lacking, some strength he was born without. . . ."

Oliver, though visibly shaken by the story, roused himself to a semblance of his earlier anger. "The moral of your story is that I've inherited your brother's weakness, is that it?" He managed a sardonic laugh. "Preaching hellfire and damnation at me—and up to your armpits in the trade yourself!"

"Goddamn it, don't play clever with me!" his father thundered. "I mean what I say. Understand that, Oliver. I am not going to lose a son as I lost a brother!"

"No? Then clean out your own stable before you come around mucking out mine!"

Matthew's face turned purple and veins stood out on his temples.

"You bloody fool! I've got too much invested to get out now!"

Oliver shrugged and closed his eyes.

Commander Jardine struggled visibly for control of his choleric rage. He lowered his heavy body into a chair close to Oliver, and fished a large black cigar from his waistcoat pocket. When he had it alight, he blew a smoke ring and studied it silently before he spoke.

"Listen to me, Oliver. I am here to help you—"

"Guilt."

"All right, guilt! *Mea culpa.* Is that what you want to hear? I am responsible for the fire and therefore for the opium and your addiction. I am responsible for the trouble the Blue Funnel line is faced with. But I'm here now to strike a bargain with you. All I ask is that you work with me. You're getting along with one hundred fifty drops of opium a day. I judge that to be several *thousand* less than you were taking when I arrived. You have a long way to go, but I can make it worth your while."

"You'll give up the opium trade, Matthew?" It slipped from my lips before I thought. I was rewarded with a black scowl.

"We will speak of that later. For the moment, I wish to deal with a more immediate problem. Your finances. As you know, I have made a great deal of money in what you both choose to regard as an evil. Much of it went to commission two new sailing vessels, the *Blue Heron* and the *Spindrift.* Beautiful things, both of them. Clippers. Like great white birds skimming along the waves." Matthew's eyes were alight with enthusiasm.

"You have to see them in motion to understand what these Americans have done. 'Virginia Built' they call them, with thin V-shaped hulls and long, sleek flanks running back to a raking stem. Oliver, I tell you they can easily do eleven knots and better, for they carry every inch of canvas possible. Ringtails, moonrakers, skysails—"

He caught himself up, aware that he was letting his enthusiasm carry him off the subject. But I noticed that Oliver's eyes were open.

"These two vessels, plus the brandy trade purchased from Margaret's father, are my assets, Oliver."

The old rogue, with his seafighter's face and brassy confidence, looked from Oliver to me, and back again. "I propose that we join forces. Amalgamate the two lines—Jardine and Company and the Blue Funnel Steam and Navigation Company—to form Jardine Steam and Navigation Company, or Jardine–Blue Funnel, as you choose; and use the profits from my enterprise to advance your interest, steamships for the Atlantic trade."

Despite my native distrust of Matthew Howard Jardine, I felt a surge of emotion. In the face of so generous an offer I could no longer doubt his distress at what he had done to Oliver, nor his deep love for his son. A man who, in his own words, "liked to be right," was prepared to go against his own nature and give way to Oliver's dream.

For a glorious moment I thought that our problems were about to be solved. And then I remembered the Curse. Dear God! Was I seriously considering linking our future to Matthew's nefarious trade, when even an indirect link in the past had brought nothing but disaster in its wake?

In the waiting silence I glanced fearfully at Oliver. Here was his dream made possible. I would have to do battle now against both of these men, and one of them, my darling, ill and in need of my support.

It is a wonder that I have any self-confidence left, for it seems I so often read a situation amiss. Far from leaping to accept his father's offer, Oliver weighed the matter, nodding.

"So we are to solve all of our problems according to expediency?" He turned his gaze on me, and his eyes held the dangerous quicksilver glow that I knew spelled trouble.

"What do you say, Margaret? Shall we accept? Forget, once and for all, this Curse you prate on about, and go where the money is?"

I sat tongue-tied. Everything within me wanted to shout

out refusal. But there was Oliver to consider. I loved him better than my life, better than anything in the world except
Charles, who was part of both of us and deserved our best efforts for his future. I had a dizzying, kaleidoscopic vision of
my father dying in the flames of Greystones—my
stepmother's willful evil that put her self-pride and her wealth
before all else—Adriana, who thrived on perverting any good
that crossed her path—and of my own poor efforts to improve my ways. Now I stood at a crossroads. The choice was
mine to make, and the eyes of the two Jardine men gave me
no quarter.

"We will accept Commander Jardine's offer," I said slowly,
choosing my words, "if he agrees to engage his vessels in a legitimate trade. On the Atlantic, or where he chooses. But not
for the smuggling of opium. I have had enough of curses."

I sat upright but sodden with fear, waiting for Oliver to
rail, weep, or whatever his condition would permit, for I had
no hope I had made a choice he could agree with. Driven by
his opium-needing restlessness, he got to his feet and paced
back and forth across the Turkey-red carpet, nodding, sneezing, but with a dignity of his own despite that.

"Then there's your answer, sir. You cannot sink your guilt
quite so easily as you had hoped. Not that your offer isn't
more than generous, and we thank you. But my wife does not
fancy the price tag attached. Nor do I."

He stopped in front of his father's chair, a faint smile on
his face. "If my affliction is so odious to you, sir, then I suggest that we give up opium together."

I loved Oliver at that moment more than ever before in
our life together. He left the room swiftly, for he was in a
pitiable state and perhaps he knew that his strength would
not withstand further pressure. I felt a twinge of pity for
Matthew Jardine, but I hurried after Oliver, up the grand
stairs, to his rooms. I helped him to undress and had Emily
bring heated bricks wrapped in flannel to place against his
back; he was shuddering and ice cold. Emily and I together
massaged his legs and his arms with liniment, for his muscles
were knotted with fearsome cramps that made him cry out.
In an hour it was time for his next portion of opium drops.
Commander Jardine, stone-faced and silent, administered
them.

I longed to crawl into Oliver's bed and hold him through
the night, but I dared not. He suffered from terrifying
dreams, and surged from one side of the bed to the other.

Emily brought me a blanket and Ned moved my chaise longue from my sitting room to Oliver's bedside. I did not know whether or not my presence made any difference to him, but it was a comfort to me, even when he woke me by crying out. I was there, close by, even if I could do nothing.

The following morning Oliver was haunted by the memory of the horrible dreams that had plagued him through the night. Matthew, for reasons of his own, decided not to further decrease the dosage of opium that day, though I believed he would have if the quarrel the previous evening had resolved his and Oliver's differences. As it was, he waited until his son's midafternoon allotment of the drug had taken effect and Oliver was relatively calm. Then, with his usual bombast, Commander Jardine called us both into my library and proposed a compromise of sorts. Perhaps it was what he had always intended, but had held in reserve so he could offer it as a concession and thus force Oliver into acceptance.

He had searched his soul, Matthew Jardine announced, and had come to realize that Oliver and I were in the right. Therefore he would give his solemn word that he would get out of the opium trade as soon as his two "Virginia Builts" arrived in Liverpool and their cargo was sold.

"And don't waste your breath telling me I'm to bring them home empty, for it's too late for that at both ends of the deal. I must buy what I have contracted for and deliver what I have promised. I'll need the money to pay my crew and time to arrange for new bookings to America."

On that point the old sea fighter was adamant. We were getting our own way of it, and we must allow him to arrange his exit from the trade as advantageously as possible. Moreover, since he was making a major concession to our consciences—his own was untroubled, he assured us blandly—Oliver must agree to one stipulation.

"We will continue as we are at present, reducing your dosage week by week until you no longer need opium in a physical sense. And then, to prevent a recurrence of your addiction, you will travel to America on a vessel of my selection. It will give you a chance to regain your strength. And to see this America which fascinates you so."

Oliver was at first too surprised to raise any real objections. And then, lethargic though he was, I sensed that the idea was taking hold in his mind as a goal, a journey to a new beginning. I pushed away my own distress at the thought of his long absence. Commander Jardine had come up with the one plan that I could believe would lead to Oliver's salvation.

How I yearned over him in the month that followed, as a mother yearns over a sickly child, with a tenderness he moved away from. His nerves were stretched so tightly that he paced and moved about continually, unable to rest except when he was exhausted and fell into shallow, dream-ridden sleep that brought its own shadows.

But the nights were worse than the days, for there was no outlet for my hurting. I longed to creep into Oliver's bed for the comfort of being close. It had been so long since he had held me and loved me. Only once, after I had finished the nightly massage of his knotted muscles, did Oliver reach out to me and draw me into his bed. In his sorry state he was incapable of making love to me or even wanting to, but he touched my cheek and held me close for a moment before he turned away, back to a twitching, yawning, weary world of his own.

His gesture moved me deeply. The knowledge that he cared for me, the hope that Adriana's revelations about me and Adriana herself were forever buried with the past, gave me the strength to exist until Oliver was well again.

CHAPTER 30

Oliver sailed from Liverpool on a springlike day in March, 1846, aboard the *Amity*, a 420-ton-burden sail packet accommodating sixteen first-class passengers, and scheduled to stop at Cork, in Ireland, before westering for America.

We said our adieus under a blue sky, rare enough in Liverpool to seem a bright omen to me, despite the heaviness of my heart. Oliver, thank God, had ceased to view me as one of the enemy bedeviling him. It had been a grueling period for all of us, dominated by Oliver's problem but still requiring a great deal of effort on my part for the arrangements necessary to unite our Blue Funnel line with Commander Jardine's interests. We were one, finally, under the name Jardine-Blue Funnel Line. Throughout the paperwork Oliver had been agreeable, and I had been watchful, with Mr.

Richard Cecil's care and knowledge to supplement my own in safeguarding our interests. I had dreaded the moment of Oliver's leave-taking and the event was as painful as I had feared, for his trust of the sea was not mine, and anything could happen before I saw him again.

"You will write to me during the voyage, Oliver, so that I have a letter by the earliest mail packet?"

"Of course, darling." He smiled down at me in the old way and my heart turned over. "You must do the same, for there will be time for one letter, at least, before I return."

I clung to him shamelessly, memorizing with my body every warm and cherished surface of him, for there were lonely months ahead. Commander Jardine harrumphed and strode about, pretending to take an interest in the vessel, but his attention was centered on Oliver.

I gave the old sea fighter a few minutes with his son, while I stood back and thought how different this day was from the day I had left Charente. My beloved Oliver was no longer the robust, sturdy man I had first seen on the dock as we boarded the *Cognac*. His hair was still a flaming red, but his eyes now were fond, not seeking, as they had been then. His face, under the deceptive warmth of freckles, was thin and wan, and his solid frame had shrunk to a spare boniness that hurt me to see.

So much had happened to us in the years since Charente. It ran through my mind in a series of flashing pictures: our strong, fateful early days of love and adventuring when we combined forces against our parents; our struggles for money and the success of the Blue Funnel Steam and Navigation Company—those seemed the halcyon days. After that, only darkness—that horrible night when Oliver had stormed into Calcutta House and raped me . . .

Perhaps my face reflected that memory. Oliver gathered me close.

"I pray that better days are coming, my love," he murmured, his breath warm in my ear. "I've done so much wrong in my life—and most of it to you, my only love. How many times have I lain awake and remembered that terrible night. . . ."

He buried his face in my neck and I whispered the same comfort that I had offered to myself when the memory recurred.

"We have Charles, Oliver. He is worth *anything* to me, so you need not scourge your soul for that."

He looked at me with a twisted smile. "And have you an excuse for me where Adriana is concerned also? Or for believing her lies? That you hated me enough to set the *Jardine* afire? Or for all that I have put you through much more recently—cursing you for not supplying me with opium?"

I opened my mouth to reply, but Oliver put a gentle hand over it. "No. I'll have no more excuses for my many failures. Only please, still love me. I want the chance to make you smile again, to come back to you the healthy, loving man you deserve. He still lives inside this poor hulk you have tended so patiently. And he loves you deeply, Margaret Jardine. I know that now. In my heart and in my mind, it is always *only* you."

Oliver's lips burned on mine with the old passion and I melted, as always. That didn't change, and I counted myself lucky. Better the suffering and agonizing that made up so much of my life than life without Oliver. I had only to endure for a few more months, and we would be together again.

We left the vessel as the tug hauled at the tow hawser, and took the phaeton to the headlands. Standing by Mersey Point, we watched the vessel drop her line. The sails rose and billowed, fitfully at first and then catching the wind. With her bow pointed toward Ireland and all sails drawing, the *Amity* soon slipped beneath the horizon. Oliver was gone.

"He's safe aboard the *Amity*," Commander Jardine assured me as we settled into the phaeton for the drive back to Calcutta House. "No doubt he knows full well why he's not aboard the *Blue Heron*, but he was canny enough not to question it."

I nodded. "I suppose the crew of the *Blue Heron* also does a brisk business in opium, on a small scale."

"Yes, well, we try to discourage it, you know."

I laughed, and he had the grace to laugh with me after a moment. I didn't think Commander Jardine fancied himself in the mother-hen role. Or on the straight side of the law. Not to his taste at all; but as I had often noted, such things change. It depends on whose ox is being gored.

For the next month I saw little of Matthew, although he gave up his rooms in Ranelagh Street and lived at Calcutta House. He was away much of the time, at Holylake occasionally, but more often in London, for what purpose I didn't know.

His two clippers, the *Blue Heron* and the *Spindrift*, had

arrived in Liverpool from the East before Oliver's departure, and I supposed that some of his time was given to the dispensing of their illicit cargoes. I did not inquire. If he was trying to book that tonnage he would have no difficulty, for the two graceful ships would be among the first such to be put into service on the Atlantic trade out of Liverpool. The problem would be to make money with them, for though they were fast and beautiful, they were built for speed at the expense of space in their holds. Fine for opium but hardly designed to carry pottery or pig iron across the Atlantic.

Then, one afternoon in late April, Matthew appeared at Calcutta House bearing a letter which had been delivered to him at Holylake. His crest of coarse, ginger-colored hair was as unruly as ever, but his cravat was neatly wrapped; he wore a lavishly embroidered satin waistcoat and a new forest-green tailcoat trimmed in braid. He looked to be on top of the world. Beaming, he handed me the letter. While I sat down to read it, he marched about the library with a glass of brandy, scarcely able to contain his elation. The letter was on palace stationery.

> My dear Commander Jardine:
> Her Majesty and the Thirteenth Duke of Norfolk have had certain conversations as to the review of your long and distinguished career and your relationship to the Howard family. It has been suggested that, at your convenience, you might arrange a meeting with me to discuss certain aspects of your heraldry.
>
> Your obedient servant,
> The Lord Privy Seal

"Well, Margaret? What do you say now?" Matthew Jardine roared. "My plan wasn't so farfetched after all, was it?" He rubbed his hands together in deep satisfaction. "I've been working on it. I still have a friend or two, you know."

"Congratulations, Matthew!" I smiled, delighted for him. "I'm sure you won't waste time arranging the meeting."

"Already done, my dear. You'll note that the letter is dated two weeks ago. Today I received confirmation of the meeting to be held a week hence, on the fifth of May, in London. I want you to go with me."

"Me? Whatever for, Matthew?"

"Ah! That's what I'm here to talk about. I was going to wait and surprise you with a *fait accompli*, but in my brain-cracking efforts to solve our problem with the steam vessels you and Oliver have set your hearts on, I had an inspiration. You must go with me to see Norfolk and help to sell my idea!"

He seized me by the hand and settled me into a chair. "Look here, Margaret. The problem, when we come down to it, is a simple one. Nobody trusts iron ships. The use of the steam engine is worry enough, though there's less resistance since steamships have proved themselves on the Irish Sea. But when you put the two together, iron *and* steam—and not paddle wheels, mind, but this newfangled screw propeller Oliver insists on—well, it's too much for most people to swallow."

"I know, Matthew. I felt that way for so long. Until I was forced to learn otherwise. You could scarcely be married to Oliver and not learn."

"Very well, then. The first thing we must do is to convince 'em that iron is not a threat! And since we can't do it by reasoning—not in the time we have before us—we must do it by illusion."

I looked at him narrowly. What was coming now? Another of Matthew Jardine's pipe dreams? But before I could ask, he thrust a sheaf of papers into my hand.

"I've prepared a report. Read it and tell me what you think."

With that he got to his feet and poured another brandy. While I read, he sat quietly across the room and waited.

Report Concerning Certain Problems
Faced by the
JARDINE-BLUE FUNNEL LINE
of Liverpool.
Prepared by
Matthew Howard Jardine, Commander, R.N., Ret.

From my observations and conversations with manufacturers, merchants, and commodity brokers involved in transatlantic shipping, it is apparent that distrust of the iron screw steamer is widespread and, in fact, not open to logical discussion. While steam is accepted for use on the Irish Sea, there is strong feeling that for relatively short distances, and where the shores are protected by the royal lifeboats, the risk is a calculated one. Waging a

fight with the North Atlantic is seen in quite a different
light. Whether or not the skepticism is justified scarcely
matters. If the Jardine-Blue Funnel Line is to conquer
that skepticism, a drastic change in public opinion is
necessary. To accomplish that end, I have several recommendations which I respectfully submit for appraisal.

1. Both the *Lady Margaret* and the *Jardine* have a
poor reputation as a result of their numerous problems. I
believe it would be wise to refit and rename them.

2. This tonnage does not create confidence because of
imagery based on the conventional view of seaworthy
ships. If both vessels had six masts, rather than three,
they would immediately take on an added impression of
reliability. The more sails the better, in this case.

3. Both vessels are black, enforcing the impression of
iron in their appearance. While black is practical for
vessels that burn coal, it is not practical if it destroys
confidence. I suggest that they should be painted white.
Granted, they will turn black soon enough and show rust
and streaking in use. But they will *be* in use, once their
threatening, black-hulled look is disguised.

4. I feel that the masters and crews of the *Lady Margaret* and the *Jardine* are not of the competence and
style best suited to our purpose. I suggest we replace
these men, ratings and officers, by Navy-trained personnel, who excel in their trade and will lend strong credibil-
ity to our cause.

5. I believe that we need royal endorsement. If we
were to steam into the Thames, take Her Majesty Queen
Victoria out for a short voyage and a royal reception,
and arrange for proper newspaper reportage, our passenger bookings, as well as our holds, would soon brim.

6. For our early voyages on the Atlantic, I suggest we
retain repair crews provided by the engine and boiler
manufacturers, to be on hand in case of breakdowns,
until all problems are ironed out.

7. When and if the vessels' machinery goes amuck,
we use sail. There is no need to keep public account of
the hours involved in either mode of locomotion. The
important thing is to keep going—and build confidence
in any way we can.

I put the report aside and looked at Matthew Jardine with
admiration.

"It's a masterful job, Commander." And then I broke into a broad grin, mirroring his own. He came lumbering across the room, clasped my waist between his broad hands, and leaned down to plant a kiss on the top of my head.

"Since we're both in the steamship business for Oliver's sake, Margaret, we'd best do all we can to make it a success. Not necessarily in what Oliver might suppose to be the most effective way."

He poured me a glass of cognac to toast our new undertaking, and then we got down to the practical aspects of the venture. Or *impractical* aspects—for I considered the matter of a royal endorsement most unlikely.

"Is it in that connection you wish me to accompany you to London, Matthew?"

Over his glass, Matthew Jardine nodded wisely. "You are to help me sell that little notion, Margaret. But leave that aside for the moment. Have you any other misgivings about the report?"

"A minor one. The captain of the *Jardine*, Captain Craigh—he is a good man, Matthew. I agree that Navy-trained personnel would lend a certain *éclat*, as well as seamanship, to the undertaking. But I would like to retain Captain Craigh."

Matthew, no doubt relieved that I had no more serious criticism, agreed, and again we grinned at each other like a pair of pirates about to board a treasure ship.

"Tell me how we're going to get this royal endorsement, Matthew, for I cannot conceive of such a thing."

"I have an audience with the Lord Privy Seal—and the Duke of Norfolk. That's all the opening I need! If things go as I foresee, we can gain their support for this venture, or at least the support of the Duke. My cousin, you know"—this time Matthew's grin was a quirky one—"though somewhat removed." With peerage almost within his grasp, Matthew could afford to be amused at himself. "Leave it to me for now, Margaret, so long as you agree in principle."

I wondered aloud what Oliver would think of all of this. Matthew waved away my misgivings.

"He wants success, and so far, it isn't even on the horizon, is it? Oliver cares about theory; he's an innovator. But it's not enough. You have to sell new ideas any way you can. This will do it." He shrugged. "Let's go ahead for now as if Oliver agrees. Time enough to pull back if he has some serious objections."

But my first excitement had had time to cool a bit; I had to go on.

"The refitting, Matthew. The additional masts, hiring maintenance crews for the engines and boilers—it's sure to cost a great deal."

Matthew Jardine leaned back, an expression of smug satisfaction on his face. "I've figured it all closely. The rerigging of each vessel and laying on that extra canvas will cost a good thirty-five thousand guineas."

"*Each* vessel." It was a horrifying sum of money.

"Margaret," Matthew Jardine sighed, "there is no making money without spending it. I made a great mistake, the greatest of my life, when I damaged the *Jardine*. All that talk about the Curse of the Flowers rolled off me like water off a duck. But *that*—what I did to Oliver—brought me up short. Enough so that I relinquished my old dream forever. I am no longer in the opium trade. I am in the steamship trade. In for a penny, in for a pound. I have arranged to sell the two clippers to raise the money we will need."

"Matthew!" I could think of nothing to say. Tears flooded my eyes, for I knew he loved those vessels as another man might love a child. No, that was wrong. He loved them, yes, but he loved Oliver more. And he loved challenge, too, for he was meeting it in high style.

I raised my glass to him. I trusted Matthew Jardine at last.

CHAPTER 31

We traveled to London in Matthew's coach, for he took great pride in it. It was a spacious, handsome affair of polished mahogany and blue enamel with silver mountings. The elegant interior, lined in heavy blue silk, had ornate silk curtains at the windows, and was luxuriously carpeted in a rich Turkish pattern. Before long, I felt sure, it would bear a coat of arms. Potter, Matthew's driver, wore dark blue livery with silver buttons and braid. We made an imposing spectacle.

I did not accompany Commander Jardine on his visit to the Lord Privy Seal, but rested in the rooms we had engaged at Morley's Hotel in Trafalgar Square. Matthew returned from his interview in high spirits, and the next afternoon we called upon the Duke of Norfolk at his London town house.

My role was not, as Matthew had earlier implied, to help in convincing Norfolk of our cause, but simply to look beautiful. The Duke, from all reports, enjoyed an excellent disposition in the company of attractive women. Accordingly I wore a new gown that I fancied greatly, of pale blue velvet with creamy lace at the bosom, and narrow belled sleeves that stopped just below the elbow, with puffs of creamy lace to the wrist. It was very new and dashing in style. Judging from appearances, its effect was not lost on the Duke, for his gaze scarcely wandered from my person. Our reception was all that Commander Jardine could have hoped for. The Duke of Norfolk was a jolly sort of man with a flush of good living on him, and a courtly manner.

"Your career and that of your family has been long and distinguished," he informed Matthew. "Experts on heraldry advise me that the past should be forgotten. With your permission, sir, we believe your hereditary title should be revived. If you accept, I am told you will be the Eighth Viscount Birkenhead."

A beatific look flooded Matthew Jardine's face, but Norfolk had not finished.

"In addition, and in recognition of past . . . inequities, shall we say . . . it has been decided to award you an earldom that relates to your illustrious career in the Royal Navy: Earl Jardine of Singapore."

Matthew Jardine had succeeded beyond his fondest dream, after years of planning! The family was reestablished! Oliver would be entitled to use the courtesy title of Viscount Birkenhead, and on Matthew's death would succeed as Earl Jardine of Singapore. Matthew Howard Jardine's cup indeed ranneth over.

The Duke was most cordial to the newly restored members of the Howard family. We sat over glasses of champagne, which may have been his favorite tipple, or perhaps what he felt the occasion demanded. Matthew, with great eloquence, outlined the project he had in mind.

Norfolk proved to be a practical man. The Howards, as Matthew had claimed, pulled together. "Yes, yes," he agreed, his eyes sliding from Matthew to me. "I quite see. Once get little Vicky aboard your steamer and . . . yes, indeed, most advantageous, I've no doubt. A capital idea, in fact, but how do you propose to go about it?"

"I have a suggestion, Your Grace."

"Jardine, you must stop that nonsense. Call me Norfolk—or better still, Billy. Everyone does."

"Thank you, Billy. Now, my idea is simplicity itself. I suggest we have a hospitality ball aboard the steamer, to benefit Her Majesty's favorite good work."

"Little Vicky, Matthew. We're all related in some way I don't understand."

Matthew, to his credit, did not by so much as a flicker reveal his elation. "Little Vicky, by all means. Well, then, tell me, does Vicky have a special charity which concerns her?"

"How the devil should I know?" Norfolk considered for a moment. "I'll get on to Peel. He has her ear. Knows everything she thinks before she thinks it, by all reports. In any case, there's bound to be something. It's a damned fine idea. Very bright of you, old boy." "Billy" included me in his expansive smile. "Brains *and* beauty in the Jardine family, if I may say so."

I smiled demurely but managed a flutter of my eyelashes to indicate that I was not immune to his masculinity. The three of us got on swimmingly, and the Duke's farewell to me was markedly affectionate.

Matthew grinned about that when we were safely ensconced in his carriage. "Norfolk will be on hand, if needed, so long as he can count on your presence, my dear." He gave me a long, thoughtful look. "You are an asset, Margaret, an ornament of the sort our family has sorely lacked."

I mulled that comment over in my mind during our return trip to Liverpool the following day. The moment I had entered the business world, I had put aside all feminine traits for fear I would not be accepted in the milieu of commerce if I revealed my feminine weakness or wiles. I began to see the situation in a different light.

There was a letter from Oliver awaiting me on my arrival home. My hands shook so in fumbling at the envelope that Emily, who had always adored Oliver, took it from me and opened it swiftly.

"There now, Miss Margaret, sit down and read your news while I fix you a nice tea. I pray Mister Oliver is on the mend. . . ."

It was a long letter and I read it again and again, laughing and weeping with sheer release of emotion. It had been written at sea.

> March 18, 1846. Aboard the *Amity*,
> vicinity of longitude 40° west.

My darling Margaret,

Ten long days since I left you. I feel the sea air is doing me a world of good, for I miss you with a need that has been sadly lacking (as you know too well) for what seems forever. Though I have enough to occupy my mind, limited as it has been of late, I find myself gazing out over the wake of the ship toward you and England, longing for the day when I shall return.

I am beginning to believe that I have underrated my father all of these years. I know now how great a debt I owe him, not only for his tireless efforts in weaning me away from that cursed drug, but for the inspiration of this voyage. I am feeling the first stirrings of renewed interest in life, and the strength to savor them. I am of a healthier color since the sun and wind have had time to do their good work. Also my appetite has come back, although conditions aboard this vessel make it a sin to consider myself and my appetite overmuch.

As you may remember, the *Amity* left Liverpool with sixteen first-class passengers aboard, and proceeded to Cork to take on Irish immigrants to America. Margaret, words cannot describe the conditions that exist for these pitiful souls. When they boarded, hordes of them, men, women, and children thin as rakes and with a pallor of malnutrition that made me appear robust by comparison, I realized how little England knows of what is happening in Ireland. Their failed potato crop, of which we hear so much, is not merely the agricultural misfortune that it appears to us to be. Those failed potatoes are the very lifeblood of the Irish, it seems, the staple that enables them to exist—or did enable them to exist, for now they are starving by the thousands. Those aboard are the luckier ones who have escaped, if escape it can be called. If the plight of their relatives at home is worse, they are not long for this world.

These poor wretches have come aboard with nothing, and little is provided for them. Only a meager portion of gruel each day, to keep body and soul together, and even that is a moot point. They exist in the top of the hold, where they live like animals on straw bunks so tightly packed that the poor devils cannot stand upright in the dark stench, and are allowed up on deck for only a short period each day.

On the fifth day out, we hit a full storm. It came from the east and great swells crashed down upon us. They were much higher than those that so nearly swamped us on the Irish Sea that memorable night aboard the *Cognac*. But of course we are in the open ocean. The storm went on for five days, and giant seas swept the decks, so that the immigrants could not come topside, even for their few minutes a day. The first thing the crew did was seal the hold so the water could not leak in, and conditions below were wretched.

Perhaps my own illness has given me an added sensibility, for the other passengers sipped their wines and remained undisturbed, while I could think of nothing but the plight of those Irish down below. Finally I parted with a fair sum of money to pay for extra rations for them, and to bribe the galley steward to see that the children are allotted a small portion of the milk from the three milch cows tethered on deck. Perhaps it helped; when the storm had passed over, the human beings who came from the holds were close to death, but only two of the infants had expired, fewer than is often the case, so the captain informs me. He, like the comfortable passengers in first-class accomodations, seems untouched by the whole matter. To be truthful, I do not quite understand my own concern, but is seems linked to thoughts of you and little Charles in such straits, and myself powerless to help you.

Dearest Margaret, when we land in New York, I shall write my impressions of that place. Until then, I remain,

Your love,
Oliver

That evening Commander Jardine, who had also received a correspondence from his son, was in fine form at dinner, and we celebrated Oliver's improved health and attitude of mind. I agreed that he should be the one to write to Oliver of his new rank. I would confine my own writing to matters of a more personal nature, for we both felt that it would be un-

wise to tell Oliver of our plans for the *Lady Margaret* and
the *Jardine* before they were more fully realized.

The next weeks saw those plans moving ahead swiftly.
Matthew, believing his new rank made all things possible,
carried through the sale of his two clippers without delay. It
proved easier than I had imagined. The *Spindrift* was sold
immediately to an immensely wealthy London sportsman, a
Royal who could afford the luxury of refitting it as a racing
yacht and fancied the novelty of owning a "Virginia Built."
The *Blue Heron* was purchased through a ship's broker by an
American shipping firm, which planned to use it, so Matthew
Jardine said with some envy in his voice, trading to the East,
out of Boston. The vessels, which had cost in excess of
twenty thousand guineas each, were sold at a respectable
profit, for both purchasers were interested in immediate possession, and the price of commissioning such ships from
America was steadily climbing.

On the strength of that money safely in hand, Matthew
wasted no time. He left immediately for Glasgow to rattle the
teeth of the yard owners who were refitting the *Jardine*. He
oversaw every detail of the new masting and ordered the
painting to go forward as swiftly as possible. In the midst of
this activity, the Duke of Norfolk came through in high style.
Upon learning of the progressive vessels being readied for
British commerce under the aegis of Lord Jardine's firm,
Queen Victoria had graciously consented to attend a ball
aboard the new steamer, to benefit the Royal Hammersmith
Hospital.

Privately, Norfolk confided to Matthew, he had got the ear
of Prince Albert. The Prince Consort was greatly interested
in all aspects of British commercial progress and was reported to be laying the groundwork even now for a great industrial fair of international proportions. Prince Albert had
expressed warm interest in the future of steam on the Atlantic, and as a result, "little Vicky" quite looked forward to
viewing the new steamers for herself.

As if all of that were not cause enough for jubilation, the
Duke of Norfolk assured Matthew that he intended to be
present for the grand occasion and "anticipated with great
pleasure seeing the lovely Viscountess Birkenhead once
again." Matthew could scarcely have been prouder if I were
his wife rather than his daughter-in-law, but I had some serious reservations on the use of that title.

To my great joy, I received a second letter from Oliver, and blessed Samuel Cunard's Royal Mail Packet Service.

New York, April 19, 1846

My darling,

How I long for you! Yet I know I must endure for another two lonely months. It seems forever and I cannot face another lengthy sail voyage. I have booked passage on a Cunard mail packet, the *Scotia*, leaving from the city of Boston on May 30, as they keep to a fixed schedule. If all goes well I shall be back with you during the third week in June. How I hope that matters have improved at home, and that my father is able to help you in the heavy task I have burdened you with.

Margaret, if anything were needed to confirm my belief in the steam vessel, it was the seemingly endless voyage I have just completed. Steam, as we know to our sorrow, presents many problems, but to my mind the difficulties of sail are far greater. To fetch our westing, the *Amity* was obliged to drive far south into latitude thirty-three north, in the vicinity of Bermuda, where we finally found a southern drift of air by which we slowly tacked and pushed our way towards New York, some six hundred miles to the north. It took us an appalling forty-one days from the time we crossed the Liverpool bar to landfall at the New Jersey Hook.

What a moment that was, my love! The hatches were opened and the reeking, greenish immigrants crawled from their quarters to hug the bulwarks and soak up everything they could of their new world. I was no different, for I longed to stretch my legs on land and see this country of which we have heard so much.

We passed the Sandy Hook signal station some hours later and our arrival was relayed by flag hoists to the Lloyd's signal station on New York's battery. The pilot boarded about half-noon and then a paddle tug took the hawser and towed us into the East River. Margaret, I fell in love with the port on first sight! Inching up the river, we passed hundreds of vessels lying to the finger piers of South Street; more foreign flags flapped off their sterns than ever we've seen in Liverpool. There was cargo heaped up in mountains everywhere, and armies of dockers working in and out of the opened holds. It was the bustle and confusion that, to my mind, spell riches.

My darling, I have now set foot in the New World and can think of nothing except how wonderful it will be when I can bring you here to see it for yourself. For all we have heard about the dirt and disarray of New York, I judge it to be far cleaner than Liverpool. And even if it were not, it has an excitement and sense of hope about it that stir me more deeply than I can say. Perhaps you will gain some idea of how strongly I feel if I tell you that I actually find myself envying those poor wretches who traveled between decks to reach this land of promise. I know full well that their lot will be a hard one, for poverty is a burden in any locale. And yet . . . they will be *here*.

It makes little sense, and I won't pursue it further, but it has a magical hold over my mind. Perhaps further acquaintance will discourage that. Be sure you will hear how I fare, in at least one more letter before I return and then, probably, endlessly, to your infinite boredom, when I come back to you a seasoned traveler after one long voyage. I think I shall listen more to my father in future when he talks of the East. I sense some of his nostalgia for it, from one view of a foreign port.

Beautiful Margaret, this place has one other effect on me. It makes me miss you more keenly than I can bear, yet bear it I must. What a strange feeling it is to have every sense intensified. Is it really this city—or that I was half numb for so long, and all that seemed real took place in my imagination and my dreams? Whichever, darling, I will never rest, no matter what our future holds, until I have you here with me. Romantic that you are, you will love it as I do.

I leave for Baltimore, Maryland, in the morning by coastal steamer, and from there will travel to Edisto Island to call on Mr. George Gore. My darling, this is an adventure I would not trade for any other, if only you were with me. Someday. In the meantime, my love, know that I think of you with every breath I take in this new country. And for all of my carry-on, it is you and England that I long to see again, for you have my heart.

Always your love,
Oliver

I sat in thought for a long time when I had finished reading and rereading Oliver's letter. It said everything I had hoped to hear. And yet there was a disturbing quality about it. Oliver was in love with a new dream. As his father had been, for so many years, in love with the East? Truly, the Jardines had a full measure of Howard blood in them, the blood of adventurers and romantics. A sense of where opportunity lay. I wanted Oliver back safely with a passion. I wanted him safe under my hand, close to my heart, where I could make him forget his dreams of glory, with love that would blot out all competition. It was a vain hope and I knew it. I would accept somewhat less, if only I could share with him, whatever came.

My mood of melancholy was dispelled by a visit from Matthew, who of late resided much of the time in Glasgow. I had fallen heir to the almost-endless chores that he thought up with reckless abandon. Matthew was giving full rein to his fertile imagination, and the results were impressive.

"These ships, Margaret, must present a spectacle that is nothing short of dazzling. A sight never before seen in London! Picture them, gliding into the Thames, sparkling in the sunlight, with flags everywhere."

He lowered his broad brow to fix me with his eyes. "*Flags*, Margaret, lots of them . . ."

And so I ordered bunting. The flag maker on the Mersey said that he had never made so many units for two ships in his life. Matthew, to his delight, was obliged to order nine more stickers to be laid on the flag loft to accommodate them. He congratulated me on my excellent judgment.

Then there was the matter of the banquet. I planned a lavish menu and purchased a sterling silver service for each of the vessels, with the new Jardine-Blue Funnel house flag embossed on every handle.

The *Lady Margaret* came into port, and as soon as the Sea Island cotton was unloaded into our warehouse on the Albert docks, I saw that she was dispatched immediately to Glasgow, where Matthew was waiting to install the three additional masts and coat her white.

There was no time to spare. A date was established for the great event—September 14th—and I had invitations engraved after approval by the Lord Privy Seal:

BUCKINGHAM PALACE

Her Majesty, the Queen, Victoria, Reg.
and
The Rt. Hon. the Earl Jardine of Singapore
request the honour of your presence
at a reception for the benefit of the
Royal Hammersmith Hospital
to be held aboard the steamers
VICTORIA REGINA and VISCOUNT
on the 14th day of September, 1846

Guests will board the steamers at the East India
Docks beginning at high Greenwich.

A reply is requested.
The Lord Privy Seal.

Beneath the excitement of all of this was the consciousness that Oliver would soon be home. I had received a short letter from him, the last before he would return, written from Old Dominion, Mr. Gore's plantation on Edisto Island. He would tell me about it on his return, Oliver said, for he had scarcely had time to view all its wonders, having just arrived. He said little about his new title, except that he was pleased for Matthew, and hoped that I enjoyed being a viscountess. The letter, though it dwelled on his love for me and his longing to see me again, made the gulf between us greater than ever. Oliver was experiencing so much that I didn't share that it frightened me. It was time he came home.

CHAPTER 32

A month to the day from the arrival of that last letter, a message was delivered at Calcutta House that the Cunard Packet, *Scotia*, had crossed the Liverpool pilot grounds. My shriek of wild excitement frightened poor Emily half to death.

"Oh, mum! Is it Mister Oliver? Has something . . . ?"

She had no need to finish, for I was dancing wildly about

the room with my skirts hiked up, half hysterical with joy
and relief.

"He's home, Emily, home safe at last! Oh, Emily . . ." I
threw my arms around her and hugged her until she gasped.

"I'll call Ned to bring round the carriage, Miss Margaret.
Now you make yourself pretty. . . ."

Emily hustled out and I flew to my wardrobe. The yellow?
No, no, Oliver always admired me in green and I had a new
green silk with a long-fringed shawl. I'd wear that. Emily
came hurrying back and dressed my hair in the style I had
adopted since Oliver's departure—a center part with long
ringlets at the sides, and the back done in a soft chignon,
pinned high. Poor Emily had a difficult time, for I found it
impossible to sit still. But when she stepped back to survey
her handiwork, she smiled.

"Ye'll do nicely. No need for artificial color on those
cheeks, either. Ye're rosy as young Charles."

I waited on the quay as the passengers debarked, craning
my neck for the first glimpse of Oliver, trying not to dither
about, but to present the facade proper for a Lady. But when
I saw him, oh, when I saw him—all of my good intentions
vanished and I flew into his arms like a hoyden, burying my
face against his, holding him with all my strength. I had no
breath even to say his name, though he was laughing and
murmuring over me.

When he raised my chin and kissed me, I thought my heart
would surely explode, and I could taste the salt of my own
tears on our lips and tongues.

"How I have dreamed of this day, my love," he murmured
finally, his arm about my waist as we walked to the carriage.

"And I, Oliver. So afraid it would never come, for I
wanted you so badly I half believed something would keep
you from me forever! Oh, darling, *darling* Oliver, never leave
me again no matter how worthy the reason, for I don't think
I can endure another long parting."

Oliver's reply was a kiss that quieted all my fears.

"Welcome home, sir," Ned beamed when he returned from
the quay with Oliver's trunk. "We've missed ye sorely, sir."

Grinning, Oliver clapped the old man on the shoulder and
helped him strap the trunk in place. "No more than I've
missed all of you, Ned." He drew a deep breath. "Ah, it's
good to be back in Liverpool."

We burst into laughter, for surely the soot-laden air of
Liverpool had to be a cultivated taste! All the same, I felt a

throb of contentment. Oliver had not grown so far away
from us in his travels as I had feared.

In the carriage I sat back. "Let me look at you, darling.
How wonderful to see you brown and healthy!"

Truly, he looked a different man from the one who had
left me almost four months ago. His face had changed
dramatically. There was a small network of wrinkles around
his eyes and across his brow. His jaw seemed more pro-
nounced, as if his ordeal had both made him older and fined
his features.

Oliver laughed and pulled me close. "How wonderful to
see you still the white and gold angel I've dreamed of these
long months." He kissed me as if he could never get enough,
and his hands, caressing me through the thin green silk,
stirred the need for him that I had put down for so long.

"Tell me," he asked at last, "do you enjoy your new status
in the world, Lady Margaret?"

"Oh, indeed, it has its uses, Lord Oliver," I said with an air
of mystery, "as you will learn. And do you fancy being a
viscount?"

"I shall have to become accustomed to it before I can say.
But yes, I shall enjoy it if it aids us in any way in our steam
venture. Margaret"—the small lines about his eyes and on his
forehead furrowed—"have you and my father managed any
help for us? Have you got on well together?"

"As for getting on together, yes, we are fast friends, I believe. Oliver, I have great respect for him, and despite all, he
is a dear man. He has done all he promised, and more. But
darling, there's so much to tell you, let us save it for later.
Please? Tell me now if you found it terribly difficult on the
voyage out. Did the craving for opium reassert itself? Do you
think it's finally gone for good?"

Oliver's answer, given without any holding back, reassured
me finally. He said he had had only fleeting thoughts of his
addiction, and then only for the first few days. There was so
much else to hold his attention. As his father had foreseen,
once his bodily need for opium had gone the change in scene,
and Oliver's own nature, had furnished a complete change of
mind.

I had asked Emily to have a cold collation prepared and left
in my private sitting room, along with champagne cooling. I
had known what I was about, for we didn't trouble even to
open one bottle of champagne. As soon as the door closed
behind us, we fell into each other's arms with no thought to

spare for anything except our need for each other. With some
last vestige of feminine prudence, I did remember to spread
my dress over the chaise longue, but the rest of our clothing
left a trail behind us to the bed.

When Oliver's arms closed about me, and his lips searched
for mine, all there is of earthly paradise was mine. I gloried
in it, the feel of him under my hands, his shoulders bronzed
and strong again, radiant health behind the desire that made
him a frantic, eager lover. There was no prolonging that first
flush of passion, for we were both afire from the very sight of
each other. I was conscious of his arms around me and the
warm weight of him against me. When he moved to enter
me, I felt that every fiber of my being was at last where it
was meant to be. I moved with him as if we were one, my
lonely longing at last at an end. All of me was filled—physi-
caly, emotionally, spiritually—with a hot contentment I had
never known before. *Oliver* . . . I cried out his name when the
final surge of passion conquered all, and we soared together to
that peak of splendor that held us fast for long moments of
bliss, and then let us subside slowly into the aftermath of
warmth and joy and fulfillment.

We lay in each other's arms for a long time; there was
nowhere else worth being. There is such a short space of time
when you know beyond any doubt where all of a lover's
thoughts may be. We savored that little hiatus in life to the
fullest. I knew that Adriana's ghost was exorcised for both of
us. No word was said, and *everything* was said, with the
movement of a leg that lay heavy with contentment across
mine, with the arm I moved luxuriously along my darling's
back; his head, as rough and curly as ever, a welcome weight
against my breast.

When finally we stirred and sat up, our eyes still unable to
leave any movement the other made, Oliver padded to the sitting room and extracted a bottle of champagne from the
bucket where it cooled, while I watched him through the
open door of the bedchamber. He brought two fat, hollow-
stemmed glasses of the bubbling nectar to the bed, and
handed me one.

"We have something to celebrate, my love. Our man-and-
wifeness, which has never before been consummated. I love
you, Margaret. I love Charles. And for the first time in my
life, I love my father. I feel as if I'm a link, an important
one, in this England of ours, joining generations to some
purpose."

It was a sentiment worth drinking to.

Oliver paced about the room, brandishing his glass. "I feel as if Charles should be here with us, perhaps in the bed with us—" He turned and laughed at the look of alarm on my face. "No, no, not literally, I suppose. But I have this feeling of cosmic relevance, that our life as a family is only now beginning, yet linked to the past and celebrating the future—oh, Margaret, does any of what I'm saying make sense?"

I smiled at him fondly, nodding in swift understanding. "You—we—know at last who we are. And why we exist."

He put his glass down and came to me. "Yes. Now we know. How wonderful that we should *both* know."

Slowly he began to fondle me, taking his time, almost dreamlike in his tenderness. His hands were as gentle as mine on Charles, his eyes full of some knowledge that had never been there before. There was a special kind of love— perhaps I had always thought it the kind of love only a woman would dream of and that a man could never know—about his hands searching my body and his eyes searching my soul. It was— different, and it touched some depths within me. My hands began to move as gently as his, my fingertips caressing the line of his strong nose, defining his temples and curling around his ears, down his sturdy column of neck and over the thatch of red hair that matted his chest. Without hurry, as if in a dream, we explored each other as lovers do, but with a specialness, a *knowing*, as if we were blind and learning our love through our fingertips. Had we done this before? Probably, but this time it was unique. It was an inside-out emotion and I almost feared it, for it was overwhelmingly strong.

It moved slowly to passion, as Oliver's tongue took over from his fingers, building, building to a dreamy desire that was, perhaps, like some opium dream, or as I imagined one to be, for all of my senses seemed to quiver with knowledge of what was to come, yet were content to wait for it, savoring every sensation along the way.

When again he slid into me I was possessed. In the sense of the occult, his creature. I knew, while we were clinging to each other, moving in a slowly mounting rhythm that had its own reason, that there were many ways of making love and perhaps I would never again know this way. But neither would I ever forget it. Nor cease to long for it again if it were not to be.

It lasted a long time, that slow building. Not a slow building of desire, for desire was the very essence of what we shared. It was the peak that we approached with long, loving strokes that seemed to last forever—yet not long enough, for nothing could be. When at last the rush came, and we clung to each other in a last intense hold on our reality, it was joy with a depth beyond my imaginings. Or Oliver's—for such an experience could not exist unshared.

How I loved this man.

We surfaced finally, but the dream lingered. It was a long time before we felt the first stirrings of hunger and the immediacy of everyday life reclaiming us. And then it was as if, released from a dream, we clutched at normalcy. Naked as blue jays, we fell upon that table of delicious food like two starvelings, stuffing ourselves, opening more champagne, toasting each other, prancing about to our own delight, and falling to again at the sight of the frothy syllabub, rich with cream and wine, which Emily, by inspiration, had furnished as dessert.

Spent though we were, there could be no sleep for us until Oliver knew of the momentous happenings that had taken place during his absence. I produced his father's report, which had started everything. Oliver settled into a chair and began to read. Soon I saw his brows draw together. No doubt he was reading about six masts instead of three. And white ships instead of black.

In the end he tossed the report aside and got to his feet to pace the sitting room. "Perhaps there's something in it, but it goes against the grain! All this frippery to disguise what is the very heart of what I'm trying to accomplish."

"Darling." I slid my arms around his neck. "Will you please reserve judgment until you see what your father and I have accomplished?"

He shook his head as a horse shakes off a buzzing fly. "It's money spent for nothing! The *Queen*, Margaret? The old man is a dreamer, this is the most farfetched dream of them all!"

I went to the small secretary desk and from a drawer took an engraved invitation for the gala to be held on September 14th.

"More than a dream, darling. She looks forward to the occasion. We have that word from the Duke of Norfolk."

Oliver sank into a chair, stunned disbelief emptying his eyes of his earlier impatience. "Queen Victoria?"

"Little Vicky, Oliver. Oh, darling, there is so much to tell you. . . ."

I began with our visit to Norfolk and his warm reception of Commander Jardine, and Oliver listened spellbound to the sequence of events that Matthew Jardine had brought about through guile and ingenuity.

"Truly, Oliver, your father has done everything possible to mend his earlier mischief. All I ask, darling, is that you go to Glasgow and see for yourself what has been accomplished."

"Poor Margaret," Oliver murmured with a rueful smile. "I went off and left you with a huge burden and you have tried your best to shoulder it. And with what results! The Queen! I can't take it in yet. But yes, we must go to Glasgow without delay. I don't believe I can rest until I see what's been going on."

He bent to kiss my face. "Now. Have you more surprises up your sleeve?"

Since I was wearing no sleeve, nor anything else, I assured him solemnly that he had now had it **all,** which was the truth. The details would reveal themselves along the way. Oliver's pride was touchy. Perhaps if I had done it all alone, he would have felt some resentment. But his father's about-face with regard to steam vessels, and the money he had contributed, left Oliver little room for anything except amazed gratitude.

We turned to the bed as groggy as a pair of drunkards, topped up not with liquor but with love and excitement and a feeling of great events shaping our lives. We clung together and slept, wrapped in each other's arms. Whichever way fate swept us, we would go together.

Two days later, when Oliver had rested, and renewed acquaintance with his small son, we traveled up to Glasgow by rail. We were fortunate enough to have a carriage to ourselves for much of the way, and Oliver talked of America. Most particularly of the Gore family and Old Dominion, their home on Edisto Island.

"Mrs. Gore insisted that I must bring 'Lady Margaret' "—he grinned down at me—"to stay at Old Dominion the next time I visit America. She's very proud of the place, and with reason. Forty-two hundred acres planted in Sea Island cotton, and a home that would delight you, my darling."

"Really?" I felt disinclined to be delighted by anything American, for Oliver's obvious infatuation with that strange foreign country made me feel left out.

"You would find the Gores quite civilized," Oliver continued, oblivious to my mood. "Mr. Gore you know, of course.

His wife is a dark-haired Virginia woman, a bit long in the nose for true beauty, but patrician, and full of quiet dignity."

"Tell me about Old Dominion. Is it a rough sort of place? I can never reconcile the idea of Mr. Gore, who is so thoroughly the gentleman, with America and slavery."

"Seeing it would not resolve your opinion, Margaret. They see it differently, of course. Their way of life depends on slavery. In the South, that is. I had no opportunity this trip, but I hope one day to tour a plantation and judge for myself. The Gores and the other wealthy plantation owners are a strange mélange of great courtesy and hardheaded worldliness, for their wealth buys them everything—and they close their eyes to the rest."

"Not too different from England, perhaps. We have our mills and our factories."

"And Ireland. I shan't forget those Irish emigrants down in the holds." Oliver shook his head. He had thought of nothing but his steam engines for so long that when he roused, the view of the rest of the world had come as a shock. Enforced idleness had given him time to look around him, but not yet time to evaluate all that he had seen.

While we rattled and swayed our way toward Glasgow, I heard more about Edisto. It was a dark and dismal day, and the dripping oil lamp fixed in the roof of the carriage gave off a nauseating odor. The thought of an American island bathed in fresh sea breezes under the blue sky seemed heaven by comparison.

"Edisto Island is a different world from ours, Margaret. Lush, green, seductive to the senses. Picture great trees festooned with long ribbons of swaying moss, jungles of yucca and myrtle and brilliant flowering vines. Yet the Gores' huge, dazzling white house sits surrounded by a boxwood garden as formal as any you might see on a large estate here in England."

"Forty-two hundred acres planted in *cotton*, Oliver? It scarcely seems possible."

"And that is but one plantation, Margaret—Old Dominion. George Gore introduced me to at least twenty other planters with similar acreage. They swear that most of them can tell blindfolded, just by the feel of a cotton boll, whose field it came from, when it was planted, and the rainfall that year! May their production continue unabated, love; it means full holds for us, so long as we can keep their trade."

"Oh, we have kept it, but Mr. Gore drove a hard bargain

after the fire. I had to lower the freighting charges for the cotton, and the price of the coal they buy from us. We are scarcely surviving. . . ."

We talked of the changes that were in store with our refurbished vessels, until I fell asleep with my head on Oliver's shoulder. I woke as the train jerked to a halt in Glasgow's Fendall Street depot.

Matthew Jardine met us for dinner at the Duke of Cranford Hotel, and a celebratory feast it was. Matthew talked thirteen to the dozen, and Oliver nodded, listening, not committing himself but not disapproving either. I left them for my bed. When Oliver joined me I woke to feel the hard-muscled warmth of him gathering me close—and remembered.

This was the hotel where I had first known Oliver Jardine in bed. Was it really only four years ago? It seemed I had lived a lifetime in those four years. I sighed in contentment and moved my body against Oliver's until he whispered, "Vixen," and we began the familiar, and ever-new, pattern of our pleasure in each other.

"Do you remember?" Oliver murmured, his lips moving along my throat. "That first night?"

It was inflammatory, that link of past with present and the remembrance of what a knowing minx I had been at sixteen. I was a woman now—and once again Oliver Jardine proved it beyond doubt as we moved together and cried out together, and clung together afterward until sleep claimed us.

It was only next morning at the shipyard that I was at last confident that Oliver had accepted his father's plan. The *Jardine*, now renamed *Viscount*, had already been painted a dazzling white. Thin morning sunlight shattered into a thousand brilliant glints and gleams that danced off polished brass. And six tall and rakish masts reached toward the sky, where there had been only three before. The *Lady Margaret*, too, now had six masts, a first coat of white, and a new name.

"Seemed only wisdom to rename her the *Victoria*," Matthew rumbled. "In view of the circumstances."

Oliver shrugged. "No doubt there's an advantage in renaming both vessels. *Anything*, if it will wipe out the 'bad-luck ship' theories that so delight our competition. Only"—he turned a rueful smile on me—"I regret that we no longer have a *Lady Margaret*."

"Oliver. Do you really consider me such a child, still? I'm interested in our vessels' welfare. Their holds full and their

reputations unblemished." I slipped my arm through his.
"Just so long as the *Victoria* pleases the Queen, I'll be well
satisfied."

He put an arm about my waist. "Next time, then. We must
have a *Lady Margaret* in our line."

I stood on tiptoe to kiss his chin. "The next one, yes. Or
the one after that."

There was only one matter on which Oliver took issue with
his father, and there he was adamant. Captain Craigh would
command the *Viscount*. But Matthew Jardine would command the *Victoria*.

The old man harrumphed and strode about, blowing out
his cheeks and bracing his shoulders, but his face was alight
with joy and pride. In a moment he and Oliver were embrac-
ing, both of them wearing foolish grins and clapping one another on the back in that way that men do to disguise their
emotions.

"And there'll be no 'Lord Jardine' about it," Matthew declared. "If I'm to command this vessel, I'll be addressed as
Commander Jardine. Only sensible!"

I left Oliver in Glasgow with Commander Jardine, discuss-
ing the new Navy-trained men to be hired for the two vessels,
and the many other preparations for the great day that would
be soon upon us. I had matters to see to in Liverpool.

I had given much thought to the several unfavorable accounts of our past travails that had appeared in the Liverpool
Commercial Telegraph. If Mr. George Gore was to be believed, America exhibited more interest in our steam venture
than did London, for I had seen few mentions of the line in
London papers. Accordingly, I posted off an invitation to the
forthcoming reception to the shipping correspondent of each
of the larger newspapers of England and Scotland. Along
with each invitation I sent a sort of advance story dealing
with the importance of the event, written as nearly like a
newspaper article as I could manage. I was determined that
England's manufacturers should know of us and be suitably
impressed by our favor in the Queen's eyes. Let us once get
the representatives of the press on hand for our spectacle,
and I had as much confidence as Matthew Jardine that they
would be influenced on our behalf.

It was bold, but I told myself that one must do what
works. And in truth, I believed that. Moreover, I had a nebu-
lous idea taking shape in my mind for a future event. As yet
I hardly dared to look at it too closely, for it was daring in

the extreme. If I worked it out properly, and all went well, it could bring us great advantage—and full holds. But that was for the future; the present had complications enough.

Three weeks before the great day, the *Victoria* and the *Viscount* arrived on the Mersey. To my eye, and the eyes of the many shipping men who came aboard out of driving curiosity, they looked like new ships. Most who came to scoff stayed to congratulate the Jardines. During those three weeks, both vessels were put through trial after trial near the Great Ormes Head pilot grounds off the Liverpool bar. And Commander Jardine, who knew all there was to know about sailing vessels, learned to handle steam.

"The tricky part is in reversing, damn it!" he explained to me. "You must learn to use the propeller as a brake, and confounded complicated it is, too. Get the engineer to bleed his steam off the main engine to the auxiliary, rotating in the opposite direction—"

He frowned at me to see if I was following, and I nodded.

"Well, that takes close to a minute, before the propeller starts to bite the other way, you see, so you have to ring for your reverse just that bit ahead of time. But I'm mastering it, never fear. By God, today, with Captain Craigh watchful as a mother hen, I maneuvered that mammoth *Victoria* as neatly as any thoroughbred at a jumping meet, easing her in and back and every way there is, till I was fairly fed up with the whole thing."

He threw back his leonine head and roared with laughter. "Can't have the damn ship plowing right up to the dock and on through, now can we? We've lived down a lot, but they'd never forgive us *that* in the London pool!"

CHAPTER 33

The great day was clear. Our two glistening vessels were off Gravesend at seven o'clock on the morning of September 14th, and from there we steamed majestically up the Thames. We were docked by ten o'clock and thousands along the embankment had watched our progress with bursts of cheers and holiday enthusiasm. Truly, we made a magnificent sight.

All of our flags, which I had feared would be too many and Matthew had insisted were exactly right, fluttered in the breeze. In contrast with the rest of the Thames pool—the rust-brown sailing barges, the grayish pall that hung over London like a veil, the murky green of the river itself—the spectacle was almost more than the eye could credit. Matthew had likened the two vessels to East Indiamen, the cathedrals of the sea, once he viewed them with their six tall masts raking upward.

"That will reassure the cravens," he declared, rubbing his hands together in satisfaction. "Steam *and* plenty of sail, right out where they can view it and take courage!"

If Matthew, Oliver, and I were jubilant, so were our directors, who were all aboard the vessels. Even the wives who had experienced the *Jardine* disaster had conquered their fears. Their wide-brimmed bonnets, colorful gowns, ribbons and flounces, fluttered in the warm breeze like butterflies in a garden. Above the music of the bands, high-pitched, excited voices exclaimed over the elegant appointments of the vessels, the notability of the occasion, and the imminent arrival of the Queen.

Oh, it was a fine day for all of us who had struggled so long, and for Liverpool as well. The Lord Mayor of the city and many other shipping men off the Mersey had traveled to London with us, anxious to share in the glory. For we were out of Liverpool, and there was great rivalry between that western port and London. To the London shipping community, no doubt, the sudden advent of two great white steamers from Liverpool appeared a near miracle. Happily, the London newspapers had for the most part ignored our many setbacks. I hoped that our present glory would do much to change the sardonic view of the Liverpool *Commercial Telegraph*, whose shipping correspondent, Gerald Shelton, had journeyed down aboard the *Victoria*. He had not dealt gently with us in the past.

With that thought in mind, I motioned Mr. Shelton to join me in my favorable position near Oliver and Commander Jardine. He looked astonished, for the royal carriage was just coming into view, and he would be in the very forefront.

"Mr. Shelton, it would seem a fine occasion to declare a ' I greeted him smilingly. "I wish you to stand here ᴇ, where you will have a fine opportunity to judge for f the Queen's response to this occasion." I tilted my

CHAPTER 34

An account of the reception and the two mammoth steamers of the Jardine-Blue Funnel Line had received great attention in leading European newspapers. Within days we were notified by a firm of solicitors representing Adriana Rantana that the demand notes she held against our firm were being called. I had had no idea of the amounts of money she had advanced to Oliver during their affair in Glasgow. The total was ruinous.

I could imagine Adriana at the Villa Rantana or the *palazzo* she had inherited in Rome, wealthy now as Croesus, but still burning for revenge. I wept and stormed, hating her with a passion. I longed to berate Oliver for allowing her to manipulate him as she had, but how could I? I knew, even if he did not, that he was a pawn in her game; control of me was the prize.

There was nothing for it but to sell off everything as quickly as possible to protect our ships. Calcutta House and all of my beloved furnishings were put up for sale and went swiftly. Matthew Jardine contributed what he had left after the exorbitant expense of the Queen's reception and the refurbishing of our two vessels.

As part of our retrenchment, it was decided that Ned and Emily should go to Holylake to help Matthew's faithful old Meredith, who had grown increasingly frail. Oliver, Charles, and I would live aboard the *Victoria*, along with Matthew Jardine and his young son, Howard. Watty, Charles's nurse, agreed to come along, for she had no one else and she loved Charles dearly.

In its way, it was a good arrangement. Oliver wanted nothing more than to be near his precious steam vessels; Matthew, as captain, would have been aboard the *Victoria* most of the time in any case. At least we were together. I will not pretend I was not desolate at losing my beloved Calcutta House, all of my treasured belongings, and my sense of roots put down. But when I cried, I made sure there was no one to hear m[...] And I smiled in Oliver's presence.

We were comfortable enough aboard the *Victoria*, though we were obliged to take over four of the cabins for our own use. Oliver and I had two, which connected, a small suite not so large as my own bedchamber at Calcutta House. Watty and the two boys settled contentedly in two of the smallest cabins. And Matthew, of course, had the captain's quarters. It meant cutting in to our passenger accommodations, but there was no help for that.

I forced myself to look to the future, and labored secretly over the scheme I was devising. Bankers and shipping men gossip; there had been no way to keep our disastrous financial situation from their ears and their ready tongues. It was essential to counteract the malicious interest which catastrophe brings in its wake. Privately, I sold my jewelry to raise the money my plan would require. Finally all was ready, and I had only to await a suitable time to reveal my efforts to Oliver and Matthew and see their faces light up with surprise and pleasure. I was becoming impatient when finally one evening, as we relaxed after dinner in Matthew's quarters, he provided the chance I had been waiting for.

"Damn ghouls," he muttered. "Everywhere I go some mope-faced ninny wants to know if we've sold our ships yet. Can't wait for us to go belly-up! I tell you, I give them a few choice words that make their ears ring. . . ."

My heart was pounding with excitement, I smiled at my two Jardine men fondly. "They'll forget all of that in a few days, Matthew. Wait until they hear what we're going to do next. They won't be able to talk of anything else!"

I had their attention and the words fairly poured out of me. "A sea race between the *Victoria* and the *Viscount*, with a prize of one thousand guineas to be awarded by the *Commercial Telegraph*! Instead of our two ships leaving weeks apart . . ."

"Margaret!"

". . . we'll have them leave together—a race from Liverpool to Charleston—"

"Margaret!" Both Jardines were on their feet, red-faced and roaring.

"It's all right, darlings! I've arranged everything. The thousand-guinea prize, the publicity, the newspapermen to come aboard, so they can write about us—"

"What?" For once, Oliver's voice drowned out his father's. "Have you taken leave of your senses, woman?"

"But Oliver—" I started to protest, but Matthew Jardine's roar overrode me.

"Newspapermen? My God, they'd crucify us! Anything could go wrong, and they'd be right there, licking their slavering chops with glee!"

"Shelton put you up to this, didn't he?" Oliver accused. "The *Commercial-Telegraph* putting up a thousand-guinea prize?" he scoffed. "They don't have to spend a copper to skew us, let alone a thousand guineas. They've been doing it right enough ever since we started out."

"Oliver, please! It's not at all like you think. If you'll just listen—"

"Listen? I don't want to hear another word on the matter. Moreover, I consider this taste of yours for continuing excitement unhealthy, Margaret. Scarcely the mark of a serious woman of business."

"Oh!" My blood seemed suddenly to boil up into my head, as hot as Oliver's vaunted steam. "You dare to say that to *me?*" I leaped to my feet and leaned from the waist, confronting the two Jardine men. "I am a partner in this business. I have worked as hard and as long as either of you. While you, Oliver, were dallying with Adriana Rantana—or taking opium! And you, Matthew, were our enemy, talking against us to anyone who'd listen—and sabotaging the *Jardine!* Sit down, both of you!"

They were so astonished that I would dare to scream back at them that they subsided, flushed with anger but stunned into silence. Oliver folded his arms across his chest and stared at me with granite-hard eyes under drawn-down brows. I ignored him.

"Matthew," I demanded, "when you came to me with an idea to further our aims, did I rant and rave before I heard you out? Even though I thought it was a pipe dream, did I not listen?"

Matthew struggled, his face choleric still. But he nodded grudgingly and shot a look at Oliver. "We'd better find out how far this has gone." He settled his heavy body in his chair and glowered at me, his face as unyielding as Oliver's.

They were a daunting sight, but I was too full of outrage to allow two oversized bullies to intimidate me further.

"Thank you, gentlemen," I purred. "Perhaps you remember the sea race between the *Sirius* and the *Great Western* some years back? I understand it occasioned intense intere̲ on both sides of the Atlantic."

"Eighteen thirty-eight," Matthew muttered. "I wagered fifty pounds on *Sirius*."

"Then why are you being so dense? Do you suppose that men won't wager on our sea race, and talk of nothing else for weeks? How long will it take the winner to cross? Which vessel is superior?"

"But there's no *point*, damn it!" Oliver pounded his fist into his palm. "Our holds are filling satisfactorily. We need only look after our proper business in a proper fashion. Not waste our time on foolishness."

"We are in a war, Oliver. You heard what your father said earlier. People are speculating on how long it will be before we're forced out of business. Let's use our weapons! Let's offer them a chance to speculate on our success! Which of our vessels is superior, and *why*? If you wager on one steam vessel against another, you must think about their merits. Since these are both our vessels," I concluded triumphantly, "we have nothing to lose."

Oliver got to his feet and prowled the sitting room like a large tiger in a small cage. "The slightest breakdown and your newspapermen will be peering over our shoulders, wagging their heads. And then informing the world of their grave misgivings."

Matthew grinned, showing his large yellow teeth. "If we wine and dine 'em well enough, mayhap they'll see what we want them to see. But they'll write what they bloody well choose."

"Matthew Jardine," I stormed, "you were the one who suggested in that paper you wrote that we take along repair crews from the companies who made the engines and boilers. Besides, if anything goes wrong with one ship, a machinery failure, or a hull or deck fracture, the other ship will be there to give assistance. We can say that it was the result of the engines being pressed to their fullest."

At last I had pierced Oliver's armor. The stubborn set of his chin relaxed as he thought. "And this thousand guineas the *Commercial-Telegraph* is giving as a prize—"

"It is to go to the captain and crew of the vessel winning the race," I interrupted. "It comes from us, of course. I sold ...ry and received enough to pay the prize and hire ...on to organize the newspaper men who will accom- ...n the voyage."

...to look at Matthew and surprised a thoughtful grin ...e. Thank God he understood the commercial world eyes. "And to betray such a knowledge of men, my sweet! Surely not learned in my bed?"

But I would have none of that. I smacked him heartily beside the ear. "Shush, you fool! Everything that matters to me in life I learned in your bed, so don't disparage it, please. I value it highly."

I kissed him close to the ear I had boxed and then on the ear and in the ear, and we proceeded from there. Perhaps it was the rowdiest lovemaking we had ever shared. We were both in a wild mood, I suppose, from other frustrations, and keyed up to every sort of lusty delight. We cavorted and clung, rollicking around the bunk and the stateroom like two bare and joyful animals, delighting in our nonsense with its undercurrent of passion held back.

When at last he took me, it was a deep-driving pleasure, rooted in our solid love for each other. Lovers and friends, linked warriors in battles against any other who threatened. Tomorrow would bring more trouble, and neither of us doubted that. But for the moment, we were one, against whatever fate could produce. We burned together and melted together and soared together. And we slept together, spoon-fashion. My last awareness before sleep took me was of the feel of Oliver Jardine's hard-muscled belly against my back as he curled protectively around me. My private fortress against the adversities of fortune.

CHAPTER 35

The final day of the race was brilliantly sunny with moderately choppy seas. We plunged through sun-dazzled water, sending up sheets of diamondlike showers of spray. Every passenger on both vessels was on deck, and despite the chill of a March morning, we were so warm from excitement that scarves were thrown back and cloaks left open. My hair came loose and streamed in the breeze, but I was too caught up in the frenzy that prevailed to bother with it. I cheered and roared with the rest as our two huge ships bored their way toward the finish, at the head of the Cooper River in Charleston.

Incredibly, there were at least five hundred small craft on hand to watch our arrival. From the moment we sighted the first tiny speck of the American coast, the *Viscount* and the *Victoria* raced in earnest, in a dead heat. Oliver and Matthew had decided that in honor of Queen Victoria, her namesake, the *Victoria*, should be the first to cross the finish line. The hysterical crowds on both ships cheered. The hundreds of small craft scudded around on the fringes. And no one suspected that far below in the bowels of the ships, the grimy engine-room hands worked furiously, Oliver among them, hand-feeding the hot, whizzing pumps with oil to keep them functioning until the contest was over.

I shrieked with the rest, and prayed in my head. Dear God, let the bearings last, don't let us fail now, within sight of our goal—and all of those watching eyes! When at last the *Victoria* pulled slowly ahead of the *Viscount* to win the race with all flags flying, tears of relief and triumph were streaming down my face. In that wildly cheering crowd, no one noticed. Someone seized me around the waist and held me high in sheer exuberance, and I looked across the throng to see Mr. Shelton grinning up at me and brandishing a bottle of champagne above his head.

Back on my feet, I was dizzy with exultation. It had worked! The mock race, the use of six masts when we had needed sail, the whole magnificent finish. It was a triumph of steam engineering, artifice, and showmanship. Around me the newsmen aboard the *Victoria* were laughing and pounding each other on the back, jubilant at our victory.

Mr. Shelton pushed his way toward me, the wide grin still on his face.

"History, Lady Birkenhead! We've seen the making of history on this voyage. The Jardines have changed the course of ocean transport forever."

He got the bottle of champagne opened, though he lost a third of it as it bubbled over onto the deck. Carefully extricating two glasses from the voluminous pockets of his cloak, he filled them with champagne and we drank to that sentiment. Strangely enough, despite our conspiracy, we both believed his words to be no more than the truth. Between us, we had staged a *tour de force* and ended up convinced by our own illusion.

Later, when Oliver finally emerged from the oily heat of the engine room, I joyously recounted Gerald Shelton's words.

"The Jardines have changed the course of ocean transport forever."

"If they only knew," he murmured, but a wry grin broke over his soot-streaked face. "Eleven days, one hour. Your Mr. Shelton will have better copy than ever he had before. That record will stand for a long time to come!"

I kissed his sweaty cheek and held him close. "And when it is broken, *you*, Oliver Jardine, will be the one to break it. You're famous, darling."

He was indeed. We were feted in Charleston and spent several days at the Gores' plantation, Old Dominion. As Oliver had told me, the house was magnificent. Built of dazzling white clapboard, it had balustraded verandas on two levels, and broad steps with a tall, white-columned portico at the front. We reached it at the end of a long drive through a formal boxwood garden. Mint, jasmine, every kind of flower scented the air, and within the house the atmosphere was one of quiet, cool luxury. Cypress floors gleamed, rich carpets glowed like jewels in the subdued light, for heavy brocade draperies were kept drawn against the sun. Fine English furniture graced every room, and the entire effect was one of great wealth and comfort.

As for the Gores themselves, I found them charming and eager to make us feel at home. Although only business acquaintances, we were accepted as welcome friends. When Oliver and Matthew returned to Charleston to see to the refitting of the vessels, the two children and I remained at Old Dominion, enjoying the Gores' hospitality.

I saw much during those weeks, and not all of it pleased me, though I was circumspect. Life on Edisto revolved around Sea Island Bulb, a strain of fine-fiber cotton brought to Edisto Island from the English colony in the Bahamas. This Sea Island cotton, which we had been carrying in our holds, was of a delicate, silky nature suitable for women's dainty fashions, and fetched high prices from the French chemise and blouse industry. It had flourished in the dark Edisto soil and as a result a rich society had sprung up on Edisto over the years. Now there were many great houses furnished with the finest that Europe had to offer, peopled by southern Americans who lived in grand style.

The Gores were gentlefolk of importance on Edisto Island and were justifiably well pleased with their way of life. But my eye and mind rebelled at the sight of the many Negro slaves who supported that way of life. No doubt the Gores

sensed a certain reservation on my part, though I tried to
hide it. They explained that although slavery had long been
outlawed in England and her colonies, the southern rural
economy could not exist without it. They were careful to let
me know that their slaves had families and their children
grew up to be field hands or were sometimes brought into the
house to work, which was considered a step up in their world.

Perhaps I would have been more receptive to the idea if I
had not accompanied Oliver when Mr. Gore took him on a
tour of the plantation. We rode in an open carriage, clip-
clopping along the hedged lanes bordering the production
fields. It was there I met Mr. Tandry, the overseer.

Luke Tandry. I still think of him with a shiver of re-
pulsion. A gaunt, hollow-cheeked man with field dust ground
into his weathered skin. He wore a tan work shirt and
breeches and a wide-brimmed black hat, and he spoke with
an accent that came from the Negroes he worked. Behind
him, we moved into the fields and through the rows of cotton
planting.

Oliver, insensitive to everything except his unending need
to learn about anything new that crossed his path, immediately set about questioning Mr. Tandry.

"The slaves, how are they managed?"

"Well, suh, let's say a new hand comes into the fields. He's
whipped up smartly and made to pick all he can that fust
day. At night we weigh it up so's his capacity for pickin' is
known. Then, suh, we find it best to keep the man to his
limit. So we weigh his bags at night in the gin house. If he's
fallin' behind, we know he's laggin' the pick and we apply the
'cat' to agree with his missin' pounds. Mind yuh now, we're
careful not to cheat. We use a recordin' book—a lash for every pound missin'."

"What's an ordinary pick weigh in at?" Oliver asked.

"About two hundred pounds, suh, per day."

Oliver shook his head in amazement. "How long are they
in the fields, then?"

The overseer looked at George Gore. Mr. Gore nodded.

"Well, suh, they start at first light. Stop at noon for fifteen
minutes to take their bacon, then they picks till it's too dark
to see. 'Les the moon is full. Then they picks onto midnight.
But most commonly 'bout seven this time o' year."

Oliver, the fool, still had not enough sense to desist. "But
see here, what about their dinner?"

Again Mr. Tandry looked to George Gore for permission to answer. This time Mr. Gore's nod came more slowly.

"When the day's pickin' is over the bags are toted to the gin house. After the hands tend to their other chores—mule and swine feedin', cuttin' wood, milkin'—why then they get to fix their vittles."

At that, even Oliver fell silent. Around us, the working slaves sang softly, incomprehensible in the light of what we had just heard. I learned later that on Edisto, at least, a singing slave was considered to be a busy slave. Singing was required, along with all else.

Unfortunately for my peace of mind, the overseer's trained eye at that moment caught sight of a large, sweating slave who stood listening, his head cocked to one side. Mr. Tandry took a threatening step toward the black man who quickly sat back on his haunches and filled his massive hands with clumps of cotton.

"Bo Daddy, yuh supposed to pick, not listen to yuh betters!"

Luke Tandry's narrow leather whip slashed down across the slave's back, drawing a thin red line of blood. He raised it for another blow, but George Gore seized his arm. At the sight of the planter's face, Mr. Tandry subsided into frozen-faced quiescence.

Oliver, not the most tactful of men when he happened on a situation that disturbed him, handed me into the open carriage next to Mr. Gore, then climbed in himself.

"Slavery was abolished in England in eighteen eleven," he observed, as we began the leisurely ride back to the house.

Mr. George Gore, a southern gentleman of impeccable courtesy, merely smiled. "At that time nearly all of the vessels engaged in slave trading came out of your home port. Liverpool slavers landed ninety percent of the African slaves in Jamaica, Barbados, Antigua, the Bahamas, and our American states of Georgia, Alabama, and South Carolina. The ancestors of my slaves came to these shores in your ships." He raised a quizzical eyebrow as he turned to face Oliver. "It seems that men from many countries go where there is profit to be found. Do you not agree?"

Oliver frowned, but before he could frame a reply, Mr. Gore continued calmly. "Now, from my observations of *your* country, I would say that British slaves have merely changed color. Our black ones live in cabins and work on the land. Your white ones live packed into the steaming, fetid alleys of

Liverpool and work nineteen hours a day in your factories."

For once Oliver had nothing to say. Mr. Gore smiled bland-ly as we clip-clopped back to his fine white house, peaceful and slumbering in the security of its delightful gardens.

I was relieved when our vessels were once again ready to put to sea. Reequipped with ventilating fans and dual pumps of American manufacturers, they steamed outward from Charleston, fully loaded with Sea Island cotton, and with ev-ery cabin occupied by a passenger elated at the prospect of traveling on one of the famous Jardine steamships. Ironically enough, we were burning the very coal we had lifted from England.

It was a peaceful and trouble-free voyage home. Ap-parently the Americans knew something about fans and pumps and bearings that we English did not. I blessed them in the days that followed, for at last I had the idyllic inter-lude I had long dreamed of. Oliver, no longer required to la-bor in the engine room, still spent many hours there, observing the workings of his beloved machinery, but without the grief that had attended our westward journey. He had time to pay attention to little Charles, and to his half brother, Howard.

Both of the children had proved to be good sailors. I scarcely know how we would have managed if they had not. Charles, almost two years of age, was usually bright-eyed and smiling, and Oliver bragged that he was fit offspring of a family born to the sea. His sturdy little legs would carry him everywhere so swiftly that at last Watty put him on a leash to save him from launching himself overboard.

I grew very fond of Howard, who was now four and a half years old, on the voyage home. He was a good-natured little fellow, solemn-eyed but quick to understand, and delighted with any attention. I spoke of it to Matthew, who looked sur-prised. Thereafter, he made it a point to spend time with his young son, taking him about the ship when he had the oppor-tunity. It appeared to benefit them both, and Howard strove to walk with his father's lumbering gait, to the amusement of the crew.

That voyage back to England was but the first of many that buoyed our hopes and started us on the slow road to fi-nancial recovery. Our two vessels were the pride of the Liver-pool basin and, indeed, were renowned everywhere for their speed and safety.

For almost four years we flourished in a climate of approbation and respect. We continued to live aboard one or the other of the ships, and with secure forward contracts— coal out, cotton in—we were at last able to consider expanding the Jardine-Blue Funnel Line. Oliver had new ideas which he wished to put into effect. Though I had my usual fears and reservations, I was prepared to go along with him, for he was my life. I wanted no more distance between us, neither physical nor of dreams and aspirations.

Aboard ship, I had little to do but enjoy my new freedom from the business world and spend more time with the rapidly growing children. By the time Charles was five and Howard nearly eight, they were inseparable, for they depended on each other for company—and both were seawise quite beyond their years, thanks to Matthew. He had begun their education early.

"See here, my lads, you must do something to justify your presence aboard this vessel. If you're to be seafaring men"—he frowned prodigiously at Howard and Charles— "you do want to be seafaring men, I suppose?"

Solemn-faced, the two little boys nodded.

"Aye, aye, sir," Matthew boomed down at them. "Let's hear it."

"Aye, aye, sir," the two small voices piped.

"Very well, then. Now, here is a spare quadrant. It is time you learned something of navigation. First of all, a seafaring man must learn to determine where he is at sea. Latitude and longitude. Let me hear you say it—latitude and longitude."

Both children, their faces rapt with attention, got out the words in their own fashion. They were very young at the time, and how much they understood of what Matthew told them is difficult to say, but if eager devotion counted for anything, they must have learned a good deal. They spent every moment that Matthew would allow trailing at his heels. I often saw the three heads bent together over some problem they were studying, and I once heard Howard refer to "resolving a traverse." Perhaps he was merely parroting Matthew. Still, both boys mastered such words as "chronometer" and "Greenwich" almost as soon as they could make sentences.

As for Matthew Jardine, I had never known him so contented. He had achieved peerage and restored his family to its proper station in life. He was again in command of a ship, and if he had less affection for the Atlantic than for his beloved South China Sea, he never said so. I believed Matthew's dreams of the East were at rest, though his memories

were certainly still green. I often came upon him telling
Howard and Charles marvelous stories of boarding parties
and cutlass battles when he served under Nelson in the war
against the French. If the two small boys learned anything of
history, it was surely a garbled version. Mixed in with tales of
Trafalgar were accounts of Commander Matthew Jardine's
exploits north of Java Head and up to the Bocca Tigris. He
told stories of Calcutta and the stench of the Hooghly River;
of life on the Singapore station and pirate junks in the China
Sea; of the long sailing route around the Cape. To the two
wide-eyed children, the confusion of locale mattered not a
whit. They soaked up the heady stuff of high adventure; they
adored Matthew and no doubt dreamed at night of battling
cutlass-wielding Malay pirates at his side.

In those four years I knew more of peace and quiet joy
than ever in my life before. But as Matthew had once said to
me, life has a way of turning you soft when the struggle
abates for long enough. So long as I was with Oliver, I felt
that I was safe from all that fate might serve up. I had almost forgotten the Curse, that legacy of my stepmother.

CHAPTER 36

It happened in October, 1850.

The *Victoria* had unloaded her tonnage of steaming coal at
Charleston and was heading for the Bahamas to pick up a
cargo of long-fiber Bahamian cotton. In the early morning of
the second day out I encountered Matthew Jardine on the
quarterdeck, frowning at the horizon. The sun was an eerie
clouded yellow, like a hole burned in the gray overcast, with
an incandescent halo around it.

"Something nasty on the way," Matthew growled. "Where's
Oliver?"

"In our cabin. What is it, Matthew? What's wrong?"

"Fetch him, Margaret," Matthew ordered, not sparing me
a glance.

I felt a sudden lump of fear gather in my throat. That terrifying night aboard the *Cognac* still lived in my memory. We
had faced storms aplenty on our Atlantic crossings, but none

had ever frightened me so thoroughly as the one on the night
Oliver had seized control of his father's ship from the panic-
stricken captain of the *Cognac*.

Then reason reasserted itself. The *Cognac* had been a small
vessel. The *Victoria* was huge and built of iron. She would
have ridden out that night on the Irish Sea without difficulty.

"Bad weather coming, sir?" Oliver greeted his father when
we joined him on the bridge.

Matthew nodded. "Bad stuff all around us. Much. The
glass has been dropping for the last three hours. There's a
howler coming, I can feel it."

I could tell that Oliver quite looked forward to some excitement, but as the day wore on, his father's watchful gravity sobered him. As for me, I needed no sobering. The
ex-Navy personnel who manned the *Victoria* had, to a man, a
careful, narrow-eyed look about them as they carried out
their duties. And the sea had a strange calmness that was ominous. There was an oiliness to the swells, a look of slow-roll-
ing weight that made me think of a waiting beast, gathering
its muscles beneath it to pounce. Yet all was quiet. The
steamer sliced its way through the uneasy calm and the glass
slipped lower and lower.

By six o'clock the first of the heavy swells started in from
the southwest, following one another, gaining steadily in
height. In another hour the seas had grown wild white beards.
They came gushing and curling over each other, chewing the
long waves into frothy layers of foam. It grew dark early, not
the velvet blackness of a moonless night, but an ominous yel-
low-gray that brought to my mind strange Eastern curses.

I could take no comfort in the shelter of our cabins. I
donned my oilskins and made my way to the bridge, wanting
to be near Oliver and Matthew. Whatever was coming toward
us was vicious, for when I looked at the glass it was already
dipping into twenty-eight inches of mercury!

"Secure below! Secure the deck and run up my lower main
with two tucks on the lines!" Commander Jardine bellowed
out his orders, throttled his engine back, and the steamer rode
to the burst of the flying seas.

Oliver, at the sight of my frightened face, pulled me close.
"It's a hurricane to the southwest. With luck, it will go by.
But we're in for some heavy weather, love."

Staring out at the night and the driven, pounding waves, I
felt that the Devil himself was in command of the elements.
Black valleys appeared around us; the seas mounted in mon-

strous thirty-foot waves that broke with a sound of thunder; the wind rose to an ungodly shriek.

"Oliver! It's going to happen again. Just like the *Cognac*, I know it is!" I was shaking with fear, linking the past to this monstrous new terror.

"No, darling, no. We'll weather it. This is no *Cognac* we're aboard. We're iron. There are no planks to work and no seams to open as there would be on a wooden ship."

But my faith in iron was a fair-weather thing. Oliver, I felt sure, was only trying to soothe me. "The plates will open! Listen to the howling—"

"*No*, Margaret. We're massive enough. The plates are watertight, with topped-over rivets. You're making yourself afraid for nothing, darling."

Suddenly, to starboard, we saw a distress rocket curve up into the fast-flowing dark clouds.

"Heave to!" Matthew ordered. "Heave to! Back the lower main and be quick on your sheets! Oliver, ring one-third ahead!"

The *Victoria* fired a rocket to acknowledge the distress call.

The steamer nosed its way in the direction from which the rocket had come and for minutes we peered into the darkness ahead. Nothing. Nothing to be seen but vast, wind-driven cliffs of water; nothing to be heard but the shrieking of the wind and the crash of the seas. And then, in a great chasm between forty-foot waves, there appeared the wreckage of a ship. In that one brief glimpse it was impossible to tell what she had been: a brig, a bark, or a fully rigged vessel. The deck was a mass of tangled lines and shredded sails, to which a few men clung desperately. As we watched, too far away to do more than stare in horror, a mountainous wave descended on the pitiful hulk, and then another close behind it. In the boiling sea there now remained only a few bits of wood and a lone man, clinging to a spar. All else had vanished.

A life ring with a line attached was shot out to the man in the water and fell far short. Oliver, at the helm, sought to bring the huge steamer closer, and another attempt was made. At that moment, the full fury of the hurricane hit us broadside and I was thrown to the deck, where I clung for my life.

The *Victoria* was picked up and tossed as if she were a matchbox in a millrace. From being borne high on the raging seas, we were plunged downward into a hugh trough. Lurching and rolling, we wallowed there. As I tried to regain my feet another mighty wave broke over our starboard bow, sweeping us fore and aft. With it went several of our lifeboats, ripped from their davits. Suddenly, over the roar of the pounding seas there was a wrenching, shuddering crash that slammed me back so that my head struck the deck forcefully.

Through a haze of pain and terror I heard Matthew Jardine shout, "My God, we've hit the coral!" The world turned into a maelstrom of crashing, rending nightmare as the seas pounded us again and again onto that underwater graveyard without mercy. For all our vaunted iron strength, the seas and the reef were stronger. We were being ground to our death on the coral! Waves like mountains lifted us off and slammed us back, while the wind, howling like a banshee, ripped our sails to shreds and snapped four of the masts as if they were toothpicks.

The full force of the hurricane probably battered us for something less than an hour, though it seemed a lifetime. When it began to lessen, I realized that beyond the crashing of the storm and the unceasing grinding of our hull on the coral reef, there was no sound from our engine room. Oliver, despite my pleas, had left me clinging to a stanchion. I told myself that it was not that he loved me less than his ship, but that he was looking to save our future—if we had one.

As soon as I was able, I made my way down to the cabin deck and was greeted by a fearful sight. The passengers, among them my own Charles with Howard and Watty, were struggling onto the deck from the cabins and saloon. Like a fool I had thought that what safety there was lay on the main deck. One glance at Watty and other others disabused me of that notion.

A male passenger carried Howard, who had a broken arm. Watty carried Charles, white-faced, with a bandage of torn pillow cover wrapped around his head.

"We're all right, mum, except for what ye see," Watty sought to reassure me. "We was flung about something awful in the cabin, but I bound 'em both up as best I could, mum."

Watty's own face was discolored with red, puffy bruises, but she assured me she had no bones broken. Then Matthew, with water streaming from his oilskins, came striding up, urging passengers to mount the companionways to the upper deck.

"Lead the way, Margaret. Take 'em to the crews' and officers' quarters; there'll be less damage there."

We had only thirty-eight passengers aboard, on their way

to the Bahamas. All were in a sorry state. Many had been cut
by broken glass from shattered mirrors and chandeliers; ten,
including young Howard, had broken limbs; and everyone
had bruises and a variety of superficial injuries. On the back
of my own head there was a lump the size of a goose egg,
and I could scarcely limp, for one of my wrenching falls had
twisted my left ankle and knee.

The ship's physician, Dr. Dugal Kintyre, did what he could
to ease the suffering of the worst-hurt passengers, setting
bones and patching wounds. Six of the able-bodied male passengers were recruited to do guard duty over the supply of
spirits aboard, at Oliver's command. The engine-room crew,
once the fires had gone out, had attempted to raid the supply
room with some success, and the sailing crew would surely
follow if the stores were left unguarded. We could ill afford
drunken crew members, for we had more than enough grief
as it was.

I learned by braving the gale that we were in dire circumstances. Oliver had inspected the lower reaches of the ship,
and any hope I had been harboring faded at the sight of his
face.

"The coral. The damned coral. If it were anything else,
maybe—but what's the use? We're impaled, Margaret! We've
got a fifty-foot hole through the two skins, and coral gouging
it larger by the hour."

It seemed incredible that coral could rip through both skins
of the *Victoria*—two layers of thick iron plates with two feet
of air space between them that made up the tough double
hull of the ship. I said as much to Oliver, but he shook his
head impatiently.

"We've got a dozen other holes as well, and more to come.
We're being ground to pieces between the seas and the reef.
We're taking water twice as fast as the pumps can handle
it. . . ."

Saving the *Victoria* was hopeless, but we were forced to remain aboard and pray that the storm would abate before she
wracked apart under our feet.

We passed a fearful night. The worst of the hurricane had
passed us, but severe seas and winds gave us no respite. Of
our twelve lifeboats, five remained intact. Two had broken
away entirely at the height of the storm and vanished. Two
were on the deck below, stove in beyond any usefulness, and
three hung partly suspended from the falls. Would five boats
be enough for all of us? The passengers and a crew of near a

hundred men? At the thought of being out on that wild sea in a small boat, riding the towering waves and crashing down into the valleys between them, buffeted by the wind and soaked to the skin, I dissolved into cowardice and thought that going down with the *Victoria* might well be the better fate. But I kept such thoughts to myself, for there was enough of dire speculation going on around me from the passengers.

Just after daybreak, in very heavy seas, we abandoned the hulk of the *Victoria*. The first lifeboat lowered was rushed by the engine-room crew. In vain Commander Jardine strove to get women and children into it, but it was cut off when only partially filled, and contained mostly drunken crew members. The other four boats were filled in orderly fashion, with passengers and crew members in each. Dr. Kintyre and the first officer went in the boat carrying the most badly hurt passengers. Watty and the two children and I, with twenty-seven others, went in the next-to-the-last lifeboat, with Oliver in charge. Commander Jardine, as captain, held to his right to be the last man off the derelict steamer. We watched the final lifeboat launched from the *Victoria*, with thirty-three aboard, and Matthew Jardine the last to board it.

The seas were running heavy, and as we pulled away from the foundering ship I felt that our lives were worth very little. Our lifeboat seemed no larger than a cork on an ocean that stretched, wide and wild, as far as the eye could see in every direction. The men at the oars had got us well away from the wreck of the *Victoria* and I was looking back when it happened.

A shout that carried over the roar of the seas arose from the lifeboat carrying Commander Jardine. The stern of the *Victoria* appeared to be swinging in a clockwise motion directly at the lifeboat. Though the men at the oars pulled for their lives, the bent propeller of the *Victoria* struck the lifeboat a blow that shattered it as if it were made of glass. While we watched, horrified, the boat and all aboard disappeared into the boiling seas.

"My father!" The words were torn from both Oliver and Howard, as if in one voice.

We turned back, searching for survivors, but there were none to be seen. Some mighty undertow caused by the shifting of the *Victoria* on the reef must have sucked them down and under the huge vessel. Though we circled for half an hour, there was no sign of a survivor. The horror of the scene would not leave my mind. Commander Jardine, that sturdy,

larger-than-life old man, was gone. I held Howard and
Charles close as they wept and could only look at Oliver with
love and pity as the tears coursed down his cheeks and my own.

The Curse. That damned, never-ending, malignant Curse.
It would see us all to our graves! I heard its evil promise in
the wail of the winds, felt its power with every wave that assailed our small craft. We were never to be free of it, no matter how we might strive. I said nothing of my conviction to
Oliver, but the closed and fearful look with which he faced
the horizon told me that he, too, believed. The Curse of the
Flowers was real. And it was ours by right of inheritance.

We survived because our boat was driven ashore on a for-
saken island with a shallow, sandy beach and a few wind-
stunted trees. Of the four lifeboats that had got safely away
from the *Victoria*, two found haven on that island. The
drunken crew members who had commandeered the first lifeboat were never heard from again. The third boat launched
was picked up by the *Flying Fox*, a small trading vessel that
plied between southern American coastal cities and the islands. Those of us who reached the island, sixty-two in all,
were rescued two days later by a slaver running from the
Bahamas to Charleston. It was a bad ship: filthy, crowded,
alive with ungodly sounds from below the decks where the
slaves were kept in chains. But it took us to Charleston in
safety. From there we made our way home to England
aboard a Cunard packet steamer, for the *Viscount* was not
due for another three weeks and we had no wish to linger.

No matter that America was beautiful and its people hospitable. Without a home, and bereft of half of our shipping
line, there could be no peace for us anywhere but back in
England, looking to our future. Whatever it might prove to be.

CHAPTER 37

We moved into Holylake on our return to England. We had
only one vessel remaining, the *Viscount*, and it was in need
of repair. Hard pressed as we were, we talked of plans to finance the building of a new steamer; Oliver felt sure that

with the insurance compensation for the *Victoria*, and our success over the past few years, we could raise the necessary money.

While we planned for the future, Lloyd's delayed payment for the *Victoria's* loss. At first they were wary, professing to be doubtful of our claim. After weeks of fruitless meetings and testimony during the winter of 1851, they took a firm stand: the *Victoria* had been lost through negligence and poor seamanship. They cited Commander Jardine's age, sixty-nine, as a contributing factor. Yet behind such allegations lurked the thinly veiled suspicion that her loss was brought about intentionally. We had been in financial difficulty from the first, and had seized on a way to extricate ourselves at Lloyd's expense. There was a hearing and Lloyd's prevailed, against all evidence and reason. They would not pay.

Without the insurance money, and with a now tarnished reputation however undeserved, we found that potential financial backers had faded away like the morning mist. We were destitute. There was no money to pay for the needed repairs to the *Viscount*, and no credit to be obtained.

We had the choice of selling our share of the Rancorne Mine or losing the *Viscount*. In Oliver's mind there was no question; the mine must be sold. To go against him would have been to put a bridgeless chasm between us—and who was to say which choice was the wiser one?

The mine was sold and the money enabled us to keep the *Viscount* in operation. But with the mine went our monopoly of transporting its coal to Charleston. The contract for the purchase of the coal still continued, but free trade now existed between England and the United States. A new American steamship company, the Collins Line, had come into existence and was heavily subsidized by the American government. They had two fast, luxurious new wooden paddle wheel steamships, the *Atlantic* and the *Arctic*, and American passengers and shippers preferred to patronize their own country's tonnage. Mr. Gore's American consortium elected to have Collins vessels transport their Edisto cotton to Liverpool and carry back the Rancorne coal to America. The *Viscount* was repaired and ready to sail, but we no longer had the forward contracts vital to our survival.

On Matthew Jardine's death, Oliver had become the Earl Jardine of Singapore and young Charles the Ninth Viscount Birkenhead. There was a certain irony in that. Matthew has amassed his fortune to achieve peerage and establish his position in the shipping world. The peerage remained, but all of his wealth had gone down with the *Victoria*. The title remained, but it was of little use to us now.

Despite our dire financial position, Oliver and I had never been closer. We had only each other to cling to, and our love flourished, though naught else would bend to our efforts. Living at Holylake was not as hateful as I had expected. Ned and Emily, who had settled contentedly at Holylake when we had moved aboard the *Victoria*, now considered the ancient fortress to be their home. In time, I, too, grew to have a reluctant fondness for the old pile. Oliver and the two children loved it and perhaps that influenced me. Yet I often dreamed at night, with the ever-present pounding of the surf in my ears, that I was back aboard the foundering *Victoria*—and woke in a sweat of cold terror.

To wipe out the memory of past fears and present trouble, Oliver proposed that we should travel to London to view the forthcoming Great Exhibition. Truth to tell, the prospect did enliven my spirits, and Emily and I spent many happy days preparing my wardrobe for the great event.

"We must be there for the opening day, for the Queen will be in attendance," Oliver stated. "Who knows what may come of it? There are sure to be many men of position and influence on hand. . . ."

I was aglow with excitement as we took our places under the vast glass domes of the Crystal Palace on the first of May, amidst the elegant throngs who came to see what the Prince Consort had wrought. *Punch* had named it the "Crystal Palace" and the name was apt. The huge edifice was constructed entirely of sparkling glass and intricate iron fretwork, rising in glorious domes high enough to accommodate full-grown elm trees within.

Under that soaring canopy, the tiny Queen appeared as magical as any princess in a fairytale, arrayed in a forthy gown of pink and silver, with a small crown and feathers adorning her heard, and the Koh-i-noor diamond at her breast. Yet for all her diminutive size in the airy, glittering palace, she was thoroughly regal as she moved along the central aisle to the triumphant music of many organs and the wild cheering of all present. I was not embarrassed to find my cheeks wet, for many around me were moved to tears by the stirring sight.

We remained in London, staying at Morley's Hotel a full week, for the Exhibition was a miracle of beauty and interest and we never wanted for entertainment. Like children at a fete, we marveled at displays from around the world; truly, there was much to see, for the Crystal Palace extended upward for three tiers, and covered eighteen acres of Hyde Park. I took special pleasure in knowing that the great edifice was the creation of Joseph Paxton, who had built my father's orchid house at Greystones so many years earlier.

Oliver was most intrigued by industrial exhibits that had to do with steam engines and their application, but I dreamed over lustrous Indian pearls and magnificent French baths. I possessed only a lounge bath, japanned on the outside in brown, and marbled within. I was grateful enough for it, set comfortably on a bath sheet in front of my bedchamber fire in drafty Holylake. But how I longed for one of the grand new French tubs on display at the Exhibition. My favorite was of copper, enameled in rosy pink and gilt. It was meant to be installed in a room set aside especially for the purpose of bathing. It had a faucet for letting cold water into the tub, and an ingeniously conceived jacket for heating the bath water within by means of a small furnace. Nor did it need to be emptied by hand, for there was a pipe to carry the water away. How I coveted a bath like that! I wondered if Oliver could devise some similar contrivance for me at Holylake, but though he nodded and smiled, he hurried me off to view another exhibit and talked to put it out of my mind.

On the last day of the Exhibition, I saw Adriana Rantana.

She stood with a group of elegant, laughing men and women some distance from us. I looked away swiftly, hoping she had not seen us, and patting my hair into place in case she had.

"Margaret darling. How marvelous to meet you here! And Oliver."

Adriana stood before us, cocking her head to one side in the way I so disliked. Her narrow amber eyes examined Oliver from head to toe and back again, slowly. "How well you look, Oliver," she purred. "So . . . virile."

She seized the hand of the tall, dark man with her. "Margaret, you remember Vittorio, I'm sure."

I hadn't recognized the handsome, worldly man at her side as one of the callow boys I had known all those summers ago at the Villa Rantana. I stood as if stricken dumb while Adriana introduced him to Oliver. I saw Oliver's jaw tighten, as he remembered Adriana's stories. The situation was quite to Adriana's liking.

"I have bought a house in London, so we are near neighbors. How is your steamship line, Oliver? I hear so many interesting accounts. . . ."

There was nothing to say; Adriana would know our position to the last sou, at least as well as we did. Oliver looked at her steadily and Vittorio maintained a distant social smile. But neither of them mattered. It was I, always, who was Adriana's game, and her eyes scarcely left mine.

"Dear Margaret. There are no friends so true as the ones we make at school, do you not agree? We must see each other more often. Are you staying long in London? No? *Quel dommage! Do* you remember the marvelous times we have had together? Ah, well, one day fate will reunite us, perhaps."

Somehow it was finally over, Adriana whirled off in a cloud of perfume, promising that she, and Vittorio too, would certainly visit us at the first opportunity.

"The four of us share so many memories! It will be quite like old times. . . ." Her devil's smile seemed to linger in the air when she had gone.

We stood in strained silence; Oliver was the first to speak.

"He is very handsome, your old friend Vittorio."

"So he is—now," I agreed. "He was a gawky, boring schoolboy when I knew him. No doubt he is still boring." I darted a glance at Oliver. "Adriana is as lovely as ever."

He gave me a sidewise smile and tucked my hand in the crook of his arm. "Oh, quite. Boring, too, wouldn't you say?"

That night I clung to Oliver like a wanton. I could not get enough of him. When we had made love once—in a desperate frenzy of desire, for such was my mood—I set myself to arouse him afresh. I was content only when he was totally engaged with me. Perhaps I chose the best medicine for what afflicted me. The second time he took me he groaned my name at the moment of ecstasy with such a wealth of love and longing that I was at last comforted. Yet I woke in the night, gripped by a nightmare of Adriana again usurping my place in Oliver's life and bed. I slithered closer to him and wrapped my arms about him, to hold us both safe from the threat. He woke and gathered me to him. . . .

It was on that night that Olivia was conceived, I decided later.

When I realized, three months later, that I was again with child, I was less than overjoyed. I would be giving yet another hostage to the Curse that never ceased to haunt us. Oliver, thank God, took away some of my pangs, for he welcomed the news of the coming event with undisguised pleasure. Olivia Victoria Jardine was born at Holylake at the end of January, 1852.

Olivia was our joy—an endless delight in the gray days we were living through. She was a beautiful baby with eyes that soon turned silver-gray, and hair that became a mass of fine, red-blonde curls. Charles, now seven, and Howard, approaching ten, were adoring and protective of her, and I felt she was destined to be greatly indulged—not least of all by her father, who delighted in her from the start.

Poor Oliver! It was well that he had something to lighten his mood, for the Jardine-Blue Funnel Line was a source of continued disappointment. He had determined that we could not succeed without some sort of subsidy, and he hit upon the idea that the *Viscount* should obtain a Royal Mail contract. The Canadian, Samuel Cunard, had long operated scheduled mail packets between Halifax, Boston, and Liverpool, and in recent years had added twice-monthly voyages to New York to his service.

"Cunard's mail subsidy now amounts to one hundred and forty-five thousand pounds annually," Oliver declared angrily. "His vessels are smaller than the *Viscount*—"

"And he has many of them," I countered. "Moreover, he has a contract with six years left to run. Oliver, you cannot hope to compete with Cunard when we have only one vessel."

"There's a lot of criticism of the favoritism being shown to Cunard over other British nationals. He has the whole pie. With this comfortable subsidy assured, he cuts freight rates in half when another ship leaves a port at the same time as his. Skims off the cream and fills his own holds first!" Oliver asserted bitterly. "Who can compete against that?"

Who indeed? Particularly when the Lords of the Admiralty, who controlled the awarding of mail contracts, had set their minds firmly against the use of iron ships in that service.

Despite my strong misgivings, Oliver would not give over. He used his title and his powerful Howard family connections to arrange meetings with various members of the Admiralty. Although he reported that much hope was held out to him, that many were sympathetic to his cause, no contract for carrying mail to America, nor anywhere else, was forthcoming.

While Oliver spent his time chasing that will-o'-the-wisp, it was left to me to do battle for what bookings could be gotten for the *Viscount*. Poor Ned was kept busy driving me from Holylake to call on business establishments that could use our services. Everywhere I pleaded our case and cut our rates as low as I dared, to enable us to keep the *Viscount* in operation.

Surprisingly, I found it less difficult than I had supposed. Remembering how Commander Jardine had taken me with him when he called on the Duke of Norfolk, I determined to learn from the experience. I made use of all of my feminine wiles to charm and cajole the men who could help me—men who were impressed by my title, as well as my natural advantages—and who were in a position to decide which ships should carry their goods.

It soon became a game at which I excelled, and I took pride in my victories. I was a novelty in the world of British shipping, and a most decorative one, it appeared. I traded on that. In addition, I employed an agent in America, found for me by my ever-faithful Mr. Richard Cecil, to aid in arranging cargoes from America to Liverpool. Despite our joint efforts, the *Viscount* often returned with her hold half empty. Perhaps it was more difficult from that end, but I often wished for a Charleston or New York woman of my own ilk, who was not averse to exerting her charm when it would work to her benefit.

And so we limped along for almost three years. Oliver was convinced that he would succeed in competing with Mr. Cunard, and relied on me to keep us afloat financially in the meantime. I thanked God nightly that Adriana Rantana had never made good her threat to visit us at Holylake. Perhaps she had found her "strong man" and married again.

CHAPTER 38

While Oliver and I struggled in our own ways to save the Jardine-Blue Funnel Line, England was becoming increasingly embroiled in a struggle of greater magnitude, a confrontation with Russia that was to culminate in war in the Crimea.

Britain had for some time been uneasily aware of the growth of the Russian Navy and the Russian threat to Constantinople. If the disintegrating Turkish empire was to lose control of Constantinople, Russia would be able to menace England's connections with India and our Eastern empire.

English public opinion was incensed by what it saw as Russia's autocratic behavior. The dispute over guardianship of the Holy Places in Palestine led to Russian occupation of two Turkish vassal states, and in October of 1853 Turkey declared war against Russia.

Under orders from Czar Nicholas I, a naval squadron from the strong Russian arsenal at Sebastopol sank the Turkish fleet in the harbor of Sinope.

Outrage in England reached fever pitch. Everywhere I went people talked of nothing else. The newspapers echoed enthusiastically the public's demand for war. In the following months The Porte—the governing body of the Turkish empire—France, and England rallied to the aid of Turkey, and the Crimean War began.

For years our Lords of the Admiralty had been convinced that iron ships had no merit. Their experts advised that an iron vessel could not resist shot unless the vessel were of such a weight that it would not float. Moreover, the shot went right through iron plates riveted together, and caused shattering when it emerged on the other side of the vessel. Should it strike a rib, the experts opined, the ship must surely go down. For that reason the Admiralty had long favored mercantile ships built of wood, with a view to arming them to serve as men-of-war if needed. As a result Mr. Cunard, whose ships were built of wood, was subsidized to carry mail—and we were not.

Oliver, as well as the owners of the Peninsular and Oriental Line, had fought for years against the theory, to no avail. American naval opinion, bowing before England's leadership in the maritime world, followed suit. Their ships were built of wood, despite President Polk's recommendations for iron.

The naval committee that found iron ships undesirable for fitting as men-of-war found the Cunard ships more suitable. Oliver chortled over that somewhat bitterly.

"They'll put four thirty-two-pounders on each side and pivot guns in the bow and stern and send them off to war! Then perhaps the rest of us will have a chance at trade."

Instead, when the Crimean War began, Cunard's largest ships were requisitioned for transport duty. In February of

1854 the Cunarders *Cambria* and *Niagara* left Liverpool carrying troops to Varna, on the Black Sea. Others soon followed, for our forces suffered huge losses from cholera before the enemy was even met; more and more mercantile ships were commissioned to transport men and horses through the Bosporus and north to the Crimea, for the campaign at the Alma and the march on Sebastopol.

With fewer ships available for the regular Atlantic trade, our business picked up rapidly. The *Viscount*'s hold was always full, with more cargo awaiting transport. Our lone ship plied the Atlantic with scarcely time for necessary repairs. Despite our new prosperity Oliver fumed, for war fever ran high in England and he was incensed that his precious ship should be accounted unfit for war service because it was of iron.

That eventually changed. The shelling of the Turkish fleet at Sinope, with every vessel shattered and all four thousand men aboard lost, had demonstrated the power of shellfire. As the Crimean War progressed, only France's iron-armored gunboats proved able to withstand that deadly fire. The *Viscount* was beating her way back to Liverpool when we were informed that the Admiralty was commissioning her for troop transport.

Oliver had got his wish. The vessel was to be fitted with four 18-pounders and carry eight gunners to man them, though there was little likelihood that ordnance would be needed. We would be traveling friendly waters until we reached the Black Sea—and the British fleet was there.

Barely two weeks later we left Liverpool aboard the *Viscount*, with a full crew and carrying two hundred men of the Coldstream Guards and 120 cases of new Enfield rifles to replace the Miniés of the Third Division in the Crimea. It was a curious voyage in many respects, colored by what was to come. Though I was not without fear, the high spirits of the Guards, in their red tunics and bearskins, half convinced me that we were invulnerable and that the Russians would soon be made aware of this. We stopped at Malta to take on fresh water, coal, and fruit, and then steamed across the Mediterranean and the Aegean, through the Dardanelles and the Sea of Marmora. But once we had passed through the narrow strait of the Bosporus, and thence into the Black Sea, the weather became as cold as the North Atlantic, and the water choppy and dark under the late October sky.

In accordance with our orders, we reported at the small

Bulgarian town of Varna. Varna, on the western shore of the Black Sea, was the pivot point of the British operation. Three hundred miles to the northeast, across the Black Sea, lay Sebastopol, the Russian naval stronghold on the coast of the Crimea. At Varna we were directed to land our troops and supplies at Balaclava, a small port south of Sebastopol, where the British had established headquarters. Though we had heard much of the British men-of-war in the Black Sea, we saw only two on the distant horizon as we made the crossing. Our ship, which loomed so large at quayside, had never seemed to me smaller or more vulnerable, despite our ordnance and the gunners who lounged about enjoying a sea voyage that required nothing of them. But at Varna, in addition to our orders, Oliver had got some encouraging news.

"The British and French have Sebastopol under seige. The Russians have sunk some of their largest ships across the mouth of the harbor to keep the allied fleet out. But at the same time, their own ships can't pass, so you are worrying for nothing, Margaret. Besides, they have only sailing vessels. They couldn't catch us in any case!"

It was in the almost landlocked harbor at Balaclava that I first saw the British and French fleets. The harbor basin was not wide, and along each side were moored the men-of-war, bristling with cannons. We nosed through the narrow passage between them and unloaded our troops and supplies in the shortest time possible.

Oliver strode about the deck, hearty and in top form, bidding the men good luck as they departed.

"I believe you wish you were going with them," I accused, half in earnest.

"Perhaps I do," he admitted with a grin. "There is a vast excitement in all of this. . . ." He waved a hand toward the panorama visible before us. Beyond the town itself, the hills reached upward, and as far as the eye could see, were dotted with white tents that appeared no larger than thimbles in the distance.

"I'd estimate that it stretches for a good twenty miles." Oliver's face, as he gazed at the distant reaches, was alight with interest. "Sebastopol can't hold out much longer. Our sixty-eight-pounders will do for her, mark my words."

The British 68-pounders were, from all reports, deadly weapons having no equal on the Russian side. All the same, I was less sanguine than Oliver. The Russians had been able to shell the Turkish fleet into shards. In the distance there was the muffled roar of cannon fire exchanged between the British guns and the Russians on the fortified hill they called the mamelon. The seige, we were told, had gone on for weeks, yet the Russians showed no sign of surrender.

"I pray you are right, Oliver, for there's a feel of snow in the air. I would hate to think of our soldiers existing in those tents once the cold weather closes in."

As soon as the disembarkation was completed, we reversed our engine and steamed slowly out of the crowded harbor, stern first, for there was no room to turn around and no berth for us within. The barometer was falling, and outside the harbor there was a stiff inshore wind that increased in strength steadily, presenting us with the danger of being driven onto the steep, rocky coast on either side of the narrow harbor inlet. The water proved to be so deep that we could find no holding ground for our anchor, and after a hasty conference, Oliver and Captain Craigh decided to put to sea without delay. I was pleased, for Sebastopol, with its huge cannons commanding the sea, was only a few miles to the north and I wished with all my heart to put distance between us. When the grim coastline of the Crimea had vanished behind the horizon I breathed a prayer of gratitude.

It was well after midnight when I woke to find that Oliver, who had been asleep at my side, was on his feet and shrugging into his clothing.

"What is it, Oliver, what's wrong?"

"Some problem below. Captain Craigh has sent for me. I'll be back as soon as I can."

With that he was gone, fastening his oilskins as he went out the door of the cabin. Almost immediately an ominous silence settled over the *Viscount*. The engine had stopped! I leaped from my warm bed and dressed quickly. Fear, never far from my mind since the disaster aboard the *Victoria*, made a hard knot somewhere inside my rib cage. I hurried out on deck and was stopped in my tracks by the force of the wind. The Black Sea was boiling around us, driven by a strong easterly wind that seemed to freeze my very teeth in my mouth. Overhead not a star could be seen, and the streaming clouds were black against an inky sky.

I heard the captain bellow, "Loose sail!" and the familiar chant as the sailing crew ran up the sails and close-hauled the vessel. We were heading as close to the wind as possible, for behind us, to the west, lay the guns of Sebastopol. When I saw Captain Craigh leave the bridge and hurry below, I followed. The heat that rose to meet me as I descended the iron stairs into the boiler room was a welcome relief from the cold wind on deck, but there was little solace to be found in the unusual quiet.

The fires were being damped down and the steam bled off. Oliver and the chief engineer were in grim-faced conference, and Captain Craigh joined them. I stood aside and listened, no longer so needful to push myself forward as I once had been. There was trouble with the steam line; it could be repaired but it would require several hours.

I returned to my cabin and went back to sleep, believing that with every hour, under steam or sail, we were on our way back to England. I had a rude awakening when I was thrown from my bunk to the floor by a huge explosion of sound that shook the *Viscount* from stem to stern.

The boilers had gone! It must be that, there was nothing else. . . . With shaking hands, fearing to see steam begin to seep into my cabin, I dressed quickly and opened the cabin door a cautious inch. There was no sign of steam, nor, for that matter, of the engine. But there was much confused shouting and racket from the deck. With the second deafening blast of sound came a great cracking of wood—and I knew. We were being fired on. Worse, we were being hit!

The main deck, as much as I could see of it in the murky predawn light, was a mad scene of noise and confusion. The sailing crew jumped to Captain Craigh's bellowed orders, and from somewhere forward came the cries of wounded men. As I stood, not knowing what to do, where to look for safety, there came the flash and roar of our own small cannon. Where was Oliver? Why would anyone be firing on us here?

There was a hellish roar and the high, keening scream of a canon ball. I watched, horrified, as the slings of the main topsail yard were hit. The reefed sail came down in a lopsided surge. Another well-placed shot carried away the funnel. My God, we were being demolished! Was Oliver lying dead somewhere out there on the deck?

Then I saw the vessel attacking us. She was a small brigantine fitted with four cannons and a pivot gun at the bow. Through the smoke and spray I could distinguish neither her name nor her colors, but I had no doubt where she came from. If the Black Sea fleet was safely sealed behind its sunken ships at Sebastopol, here was a renegade of shallow enough draft to find a way through.

The cannonading seemed to go on and on. Though our

masts still stood, the sails and yards were in wreckage, and nowhere could I see Oliver. The small craft took several hits from our cannons, but they were above the waterline and did little apparent damage, missing both masts. She appeared no larger than a troublesome gnat as she darted about. Yet within a half hour, all of our cannons were demolished by her fire and their gunners lay dead or badly wounded in a fearful mess of iron and blood.

Only then did silence fall. Just as I saw Oliver, soot-stained and filthy, emerge on deck from below, we were hailed by the brigantine, *Vanya*.

"Stand by for boarding."

We had little choice. With no steam, no weapons, and our rigging in tatters, we were immobile and defenseless.

Oliver made his way across the hellish deck toward me, speaking to the grim-faced sailing crew on the way. I saw him stop in his tracks once, as a seaman spoke to him urgently, and then he was at my side. He spoke hurriedly.

"Margaret, Captain Craigh is dead. Struck through the head by a shard of iron, so the helmsman tells me. The steam line is repaired, but without a funnel we can't fire the boilers. I had hoped to appear as one of the seamen, but without Captain Craigh I shall have to take charge. Go to our cabin and remain there. Stay out of sight if you can."

I was prepared to resist, but one clance at Oliver's grim face changed my mind. I repaired to my cabin and bolted the door. And there I sat, in a welter of fear and anxiety, trying to interpret the sounds on deck, wishing I could be invisible, wishing I were a man, and so could witness what was going on. They were Russian, I was sure only of that. But the call to stand by had been in English, heavily accented. So an English-speaking officer was in charge. That made it more likely that the small ship was a part of the Russian fleet and not a pirate. I could find little to choose between the two. At least the steam line was repaired. If only we could get away somehow!

Mixed in with my confused fears was shame that so small a vessel could have taken us so easily. It had come up on us in the dark, without lights, I had no doubt, and fired without warning. Barbarians! But that was not a comforting thought, and I paced my confined area, ready at one moment to open the door boldly and stride out—and the next fearful of the kind of men who were surely aboard us by now. I had heard the shouts as the grappling hooks were made fast and the grating sound of the boarding, for the small boat that put out from the brigantine bumped against our side in the rough seas.

I was released from my exile shortly thereafter by a general search of the *Viscount*. The cabin door was tried and then a command came in a language I had never heard before—or at least not so guttural and coarse a version of it. I could understand the heavy blow that hit the door, however, and I hastened to unbolt it before it was stove in.

Two burly, dark-haired men in common seamen's garb stood without. They looked at me in open-mouthed astonishment that slowly changed to grins that I liked far less. One of them took me firmly by the arm, and when I jerked away, fetched me a blow on the side of the head that knocked off the weatherproof hat I still wore, and made my ears ring.

No doubt he saw the new fear that flared within me, for his grin grew broader and with one hand he ripped away the oilskins that I had counted my best protection—and not only against the weather. After one delighted leer he hauled me to him, and his breath, reeking of onion and fish, seemed to smother me in a sickening miasma. I switched my head aside, but he succeeded in planting a wet and revolting kiss on my mouth. While I struggled and kicked, his mate shouted at him in unintelligible jargon. There was a short, sharp argument, but in the end my captor shrugged and gave me an "I can wait" leer. Stumbling along with my arm pinioned in his large and hairy fist, I was trotted to the deck by two grinning apes who evidently considered me booty of war!

On the deck stood the bloody, battered crew of the *Viscount*, lined up before three officers from the brigantine, trim and untouched in their white uniforms. The one commanding, or so I surmised him to be, for the other two stood slightly behind him, looked up as we interrupted the tableau. His gaze claimed mine for one moment in utter surprise, and something in that look made me realize that my hair had fallen loose and now tumbled over my shoulders. I tossed it back and faced him defiantly.

Oliver stepped forward and said to the commanding officer, his voice shaking with fury, "Your men are manhandling my wife. Please be good enough to call them off."

The Russian officer spoke in a quick, harsh voice. The hand that had been bruising my arm dropped immediately and I stumbled across the deck to stand by Oliver.

As if there had been no interruption, the officer returned to matters at hand.

"We could have destroyed you, as you see. We prefer to claim you as a prize." His smile was thin. "We hear much of steamers and admire them. When our informants in Balaclava reported your arrival we readied ourselves. God was with us, no doubt."

He turned his steely gaze on Oliver. "You were second in command of this vessel?" He peered again at the ship's papers in his hand. "Jardine?"

"Second in command and owner. Earl Oliver Howard Jardine of Singapore." Despite his filthy and disheveled appearance, there was dignity in Oliver's stance and voice. "My wife, Countess Jardine."

The Russian officer bowed. Plainly he considered the English a race apart if such unlikely specimens represented their aristocracy, but he had more immediate questions in mind.

"Why did you stop? You have trouble with your steam apparatus, yes?"

Oliver shrugged. "A vital part broke and cannot be repaired. Such things happen often, which is why we carry sail. It can be replaced in Liverpool."

"In Liverpool. Indeed? But you are not going to Liverpool; have I not been clear? You are going to Sebastopol."

There was a loud groan from our crew and wide smiles from the seamen from the Russian brigantine. Though they might not understand English—almost certainly did not—they understood the intent.

The Russians were efficient. Our colors came down from the gaff and a prize crew of four, commanded by an officer, Lieutenant Platov, was left on board to conduct us back to Sebastopol. Among them was the seaman who had dragged me from my cabin. The Vanya, close-hauled on a starboard tack, was soon far in the distance. Our sailing crew was put to work repairing the rigging under the watchful eyes of three of the Russian seamen. The engine-room crew, along with five gunners who had survived the battle, were locked in the boiler room below, under the guard of the fourth Russian seaman. Unless a British man-of-war sighted us and came to our rescue, we would shortly be on our way to Russia.

Three gunners and four of our crew, in addition to Captain Craigh had died in battle with the Vanya. Three other men were wounded, though none seriously. We were allowed to give our dead a proper burial at sea. Oliver, in his whites, read the Church of England service over the bodies of the eight men. Long planks, placed side by side, each with one end resting on the deck and the other on the bulwarks, served as their biers. When the brief service was over the planks were raised, and the bodies, sewn into their hammocks, slid to their watery graves. My thoughts turned to Matthew Jardine, who had had no funeral rites. I hoped he rested easy.

I judged Lieutenant Platov to be in his early thirties and overeager to succeed in this command. The expression in his darting dark eyes changed rapidly from haughtiness as he surveyed the work in hand to an almost childlike curiosity about anything new to him. He had a full, dark beard and strutted about, ramrod straight, barking his orders with a harsh manner and chilly eye. He made it clear that both Oliver and I were to call him "sir," and his own men, as well as ours, jumped to his command, or suffered.

Lieutenant Platov had examined the *Viscount's* machinery with great interest. It was ambition rather than scientific curiosity which inspired him. Mr. McConnish, the chief engineer, fiddled something or other which he displayed as the broken part that had caused the engine to fail. Platov nodded wisely at the welter of misinformation Mr. McConnish rattled off in a Scottish accent that even I was at a loss to understand.

It was impossible to avoid Platov's company, for he was a snob and found enormous interest in having two captives who bore titles. Moreover, he was determined to learn all that could be learned about a steam vessel in the time available. While repairs to the rigging went on, he kept thinking of new questions for Oliver to answer.

How fast could the *Viscount* travel when under steam? How many trips to America had she made? How many days outward bound? How many days on the return voyage? How much coal did she burn and what kind? How, precisely, did the steam drive the engine and turn the screw propeller?

The young lieutenant had had a classical education and spoke French fluently, but his English, like Oliver's French, was halting. Soon it was I who answered his many questions.

It was apparent that by the end of this voyage, Platov hoped to appear an authority on steam vessels among his comrades. But his aspirations did not stop there.

"Lady Jardine"—he delighted in rolling that name off his tongue—"could the *Viscount* not somehow be made to operate again? Perhaps your men had not enough time to solve the problem of the repair?"

At that question I frowned, as if thinking deeply. In truth, I was thinking, though not along the lines Platov had in mind. I decided there was little to be lost by exploring further the glimmer of an idea that had come to me.

"Perhaps you are right, sir. No doubt the engine could be fixed in time. But there would be no point, sir," I said regretfully. "The funnel was shattered, as you know. Without a funnel a steamship cannot function. There must be a way to send out the smoke from the burning coal, sir."

The more "sirs" the better, if they would soothe Platov, for what I had in mind surely would not.

"Ah, yes," he agreed, nodding. "A very great problem."

"Though not an insurmountable problem, sir. No doubt my husband could construct a new funnel if he set his mind to it."

"Indeed?" Platov fell silent. Shortly thereafter he examined the remains of the funnel, peering down the flue hole and looking doubtful.

Within the hour Oliver was instructed to set to work at once and construct a new funnel. "I wish the ship to be in the best possible condition when I deliver her," Platov said. "Prove your worth now and no doubt you will be better treated on your arrival."

Oliver, not too surprisingly, looked stupefied. "A new funnel?"

I was terrified that he might give the show away by looking too pleased at the suggestion, and squeezed his hand very hard. He obliged by frowning thoughtfully at the horizon and shaking his head in doubt.

"Hmmmm, well, I suppose I could try. Perhaps I could jury-rig a funnel of sorts that might serve. . . ."

"Jury-rig?" Platov looked at me. "What does that mean, jury-rig?"

"My husband means that perhaps he could make a funnel that would function satisfactorily, though it might be unconventional in appearance, sir."

Platov smiled and rubbed his hands together in satisfaction. "Very good. After, we will see what can be done about the engine."

Oliver needed no further encouragement. For a time Platov watched carefully as Oliver found what was left of the funnel and took measurements in a businesslike fashion. I stayed close to Platov's side, a veritable fountain of information on the use of steam engines in ships, although I made sure the facts imparted were of a general nature. I had no wish for Platov to understand more than was necessary to maintain his interest.

When Oliver said that he would need to go to the boiler room to continue his work, Platov nodded and called Kurofsky, the seaman who had tried to molest me, and detailed him to keep an eye on Oliver while he was below. That was not too bad. Kurofsky knew no English. If Oliver had a plan in mind he could speak freely with the men in the engine room.

I was invited to dine with Lieutenant Platov in the captain's quarters in half an hour. It was in the nature of a royal command and I accepted prettily. Poor Oliver would be eating hurriedly in the engine room, under the eyes of Kurofsky and his fellow guard.

I was in a fever of anxiety. How long would it take us to reach the Russian coast? Would there be enough time for Oliver to complete a funnel? Would we be able to overpower five armed men with no weapons except the belaying pins or lengths of pipe that might come to hand? We outnumbered them greatly, but they knew it and never seemed even to blink. In our favor was the fact that our progress was slow, for only some of the rigging had proved to be reparable, and the wind had shifted so that we were obliged to tack in order to steer for Sebastopol.

Also, I realized with surprise, Platov was in no hurry. Much more than he wanted to arrive with his prize, he wanted to arrive with it in steaming condition. Once he saw the funnel replaced, he would be after Oliver to repair the "broken part" of the steam apparatus. So our tacks were long and our sails were reefed. If allowing our men more time would accomplish Platov's ambition, he was giving us all possible leeway to achieve it for him.

Platov had retired to his quarters, no doubt to ready himself for dinner with a countess. I took the opportunity to visit the galley. The cooks looked at me in some surprise as I nosed about, searching for a knife what would suit me. I chose one and was about to slip it into the pocket of my dress when the head cook, with an evil smile, held out a long, thin knife as sharp-pointed as a stiletto.

"Filleting knife, m'lady. Handy if you need it fast and

easy-sliding like. Go for the neck, straight across if you can.
Or behind the ear, that's next best."

To illustrate, he tickled his own neck with the tip of the
blade and handed it to me with a conspiratorial smile. "Good
luck, m'lady."

Wordless, I took the knife and fled, trembling within at the
picture he had conjured up in my mind. And yet I was grateful for the advice and the way he had forced me to face my
purpose—if I didn't want to end up in Russia. With
Kurofsky.

At dinner I entertained Platov with stories of the speed of
the *Viscount,* the directness of her course, and how our
Queen herself had called her "the finest steamer in the
world." I considered it unnecessary to mention the *Victoria*—it was the sentiment that counted.

"She will be most unhappy to lose so fine a vessel, I am
sure," Platov commented smugly, and relapsed into smiling
silence, no doubt picturing himself arriving at Sebastopol in
triumph. We shared numerous glasses of cognac before we
arose from the table. My head for it was considerably better
than Platov's, I noticed.

It was beginning dusk when Oliver, with two of the engine
crew and the ever-present Kurofsky, emerged onto the deck
with a strange device. It was a funnel made of a patchwork
of sheet iron, bent and riveted into shape.

"Aha! The jury-rig," Platov exclaimed, rubbing his hands
together.

The funnel was fitted into place and a collar attached at
the joint, under Platov's supervision. Kurofsky contented himself with sending steaming glances in my direction.

Platov was in a great state of excitement. "So we make all
progress. Now let us see about this steam engine. Perhaps I
can be of help in solving the problem," he suggested loftily,
no doubt buoyed up by cognac.

He followed Oliver below, waving Kurofsky to see to matters on deck in his absence. I hurried for safety toward my
cabin, but the shaggy Russian had been waiting for his prize
too long to let me escape so easily. He was hard on my heels,
pushing through the doorway before I could slide the bolt.

He slammed one huge hand over my mouth and locked the
other around my waist. I understood no word of what he
said, nor did I need to. He eyes burned down into mine, and
I ceased to be afraid for my honor and feared for my very
life.

He was a beast, a great hairy brute who reeked of fish and less savory stenches. He held me fast while he lit the oil lamp. When I flailed about feebly he clouted both sides of my head with a hand that felt like a sledge hammer. My knees sagged under me and he pushed me down and straddled me on the floor. I struggled to free myself as he loosened his nether garments, and found my left arm twisted up beneath me and tugged until I thought my shoulder would surely snap. When he took me I was half unconscious from the bone-cracking pain in my shoulder. Plunging and grunting like some hairy pig, he achieved his pleasure.

When he was quite finished—a lifetime later—he rolled over onto his back beside me on the floor and turned his face to grin at me. The stench of his breath, the dizzying pain in my shoulder and my head, the sick disgust inside me—they all came together in a mounting wave of nausea and my stomach revolted. There was a chamber pot in a small compartment under the bunk and I managed to fetch it out before I retched and vomited.

I was heaving and gasping and crying all at once, more wretched than I had ever been in my life before, and that pig lay there watching me, a contented smile on his face. I looked up once to see his eyes on me, and I knew, beyond a doubt, that the moment I was finished being ill he was going to take me again. I made up my mind that I would die before that happened.

The knife was in my pocket. While wiping my mouth on my skirt I groped for it. Kurofsky rolled lazily toward me, confident of his power. For one fraction of a moment the lamplight caught and gleamed on the blade as I brought it up. But he was off guard and off-balance. I lunged with the strength of desperation. The knife slid home, into the side of his throat, and I pulled it toward me, still imbedded. I was faintly astonished when it sliced as easily as if I were cutting a melon. And then blood spurted everywhere. Kurofsky fell forward, jerking and flailing, half across me. I felt his blood pumping out—onto me—warm and sticky, soaking into my dress, onto my body.

I struggled free of him and crawled across the small cabin to where the washstand stood, and when I was strong enough pulled myself to my feet. There was some water in the covered bucket. I took off all of my clothing and spread my dress and petticoats over the horror on the floor so that there was nothing but a hump to be seen lying there. Then I began to wash. I must have washed for a very long time, for I became icy cold and started to shake. It was interesting, I thought, the way my hands shook, and my arms and all of my body. I giggled about it. Oliver would be amused. I stopped giggling because I was so very cold. I took my time dressing properly in clean garments. It was difficult to fasten them with shaking hands, but I was in no hurry.

Finally I was fastened and my hair was brushed and pinned. It looked quite nice, I thought. I put on my oilskins and gathered up my reticule and toilet articles, for I would not be coming back to this cabin. There was a good reason for this that I could not remember, but I knew that it was so. I unbolted the door and closed it carefully behind me.

On deck, through the wind-driven spray and the darkness, I could see lights winking in the distance, far off and high. I frowned, mildly puzzled. The sight was an unfamiliar one. I must ask Oliver where we were. Suddenly, under my feet, the deck pulsed and vibrated. The familiar sound of the engine filled my ears and snapped me back to sanity.

I ran along the deck and there was the sailing crew scrambling aloft; the *Viscount* was coming about, heading away from those distant lights. In a rush I remembered Kurofsky on my cabin floor. Platov accompanying Oliver to the engine room. And the funnel repaired. Those were the lights of Sebastopol receding behind us.

"We're going home!" I shouted out into the darkness. "Do you hear that, damn you all? We're going *home!*"

"Margaret!" Oliver called, running to me along the deck. "I was coming to find you." His arms were around me, holding me close. "They've gone, darling. At least—"

He looked around and I suddenly noticed the grinning sailors standing a decent distance away. "Avast there," Oliver instructed, "get on with the search, and look sharp about it. He's dangerous—"

"Kurofsky?" I interrupted Oliver in an urgent whisper. "He is in my cabin. Dead." The whisper wouldn't hold and I heard my own voice climbing. "I killed him. I got a filleting knife from the cook and I killed the Russian. A filleting knife, Oliver—"

I poured out the story to Oliver in a kind of sobbing hysteria, while he held me tight and rocked me back and forth. When at last I could control my shaking, he took me to the captain's quarters, then left with the seamen to deal with the remains of the Russian on my cabin floor. But not before he reassured me that we were free and safe. They had taken Platov first, in the engine room, and then the guard at the door, so they had had two guns. One of the Russian seamen on deck had been killed in the scuffle that followed, and Kurofsky had vanished—as I knew only too well. Platov and the other two Russian seamen had been put out in a small boat with oars in sight of Sebastopol.

I collapsed onto the bed in the captain's quarters and waited for Oliver to return. The sound of the engines, thrumming steadily, lulled me. We were going home . . . going home. . . .

CHAPTER 39

Though we received compensation from the government, the repairs to the *Viscount* had proved to be costly and painfully slow. By the time the vessel was again seaworthy, she was no longer needed as a troop carrier. The war in the Crimea had virtually ended with a victory for the allies in the winter of 1855. The *Viscount* was no longer needed—but neither were the other merchant ships which had been used as transport. And so the old competition for full holds began again.

We were hard pressed to make ends meet, and trouble dogged us on every front. The *Viscount* was often laid up for repairs, minor but time-consuming, and therefore disastrous financially. Holylake, too, needed extensive work, but with the two boys now in school and a governess living at Holylake to instruct Olivia, there was no money to spend on house or grounds. We were existing, but falling behind month by month, as things wore out or broke down, and we could do little about it. Such was the state of affairs that gray January day in 1856 when Adriana Rantana arrived at Holylake.

She swept into our lives, her tawny cheeks flushed from excitement or the chill wind that blew from the sea, as beautiful and impossible as ever. Oliver and I had been going over the state of our finances and I had thought that matters could hardly be worse. With Adriana's arrival they became worse and much worse almost immediately.

"Darlings, are you very angry with me? To tell you I

would come—when was it? Yes, of course, at the Exhibition, and then to let almost five years go by!"

She extended both hands to me and I took them. I scarcely knew what else to do. "Margaret, *you* will forgive me, for you understand such things. I married again, you see—a quite wonderful man, and we were desperately happy for ages. More than a year, I think. Then things began to go wrong, as they do. But you understand, I know. Getting rid of him was tiresome. I'm spiritually exhausted, I assure you. The moment I thought of you—dear Margaret and Oliver—I longed for you both. What a blessed relief to come and relax with you at Holylake, away from that frantic life that has worn me to a wraith."

I felt there was nothing to do but invite her to dine with us. Oliver seemed surprised at the invitation, but followed my lead. If Adriana noticed a lack of warmth, she overwhelmed it with her own formidable charm. My misgivings grew in proportion, for I knew Adriana. Charm was a weapon to be employed for a purpose. Oliver treated her with amused tolerance, but I could feel the sword over my head.

I had not long to wait before it fell.

We had finished dinner and were lingering at the table over cognac. Quite suddenly Adriana's gaiety vanished, as if she had finished with that role. She leaned back in her chair and surveyed Oliver and me with her old look of mocking amusement.

"I've been bored, darlings. More bored than you can conceive of. So I've thought of an amusement we can all enjoy."

Adriana's brandy-colored eyes sought us out in turn, glinting with malicious amusement.

"Have you missed me, Oliver? I think you have. We were marvelous lovers, were we not? And Margaret, darling, what of you?"

She leaned toward me along the table and slid her hand over mine before I had wit or strength to move it. "I have missed you, Margaret—you most of all."

Snatching my hand free, I pushed my chair back from the table. Adriana threw her head back and laughed. Though she spoke to Oliver, her eyes were fixed on me.

"Do you know, Oliver, this child still has a provincial notion that I am somehow a threat to her where you are concerned. That I have come to lure you away, perhaps. . . ."

Adriana's smile was lazy. "Ridiculous. What I want, of course, is simply to join you."

Oliver looked at her, a tiny frown creasing his forehead. "Join us? You mean, our firm. . . ?"

The lazy smile grew indulgent. "That too, if you wish, darling. You know that I have all of this boring money, and—you do need money, don't you?"

Oliver nodded slowly, his eyes steady on her. "You know that well enough, I'm sure."

"Well, then? What could be more reasonable than that I wish to share it with my two lovers?"

I moaned and Adriana left her chair quickly and came to me. "Now darling, don't be a child. Oliver understands these things." She stroked my hair and I flung myself away from her.

Oliver was staring at me, his face wiped clean of all expression.

"Margaret? What is she saying?"

While I struggled for words, Adriana interrupted. "Oliver, don't be difficult. Surely you know that Margaret and I have been lovers for years. Since Berri."

"No! That isn't true!" I pushed the words out in strangled gasps, for Oliver's expression was truly frightening. "It was only one summer, Oliver. . . . I was a fool. A very young and innocent one, please believe that. . . ."

Adriana laughed, tossing her head back derisively. "Margaret, really! *Still* the little white and gold angel? How pretentious you are, darling. Of course you were a dream, but . . . innocent? Now really!"

I ignored her and crossed to Oliver, who was on his feet, staring at me as if I were a stranger.

"Oliver, you must see what she's trying to do! Don't listen to her."

But Oliver did listen to her, because Adriana began to speak in a quiet, insinuating voice that went on and on, relating incidents I had never thought to hear repeated, had almost managed to put out of my mind. God knows, I had tried. At last I fled from the room, my face burning, as the old memories came flooding back with all the attendant feelings of guilt and shame I had known at the outset.

I lay on my bed in the dark for a long time, weeping and sick at heart. I had seen the look on Oliver's face. I had always felt, from my first meeting with Oliver Jardine, that something in his nature could never accept my past relationship with Adriana Rantana. He had viewed me at the begin-

ning as an angelic innocent. Our stormy years together had
taught him otherwise. And yet that illusion still lived deep
within him. His love for me would not survive this blow.

Perhaps a half hour later I heard Oliver moving about in
his bedroom. I would have to face him sooner or later. I
composed myself as best I could and crossed the small sitting
room that adjoined our bedrooms. He neither looked at me
nor spoke, but moved purposefully around the room.

"Oliver, please stop and think, darling. I was fifteen, a
child who knew nothing when I fell in with that she-devil."

I might as well have not spoken. Oliver took his heavy coat
from the wardrobe, put it on, and strode about picking up a
few possessions and shoving them into the pockets. Then he
took up the lamp.

"Oliver, what are you doing? Please, darling, talk with
me."

He left the room and I ran after him along the damp and
chilly halls of Holylake to the room where Olivia slept.
Shielding the lamplight so that it would not wake her, he stood
for a long moment staring down at his daughter. He bent to
kiss her forehead and Olivia stirred. The red-gold head turned
on the pillow and she opened her eyes.

"Papa?"

He went completely still. But Olivia smiled and went back
to sleep. Oliver braced his shoulders and marched out of the
room. I followed, pleading, while he roused Ned and told
him that they were driving to Liverpool that night. He never
once looked at me or spoke, though I wept and pleaded without pride.

Nothing availed. He went out the door and climbed into
the carriage without a backward glance. Ned whipped up the
horses. I watched, at one with the blackness around me, as
they disappeared into the winter night.

CHAPTER 40

Oliver left and Adriana remained at Holylake. She refused to
leave at my demand and threatened, if I had her ejected
bodily, to ruin my reputation not only in the business world

at large but within my own family. My children would learn why their father no longer lived at Holylake. I neither spoke to her nor acknowledged her presence. It made no difference to her. She had the insolence of great wealth and no idea that anything in life should or could be arranged contrary to her wishes. So once again Adriana Rantana made her home under my roof, and came and went as she chose. If I had believed, with Oliver's, leaving me, that she could no longer manipulate me through blackmail, she had proved me wrong.

Every day I looked for Oliver's return, or at least some word from him. With Charles and Howard away at public school, there was only little Olivia to question me. I told her that Oliver had gone to Glasgow to tend to matters of business.

Three weeks after Oliver's departure, Adriana went to Liverpool. When three days had passed and she had not returned, I was in despair. In my distraught, irrational state I believed that she had found Oliver and they were together. Then, in the middle of the night, Adriana arrived back at Holylake and stormed into my rooms.

"Margaret! Wake up!"

While I struggled from sleep, she lighted a lamp and stood by my bed, still in her traveling cloak and hat, and for the first time I saw Adriana Rantana shaken out of her superb self-confidence.

"He's gone! Oliver has gone to America!"

To America. To America. From a great distance I seemed to hear her words like a death knell ringing in my mind. I wondered why I had not thought of America earlier. It had fascinated him from the start; and now he had gone there, where people went to start a new life—leaving all of us behind.

The story poured from her. "He booked passage on an American steam vessel—the *Virtue*—two days after he left Holylake. Margaret, he has left everything, without a backward glance."

"What did you expect?" I asked in a voice as cold as my heart. "That he would leave me, his children—and go with you?"

Her eyes flickered and I knew on the instant that she had expected exactly that. I laughed. "You are a fool, Adriana. What you have managed to accomplish is known as fouling your own nest!"

"But his steamship company! How can he have walked away?"

She really did not know. She had wanted to damage me in Oliver's eyes, but she had no idea of the forces she had loosed. What Adriana considered mildly decadent, Oliver considered morally reprehensible. And yet that was the smallest part of the blow she had dealt both Oliver and me.

For all her Machiavellian tactics, Adriana understood nothing of Oliver Jardine. She had thought to destroy his "white and gold angel" once and for all. Instead, she had achieved something she had never contemplated—because she would never have considered it of importance. But I knew Oliver—his ego, the quality of his passion for me. With her sly, insinuating account of that long-ago summer, Adriana had changed me from a man's woman—Oliver's woman—to a creature that another female could possess. Worth nothing, and any man who had loved me must be a dupe and a fool!

How to explain any of that to Adriana, even if I had wanted to? Or that, by now, Oliver must realize that over the years she had used him time and again, in her efforts to get at me. Small wonder he had walked away! The ends of the earth wouldn't be too far, if it meant escaping Adriana. I turned my back to her and feigned sleep.

She stood silent for what seemed a long time before she turned out the lamp and closed my door behind her.

But in the morning, the nightmare was still to be dealt with and Adriana gave me no quarter. She seated herself at the breakfast table and when we were alone, began to organize my life as I would live it in the years to come.

"The matter of your livelihood cannot be allowed to drift on without attention, Margaret," she said crisply, very much the woman of affairs. "You have children to think of. You must take the reins in your hands again, and this time you will have help, I promise you. Fetch your account books. Explain them to me so I may see what needs to be done."

My first, overriding impulse was to seize Adriana by her hair and throw her forcibly out of my house. But the thought of my son and daughter, and of Howard, almost another son, restrained me. The financial state of the Jardine-Blue Funnel Line was deteriorating steadily, and with Oliver gone its decline would accelerate. How was I to provide for my family?

And so it began. Adriana Rantana, bored with drifting from bed to bed throughout the pleasure spots of Europe, set about taking over Oliver's role in managing the Jardine-Blue Funnel Line. With her services came a limitless amount of money. Our creditors were paid off and a new vessel ordered, more splendid than the *Viscount*. Its lines were laid down that May on the Clydeside. The *Viscount* was refurbished and Adriana made use of her extensive financial connections to see that its holds were filled.

Eventually I became accustomed to the order of things. Adriana and I worked well enough together and, surprisingly, despite the vast amounts of money she was pouring into the firm, she asked nothing in return. The months went by and a guarded pseudo-friendship grew up between us, based on the necessity of dealing with problems and decisions as they arose.

It was a surface truce; there was no warmth or trust involved, merely convenience. In the back of my mind, the memory of the dreadful blow she had dealt me seemed never to diminish. I knew she was trying to buy or cajole me back to her, but I scarcely cared what she thought she might achieve; while I knew my own heart, there was no fathoming hers. It was an uneasy peace, but the only option I had. Without Adriana's help and wealth, I and those I loved would have lost everything in short order.

Holylake was slowly renovated and life thereby became more pleasant in a physical sense. The sea still reverberated within and without, but the drafts and dampness were sealed out, the chimneys and fireplaces made to function properly. Fine carpeting and draperies replaced threadbare ones, and new heaters spread warmth throughout the ancient stone.

It was a strange interlude, for I lived with a deep grief that I sought to bury under the mundane. Yet on the surface I existed pleasantly enough, constantly busy in small ways, and occupied mentally by the larger events of building the Jardine-Blue Funnel Line into a powerful force in the shipping world. Our new ship, the *Matthew J*, was launched in February of 1857. Adriana had wanted to call her the *Lady Margaret II*, but I would have none of that. This vessel must commemorate Matthew Jardine, whom I missed of late nearly as much as I missed his son.

We heard news of Oliver indirectly. He had gone to New York; he had found work aboard a coastal steamer that plied between Charleston and St. Augustine; later he was employed on a coastal steamer carrying goods and passengers to ports along the east coast.

In time small amounts of money began to arrive from him through our solicitors. Aside from a terse note that accompanied the first sum, stating that all money received from him was to be used solely for the children, and that he hoped to send larger amounts in the future, there was no word from him.

Oliver had been gone for sixteen months when Adriana and I went to Liverpool for the first departure of our fine new vessel, the *Matthew J*, with full holds, for New York. On our return to Holylake, Adriana, who had been in a strange mood all of the afternoon and evening, imparted her latest news of Oliver.

"He is living in Charleston," she said, her eyes at once hooded and watchful. "With a woman. A Mrs. Coral Ewell."

The words hit me like a blow to the heart and I took refuge in stupidity. "Mrs. *Cora* Ewell. Has she no proper name, no husband?"

Adriana shrugged. "She's a widow. I am not responsible for the way my informants deliver their information. I know only that she is twenty-three years old and lost her husband some time ago. She and Oliver do not live together in the sense that they share a house. I doubt that Charleston society would smile on that. They are discreet—but for all practical purposes . . ."

The amused tilt of Adriana's eyebrows had never seemed more Italian. Nor more cynical.

"How long . . . ?" I found the words impossible to utter.

"How long have they been lovers? Something over six months, I gather. What difference?" She smiled at me, her full lips canted to one side. "Well, Margaret? Are you going to storm off across the Atlantic, to tear him from her bosom—if you will forgive so unfortunate a choice of words?"

I sat, frozen in my shock. "Twenty-three . . . so young?" I was nearing my thirty-second birthday and feeling as if I were double that age. *She* would be young and fresh. . . .

But Adriana chortled with amusement. "The greater fool Oliver! Is he not thirty-seven, fourteen years older than his new paramour? No doubt she has him always on the run!"

I could not join in her mockery.

Adriana yawned prodigiously and stretched like a sleek and tawny cat. "So much for Oliver. I'm for bed, darling. See you in the morning."

I sat for a long time and perhaps I wept a little. It was one thing to know that Oliver was lost to me. Another to know that he had found a new love. And a new love so much younger than I. There was a bleak, bitter taste to that, and I could not put it out of my mind. By comparison, Adriana

Rantana seemed an old and familiar threat, a *known* threat, as powerless and bereft as I was now.

I mounted the grand stairs slowly, full of my misery. I wondered if Cora Ewell was fair or dark, tall and bold or tiny and demure. I thought the latter, for Oliver was always more admiring of delicate, ladylike types. Except in bed, my mind supplied, and I found myself in my bedchamber with a haze of tears in my eyes.

I could picture them. I could picture Oliver all too clearly, all the time, every day, every hour. I saw the lithe lines of the man, his confident stride and the swing of his shoulders. I visualized his red head tilted toward *her*—whoever she was, this Cora Ewell—smiling on her as he had once smiled on me, and tumbling her—oh, God, I prayed, stop me from this folly. . . .

I undressed like an automaton in the lamplight, dropping my clothes a piece at a time. Cora. Was she fuller of bosom, slimmer of waist than I? Oh, no doubt, for she was a mere girl, after all. Were her thighs smoother, her hair softer, her eyes more loving?

I rose in the morning exhausted, wan, and with dark circles under my eyes.

Adriana, by contrast, was bright of eye and full of lighthearted chatter at breakfast. She was tender and affectionate and kept covering my hand with hers.

I understood what was in her mind. Oliver, sometimes her lover but always her rival, had been removed. Now, at last, I would turn to her. Wearily I told her that we would not be lovers and live together in the garden of delight she pictured and wanted and demanded and fought for.

Again life at Holylake went back to being an armed truce. Adriana and I were pleasant to one another on the surface, civilized in every respect before the servants, but there was an undercurrent of enmity that was defensive on my side, furious on hers. And the months went by. They drifted into one another in a curious way, where nothing changes on the surface but everything changes below, in time. I had no idea what went on in Adriana's devious mind except that it would no doubt do me a damage in the end. I couldn't help that. I was existing in the only way possible for me, spending more time with Olivia, and with Charles and Howard when they were home for school holidays. And enduring the reminiscing of the two boys when they talked of Matthew and Oliver and the days aboard the *Victoria*.

It seemed a world away, a world that could never be re-captured, a world in which Oliver existed and I could never again enter.

CHAPTER 41

Oliver Jardine arrived at the oak door of Holylake in a han-som cab on April 30, 1860, without luggage—as empty-handed as he had left, except for gifts for the children. He had been gone for four years and three months. I had missed him every day of that long, weary time.

I was coming along the corridor from the library when I heard Emily scream—and then Oliver's voice. Oliver! I stood stock-still for one stunned moment. Then I flew along the corridor and across the long stone hall and into his arms. Perhaps he had planned to be coolly reserved, but I gave him no opportunity. I hugged and clung and twined myself around him until he began to laugh and pulled gently away, to study me at arm's length.

"Margaret. Beautiful Margaret. You *are* still beautiful, More so than I remembered."

After that, everything happened as if in a dream. We walked, laughing, arms about each other, into the library, with a beaming Emily following after. Master Oliver must eat, must drink, have a pot of nice hot tea, or mayhap a glass of scotch, sir? Laughing, Oliver accepted scotch and Emily bustled off to spread the happy news of his arrival home. By a stroke of great good fortune Adriana was in London for a week. She went there, or elsewhere, to Rome, Paris, even to Saint Petersburg, from time to time. I never inquired the reason and she did not say, but I knew she had friends every-where, perhaps more obliging than I.

Howard and Charles were away at school. Olivia, who had been scarcely four when Oliver left, did not recognize her fa-ther. But Lady Olivia Jardine was not a girl to languish in the shadows, and before many minutes she was on his lap. Her pinny rucked up and her eight-year-old legs swinging happily, she giggled at Oliver's teasing. At that moment I knew that

Oliver, whatever might happen between us in future, was home to stay.

Certainly there was great strain between us. Our conversation was of events and excitements, but nothing of *us*. Oliver told me of his adventures in America—of New York and Charleston and Savannah and the coastal trade—but there was no mention of Mrs. Cora Ewell. He listened to the story of our progress and the solid position the Jardine-Blue Funnel Line now held in the Liverpool shipping community. At my first mention of Adriana his face darkened, but I swept on with my account. Let him think what he wished. If he wanted to know more, he could ask, and then we should have an exchange of information. Finally, when dinner was long over and it was time to retire, we mounted the grand stairs and walked along the hall to our bedchambers. Inside the door Oliver halted, surveying me.

"Are you quite sure you wish me to share this suite as we used to?"

I stared at him, open-mouthed. "But where else would you sleep?"

He shrugged. "Perhaps I'm usurping Adriana's place."

I ceased unbuttoning my dress and walked over to face him, eye to eye.

"Oliver. Let us settle this now, once and for all. What Adriana told you four years ago was quite true. But it was true *almost twenty years ago*. Can you not grasp that important fact? I was fifteen, Oliver, when I was seduced by Adriana. I am not making excuses, please understand, merely relating facts. But perhaps you wish to hear it in detail? A somewhat truer account than Adriana would have presented, I'm sure."

I made him listen. I told him all of it. And I made it quite clear to him that I had resisted Adriana many times over the years, when my life would have been easier for yielding.

He sat on the side of my chaise longue, head down, listening to every word. When I had finished he stood up and put his arms around me, holding me close.

"Margaret. I've been a fool. I know that. But there was something . . . something to do with my pride. . . . Part of it was that a *woman* could have you. . . ."

I brushed his lips with a gentle finger. "Can we not forget it, please, Oliver?"

In bed, our old familiar passion came rushing back, sweeping all before it. Oliver! My heart kept singing his name. Ol-

iver, with his hands and lips at my breast, Oliver's strong
body, a little more solid, heavier of limb, but still familiar,
still all that I desired, in every line and muscle and lithe detail. I loved and was loved and the past was forgotten—all
the unhappiness and injustice were over and done, wiped out
by this love that would never release me from its grip. I
wrapped myself around him knowing I would never let him
go, conscious of all of him, within and without, wanting no
more—and no less. When at last we were spent and lay side
by side, touching arms, touching legs, Oliver rose on one elbow and peered down into my eyes.

"She couldn't do that to you."

I lay silent. The past, that old dead past, still rankled, and
I had no way to wipe it from his mind.

"Well?" he persisted. "Am I better than Adriana to you?"

"Am I better than Cora Ewell to you?"

He flopped down beside me and stared at the ceiling.

"How did you know about that?"

"There are no secrets, Oliver. Things to be forgiven.
Things to be forgotten. Perhaps things that should never be
mentioned, even once. Or if mentioned once, then never
again."

There was a long silence. Then Oliver rolled toward me
and pulled me to him, tucking my head under his chin.

"Margaret, at this moment I count myself the luckiest man
in the world. Luckier than I have any right to be. I love you.
Only you. I will always love you."

There was nothing else I wanted of life. My old dream of
achievement? I had proved what I had to prove and could
rest easy. My children? I loved them dearly, but I couldn't
live their lives. I had what I wanted and couldn't live without,
safe in my bed and my arms. I wriggled closer and slept,
warm and contented.

CHAPTER 42

Against all probability, Adriana remained at Holylake. She
returned from her sojourn in London and greeted Oliver most
affably, as an old friend and no more than that. I wished, and

Oliver fervently hoped, that she would leave. But with thousands of pounds of her money invested in the Jardine-Blue Funnel Line, it was difficult to make her do so. Moreover, we had two more vessels being built to our order and Adriana was far more involved with their building than I was.

She was gracious in every respect, insisting that Oliver again take charge of our affairs, relinquishing all control, announcing herself ready to help in any ways that she could, but not putting herself forward. It was most surprising and, so far as I could see, genuine. Had Adriana mellowed? When I thought about it I found it impossible to believe. But against that I had the evidence of my own senses. I had never known her to be so tolerant and easy of manner.

Howard and Charles came home from school for the summer holidays and our household was complete. They adored Oliver, as did Olivia, and whenever he was about the house he always had two or three of them following him, asking questions about America, about new developments in steam engineering—and when they could go to sea.

Poor Olivia was jealous, for she alone had never known her grandfather Matthew, and hated being the one who had not been on the *Victoria* with him, hearing his stories of Trafalgar, East Indiamen, and the China Seas. Howard and Charles, the devils, though far too old to delight in teasing her, delighted in playing "Remember when he told us about," recounting some marvelous tale of Malay pirates, or how Charles, when only four, had learned to read the compass and follow in his grandfather's footsteps, piping out orders immediately Matthew had bellowed them to the crew.

The two boys were tall now, and inseparable when at home. Howard was a fine-looking boy, fond of sports and gregarious by nature, with hair that had darkened to a russet-brown. He would be eighteen in September and had the large frame and head of his father. Charles, just fifteen, was somewhat smaller of bone but showed promise of being as tall as Oliver. His hair was as coppery as Oliver's had been when I first met him, and he bemoaned the freckles that spattered his nose.

And Olivia? She was everyone's darling. She bounced, she shouted, she laughed and ran and was a live ray of sunshine in somber Holylake. Moreover, at eight, she was determined to become a boy as soon as she could manage it, despite the fact that she was fine-boned and feminine everywhere but in her heart!

We were happy in those months after Oliver's return. But perhaps happiness—other people's—was the one thing Adriana could not endure. I had known her longest and best; I should have been wiser; but my own happiness blinded me to danger. Innocence, as I had learned long ago, was no protection, and Adriana Rantana was a woman who knew no rules.

It was nearing the end of August. I woke in the night and didn't know why. I'd heard something, a cry? I reached out for Oliver and he wasn't there. Alarmed, I struggled to my feet and went out into the long dim upper corridor. Even in August, Holylake was chill underfoot. Again I heard sounds, raised voices. Oliver—and Adriana! A kaleidoscope of images flooded my mind as I ran along the corridor. Images out of the past: Oliver and Adriana in Glasgow, in that bed; Oliver and Adriana in Calcutta House. Yet none of those images had substance, for above all else, I trusted Oliver at last.

Charles's room. They were in Charles's room! I arrived at the open door to witness a tableau I would never forget. My son—my *son*—crouched on his bed, a sheet clutched to cover himself, and Adriana, naked as the day she was born, standing beside that bed with her long hair cascading over her shoulders, her hands on her hips, facing Oliver and laughing!

". . . Jealousy, Oliver, *that* is what sickens you! Locked to that little blonde devil of yours but longing to be between *my* legs, and envying your fine, strong son!"

Oliver advanced on her, and Adriana backed away from him, swinging her hips, glancing at Charles out of the corner of her eye.

"Shall we show him what a man you are, beautiful Charles? Come, darling, think of all the lovely things I've taught you. . . ."

Her voice was low, caressing, vicious, and she moved with a shameless, sensuous rhythm that held Charles's eyes riveted—a snake mesmerizing a bird.

I scarcely saw the blow, it was so swift. The back of Oliver's hand lashed out and struck her full in the face. Adriana went down like a felled tree. Her head struck the stone floor in front of the fireplace with a sharp, sickening sound and she lay still.

I stood paralyzed in the silence that filled the room. Charles, my darling, stared at me from a flushed and terrified face. Oliver dropped to his knees beside Adriana, feeling for a pulse in her wrist, the pump of her heart. Adriana's mass of tawny hair was turning red and redder; a puddle of blood inched its way along the stone apron of the fireplace. I blocked Charles's view as Oliver turned her enough so that we could see, then gently laid her back as she had fallen. The back of her head was split like a melon.

The rest of that night was a ghastly nightmare.

Oliver, gray of face, stared at me as the reality of our situation sank slowly into our minds. He got to his feet like an old man, looking down at the hand that had struck Adriana as if it belonged to a stranger. Then Charles moved on the bed behind me and Oliver's head came up swiftly. He looked at his son and I saw spots of hectic color flush his cheekbones, resolve wipe the emptiness from his eyes.

"Charles!" Oliver picked up Charles's nightshirt from the floor and tossed it onto the bed. "Put this on and go immediately to Adriana's room. You are to sleep there tonight."

Oliver strode about like a demented stage director, giving instructions. "Forget everything that happened here tonight. You know nothing, heard nothing. You went to bed and fell asleep immediately. You learned of Miss Rantana's tragic accident in the morning. Do you understand me, Charles?"

Charles, the frightened child within staring out through tear-glazed eyes, nodded.

"Margaret, go with him. Start bringing every possession of Adriana's from that room." As he spoke, Oliver was opening the wardrobe and taking out Charles's clothing, gathering up his brushes and his books, all the detritus of boyhood, and heaping everything on the bed.

I seized an armful of clothing and followed Charles along the corridor to what had been Adriana's room. But before I returned to Oliver and that death chamber, I hurried to my own rooms and poured a small glass of cognac for Charles. He was in Adriana's bed, shuddering under the covers pulled up to his chin. His eyes, huge and staring, looked at me as if he didn't recognize me. Adriana was dead, and I was sorrier than words could tell. But in that instant, looking at Charles and realizing what Adriana had done—and the evil she had intended—I could have killed her myself without a second thought. I knew that her seduction of fifteen-year-old Charles had not been merely the action of an older woman amusing herself with a young boy. I knew with utmost certainty that her purpose had been to enslave our innocent son, to use him against us—especially me. That would have been her ultimate revenge.

"Here, darling," I told Charles, holding the glass of cognac to his lips. "Drink this quickly. It will make you sleep."

Charles gagged, but got it down. I arranged the covers around his shaking shoulders—so broad, my man-child's—and kissed his clammy forehead. "It will be all right, Charles. Remember your father's words when morning comes, but for now try not to think."

Oliver and I were occupied in rearranging the two bed-chambers when I turned to find Emily in a woolen robe and nightcap, and behind her, Ned in his nightshirt, staring in through the doorway of the room that had been Charles's. Adriana's sprawled legs were clearly in view.

Oliver edged me into the corridor and closed the door firmly behind us. "I suggest we go to the library. Ned, Emily, we are in an ugly situation. I had hoped not to drag you into it."

In the library, with a fire in the grate for what warmth it could restore to my icy limbs, Oliver was in command of our audience.

"I had not intended to tell this story to anyone. Now it appears I have no choice. And I believe that I can trust you. But before I do, I want your solemn promise, as God is your witness, that you will not in any way reveal what I am about to tell you. Ned?"

Ned raised his right hand. "My oath, m'lord, as God's my witness."

"Emily?"

"Yes, m'lord. As God's my witness."

Oliver told it succinctly, wasting no words on emotion. Only his strained face and set shoulders revealed the tightly controlled havoc within. There was a moment of silence when he finished.

"We'll help ye, m'lord. We'll help in any way we can," Ned said. Emily, beside him, nodded.

Something within Oliver faltered for a moment. Kindness, that normal human emotion, pierced his iron resolve. "Thank you both, more than I can say." Then he cleared his throat and the granite-hard determination returned to his features.

"We must finish changing around the bedchambers. Charles is to be kept out of this entirely. We will discover Miss Rantana's death in the morning and notify the authorities. She has suffered a tragic accident and in the investigation—there is sure to be one—it is important that the other servants say nothing beyond what is necessary. There must be no mention of the changing of bedchambers. You understand?"

"Mayhap Miss Rantana saw a mouse in her room, m'lord?" Emily ventured. "She has a fear of them and would carry on something dreadful about a thing like that, sir."

Oliver looked at her with gratitude. "Perhaps you'll mention that to the servants, Emily?"

"I'll explain to Howard and Olivia," I said quickly. "And tell them that there is no need to mention it to anyone. . . ."

Emily's eyes met mine and she nodded. "No need at all, m'lady. A simple enough thing. The whole household knows Miss Rantana had her ways, m'lady."

So Emily would take care of the servants. That would help, but I was far from happy about the course Oliver was determined on. Too many things could go wrong. Yet I could suggest nothing better, and if I could, he would not be moved. To try would only confirm him in his stubbornness. We were committed to a lie of enormous dimensions and enormous danger.

With Ned and Emily's help we completed the changing of the bedchambers; Emily and I looked at them with a critical eye and judged them adequate. Neither of us looked at Adriana, or we could not have borne what we were about.

I had known her for almost twenty years. Through all of that time she had manipulated my life to suit her whims. But now, in death, Adriana Rantana could ruin it beyond mending. I felt it in my soul. In bed, when sleep would not come in the few hours left to it, I thought of the summer day so many years earlier when I had gone with her, by boat, to the Villa Rantana. She had astonished me that day by telling me that she loved the Villa Rantana best of all the Rantana properties, because of its atmosphere of "secrecy and power." Secrecy and power. Those words defined Adriana's life. And perhaps her death.

If she had died in the same way in her native Italy, all might have gone differently. She could have been spirited out of the house and into a grave on some Tuscan hillside. But this was England. Next day the police came from Liverpool and a plodding but thorough investigation was begun. Charles, on the fringes with the other two young people, looked white and drawn. But so did we all.

We existed for five days in a state of suspended animation, dreading every knock on the door, fearful that our guilt was writ large in scarlet on our foreheads. On the sixth day the

blow fell. There was a contusion on the front of Miss Rantana's face. Miss Rantana had fallen and hit the back of her
head on the stone apron of the fireplace. Such a fall could
not account for the contusion. Could we? No, indeed, we
could not, we were as mystified as the police.

In the end that proved to be a minor consideration. There
had been an autopsy, since Adriana's death was a violent one,
and the Home Office analyst was thorough. Adriana Rantana
had had sexual intercourse shortly before her death. With
whom? The police were chillingly polite, but at Holylake
there were a limited number of choices. And one obvious
one.

Earl Oliver Howard Jardine of Singapore was indicted on
the capital charge of murder. Inspector Rolfe, who had led
the investigation, hesitated to put a peer of the realm in the
common jail and Oliver was allowed to remain at home, on
two thousand pounds' bail, pending trial. As a peer of the
realm, he was not to appear before the Queen's Bench in the
ordinary way, but would be tried in the House of Lords.
Trial date was set for November 18th, three months away.

Troubles now came thick and fast, treading on each other's
heels. A corps of solicitors representing the Rantana interests
arrived in Liverpool, hot-eyed behind their frozen legal faces.
They immediately canceled the contracts for the two new
vessels under construction and showed a keen interest in de-
termining what part of the Jardine-Blue Funnel Line was in
their late client's name. They gave eulogistic interviews to the
press regarding Miss Rantana's beauty, wealth, and impeccable family background. We, the Jardines, were painted as vil-
lains. Though the insinuations fell just short of libel, we
appeared to be monsters of greed who had long cultivated
Miss Rantana because of her wealth and generosity. Who
knows, they may even have believed their own tales.

The press seized on the story with enthusiasm, objecting to
bail having been granted, and warning Lord Jardine that his
freedom was only temporary. No doubt it was glorious sport
for them. There had been no other case involving the capital
charge before the House of Lords in twenty years. Although
Lord Cardigan had gone free, the press pointed out with rel-
ish that scarcely a century earlier the Lords had sent Ferrers
to the gallows and Lovat to the block.

The circumstances might have been made to order for
creating a furor in the newspapers. A beautiful and wealthy
victim, an ancient and dismal home—there at least the press

had the right of it—and a wife of some sixteen years' standing who was so mistaken in her trust of her husband that she was supporting him in a scandalous misadventure. The fact that I was a notable figure in the business world served only to illustrate that women who were too forward in such matters brought trouble on their own heads and households. I thanked God daily that Howard and Charles were back at Harrow, and away from the worst of it.

We had engaged a leading firm of solicitors, Priory, Hull and Greene, to represent Oliver at the inquest. For the trial Mr. Fraser Priory, the senior partner, recommended that Sir Kenneth Champfield, Q.C., be briefed to lead for the defense. We agreed gladly, for his reputation in the courtroom was unequaled. Sir Kenneth accepted the brief and returned all other work to devote himself to Oliver's case. For juniors he would have Mr. Dunton Bird and Mr. Thomas Bicksler; a strong representation, Mr. Priory assured me. We would need all the strength possible, for the Solicitor-General himself, Sir William Cartwright, Q.C., was to lead for the Crown.

Some while after Sir Kenneth Champfield had accepted the brief and had talked with Oliver, he sent word that he wished to see me privately on a matter of grave importance. He would wait on me in his chambers, at my convenience. I was shown into his presence by his clerk and seated with utmost courtesy by the great man. Though I was trembling within, as I had been ever since Adriana's death, I strove to appear composed.

Sir Kenneth Champfield, a man of imposing stature and resonant voice, had a manner that would charm birds out of trees—and the coldest blue eyes I had ever seen. When the amenities had been observed, he wasted no time coming to the point.

"Lady Jardine, I find I have a strong sense of disbelief in your husband's story. If *I* find difficulty with it, I assure you he will not fare better during his trial. Yet nothing I say appears to be of any avail. Lord Jardine refuses to discuss the matter, other than to maintain that he visited Miss Rantana in her bedchamber after you were asleep, and left her an hour later, comfortably abed and in good health. I regret, madam, the necessity to speak to you of so painful a matter. . . ."

I waved that away. I had pain aplenty, but Oliver's supposed infidelity was the smallest part of it. No doubt Sir Kenneth noted that and was confirmed in his opinion that he was not being told the truth.

"I will, naturally, undertake the defense on those grounds, if Lord Jardine cannot be swayed. In that case, as I have warned him, and am now warning you, the likelihood is strong—almost certain—that he will be adjudged guilty on the capital charge. Unless, Lady Jardine, you are prepared to add something to my knowledge of this case?"

I shook my head, afraid my voice would betray me, and unable to meet those keen blue eyes for fear they would read my mind.

Sir Kenneth sat forward. "Lady Jardine, I will not press you on this matter again, but consider. The authorities do not believe that Miss Rantana slipped and fell to her death unassisted. Her face bore the clear imprint of a blow inflicted shortly before she died. A blow was struck—and is left unexplained. The Crown is right to consider that there is a strong suspicion there of cause and effect. Now, let us suppose that the blow was struck instinctively, under circumstances that would make it a normal and easy-to-understand reaction, under the stress of great emotion. The sudden shock of discovering love betrayed. A flash of angry jealousy that lashes out without premeditation. Then the matter becomes understandable, perhaps even . . . condonable. Miss Rantana loses her balance and falls, striking her head. Clearly an accident, Lady Jardine, and there is a strong defense to be made under such circumstances."

He sat back and looked at me, his eyes willing me to speak. "Madam, what have you to say?"

I felt a rush of blood to the head and for a moment was quite dizzy. This man believed that *I* was responsible for Adriana's death! That Oliver was protecting me. I realized, with cold horror, that Sir Kenneth would not be alone in that view. All the world would hear and read of Oliver's indefensible stand and conclude that there had been a dreadful quarrel of some sort; that I had discovered the lovers and had struck Adriana in my fury; that my husband, out of remorse, was shouldering the blame—and I was allowing it.

What had I to say? Sir Kenneth asked. I had nothing to say. Oliver had sworn that if I revealed the truth and he went free as a result, he would walk out of my life forever. He would rather go to the gallows than have Charles involved in grief that was not of his own making. I had been close, despite that, to telling Sir Kenneth the true story. Better to lose Oliver's love and save his life than to lose him to the gallows.

But another way had opened up before me. Oliver would not hang, for Sir Kenneth Champfield would save him. Whether he knew it or not, he would offer me up as the villain—through innuendo. I could bear the dishonor gladly if it would save both Oliver and Charles. I had only to feed Sir Kenneth's suspicions, encourage his contempt. His professional pride would do the rest. No English jury—including the members of the House of Lords—would convict a man shown to be protecting his wife, however ill-advisedly. Sir Kenneth Champfield would seize on that defense rather than lose a case, and a client to the gallows.

I dabbed at dry eyes. "I know nothing!" I declared defiantly. "Nothing beyond what my husband has told you. I cannot think what you are trying to get at, Sir Kenneth."

I made a show of looking haughty and virtuous. "I was asleep the entire night and nothing wakened me. No doubt the disgusting facts are exactly as my husband has presented them. I fail to see why you should choose to think otherwise. Certainly *I* was in no way involved. . . ."

I sounded despicably false and self-serving to my own ears, and prayed that I sounded worse to Sir Kenneth. His face closed against me and the scathing blue eyes made me feel that he would consider it a pleasure—no, a duty—to expose my perfidy for all the world to see.

With frigid politeness he saw me to the door and I made my escape, shivering from the chill of his contempt—but not before I had managed a sly and secretive smile that defied him to prove me a liar. It would be a small price to pay if only it would save Oliver.

CHAPTER 43

November 18th arrived, a chill gray day well suited to the business at hand. We had gone to London two days beforehand and were comfortable enough at the Royal York Hotel. I longed to reassure Oliver that all would be well, but the words had no substance for him and I could not tell him why

I felt so strongly that he would go free without betraying what was to come. I could only pray that Sir Kenneth Champfield would prove to be the man I thought him to be—and sacrifice me to save Oliver.

From the furor that the newspapers had been making of the case I knew that it would be a spectacle like no other I had witnessed. As my carriage approached the Houses of Parliament, I was seized with foreboding and grateful to have Emily, a staunch ally, at my side. Oliver was to arrive sometime later, but Emily and I must be in our seats before that. I felt there could be no lonelier woman in all of England than I, as my carriage rolled toward Whitehall. Everywhere, the police sought to control the spectators swarming, on foot and in fine carriages, toward the House of Lords. For them it was a Roman holiday; for me, perhaps not so different, for I was to be thrown to the lions unless I had misjudged Sir Kenneth Champfield.

The trial was to be held in the Painted Chamber of Westminster, where the House of Lords had met since the fire of 1834. The chamber was soon crowded, the benches and galleries filled, and members of the House of Commons admitted to stand where they could find room. Everywhere I looked my eye met crimson: on upholstered benches, draped galleries, and carpeted floor. Under the gilt chandeliers, the peers took their places, decorations and orders glittering on their robes, their cocked hats adding an almost frivolous note to the occasion. Another time I would have reveled in the color and excitement, but this was not another time. Emily clutched my hand and nodded toward the Queen's Ladies-in-Waiting, arrayed in gorgeous silks and satins, who were on hand in a bevy—for amusement I suppose, for the Queen, mercifully, had declined to attend.

Quiet fell over the Chamber as the procession began, led by the purse-bearer. It was a display of medieval pageantry so weighty, so full of import, that it added to my terror. Following the purse-bearer came the Sergeant carrying the mace. Then, with measured steps, the Garter King-at-Arms, bearing the scepter. Behind him the Gentleman Usher of the Black Rod, with the thin white staff that would be snapped in two at the end of the proceedings. The Lord Chancellor followed, grave of face. He would preside.

The weight of long tradition filled the room, half suffocating me, crushing my meager store of courage. Oliver, my Oliver, must somehow stand against this awesome show of power. The Lord Chancellor took his seat just below the empty throne. There were opening prayers, and then the business of the day got underway: the reading of the royal commission and the indictment against Oliver.

At last Oliver was conducted into the chamber. His hair was aflame under the chandeliers, his head high and cocked to one side like some pirate taken and defiant in the face of the rope from the yardarm. He took the seat provided for him near Sir Kenneth at the side of the bar. Sir William Cartwright, for the Crown, sat at the other side of the bar.

The Deputy Clerk addressed Oliver. "How say you, my lord? Are you guilty of the capital charge, or not guilty?"

Oliver's eyes faced down the packed banks of spectators; his voice rose firmly so that all might hear. "Not guilty, my lords."

"How will your lordship be tried?"

"By God and my Peers."

And they began. Sir William Cartwright made his opening address for the Crown, stating the case against Oliver baldly. I realized there was no other way to state it. I cringed and clung to Emily's cold hand, bracing myself for what was yet to come. Sir William called his first witness, Constable Dunn, who had come to Holylake to investigate Adriana's death. His testimony, and that of Inspector Rolfe, who followed, was couched in official language that made the matter sound almost impersonal. Not so the testimony of Sir Arthur Bellington, the Home Office analyst. He had done the autopsy of Adriana's body, and he proceeded to tell all the world that she had had sexual relations shortly before her death; had been struck in the face prior to her death; and had suffered a severe fracture of her skull resulting in almost-instantaneous death.

While the facts were sensational enough for the most morbid taste, the conduct of the trial was not, for Sir Kenneth Champfield took issue with nothing. As the witnesses for the prosecution appeared, one after the other, he waived the right to cross-examine. I felt physically ill, yet scarcely knew whether it was because he seemed to accept everything, or because I dreaded that what was coming would be the more dramatic by contrast.

At last Sir William Cartwright sat down, his witnesses all having had their say, unchallenged. Sir Kenneth Champfield rose. I braced myself. God alone could help me now, and I

had no great hope of Him, for there could be no easy answers.

"I have one witness to call, my lords, and one only. He is
waiting now in the anteroom. I ask that Charles Millbrook
Jardine, Viscount Birkenhead, son of the defendant—"

He got no further. Oliver was on his feet, shouting, "No! I
will not have it!"

The entire chamber erupted into excited buzzing and the
Lord Chancellor had some difficulty restoring order. Poor
Emily was waving smelling salts under my nose as I sought to
push her hand away. God knows my heart was pounding and
my brain in turmoil, but I was not about to faint. Not with
Oliver in such distress and Charles—my own darling
Charles—could it be that he was actually about to appear in
front of this avid crowd?

I had not long to wait and wonder. In dead silence, except
for a general rustling of robes like a vast whispering throughout the chamber as everyone craned forward to see, the Yeo-
man Usher in his medieval dress conducted Charles to the
bar of the chamber. Charles—he seemed so tall suddenly—
bowed to the Lord Chancellor and then to the peers on each
side. Before my wondering eyes he faced the assembly in the
Painted Chamber, his color high but his eyes steadfast. As for
myself, I could only marvel at the look he exchanged with
Oliver, at once proud and defiant. My son was a child no
longer.

Charles Millbrook Jardine was sworn and a stool was provided for him near his father. Oliver reached out and
clutched Charles's hand. My heart turned over slowly at the
sight of the two of them, so like, and the bond that seemed,
almost visibly, to bind them close.

"My lords," Sir Kenneth Champfield commenced, "late
yesterday I received a communication from the son of the defendant, which I have in my possession. I will, in good time,
read it to the assembly here gathered, because it casts a new
light on the puzzle that confronts us. The author of this communication, Charles Jardine, Viscount Birkenhead, having
hand-delivered the missive to my chambers, has made himself
available to testify on behalf of the defendant, his father."

I never knew the pain and joy of motherhood more poi-
gnantly than at that moment. Charles's head, as brilliantly
plumaged as Oliver's, held as high; two faces, white beneath
their spattering of freckles; two pairs of steady eyes glinting
under the brass chandeliers as they turned to look at each

other. I heard the rustle and sigh that went through the chambers. Perhaps it was only anticipation, but I felt it was another sentiment, nearer the one in my heart.

Charles stood facing the assembly to tell, in a voice that gained strength after the first halting phrases, the story of the night of Adriana's death. Sir Kenneth led him through it when he hesitated or faltered. After he had once begun, Charles seemed scarcely to see the rapt faces around him, for he was back in time, reliving that horrible night. It showed on his face, told in his voice. There was shame, for he felt his own role keenly, but he seemed determined to spare himself nothing. Nor did he spare Adriana.

Those who had come for titillation got it in full measure. Charles, for all of his youthful insecurities, was no coward and no fool. His father's life was at stake and he was determined to tell the whole truth, at the expense of delicacy if need be. Afterward there might be snickers and feverish gossip, but while Charles spoke there was only breathless silence.

When he had finished and sat down, Sir Kenenth thanked him gravely and turned to address the chamber.

"My lords, you have heard a true account of the tragic events that led to the death of Adriana Rantana. The written account which young Viscount Birkenhead furnished me corroborates what you have heard in every detail. It is here for your examination if you so desire. However, I feel that the circumstances of this trial have altered drastically. What we must deal with now is the fact of an accidental death and the loyal effort of a father—and a mother—to protect a young man. I cannot bring myself to say 'boy' despite his tender years, for I think you will agree that, Viscount Birkenhead is a man in every sense of the word. And so I say, the efforts of a father and mother to protect a young man from grave moral danger and from scandal resulting from a distressing accident. True, there has been dishonesty on the part of Lord Jardine in his efforts to protect his son. But surely any one of us here assembled, seeing our child so threatened, would have taken the same steps that Oliver Howard Jardine saw to be his plain duty.

"Miss Rantana is dead and that is a fact to be regretted. But Lord Jardine neither wished nor caused her death, except in the broadest sense. There are accidents of fate, my lords, which no man can be expected to foresee, or to guard against. This was such an accident. Let us be grateful that none of us has been put to the test set before Lord Jardine.

Let us hope that each of us, if so tested, would rise to the occasion with as much courage and determination to protect the sanctity of our home. And let us not reward honor . . . yes, *honor*—with a demand for vengeance! I believe, my lords, that this is a time for mercy, for all concerned have suffered greatly in the past few months."

When Sir Kenneth finished speaking, there was a general exhalation of breath throughout the chamber, and again an excited buzz of talk broke out.

The spectators were cleared from the galleries, and Oliver and Charles were escorted into the antechamber. The Lord Chancellor then addressed the peers.

"My lords, you have witnessed here today a most surprising turn of events; testimony casting an entirely new light on a distressing situation involving delicate considerations of a moral man's response to an attack on the sanctity of his home. . . ."

There was much more of it, but I scarcely heard it for my own heart was pounding in my ears. I remember that the Lord Chancellor finished by counseling the peers to make their decision according to the laws of the land—and their hearts. It was, he said, his own opinion that a jury would find for the defendant in an ordinary court, in view of the unusual circumstances.

While Oliver and Charles still waited in the anteroom, the spectators were allowed to reenter the chamber and the Lord Chancellor rose and took the vote. One by one, he asked each peer for his decision.

". . . how says your lordship? Is Earl Oliver Howard Jardine of Singapore guilty of the charge of which he stands indicted, or not guilty?"

And one by one, each peer rose and removed his cocked hat, placed his right hand on his heart, and responded, "Not guilty, upon my honor."

Not one dissenting vote! I felt as if my body had been turned to some lighter-than-air substance, to gossamer fluff, and as if I were floating over the heads of the whole assemblage shouting out hosannas!

Oliver was led back to the bar. The Lord Chancellor, his old eyes bright, spoke in a strong, proud voice.

"Lord Jardine you have been tried by a jury of your peers, and I have the pleasure of informing you that their lordships have unanimously declared you to be not guilty of the charge on which you were indicted. You stand acquitted."

There was a modest cheer from the spectators and then the company rustled to its feet, milling about in a hum of excited talk. As the others filed out into the late November afternoon, Emily and I hurried forward to claim our heroes.

CHAPTER 44

We lost the *Matthew J* to the Rantana interests. The vessel was part of the Jardine-Blue Funnel Line, but Adriana's money had paid for it and its ownership was in her name. The two new ships Adriana had ordered built were canceled by the Rantana solicitors; we were once again left with only the *Viscount*, now fifteen years old. And so we struggled on—to keep her holds filled, to keep Charles in Harrow and Howard at Oxford, and to maintain our household, which now included Miss Chulds, governess-schoolmistress for Olivia. What a long struggle it had been, and yet we seemed no nearer our goal. But a successful and profitable steamship line was Oliver's dream, his only dream, and it was unchanging. I said nothing to discourage him and we lived in hope— of what, I couldn't have said.

The American Civil War saved us. In 1862, the talk among shipowners in Liverpool and London was of nothing but the enormous fortunes being made by supplying the American South with arms and supplies. For several years our vessels had been going to New York rather than to Charleston because of the cargoes we carried. Oliver, listening to the accounts of huge profits and little risk, now determined that we should again go to Charleston, despite President Lincoln's proclaimed closing of the southern ports.

Certainly in England no one took the proclamation of a blockade seriously. How could a nation "blockade" its own ports? our newspapers asked, and quoted the Treaty of Paris to substantiate their view. A blockade can exist only between independent nations, and to be recognized by foreign powers, it must be effective.

"They haven't got the fleet for it," Oliver scoffed. "From Cape Henry to the Mexican border is nearly four thousand miles. It's a 'paper' blockade, Margaret, empty talk. What's

real is the *market*. There's a fortune there for the taking! Our
Lancashire mills are crying for southern cotton. The South
needs manufactured goods, but the North has all the
factories. Guns, ammunition, cloth for uniforms, boots, iron
rails to keep their railroads running—the South will buy anything we bring in and pay handsomely for the privilege."

I eyed him dubiously, for I felt it could not be as safe as
he professed. "Are there no Federal gunboats patroling their
waters? Surely they don't stand idly by and let British vessels
come and go as they please."

"Oh, there are a few about, from all accounts, but they can
do little to stop a determined captain. Everyone who has run
the gantlet talks of the huge profits and laughs at the risks. I
tell you, Margaret, this is the trade for us. In six months we
can make a fortune—thirty thousand pounds each way."

I soon became caught up in Oliver's enthusiasm. Together
we determined what our cargo should be and filled the *Viscount* on our own account. On her first voyage to Charleston,
the *Viscount* would carry four hundred barrels of gunpowder,
ten thousand rifles, medical supplies, and quantities of boots
and cloth, as well as a large assortment of fashionable clothing, for which there was said to be much demand. Oliver was
determined to go along as supercargo, in charge of our cargo
and the business affairs connected with its sale in America.

I, too, was determined to go along, for I remembered the
existence somewhere in South Carolina of a Mrs. Cora Ewell
who had once come close to claiming my husband forever. I
did not intend to allow her a second opportunity. Charles,
who had finished his final year at Harrow and was home for
the summer, persuaded his father to allow him to accompany
us. Howard, who was now almost twenty and had completed
two years at Oxford, expressed a wish to try his hand at arranging future cargoes while we were away. He had a head
for such matters and I was happy enough to give him the opportunity to gain experience. Only little Olivia was unhappy,
for she wished to make the voyage with us; if Oliver would
have yielded, I would not. I did not for a moment suppose
that running the blockade would be the easy feat he proclaimed it to be, and I did not want Olivia's young life in
jeopardy.

We were all happy to be at sea again. My old fears had
faded and I was excited at the prospect of wealth at the end
of the journey. We met only one storm on the Atlantic, and
that no more severe than a summer squall, nothing by com-

parison with some I had lived through. Our arrival in Nassau's blue waters unscathed by Yankee warships, which we had sighted only at a great distance, seemed a good omen.

I found Nassau a bewildering place: raw, hot, colorful, and bustling with activity. It was the center of the thriving trade with the southern ports, the place where we would prepare for our run. I had little to do during our stay on the island but laze away the days and watch the ceaseless activity that went on around me. Oliver and Charles, scarcely able to contain their excitement, were like two boys playing at pirates.

Our third day in Nassau, Oliver sent Charles to tell me news which he must have thought would upset me. Poor Charles, flushed of face, found me on the veranda of the small hotel where we were staying while our preparations were in progress.

"Mother, there is something you must know, and . . ." He hesitated and seated himself beside me on the wicker settee where I had been whiling away a hot afternoon, watching the passing scene. "Well—it's that the *Viscount* must be painted." He darted a worried look at me. "Gray."

"Gray? But—"

"To escape being seen at night, Mother. You see, here they have decided the exact shade of gray that will blend into the darkness. That's quite important, you know. And we—all of us who will be on deck—must wear gray clothing."

Despite the tremor of foreboding that such preparations conjured up, I smiled into Charles's worried face. "Why, how exciting, darling. Now, what do I have that would serve . . . ?"

Charles's face broke into the sunny grin that I so loved. "I *told* him that you'd understand at once! Women are practical, I feel; and you most of all, Mother."

It was one of the nicest compliments I had ever received.

Charles was growing so tall, I mused, as I watched him race off to whatever chore Oliver had set him. At seventeen he was broad of shoulder, like his father, though he had much filling in to do. In fact, Charles was like Oliver in every respect, except that perhaps his nature was sunnier. That might change in time, when life had tried him more sorely. Then I remembered the decision he had had to make before he paid his visit to Sir Kenneth Champfield—and the House of Lords. For a boy who had been only fifteen at the time, horribly embarrassed as well as frightened at his own part in Adriana's death, he had shown remarkable courage. I could

well afford to feel pride in Charles, equal to my love for him.
But he was growing up so swiftly.

Our new captain was rakish Jack Grantham, who enjoyed
a reputation as one of the finest and most fearless ship's captains in the business of blockade-running. He had never yet
been taken; I hoped his record of success would remain un-
broken. The pilot, Duane Evans, had been born and raised in
the Carolinas and was familiar with every inlet, harbor, bar,
shoal, and landmark from Cape Henry to Galveston, if all of
the stories told were to be believed.

I was excited by the atmosphere of Nassau and by the adventure to come. Yet the Union fleet was not so easy an ad-
versary as Oliver had led me to suppose. It had succeeded in
closing Port Royal and New Orleans, and controlled much of
North Carolina's coastline—none of which appeared to trouble the wild assembly of profiteers who did business out of
Nassau.

On Captain Grantham's advice, everything aloft was taken
down except for the mainmast, with a crow's nest atop for a
lookout. And the *Viscount* was painted a dull gray.

"Like that, the right shade of gray and not much sticking
upward, they ain't likely to see us on a moonless night. "I've
gone through like we was invisible, ma'am, not twenty-five
yards from a blockade ship lyin' there waitin' in the dark,
like a cat at a mousehole."

"And I am to wear gray too, I understand?" I asked,
laughing.

Captain Grantham did not so much as smile. "If you're
goin' to be on deck, yes, indeed, ma'am. Black won't do,
mind. You can see a black outline a lot clearer. Gray it has
to be if you value your ship."

On the advice of our new captain and pilot, we would go
to Wilmington, North Carolina, rather than to Charleston.
And so one night when the moon was right, we stole out of
Nassau and steamed northwestward, bound for Wilmington.

From the outset, it was a time of tension and little sleep.
Union vessels were now making a practice of seizing any
British ship traveling between Nassau or Bermuda and the
southern ports, on the premise that she would be a blockade-
runner. Occasionally we sighted vessels in the distance and altered course, but we were not pursued. On the night of the
third day we ran without lights, a ghost ship with tarpaulins
covering even the engine-room hatchways and the binnacle.
Not so much as the light from a pipe was to be seen on the

Viscount, and anything said was said in a whisper. Only the sound of the engines broke the stillness, and that sounded loud as thunder.

"That's steady sound, ma'am," Captain Jack, as he liked to be called, explained. "Mixes right in with the sound of their own ships and the sea. A voice carries different over water."

We were heading for the New Inlet of the Cape Fear River. The Union blockaders would be positioned in a cordon guarding the entry to the river mouth. Rather than head suicidally through their midst, we would approach from the north and inch our way toward the New Inlet in the deep water close to the shore—and inside the line of the warships. Or so we hoped.

Oliver and Charles, with Captain Jack and Duane Evans, the pilot, stared out into the darkness from the bridge. I followed the example of the crew and crouched low behind the bulwarks. There was a whispered conference on the bridge and then the *Viscount* slowed and stopped to allow the leadsman in the fore-chains to take a sounding. Again the engines started and we moved on into the darkness; I thought our direction changed slightly but could not be sure.

An hour dragged by and every moment of it I was braced to hear a shout, followed by the crash of guns firing on us. But all was still. Again the engines stopped for another sounding. This time the leadsman's reading satisfied the pilot, and when the engines resumed their steady pulsing, it was at minimum speed. There was a breathless quality aboard the ship as we crept onward along the dark road of the sea.

I heard a whisper of sound from the bridge and raised my head above the bulwarks to peer into the blackness around us. There, on our port bow, I could make out the faint outline of a long, low vessel, silent and unmoving. As we slid by her, my heart pounded erratically and I ceased breathing momentarily. We were less than a hundred yards away and it seemed impossible that we would not be seen. But there was neither sound nor light from the long, dark gunboat, for that is what it was. I blessed Captain Jack's knowledge of his business. With the land to our starboard side, our lead-gray ship blended into the background of the low, woody shore, making us invisible.

I prayed we had not much further to go to reach safety under the guns of Fort Fisher. When I could stand my solitude no longer, I stole diligently up to the bridge, to be near Oliver. He squeezed the hand I slipped into his and I saw the

brief flash of his teeth as he grinned down at me. To my
amazement I realized that I, too, was enjoying the hot little
flame of danger warming me from within. Life had been
growing stale, and this clandestine adventure was giving it excitement once again. Then Oliver's hand tightened on mine.

The shadowy shape of a cruiser loomed out of the
darkness ahead. She was moving slowly, low in the water
with no light showing, and was about to cross our bow. At a
muttered order from Captain Jack down the tube, our engines went dead. We lay silent while the dark shadow passed
before us and disappeared into the gloom.

There was a whispered conference between Captain Jack
and the pilot. Dawn was not far off and we had to make for
safety as swiftly as we dared, in close to the dim white line of
surf. As the first streaks of light appeared in the eastern sky,
I searched the flat, monotonous shoreline for sight of the
Mound, a low hill that was the only identifiable feature that
would indicate our nearness to Fort Fisher. Long before I
saw it the pilot ceased his straining into the faint light and
called out, "There she is, there's the Mound," in a voice
hoarse with relief. When at last I, too, discerned the Mound,
I could scarcely believe that that tiny hillock could be the
landmark we sought; it was barely as high as a well-grown
tree!

Then, to my dismay, we changed course and headed further away from the shore, to round the North Breaker Shoal.
And there in the gathering light was a Yankee cruiser to our
port, steaming straight for us! There was no longer need for
quiet, for there was no darkness to protect us now. Captain
Jack Grantham shouted down the tube for full steam, and the
Viscount clawed her way toward the New Inlet of the Cape
Fear. The cruiser began firing shells that fell short, but she
was gaining on us. Though smaller, she was heavily armed,
and with four hundred barrels of gunpowder aboard, we
could afford to take no direct hits. Fortunately Fort Fisher
was on guard. Soon their great Columbiads were sending
shells past us, driving off our pursuer. When finally we rounded the point and came safely to anchor off Fort Fisher, I
could scarcely believe we had come unscathed through that
night of excitement and terror.

We stopped only briefly at the fort, and then steamed up
the Cape Fear River to Wilmington and a royal welcome. It
was a time of triumph and we celebrated it in the accepted
way, by offering a hospitable feast aboard the Viscount for

important businessmen and officials of the town the night following our arrival. We remained in Wilmington for scarcely a week, while Oliver easily sold our entire cargo at astonishing prices and took aboard all the cotton the vessel could carry. Even the decks were piled so high with cotton bales and hogsheads of tobacco that I feared we would founder when we reached the open sea—if we did.

As if to quiet my misgivings about blockade-running as a business, we easily evaded the cordon of Yankee cruisers on the moonless night when we stole out of Wilmington, past Fort Fisher and into open water. The return voyage to Nassau was as peaceful as one could ask, and it confirmed Oliver in his opinion that there was much money to be made and little risk in our new undertaking.

We dropped the captain and pilot at Nassau, where they would immediately ship out again on their next voyage to Wilmington. With our masts restored and our ship overheavy with cargo, we made our way safely back to Liverpool. On the two legs of the voyage we had made the huge net profit of forty thousand pounds.

Oliver made immediate preparations for a second voyage, but I was unwilling to leave Olivia again so soon. Howard returned to Oxford, but Charles wanted to go with Oliver. He loved the sea and the excitement of running the blockade. He would go to the university later, he proclaimed. I protested, but Oliver sided with Charles.

"Charles will make his way, Margaret, though not perhaps as a scholar, as you seem to wish. He is learning other things, more important for him than what comes from books. Charles is a Jardine. The sea is in his blood."

I had no choice but to let him go with as good grace as I could manage.

Again the *Viscount* returned to Liverpool with huge profits and again Oliver assured me that the dangers were slight, with a good captain and pilot aboard. He had nothing but praise for Charles, who was learning quickly, it appeared.

"He would make my father proud, Margaret, as you should be! He can turn his hand to anything and never misses a chance to learn more. You should see him up on the crosstrees, guiding the *Viscount* through shoal waters. Or right by my side when I negotiate for the sale of goods we take into Wilmington. He is learning everything the pilot can teach him of the waters around Nassau and the Carolina coast. After this next voyage we will be in a position to buy another ship; then Charles will go aboard as supercargo."

Olivia, hearing all of this high praise of Charles, coaxed to go along, wanting to show her father that Charles was not the only one deserving of his admiration. And go along we did, both of us, on the third voyage.

Matters went well from the outset. We carried every ounce of cargo the *Viscount* could accommodate, and Olivia proved to be a good sailor after the first few days on the rough Atlantic. In Nassau we were again able to hire Captain Jack Grantham, and Duane Evans as pilot. Yet other things had changed, as I was soon to learn.

It was the spring of 1864. The South was now desperate for every sort of goods and supplies from abroad, for her position had become perilous. The North, with its industrial resources working at full production, could feed and clothe its troops, supply them with guns and ammunition, and mass swift new cruisers to guard the entries to the beleaguered southern ports. The Union fleet now ranged the Atlantic and hovered near the British ports of Nassau and Bermuda, ready to pounce on any ship that ventured forth carrying supplies for the South. In recent months many blockade-runners had been captured and destroyed by fast Yankee cruisers, which lay in wait for them when they were a few hundred miles out to sea, too far to double back to the safety of Nassau or Bermuda, and far from the southern coast.

Captain Jack Grantham and Oliver scoffed at such tales, claiming much faith in the speed of our old *Viscount*.

"They won't catch us, ma'am, count on it," the captain said with a laugh when I sought to question him on our chances. "Old she may be, but the *Viscount* can show her heels to the best of 'em!"

Oliver looked proud at those words. "She's in top shape, Margaret, everything replaced that was worn or wearing. She won't fail us when we need her, never fear."

"But could we not carry some armament, Oliver," I pleaded, "as we did in the Black Sea? With Olivia aboard—"

Captain Grantham scotched that idea swiftly. "No, ma'am. Any blockade-runner that makes armed resistance is liker than not to be posted as pirates. You won't see me, nor no other sensible man, aboard anythin' carryin' guns, ma'am."

Duane Evans, the pilot, approached me later, offering comfort. "Don't you fret too much about the young 'un, ma'am. Blockade-runnin' is hard on the nerves right enough, but it ain't half so dangerous as it looks. Why, I've sat out there most of a day more than once, waitin' for dark so's we could make your run—and not a blockader even noticed us! And then when we go in, see, we're moving fast and it's not easy to hit us in the dark with their own decks heavin' up and down. The odds is in our favor, ma'am, all the way."

When we set out from Nassau my doubts were finally at rest. This voyage would be as safe as such ventures could be. All the same, I decided, Olivia's first experience of blockade-running would be her last, and mine as well. The second day out, the lookout spotted what he thought was an unknown vessel burning a great distance off. An hour later we could see she was a Union cruiser burning soft coal, and in hot pursuit of a blockade-runner making for Nassau.

We altered course slightly to stay well away and raced along through a calm blue sea under brilliant sunshine. My courage increased considerably for we saw no other ships, near or far. No doubt the stories I had heard in Nassau were put about by other blockade-runners hoping to discourage competition. The afternoon of the third day turned dark and overcast and we clawed our way at top speed, hoping to make Wilmington before dawn.

Once again, with all signs of light on the *Viscount* extinguished, we made our way through blackness. Olivia wished to be on the bridge with her father and Charles, but Oliver instructed her to stay with me. In a fever of excitement, she sheltered under my arm like a baby chick as we crouched below the bulwarks. This time, the tension and danger lacked all pleasurable excitement for me, for I had Olivia to fear for, and such hostages to fortune drain away the courage. Silently I cursed myself for a fool for not insisting that she stay behind in Nassau, though there had been several cases of yellow fever there. I had thought of the Curse of the Flowers that hung over our family and weighed the relative dangers of yellow fever against capture by Yankee blockaders. Soothed by Captain Jack and Duane Evans, I had chosen the latter as the safer risk. Now I was far less sure, for there was a storm brewing, and an occasional flash of lightning threatened to make us clearly visible to any Yankee vessel that might be nearby.

After one such flare that seemed to last for minutes, there was a quickening of movement on the bridge of the *Viscount*. I raised my head to peer over the bulwarks and was rewarded with the sight of a train of sparks shooting upward, followed by a great brilliant glare of white light. A rocket, a Drummond light, revealed the clear outline of a large steam cruiser off our port stern. And revealed us equally clearly to them. Three more rockets followed in close succession, launched in our direction—alerting other blockaders to our position. I heard Captain Grantham shout down the tube for full steam, and a moment later the scream of a shell. It plowed the water astern as the *Viscount* leaped forward.

I scarcely know what happened after that, for I hugged a trembling Olivia to me, assuring her that it would be all right, not to be frightened, and over her head tried to watch Oliver and Charles on the bridge. We were beating through the rising seas, making for the New Inlet. With dread, I remembered that we had yet to head away from shore to avoid the North Breaker Shoal. Even as I thought it, we altered course abruptly. Behind us the Union cruiser, confident that we carried no guns, was fully lighted and in hot pursuit. There was a dreadful roar and our one mast came crashing down, carrying the crosstrees with it. Surely the lookout would have come down when the firing started? I had little time to think of that, for we took another hit as the pursuing cruiser gained on us, striving to edge us further out to sea and into the jaws of the blockade fleet. I wanted to be with Oliver and Charles if I were about to die, yet I dared not take Olivia up to the bridge, to exposure to greater danger.

There was a dreadful, wracking hit that made the iron of the vessel ring and shudder, and almost simultaneously we again altered course. I prayed we had passed the shoal and would soon be within range of Fort Fisher's guns. And cursed Oliver and myself for being such fools as to believe the old *Viscount* could still outrun newer, lighter vessels like the one attacking us.

There came a bone-crashing thud from below and the *Viscount* rang like an iron bell struck with a mallet. We had run aground. I heard the engines reverse—and strain. But we didn't move. Our bow was dug in. And then . . . oh, God . . . the engines stopped—I was back on the coral again on the *Victoria*, with the seas crashing around me. . . . I felt Olivia stir in my arms and fought my way up from the swirling panic that threatened to claim me. I couldn't afford panic or the pain of old terrors; I was in a new nightmare and I had Olivia to think of.

We were stuck fast, there was no hope that the *Viscount* could be floated off without a flood tide—if at all—and the

Yankee ship was closing the distance between us. Her guns would find us like ducks in a millpond. I seized Olivia by the hand and we ran toward Oliver and the others as our lights came on to show the flag coming down from the gaff. We were surrendering. I thanked God, for we had no other choice except death, and everything I loved was aboard this old ship.

The Union cruiser came close enough so I could hear the skirl of the bosun's pipes and the cry "boarders away!" A boat put out from the other ship, and it seemed only moments before the Federal bluejackets were swarming aboard. They strutted about, delighted with their prize, for it was worth a fortune to them, each man getting a share. The lieutenant in charge was courteous enough, if smug, and when he discovered that Oliver and I were wed, and our two children were aboard, he looked us over with some interest.

"You English are different, all right," he said. "I'd never bring my Mary along on a jaunt like this. Not that she'd want to come! Got too much sense."

"What will you do with us?" I asked, a quaver in my voice that I did not have to assume.

The young lieutenant looked taken aback at that, for he had not, I was sure, expected to be faced with a family. I followed up my advantage swiftly, slight as it was.

"Can you not just put us out in a small boat? You have our ship and all the cargo, worth a fortune, as you know. We have nothing. Please—let us go."

"The captain and pilot go to prison," he said sternly. "Safely away, so they won't get up to any more of this kind of work."

"No more can we," I assured him, "for all our wealth is right here in your custody. We'll make our way back to England however we can. Surely the Union navy does not need women and children as prisoners?"

It seemed a reasonable plea, for apart from captains and pilots who knew the southern coast, what interest could the Union have in taking civilian prisoners, a bother that served no purpose? Ships and cargoes and men knowledgeable of the waters around Wilmington and Charleston would be the prizes, I reasoned. I thanked God for Charles's youthful English face—and Oliver's silence. After one startled sidelong glance at me, he had said nothing.

The young lieutenant was noncommittal. He hurried off to see that the crew, and most particularly the pilot and captain, were safely headed back to the *Niphon*, for that was the name of the Union vessel that had captured us. We waited in silent apprehension; but Oliver squeezed my hand, which he gripped tightly throughout the whole ordeal, and sent me a quick, rakish grin that seemed to understand and urge me on.

When Lieutenant Traves, as we heard him addressed, returned to our little group, his manner was gruff. He looked at me and avoided Oliver's eye, fearing censure for weakness, I had no doubt.

"I have decided that the four of you are of no use to us," he declared in a voice that seemed to disdain us. "I have had a lifeboat readied; you are free to make your way ashore as best you can, and to take your personal possessions with you."

As he was about to turn away, Oliver reached out to grasp his shoulder. "Lieutenant Traves, if ever you or any of yours should come to England, you will always be well received at Holylake, the seat of the Jardine family. Remember the name. Holylake. We will make you welcome."

There was an instant of uneasy rapport between the two men, then Lieutenant Traves nodded abruptly and walked away, shouting to one of his men to cast off. A prize crew was left on board to take over the *Viscount* for the Federal government. She would be towed off the shoal at full tide. As for the four Jardines, all who were permitted to go free at that moment, we boarded the lifeboat. Oliver and Charles took the oars; with lanterns flaring at either end of the boat, and Olivia and I huddled together with our belongings piled around us, we pulled away from the side, leaving the *Viscount* to her fate.

After a time the sea became calmer, and despite our plight the four of us grinned at each other like fools, grateful that we had escaped with our lives and our liberty. Gone was our faithful old *Viscount*, our investment, and the profits we had counted on. It was a heavy blow, yet it seemed a mere trifle when put next to the fact that all four of us were safe and healthy and together, and not confined to some improbable northern prison.

Fort Fisher was near. Oliver and Charles pulled at the oars and Olivia slept, exhausted by excitement, with her head in my lap. And I? I thought of the Curse . . . and judged it defeated. For the moment, at least.

CHAPTER 45

We stayed overnight in Fort Fisher. Colonel Lamb, the commander of the fort, provided transport up the Cape Fear, the twenty-eight miles to Wilmington, and made arrangements for us to stay with a Mrs. Decie Bruce, a friend of his wife. We were fortunate that Mrs. Bruce took us in, for the town was overcrowded, teeming with every sort of freebooter and opportunist, as well as hundreds of wounded Confederate soldiers who took whatever shelter was provided, often rough and primitive. The good people of Wilmington went hungry to feed them, and exhausted themselves in tending to the many who had no one else to help them. Pervading all was the sense of a lost cause, of privation and unending courage and integrity gone for naught.

Everywhere I went I saw sad-eyed, seeking men and women, young and old, searching the long rows of wounded for the face they sought, and then, in desperation, examining the new red mounds of earth with their small markers. Sometimes I felt my heart would break for them, traveling on, their tired eyes darting about so as not to miss any face, any clue; hoping, at every overheard snatch of conversation from a soldier or his family, to find a new destination to search for their own.

Once again I yearned to go home. There was more heartbreak here than I could bear. Yet it was only the beginning of heartbreak, reason told me. Olivia, like a little twelve-year-old wraith, drifted at my side, wide-eyed at all she saw. Charles seemed to have found friends and a social life of sorts. As for Oliver, he had learned that the *Viscount* had been taken to the Federal naval supply station at Port Royal, in South Carolina. From there she would go to a northern port and be auctioned, with half of her price going to the Federal government and half to the officers and crew of the *Niphon*, which had made the capture.

Oliver racked his brain for a way to reclaim the *Viscount*, and in the meantime sought to make arrangements for passage back to Nassau for us. From there we would return to

339

Liverpool. We had been in Wilmington three days when Oliver and Charles returned to the Bruce home, full of excitement.

"Margaret, good news! I've met some capital fellows from home who are living here on Market Street and running the blockade as a regular thing. Making a fortune, too, from all reports. They'll get us to Nassau on their next trip out. In the meantime, we're invited to dine with them tomorrow evening."

"They're said to be royal naval officers on temporary leave," Charles confided, glowing with enthusiasm. "But of course they don't talk about it, or ever use their real names. The one who calls himself Captain Hackett is a very dashing sort of fellow. They say he won the Victoria Cross for something heroic he did in the Crimea." Charles laughed down at me from his new height. "Wear your prettiest gown, Mother. They're a fashionable lot, I warn you."

Mrs. Decie Bruce, too, was intrigued at hearing of our invitation from "the English gentlemen."

"How exciting, Lady Jardine! Invitations there are much in demand, I assure you. I hear they've spent a fortune on furnishings, and set a fine table, too. Of course, I have seen them about and they do dress well, most extravagantly, yet with a foreign look. Rather as if they were very expensive grooms. Or perhaps coachmen. But you are English too, so perhaps the style will seem quite usual to you."

I dressed carefully for what appeared to be an engagement of some importance to the men in my family. I was grateful to the young Federal lieutenant who had let us take our trunks from the *Viscount,* for I had a most flattering gown of French blue satin, with a looped and ruffled skirt over whalebone hoops. With my hair piled in cascading ringlets that hung on my neck in back, and a white ostrich-feather fan, I felt grand enough for any company. Charles, who was not given to fussing overmuch with his appearance, took particular care with his toilette for the event. The gentlemen with whom we were to dine must indeed be "a fashionable lot"!

The house on Market Street was ablaze with lights and activity. The five gentlemen who lived therein, our hosts, were resplendent in the newest and best of civilian clothing. They welcomed us warmly and I immediately believed they did indeed make a fortune from their blockade-running—and spent it, too. Everything in the house was of the finest quality and workmanship and would have brought a pretty price in

Wilmington, for the prices for even plain things were astronomical.

"Captain Hackett," whom Oliver had told me was the younger son of a British earl, was a tall and debonair man with laughing eyes and a handsome, disciplined face. I had no doubt that he broke many a feminine heart wherever he went. He escorted us around, introducing us to the assemblage.

Colonel and Mrs. Lamb were in attendance, as well as many of Wilmington's more notable gentry, and a sprinkling of merchants who no doubt bought much of the goods our hosts brought through the blockade. Charles seemed at home with both the gentlemen-adventurers and the young Confederate officers who added gaiety to the company. And at dinner he sat next to a small, darkly attractive girl with huge blue eyes fringed with thick, dark lashes. Certainly the "English gentlemen" enjoyed good living, for we had oysters and champage, as well as poultry and beef, excellent butter, fresh fruits and vegetables, and real coffee—all of them difficult to obtain in Wilmington and exorbitant in price. Moreover, we ate from the finest bone china at a table set with damask, heavy silver, and crystal glasses kept filled with first-class wines.

After dinner a Negro minstrel band played lively music for our entertainment and I could scarcely keep my feet from tapping. Charles, I noted, sat with his dinner partner during the entertainment. I felt a twinge of motherly jealousy—or perhaps a sense of impending loss—as I noted his red head bent solicitously toward her dark one rather often, and the eagerness with which he fetched and carried for her comfort.

Soon after the musical presentation was over, he brought his friend to where Oliver and I were admiring a rather fine Sèvres vase.

"Mother, Father, may I present Miss Diana Van Hotton of New York? Miss Van Hotton, like us, is trapped in Wilmington by the war and hopes to go to Nassau quite soon."

The dark-haired girl curtseyed prettily, her fringed-gentian eyes wide with excitement. "Captain Hackett has promised that I shall be on the next trip out—and then, *home!*"

I felt a bond with Miss Van Hotton, for I recognized her longing. "Then perhaps we shall be shipmates. Have you been in Wilmington for long, Miss Van Hotton?"

"Almost a year." Her face was suddenly sad. "It seemed such a lark when I came here with a friend from school. But that was before things became so awful. Twice before I thought I could get passage out, but both times there were far too many others ahead of me. They carry only a few passengers each trip, you know." The wide smile flashed again. "This time I shall be lucky, I feel it!"

"And so shall I, if we travel on the same ship," Charles said with a gallantry that quite amazed me.

"Van Hotton," Oliver said in a thoughtful voice. "There is a Cyrus Van Hotton of whom I have heard a good deal, a leader in the American shipping industry."

"He is my father. Poor Daddy. He has been frantic these past months. A good Yankee, you know, and mistrustful of all southerners. Though I don't admit that to everyone." She turned a dazzling smile on Charles. "It's different to admit it to you, for you are not really a part of our sad trouble, are you?"

Poor Charles. I could see him melting under the blue fire of Diana Van Hotton's eyes. He was hopelessly smitten, and I prayed she would not be too hard on him.

It was a fascinating evening in every respect. Captain Hackett regaled the company with tales of escapades with Yankee blockaders and his friends joined in, topping each other's accounts of perilous escapes and near disasters on the run from Nassau to Wilmington. Captain Hackett addressed us as Lord and Lady Jardine, but made no reference to his own true identity, even when Oliver told of our escape from the Russians off Sebastopol in the Crimea. From his courteous interest, one might think his only knowledge of that sad war was what he had read in the English press. Yet Oliver recognized him and informed me privately that his lustrous reputation in England was all that Charles had surmised. All in all, a most intriguing gentleman.

From that night onward, Charles spent whatever time he could at the house on Market Street, or in the company of Miss Diana Van Hotton. It now appeared certain that we should be going to Nassau on the same voyage, which delighted Charles.

Luckily, Olivia, too, had a companion. Mrs. Decie Bruce, our kind hostess, had two young daughters near Olivia's age, and the three girls kept each other entertained. Mrs. Bruce, whose husband was fighting in Virginia, regretted the fact that there was very limited social life in Wilmington at the moment, but I accompanied her to the City Hall, where many Wilmington women gathered to make underwear and haversacks for the men at the front. And it was there that I saw Mrs. Cora Ewell.

The place was a hive of feminine activity and my sewing skills were limited, so perhaps I concentrated more on my stitches than on the conversation. But I heard the name Ewell clearly and paid attention thereafter. Cora Ewell, it developed, was sitting with a group of women nearby, who were making powder bags for the Columbiads at Fort Fisher. I looked over and knew instinctively which one she was. Perhaps I should have been flattered. She was somewhat taller than I, but her hair was the same pale corn color, and her figure, too, resembled mine. I might have found some bitter amusement in that—except for the small boy who sat by her chair playing with toy soldiers. A small red-haired boy who looked to be about six years of age. I felt sickness rising in my throat as realization swept over me. There could be no mistake. He was too like Oliver. Too like Charles at that age.

It was the one thing I had never considered. That Oliver, in his idyll with this American woman, might have fathered a child. I couldn't take my eyes from them, that pretty domestic picture of the woman sewing and the child playing at her skirts.

Cora Ewell looked up and our eyes met. It lasted only a fraction of time before she looked casually away. But she knew. God, how I hated her at that moment. Tears flooded my eyes and I quickly jabbed my needle into my finger, making the blood flow. If I was going to cry, I must have a reason, and Cora Ewell and her wretched child could not be the apparent one, not before these women. No doubt they knew, perhaps had even led the conversation for my benfit.

After that first hot rush of shock and wrenching jealousy I felt a new emotion take hold of me. Hatred. Hatred of Oliver; implacable, black as sin. *His* sin! I made light of my bleeding finger and bravely continued my sewing, impervious to everything except the cold, firece loathing that roiled within me. Somehow I endured the remainder of that afternoon without betraying my new knowledge, arming myself against all feeling except for this hatred that twisted and gnawed at my vitals. As we were ready to leave the City Hall, I heard Cora Ewell call to her son. Vance, his name was Vance. Vance Ewell. Vance Jardine.

At the dinner table, Oliver was full of news. We would be

leaving for Nassau within the week on Captain Hackett's vessel, *Vanity*.

"A twin-screw steamer, two hundred fifty horsepower, built on the Clyde especially for blockade-running. She's made six round trips so far and never been caught!"

I smiled because it was expected of me. "How wonderful."

"I don't think so," Olivia pouted. "I like it here. No dumb lessons with Miss Chulds."

"Diana will be on the same voyage," Charles volunteered, looking well content at the thought.

So Miss Van Hotton was now "Diana."

"You will hate to part with your friend, Charles," I observed, and caught a quick look from Charles to Oliver.

"Well, perhaps they won't be parting quite yet," Oliver said, smiling and sounding brisk. "I think we, too, should go to New York, Margaret, before we return to Liverpool. There is a chance I may be able to reclaim the *Viscount*. It will cost a fair amount of money, no doubt, but—"

"Diana believes that her father will help us," Charles broke in. "He has been of considerable service to the Union government and has many influential friends."

"Including the Secretary of the Navy, Mr. Gideon Welles," Oliver supplied.

"Oh." It was all happening so swiftly that I scarcely knew what to think. "How much money will it take, Oliver?"

He shrugged. "What difference, so long as we have it? I want the *Viscount* back."

"Would we not be better to start anew, commission a new ship?"

"I want the *Viscount*, Margaret. There will be a new ship in time. We have money to work with now, despite our recent loss. I'll find backers, but first I must have the *Viscount*." There was finality in his voice and he turned his attention to Olivia. "Well, Livia, what do you say now? No lessons for a while yet, but a visit to New York."

The talk went on around me while I pondered this new development. Miss Van Hotton thought her father might be able to help us? I looked at Charles thoughtfully, aware that he had changed a great deal since we had left Liverpool. There was a new look of confidence and strength about him. Despite our ordeals, he had filled out, become tall and brawny. His hair had darkened, but sun-lightened streaks of bright red still gleamed in it. His skin, less fair than Oliver's, was tanned a warm golden brown. He was handsome, this large nineteen-year-old son of mine; a man now, and it had happened so gradually that I had scarcely been aware of the changing. There was Charles—and there was Vance. Suddenly I felt ill, and excused myself from the table.

We were getting ready for bed when Oliver again broached the subject of New York.

"How do you feel about it, Margaret?"

I shrugged. "You and Charles are happy. I suppose I am, too."

"I'm growing impatient here. I want to get back to Liverpool, but with my ship!" He reached out for me. "You understand, don't you, darling?"

I eluded his hands. "Perfectly. And I understand why you are anxious to leave Wilmington. Will you say good-bye to Vance before we go?"

In the silence that grew around us, Oliver flushed a deep red that suffused his face. "Vance?" he repeated stupidly.

"Your son. You do remember Cora Ewell, I suppose? And the child she bore you?"

He started to bluster but thought better of that at the sight of my face. Sinking down on the side of the bed, he buried his head in his hands. "How did you find out?"

"It wasn't difficult. I had only to see him. And her, of course. You run to type, Oliver."

He got to his feet and approached me, his arms outstretched. "Margaret, try to understand. It happened . . . but it's long over."

"So I believed. But it's *not* over. It can never be over, for she bore you a son. He—they—have a claim on you, on your heart, a second family. . . ."

When there had been only Cora Ewell, some strange American woman he had taken up with, I had been able to tell myself that these things happened. Oliver was a man, and he had been away four years. But a child, a son, no! What had been only a shadowy liaison now had substance. Cora Ewell and her son somehow diminished me and my children.

My eyes felt feverish with unshed tears. There was a bitter taste in my throat—hatred, jealousy. When Oliver reached for me I evaded him.

"Margaret, please . . . try to forgive me. As I have always forgiven you."

"Oh? For what? The looseness of my morals before you met me? Forgiveness that took the form of rape, and left me with a child that you wouldn't give your name until I forced you? Forgiveness that took its solace in Adriana's bed?" I laughed. "Or are you now telling me that you forgive me for *Adriana*? Those long four years when I struggled on without you were forgiveness, Oliver? And this Vance child merely a by-blow, to be overlooked because of that generosity on your part? Dear God!"

It all spewed out, all the hurt and outrage and damage I had suffered through this monster of selfishness I had thought I loved and trusted. When it was spent there was nothing left inside, neither love nor hurt, but simply emptiness of soul. I had wanted Oliver Jardine for more than twenty years and now I no longer wanted him. I felt there was nothing there worth wanting.

In the days that followed I thought of my position. I would be thirty-nine years old in another few months. Hardly an age to consider my life finished. Perhaps I would find someone new in time. A lover. Someone whom I would care for to a degree, but not deeply. Never again deeply, for that was a fool's game. I had neither energy nor interest to pursue the thought, for everything within me drained away in silent mourning, like blood from a wound that wouldn't be staunched.

CHAPTER 46

At eleven o'clock of an overcast and pitch-black night, we weighed anchor and slipped out of the mouth of the Cape Fear River. Once over the bar we were fair game for the more-than-twenty blockade vessels that Fort Fisher had advised us were cordoning the inlet.

"The blacker the night, the closer in they get," Captain Hackett had said with a laugh as we steamed out of the river. "Little good it will do them tonight. I feel lucky."

I hoped that his confidence was well-founded, for I wished only to be away from Wilmington and its memories. Yet perhaps what I needed was fresh sea air, for some of my inner burden lightened as we edged along the coast and eastward. Soon we headed straight out to sea, passing once between two large black hulks that failed to see us. When morning light came there was nothing in sight in any direction, and I breathed a sigh of relief.

The weather was dark and overcast, with low-lying clouds that seemed to press down on the sea. We caught the Gulf Stream and traveled along it with that remarkable current speeding us on our way. Late that afternoon the overcast cleared considerably, and not long afterward the lookout cried "Sail ho!" In a short time the topsails of a large steam frigate appeared over the edge of the horizon. She followed us until darkness fell, but though she had both steam and full canvas up, she was no match for the fleet-winged *Vanity*.

Charles divided his time between hero-worshiping Captain Hackett and staying close to Diana Van Hotton. I believe he was happier than ever before in his life. And we arrived in Nassau without further difficulty, though we changed course several times to give a wide berth to prowling Union vessels.

We were able to catch a fast steam packet to New York the following day, and I for one left Nassau behind with no regrets. Charles continued his idyll with Diana, and I gave my attention to Olivia when she was not with Oliver. With Oliver I was civil and distant. He was no longer a part of my inner life, but I would maintain the surface appearances as well as possible. After a few attempts to win me over, he seemed to accept the situation. What he felt I had no idea; nor did I care.

We were made welcome in New York by Mr. and Mrs. Van Hotton, both of whom were on hand to greet their daughter. I did not know what they thought of Diana bringing along four house guests with her, but somehow we were soon ensconced in the Van Hottons' luxurious Fifth Avenue mansion and made to feel honored guests.

Perhaps Oliver's title helped, but to do Mr. Van Hotton justice, it was more likely a case of shared interests. As for me, the Van Hottons must have decided that I was one of the cold Englishwomen of whom they had heard, and though they were punctiliously polite, there was little real warmth between us. I regretted that, for they seemed kind and charming people. The fault was with me, and the chill within me was both too deep to be rooted out and too intense to be overlooked.

At dinner that first night, Mr. Van Hotton and Oliver

talked of generalities concerning ships and shipping, but there was an eagerness about it that augured well for our hopes of the New Yorker's help in reclaiming the *Viscount*. The fact that we had been blockade-runners seemed to bother Mr. Van Hotton not a whit; he was clearly a man who understood the exigencies of business, wars notwithstanding. I was sure all would have been quite different if we had not been English. Somehow, despite the anti-English feeling that existed in the North, we were regarded as entrepreneurs, rather than traitors to the northern cause. And, of course, both of the Van Hottons were of a mind to view British blockade-runners with affection, for Diana was at home at last, thanks to one of the most successful of them.

"Cyrus is going to help us, Margaret," Oliver exulted the evening of our second day in New York. "It may take some time, but he is sure he can arrange for me to buy back the *Viscount*. In fact, he is quite curious himself to see it, for he was astonished to hear that it is nineteen years old and embodies so many principles only now being accepted in the United States. Or anywhere, for that matter."

"Is Gideon Welles truly his friend? That almost ensures success, does it not?"

"Van Hotton assures me that before Welles was Secretary of the Navy they had many business dealings together. And more recently he has been of great help to Welles in obtaining a number of vessels for the Union fleet."

With Oliver in so elated a mood, I thought it time to speak of Charles and Diana Van Hotton. "You do realize that they are serious, don't you? I can't help worrying. Charles is so young."

At that, Oliver shouted with laughter. "He's nineteen, for God's sake! How old were you when you bore him, pray tell? All of twenty? No, by God, you weren't twenty for another—what—six months?"

"How old is Diana? She looks to be very young."

"Everyone looks very young from our vantage point, my dear. She will be nineteen in another two months, according to her father, who should know. Stop worrying about them, Margaret. Charles has a good head on him, that I can vouch for. And the girl seems likable enough. Pretty little thing, too."

"Ye-es. Perhaps a bit willful under her pretty ways, though."

Oliver raised amused eyebrows. "A trait you would naturally recognize, my dear. I suppose Charles can contend with it. As I have, for so many years!"

With that he reached out for me, as if our surface camaraderie had changed anything. I turned quickly to the mirror and fixed my earrings in place, for it was almost dinner time and the Van Hottons were at least as formal as the British are said to be. Oliver regarded me in the mirror for a moment and then turned away silently to don his jacket.

Incredible as it seemed to me, we remained as the Van Hottons' house guests for a full two months. Arrangements for reclaiming the *Viscount* took time and the Van Hottons would not hear of us moving to a hotel. They entertained for us lavishly, and I must say that I met a variety of lively, delightful people, several of whom I felt would be friends always. Strangely, when I was not in Oliver's immediate presence, I was my normal self, able to exhibit the warmth and interest and merriment that had always been a part of me.

It was only when he was at my side, or when we were alone, that the pall descended over me, like a blanket extinguishing a light. I began to avoid him as much as possible on social occasions, for I did not care for the new me, and wished to obliterate her in laughter and gaiety.

We had been in New York for a month when Charles came to me, looking resolute and especially tall and stalwart.

"Mother? I need to talk with you, I think."

We were in the privacy of a sitting room of the suite the Van Hottons had provided us, and Oliver was off somewhere with Cyrus, as he insisted that we call him. Charles seated himself in a capacious lounge chair and leaned forward with his arms on his knees.

"Diana and I wish to marry, Mother. We are very much in love and she is willing to return to Holylake with us. I believe you like her, don't you?"

"Of course I do, Charles. She is a delightful girl in every way. But darling . . . you were going to go to Oxford, as Howard is."

He grinned at me, as Oliver had so often done in the past, and my heart turned over.

"No, Mother. You thought I was because you wanted to believe it. But I'm a seafaring man. Like Grandfather. Like Father."

"Like all of the Jardines, no doubt," I observed acidly, and immediately regretted it. "Yes, yes, Charles, I do understand that, only—"

"Only you would like me to complete my schooling first?"

He shook his head. "I'm no scholar, Mother. Howard is; perhaps he should have been your son."

"No, Charles. I could never be disappointed in you in any way, or wish for a finer son in any way. I only want you to be sure, darling."

Charles got to his feet and grinned down at me. "Oh, I'm sure, Mother. You must have seen that. Why, I knew Diana was the woman for me from the first moment I met her. Well—no doubt that sounds peculiar to you."

I shook my head mutely, remembering the quay at Charente and my first sight of Oliver Jardine. And all that had happened since that far-off day. But there was no way to say it. And if I could have, what difference? I hadn't looked back, had I? Until a scarce two months ago.

I got to my feet and put my hands on my tall son's shoulders.

"Darling Charles. Perhaps I understand better than you think. I wish you every happiness with Diana and shall look forward to welcoming her as a daughter in our family."

Charles's joyous smile was my reward. "Mama, I love you," he said, and kissed me on the cheek before he raced for the door. "I *told* Diana you were a wonder. We're going to ask her father right away."

He was gone from my room. I cried a little, but whether from a mixture of happiness for Charles and sadness at the prospect of losing him, or for my own lost dreams, I was incapable of knowing.

CHAPTER 47

Diana Elizabeth Van Hotton and Charles Millbrook Jardine, Viscount Birkenhead, were married on the eleventh of September, 1864, in the Fifth Avenue Presbyterian Church. The New York press was eloquent on the brilliance of the match, the beauty of the bride, the "aristocratic charm" of the groom, and the elegance of the entire undertaking. The Van Hottons spared no expense in providing a lavish celebration, and it was, in fact, as beautiful a wedding as the newspapers declared it to be.

During the course of the wedding preparations Dorrie Van Hotton and I finally became closer, for I felt deeply for her. I knew how bereft I should feel if our roles had been reversed, and Charles were going to live in America. But the Van Hottons were good-natured people and would do nothing to dampen the young people's pleasure. They insisted that they would visit often in England and that Diana and Charles would visit America. Too, they were naïvely pleased that their daughter was marrying a viscount, albeit a very impoverished one. For myself, I was simply pleased that Diana and Charles were so in love, and prayed the years would be kind to them.

Because the young people would so soon be going to England, they did not take a wedding trip, but stayed at the Van Hotton house in a luxurious suite which had been especially refurbished for them. Three weeks after the wedding, the *Viscount* arrived in New York. Cyrus Van Hotton had been successful in his efforts. Reclaiming her would cost thirty thousand pounds, and Oliver considered that he had got a good bargain. The two men, Oliver and Cyrus, were like a pair of triumphant children who had won a great prize. Together they spent hours going over the vessel, deciding what must be done to put her in good order.

Our own affection for the old steamer was one thing; but to hear Mr. Van Hotton after his inspection tour was most gratifying. We sat long at the table that evening, for I was as interested as Oliver in the American shipowner's opinion.

"Well, Oliver and Margaret" (we had finally convinced him to stop calling us Lord Oliver and Lady Margaret, though I suspected he preferred to), "for a steamer that's nineteen years old, it's quite a vessel. Far ahead of its time, no mistake about that. And it still has many a quality as up-to-date as you could ask for."

Cyrus Van Hotton nodded portentously and leaned back to light up a fat cigar. When he had it going to his satisfaction, he fixed Oliver with his keen brown-button eyes.

"Now that we're related, in a manner of speaking, I'm of a mind to foster the relationship in a business way, if such a thing interests you. There are the young people to think of."

He ceased speaking to puff thoughtfully on his cigar. I sensed a breathless waiting in Oliver and a growing excitement within my own breast.

"There's naught to be done until this war ends," Cyrus Van Hotton continued. "But once it's over, and pray the

Lord that will be soon, I'm thinking we might put together an
American-British consortium, between us. Why should we let
Sam Cunard keep on skimming off the cream, eh? He's had it
all to himself long enough. Time for us lean and hungry
ones"—Cyrus Van Hotton laughed and patted his corpulent
front—"to share the feast."

"It sounds of interest," Oliver said cautiously. "I have a
few ideas I'd like to see put into practice. . . ."

"Exactly. You're a man of ideas, of vision, judging from
what I saw this afternoon. But you've been hog-tied by trying
to go it without the backing you need. Now, if this idea of
mine works out, we'll raise money on this side of the Atlantic
and you do what you can on your side. We'll start out big
enough to give 'em all a run for their money. I know men
who'd welcome a chance to get in on such a venture, with
someone like you behind it—a man who knows the sea and
ships. And not to forget Charles, as well. We've spent some
time talking. He's quite a young man. But you know that, I
guess. I like his style and enthusiasm. Tells me he grew up on
a ship, and in that family seat of yours, Holylake, with the
sea all around it, so I guess he's got it in the blood, all right."

"A sealord." Oliver murmured it, a faraway look in his
eyes.

"Eh? What's that?"

"An expression of my father's. He was with Nelson at
Trafalgar, and a seaman all of his life. Commander of a ship
of the line on the Singapore station for years, before he retired and went into the commercial side of the business. He
said that we Jardines came from a long line of seafarers—
there was a pirate way back there somewhere—and were
born to be sealords."

Cyrus Van Hotton stared at Oliver, and then slammed his
hand down on the damask-covered table.

"Sealords, eh! Well, now, I like the sound of that. It fits
how I think of you and Charles. Yes, sir, born to be sealords.
And an earl and a viscount, to boot!" He grinned at us.
"That kind of thing does no harm when you want to raise
money in this country, you know. But you'll see, once this
war is over."

We sailed for Liverpool on the ninth of October, 1864,
taking a new daughter-in-law with us. Through Mr. Van Hotton's influence we had full holds and great hope for the future. Poor Diana was seasick for the first two days, but after
that took to the sea as if she had been raised on a ship, like

her new husband. I wondered, with a few qualms, how well she would like Holylake, after the luxury she was used to. Judging from her radiant face, so long as she had Charles nearby, she would accept whatever else might come.

Being back on the old *Viscount* was almost—not quite—like coming home. The ship held so many memories for me. Happy ones and unhappy ones, of quarrels and loving, of terrors lived through and dangers overcome. On this vessel Oliver had almost died of his burns—and I had been raped by a Russian seaman. With or without Oliver, I had struggled and fought to keep her holds filled, and a long, hard struggle it had been. The *Viscount* had survived, but the love that had kept her going for all of those years had died somewhere along the way.

And always before me were the tender, loving faces of Diana and Charles, reminding me of all that was lost. I stood on the deck alone one night, watching the moon behind scudding clouds. Further along the deck Charles and Diana watched the moon too, bundled against the spray and sheltering close to each other. Their heads were together, Charles's arms around Diana—and then they turned and went to their cabin.

I felt slow tears filling my eyes, cold loneliness stealing through my bones. All I could think of was what I had lost. Compared to that, the inner anger that had sustained me for so many months was bitter, sour fare. I bowed my head in my hands and wept, salt tears mingling with the spray on my face.

Suddenly I was grasped from behind by strong arms that pulled me close and turned me around. Oliver's face, warm in spite of the night wind and spray, rested against mine as he held me silently, his arms cradling and rocking me like the lost child that I was, inside.

When finally he spoke, it was something I thought I didn't want to hear.

"Do you remember the night when I first came back to Holylake? I asked you about Adriana . . . and you asked me about Cora Ewell?"

It took me a while to answer, but I got it out finally.

"Yes."

"Do you remember what I told you that night? That I loved you . . . and only you. That I would always love you. Do you remember that?"

"Yes," I whispered past the lump in my throat.

"That's why I came back, Margaret. That's why I'll stay. Whatever it was that started that day on the quay at Charente changed my life forever." He paused. "Can you say the same?"

"Yes."

His lips came down on mine in a hot, searing testament to his words. All the pent-up misery in me broke and drained away as I strained toward him. *Oliver*.

"Come." His arm about me, he led me back to our cabin and turned on the lamp. I looked around and it was no longer the strange, confining prison where I had turned my back on him—as it had been since we'd boarded in New York. It was *home* . . . and *we* were home . . . and a wild joy started to well up inside me.

With tender hands he undressed me, his eyes never leaving mine. And once in bed, close to him again, against that strong, familiar body that had the power to start and stop my life, I knew that I belonged to Oliver Jardine for the rest of my days—and probably in the hereafter.

It was strange love that we made, a long feast after famine; sanctuary. Over the years Oliver and I had made love in many ways, frolicked and fought and lusted; partaken of each other at times with a desperate urgency. This was love restored, when we had thought it gone forever, and there was gratitude and thanksgiving in our joining; a slow savoring of the feel of each other again. This was *us*—Oliver and Margaret, locked in heart-stopping passion that built and built to a final crescendo; part of the past . . . and the beginning of the next time.

When at last we lay spent, when Oliver's arms were locked about me in sleep, I looked around our familiar cabin. We were not alone. The shadow of Matthew was there; Adriana; Cora Ewell and her son. They were a part of our life, they had touched it, but they were outside it and always would be. We would go on fighting for our shipping line, perhaps with the help of Cyrus Van Hotton. Our children would follow after us, with their own strivings and triumphs. But all of that was apart from us, outside. Within, there were only—Oliver and Margaret Jardine.

Oliver stirred and murmured my name. I arranged myself close against his warmth, breathed the safe, familiar scent of him—and slept.

FOR YOUR FUTURE ENJOYMENT—
A SELECTION FROM

THE TIDES
OF DESTINY

Here is an enthralling scene from the continuing saga of the powerful Jardine family—their tragedies, their triumphs, and the empire they created. Watch for the complete novel coming to you soon in a Signet edition.

THE TIDES OF DESTINY

by Janet Gregory

Olivia Jardine clattered along the chilly stone corridor of Holylake, out the back door, and into the walled kitchen garden. Although it was five o'clock, the rare spring sunlight still had warmth. Instead of tying the scarf over her red-gold hair, she stuffed it into her coat pocket, and closed the high wooden gate of the kitchen garden behind her. At sixteen, Olivia was tall and willowy, with imperious gray eyes and an eager, headstrong disposition. Her creamy skin curved over wide cheekbones with faint violet shadows below; her jaw was delicately chiseled, slightly squared. A distinctive, aristocratic face; with its frame of gleaming red-gold hair it compelled attention like some brilliant exotic flower on a slim stem.

A narrow path bordered by prickly hedgerows wound across the stony meadows of Holylake, and Olivia followed it. Behind her, slanting rays of sunlight softened the craggy harshness of the ancient priory-fortress. She was happy to be home again. The spring holidays stretched before her, idyllic by comparison with life at the boarding school that she considered unutterably dreary. That Holylake was drearier—grimly barren, sea-battered, falling into ruin which there was never enough money to repair —took away none of its charm for her. It was home, the only home she knew; it was warmed by the presence of the father and mother she loved; and now Charles and his bride, Diana, lived there too.

Diana. Olivia's step quickened. It was wonderful to have Diana at Holylake. Though she was five years older,

357

and an American, there was a bond of affection between them, Olivia reflected happily, that made such differences unimportant. Moreover, Diana had confided that if all went well, Olivia would become an aunt in October. An aunt at sixteen. There was deep satisfaction in that. It helped to calm some of her constant inner rage of impatience—to be acknowledged an adult, to be free of the tiresome strictures of school and teachers, to taste the joys and excitement of real life.

Olivia had arrived home from school a day earlier than expected. Her mother, father, and brother Charles were in Liverpool, and Diana had told Emily, the housekeeper, that she was going for a walk across the meadows. Olivia, incapable of patiently awaiting any event, set out to overtake and surprise the older girl. The path twisted, and at every turn she hoped to see Diana just ahead. Then she would call out, Diana would turn around, unable to believe her eyes; they would run toward each other and embrace. . . .

Olivia Jardine rounded a turn in the path and Diana hurtled headlong into her, bent half double, gasping for breath.

"Diana, what is it? What's wrong?"

Diana raised glazed eyes, empty of recognition, empty of everything save fear.

"I didn't heed her. I didn't go. Oh, *dearest* Charles, how could I leave him?" Diana's voice sank to a whimper. "I'm afraid. Now that it's too late. She warned me . . . she said go—"

Olivia grasped the hysterical girl's shoulders, seeking to steady her. "What are you saying, Diana? Go where? Who has been frightening you this way?"

But Diana shook her head, sobbing. "Too late. It's too late!" She tugged free of Olivia's grasp and half stumbled, half ran along the path back to Holylake.

Olivia stood perfectly still, her jaw suddenly clearly defined under the rounded flesh of youth. Whatever had upset Diana was ahead somewhere. With protective fury rising in waves that set her blood pounding in her ears, Olivia started along the path at a run. She would deal with whoever had troubled Diana, that mildest, sweetest, most lovable of sisters-in-law.

She nearly raced past the old crone who was half hidden in the hedgerow a hundred yards further along the path. She wasn't meant to rush by, though, Olivia realized a moment later. The old woman had been waiting for her! There was a glint of malicious amusement in the deep-set black eyes peering at her from a clutch of shawls.

"Good day, m'lady. Eh, ye're in a great tear now, are ye?" The old head bobbed and nodded. "More's the pity, more's the pity. If ye had a bit o' time, like—and mayhap a small piece o' siller to spare a poor soul—ah, the things I could tell ye!"

The cozening, overly familiar voice made Olivia's gorge rise. She need look no further for the source of Diana's fears!

"What are you doing on our land? You have no business here, you're not one of our people!"

"Do ye say so, m'lady? Yet I've been here longer than ye. Or yer mother, or her mother before her. Mayhap I'll be here after ye're all gone."

"You're an impudent, lying old gypsy!"

"Oh, no, m'lady. I've lived right here on this land all me years. But as fer the Romany now, ye'll be one o' theirs afore me! It's in yer fate."

"I will be a gypsy? How dare you!" Olivia's silver-gray eyes were incandescent with fury. She slashed at the old crone but succeeded only in disarranging one of her shawls as the woman dodged away, cackling.

"Eh, but she's in a temper now, right enough," Olivia's tormenter observed from a safe distance. "Don't like that, she don't! It's God's truth all the same. Ye'll see!"

Then, before Olivia's furious eyes, the spiteful virago suddenly became a harmless, fawning old countrywoman.

"Oh, m'lady, I pray ye forgive a foolish old woman," she entreated, again approaching Olivia. "I've the true gift, ye see. The second sight, some calls it. And sometimes it do take me strange-like."

Olivia Jardine planted her fists on her hips and shook back her gleaming hair.

"Forgive you? Hah! When my brother learns how you've terrified his wife with your lies—"

"Oh, no, m'lady, I swear, 'twas God's own truth, all that I told her ladyship! I warned her—"

Olivia Jardine, in a frenzy of growing fear for Diana, seized and shook the old woman by her shoulders. "You spiteful creature, what kind of foolish tale did you tell her? Something dangerous, I'll be bound. If you've done her unborn child a damage, you'll answer to my brother!"

"Oh, no, m'lady, ye can't lay *that* to me! 'Tisn't my Curse, but yer own. I warned her, I did, and she paid me no heed. But ye'll not put the blame fer that on me!"

"Blame for *what*?" Olivia asked, with a chill starting along her spine. Somehow the old hag's righteous indignation was more frightening than her spite.

The woman looked bewildered. "Why, the Curse. It's naught to do with me. It came with *her*. She brought it . . . and she passed it along to all o' ye."

"What? to the Jardines?" Olivia forced a laugh. "Oh, really! What a tale. Who is supposed to have laid this curse on us, pray tell?"

The old crone ignored her words, nodding with simple-minded eagerness. "Aye, she did, laid it on the lot o' ye. I heard her, I was right there. Oh, she were a tartar, she were, and I served her well, fer I was that afeared o' her—"

"I don't know what you're talking about," Olivia interrupted impatiently. "No one but my parents has lived at Holylake for years."

"Why, her, m'lady, the Old Mistress, her as brought the Curse. An' now it's on the young, dark-haired one. I warned her, last All Saints' Day it were. I saw it on her then, clear as clear. All wreathed around in poison flowers, she was. That's what it's called, see, the Curse o' the Flowers."

The old head shook in relentless judgment. "She didn't leave, though I told her 'twould be her doom and death if she stayed."

Olivia fell silent, white-faced and drained of strength. The Curse of the Flowers. It was ridiculous, a packet of lies. She would soon talk Diana out of her foolish fears! Yet something about the tale was eerily convincing. In the depths of her mind, a long-dismissed memory stirred. Once when she was very young she had overheard her mother ranting and railing against some shameful curse said to afflict the family. It had frightened her at the time, but then she had forgotten it.

None of it was any excuse for this old fool trying to link some hand-me-down curse to poor Diana.

"You have caused my sister-in-law a great deal of anguish with your foolish talk! You're a wicked, depraved creature."

"Aye, no doubt, m'lady." For a moment the malicious smirk was back on the old face. "But 'tis the pot calling the kettle black. Ye have sins enough o' yer own still to come. Ye're born to a wild family and ye'll add a fair share to its fame."

"What do you know of me?" Olivia scoffed. Her curiosity was piqued, but she was reluctant to let this old woman know it.

A brown, clawlike hand darted out and seized Olivia's, turning it palm up. "Eh, ye're a wild one, right enough."

Bright black eyes half hidden by folds of flesh darted to Olivia's face. "I see ye decked out in fine satins and laces. Fine as any duchess, ye are. Ah, but wait—not a duchess after all, but more like a harlot! Aye, a harlot with her red head held high and mighty."

The old crone cackled. "Ye've a comedown waitin' fer ye there, yer ladyship. I see ye trundlin' off in a cart with a dark man . . . a man with no name. . . ."

Olivia snatched back her hand. "Ugh—you're disgusting! Pretending to read the future, when all you want is a chance to insult your betters."

"Eh, ye're a prickly one, ye are. An' yer own contrary nature will cause ye to lie down in many a hard bed—"

"Poof!" Olivia interrupted. "Do you never see anything pleasant, then? Nothing but misery and disasters?"

"I only tells the good things to them as listens to me," the woman said, cackling with amusement. "Still, fer all ye're such a scoffer . . . aye, ye'll find yer happiness one day. I see a child—"

"Don't talk to me of children," Olivia said impatiently. "Tell me who I'll wed! Will he be handsome? Will I wed as young as Diana?"

"No, ye will not. Nor die as young, neither!"

"Die? Diana? Oh, no . . ."

The old woman shrugged. "God and the Devil arranges such matters betwixt 'em. Ye can't change it."

"I don't believe you about Diana. There *is* no Curse! None of this is true," Olivia shouted defiantly, her eyes shiny with fear and unshed tears.

"Oh, ah? And do ye think to escape the Curse yerself,

m'lady? Why, I have no doubt the Old Mistress intended it fer you, special, if ever ye was born!"

"Stop, stop!" Olivia cried as panicky fear began to build inside her. But there was no respite.

"Ye'll turn yer back on them as loves ye. Ye'll dance to whatever tune the Devil pipes. Ye'll bear yer child on a pile o' straw...."

Olivia clapped her hands over her ears and fled back along the path to Holylake. But the old crone's words followed her.

"Ye'll find a way to end the Curse. But not fer many and many a year ... too late fer ye and some as loved ye...."

Janet Gregory was born in Buffalo, New York. She is the author of eight suspense novels set in Montreal and in the Palm Beaches where she now lives. Her previous books have been published in nine countries and have also been serialized in leading magazines.

More Bestsellers from SIGNET